Really, Really, Really, Really, Weird Stories
Contents ©1999 by John Shirley
Cover, cover design, and interior artwork ©1999 Alan M. Clark
Interior design and composition by John Tynes

The publisher would like to thank the following for indespensible help and support. William K. Shafer, Alan Beatts, John Pelan, Matt Johnson, John Tynes, John Shirley and Paula Guran.

First Edition
Printed in the United States of America
Limited Edition ISBN 1-892389-01-0
Trade Edition ISBN 1-892389-02-9

Night Shade Books
870 East El Camino Real #133
Mountain View, CA 98040
www.nightshadebooks.com
night@nightshadebooks.com

Really,
Really,
Really,
Really,

WEIRD STORIES

JOHN
SHIRLEY

NIGHT SHADE BOOKS
MOUNTAIN VIEW,

this book is dedicated
to these really weird people

Micky Shirley, Ivan Stang, Paul Mavrides, Harry S. Robins, Rudy Rucker, Shikhar, Gene a Texas Fan, Jan My Man in Germany, LadyCro, Marc Laidlaw, Richard Kadrey, Paula Guran, Mark Ziesing, Tim Powers, Serena Powers, Art Cover, Steve Brown, Richard Smoley, Michael and Misha Chocholak, DC Moon, Robert Sheckley, Ed Kramer, Corby Simpson, Mark Sten, Dona Bolt, Jeff Bolt, Dale van Wormer, Charlene Zaharakis, Jon Newton, Jim Baldwin, Katherine Dunn, Julia Solis, John Roome, Don Roeser, Eric Bloom, Ted Oliphant, Greg Bishop, Tim Brigham, and the Reverend Nanzi Regalia.

THE AUTHOR WANTS
TO TELL YOU . . .

This collection is in four sections. The first one is REALLY WEIRD STO-
RIES; second one is REALLY, REALLY WEIRD STORIES; third one is
REALLY, REALLY, REALLY WEIRD STORIES; last one is REALLY, RE-
ALLY, REALLY, *REALLY* WEIRD STORIES. I've tried to arrange the
stories in just that way—so that the stories in each section are "weirder"
than the ones in the last.

As for why . . .

The idea for this collection came to me when Paula Guran said, "Yeah,
I read that *Lot Five* story. Shirley, that was a really weird story."

I muttered, "You think *that's* weird?" Then I thought: Well, it is but—
it's all relative. I mean, you could stack up stories according to weirdness
if you chose to. That wouldn't be any kind of measure of quality, but,
yeah, it would be *really fun* to do.

And so it has been. This collection is gimmicky, it's a sort of high concept
collection, and that doesn't justify its existence. The entertainment element
does, perhaps, but I like to think it has more going for it than that.

Having said that . . .

I'm really into this experiment: this journey. How far can we go, and
still take our reference points with us? How far can we go without getting lost—or if we get lost, can we find our way back? Does it matter?
Isn't the point to be aware, to be real, to know who you are, whatever
relative normality or so-called weirdness goes down?

Or is the point just to have one motherfucker of a ride?

You decide if it's a good ride. And you can decide if I stacked these up
right: if each section is weirder than the last. Let me know what you
think. *Weird* is obviously relative, and this "stacking" wasn't half so easy
as I thought it'd be. Some stories are in a particular section of relative
weirdness because of the *way* they're written rather than because of

what happens in them. Not everyone will agree about the comparative weirdness of these stories. Within given sections, stories are arranged for other reasons, having to do with pacing and tone and variety. It should be noted that this collection is no particular genre; it's several genres.

Many of the stories in this book have never been published before—or in some cases were what I think of as *barely* published. Some of the former group were judged—not by me—to be too weird to be published . . . till now.

There are a few stories that should, by rights, be in this book but were unavailable for contractual reasons. But, for the most part, these are the weirdest stories I ever wrote; especially, as you might suppose, those in the last section.

As I was compiling this book, over a couple of weeks (I had other stuff to do too), I was mostly listening to the following music:

Monster Magnet's *Powertrip* album, Nick Cave's *Murder Ballads*, Lou Reed's boxed set and *Live in London*, Frank Zappa's *Hot Rats*, various things by King Crimson, various cuts by Bauhaus and by Peter Murphy, PJ Harvey, the band Poe, Iggy and the Stooges and Iggy's recent solo albums, Hound Dog Taylor, John Lee Hooker, the Oblivion Seekers, Big Mama Thornton, Frank Sinatra (60s stuff), Cake (my kids made me; I liked it), *We Will Fall* (Iggy tribute CD), Trust/Obey, Patti Smith, Cracker, The Cramps, Tilt, The Sick, Witchman, Mudhoney, Rolling Stones, Johnny Cash, and the new Blue Öyster Cult album—*Heaven Forbid*.

Have a weird day. Have a *really* weird day.

John Shirley

For more about the really weird author,
you are invited to visit the official
John Shirley Web Site:

http://www.darkecho.com/JohnShirley

or contact him via email:

darkecho@aol.com

∞ ∞ ∞

The first time I saw
the dum dum boys
I was fascinated
They just stood in front
of the old drug store
I was most impressed
No one else was impressed
Not at all
—Iggy Pop, "Dum Dum Boys"

Really

WEIRD
STORIES

"I Want To Get Married,"
Says the World's Smallest Man!

"You a fucking ho," Delbert said. "You don't come at me like that, not a fuckin ho."

"Fuck you, Delbert, who turned me out? You busted me out there on Capp Street when it was fucking thirty degrees—I ain'a motherfucking tossup like yo' nigger bitch cousins, I'm a white girl, motherfucker, I don't come out of that—"

"Don't be talkin that shit. You was already a fucking whore, you fucked that *ess ay* motherfucker CheeChee—"

"Sure so he didn't beat my fucking head in. Where were you? Where were you when he was slapping me and shit? Hittin' the fuckin' pipe, Delbert. Shit you knew what was going on—Where you going now goddamnit?"

Delbert was mumbling over the loose knob of the hotel room's door, trying to get out into the hall. The knob was about ready to come off. Brandy was glad Delbert was going because that meant he wasn't going to work himself up to knocking her around, but at the same time she didn't want to be left alone, just her and the fucked-up TV that was more or less a radio now because the picture was so slanty you couldn't make it out, a two-week-old *Weekly World Inquirer,* and one can of Colt Malt stashed on the window ledge. And something else, he was going to get some money, maybe get an out-front from Terrence, and do some rock. She shouted after him, "You going to hit that pipe without me again? You suckin' it all up, microwavin' that pipe, fuckin' it up the way you do it, and Terrence going to kick yo' ass if you smoke what he give you to sell—"

But he'd got the door open, yelling, "SHUT UP WOMAN I BITCH-SLAP YOU!" as he slammed it behind him with that soap-opera timing.

"*Fuck* you, you better bring me some fuckin . . ." She let her voice trail off as his steps receded down the hall, " . . . dope."

The fight had used her up. She felt that plunge feeling again, like nothing was any use so why try; and what she wanted was to go back to bed. She thought, maybe I get my baby out of Foster Care Hold, that place's just like prison. Shit Candy's not a baby anymore, she's ten, and she's half-white, looks more white than anything else, she'll be OK.

Brandy got up off the edge of the bed, walked across the chilly room, hugging herself, feeling her sharp hips under her fingers, as she went to the window. She looked out through the little cigarette-burn hole, just in time to see Delbert walk his skinny black ass out the front door, right up to Terrence. "The man's going to go off on you one of these days, Delbert, you be a dead nigger before you hit the emergency room, you fucking asshole," she said, aloud, taking satisfaction in it.

There was no reason, she thought, to be looking out the burn-hole instead of just lifting the shade; she didn't have anything to be paranoid about, there wasn't even any fucking crumbles of dope in the house, she hadn't had any hubba in two days, and now she was laying awake at night thinking about it, not wanting to go out and turn a trick for it because she had that really bad lady trouble, and the pain when they fucked her was like stabbing her pussy, the infection—

There it was, soon as she started thinking about it, the itching starts up bad again, itching and burning in her cunt. Ow Ow. Ow. Shit, go to the clinic, go to the clinic. She didn't have the energy. They made you wait so long. Treated you like a fucking whore.

She turned to the burn-hole again, saw Terrence walking along with Delbert, Terrence shaking his head. No more credit. Delbert'd be back up here, beat her till she'd hit the streets again. She turned away from the cigarette hole. Looking out through the tiny burn-hole was a tweakin' habit. Like picking holes in your skin trying to get coke bugs. Once she'd spent a whole day, eight hours straight staring out through that hole, picking her skin bloody, staring, turning away only to hit the crack pipe. That was when Delbert was dealing and they were flush with dope. Fucking cocaine made you tweaky, it was funny stuff. Maybe Delbert's cousin Darius would give her some. For some head. Her stomach lurched. She went back to the bed, looked again at the *Inquirer* article she'd been laboriously reading:

I WANT TO GET MARRIED,
SAYS WORLD'S SMALLEST MAN!
Ross Taraval, the world's smallest man, wants to get married—and he's one eligible bachelor! He weighs only seventeen pounds and

is only 28 inches high but he has a budding career as an entertainer and he's got plenty of love to give, he tells us. "I want a wife to share my success," said Ross, 24, who has starred in two films shot in Mexico, making him a star, or anyway a comet, in that enterprising land. Recently he was given a "small" role in a Hollywood film. "There's more to me than meets the eye," Ross said. "The doctors say I could have children—and I'd support my new wife in real style! And listen, I want a full-sized wife. That's what a real man wants—and I can handle her—just let me climb aboard! I've got so much love to give and there's a real man inside this little body wanting to give it to the right woman!"

Ross, who was abandoned at three years old, was raised by nuns in Miami. After attracting attention in the *Trafalgar Book of World Records*, Ross was contacted by his manager, six-foot-five-inch Benny Chafin, who could carry Ross in his overcoat pocket if he wanted to. Chafin trained Ross in singing and dancing and soon found him work in nightclubs and TV endorsements.

"I've got my eye on a beautiful house in the Hollywood Hills for the right lady," Ross said.

There was a picture of the little guy standing next to his manager—not even coming up to the manager's crotch height. The manager, now, was cute, he looked kind of like Geraldo Rivera, Brandy thought. There was a little box at the bottom of the article. It said:

If you think you'd be a likely life-mate for Ross and would like to get in touch with him, you may write him care of the Weekly World Inquirer *and we'll forward your letter to him. Address your correspondence to . . .*

Huh. Stupid idea.

She heard Delbert's footsteps in the hall . . .

There was a stamp on the letter from her sister that hadn't been canceled. She could peel it off.

"I think I got you a job at Universal Studios!" Benny said, striding breathlessly in.

"Really?" Ross's heart thumped. He climbed arduously down off the chair he'd been squatting in to watch TV. The Sleepytime Inn had a Playboy Channel.

He hurried over to Benny, who was taking off his coat. It was May in Los Angeles, and sort of cold there. The cold made Ross's joints ache. Benny had said it was always warm in LA, but it wasn't now. It was cloudy and windy.

It took Ross a long time to get across the floor to Benny, and Ross was impatient to know what was going on, so he started shouting questions through his wheezing before he got there.

"What movie am I in?" he asked. "Does it have Arnold Schwarzanegger?"

"Ross, slow down, you'll get your asthma started. No, it's not a movie. It's at their theme park. They want you to play King of the Wonksters for the tourists. It's a live show."

Ross stopped in the middle of the floor, panting, confused. "What're Wonksters?"

"They're . . . sort of like Ewoks. Little outer space guys. Universal's got a movie coming out about 'em at Christmas so this'd be next summer—if the movie hits—and—"

"Next summer! I need some work now! Those bastards! You said I could be in a buddy picture with Arnold Schwarzanegger!"

"I spoke to his agent. He already did a buddy picture with a little guy. He doesn't want to do that again."

"You said I could meet him!"

"You're going to be around Hollywood for a long time, you'll meet your hero, Ross, calm down, all right? You don't want to have an attack. Maybe we can get a photo op or something with him—"

Benny had turned away, was frowning over the papers in his briefcase.

"We're not even sleeping in Hollywood!" Ross burst out. He'd been saving this all morning, having heard it from the maid. "We're . . . "

"Hey, we're in LA, OK? It doesn't matter where you live as long as you can drive to the studios. Most of 'em aren't actually in Hollywood, Ross, they're in Burbank or Culver City—"

"Mary, Mother of God! I want to go out in Hollywood! You're out getting wild with all the girls! No? You are! And leaving me here!"

Benny turned to him, his cheeks mottling. He cocked a hip, slightly, and Ross backed away. He knew, from the times he had run away from the mission, how people stood when they were going to kick you.

He'd spent six weeks in the mission hospital, after one kick stove in his ribs, and he wasn't quite right from it yet. He most definitely knew when they were going to kick you.

But Benny made that long exhalation through his nose that meant he was trying to keep his temper. He'd never kicked Ross, or hurt him at all, he probably never would. He'd done nothing but help him, after all.

"I'm sorry, Benny," Ross said. "Can we have a Big Mac and watch Playboy channel?"

"Sure. We deserve a break, right?" He'd turned back to his briefcase, sorting papers. "I had a letter here for you, from those people at the *World Inquirer*."

"I don't like those people."

"They're bloodsuckers. But the publicity is good, so whatever it is, we play along. We'll get a TV commercial or something out of it."

"I hope you are not mad at me, Benny . . ."

"I'm not mad at you. Hey, here it is. Your letter."

There was something off about his face, Brandy thought. His nose seemed crooked or something. His features a little distorted. Must be from being a dwarf, or a midget, or whatever he was.

She tried to picture cuddling with him, think of him as cute, like a kid, but when she pictured him unzipping his pants, she got a skin-crawling feeling . . .

Hit the pipe a few times, anything's all right.

She pushed the pipe to the back of her mind. She had to play this carefully.

They were sitting in the corner booth of a Denny's restaurant. Ross, actually, was standing on the leatherette seat, leaning on the table like it was a bar, but the people who passed probably thought he was sitting. They also probably thought he was her kid. Shit, he was twenty-eight inches high. His head, though, was almost normal sized. Too big for his body. He was wearing a stiffly pressed suit and tie, with a hanky tucked in the pocket; he looked like a little kid going to Sunday School. "Did a lot of women write to you?" she asked.

"Not too many. The ones that did are too big and fat or old, except you. Or they were black. I don't want a black wife. I liked you, because your hair is blonde, and your letter was very nice, the handwriting was nice, the stationery was very nice. Smelled nice too."

But he was talking sort of distractedly. She could see he was staring at the scabs on her cheeks. There were only a few, really.

"I guess you're looking at my skin—" she began.

"No no no! It's fine. Fine." His voice sounded like it was coming through a little tube from the next room. He smiled at her. He had nice teeth.

"It's OK to notice it," Brandy said. "My . . . my sister has this crazy Siamese cat. You know how the little fuh—" Watch your language, she told herself. "You know how they are. I bent over to pet him and he jumped up and scratched me . . . "

Ross nodded. He seemed to buy it. Maybe where he was from they didn't have a lot of hubba-heads picking at their skin all the time.

"There was a cat," he said absently, "who scared me, at the mission. Big and fat and mean." He scowled and muttered something else in his munchkin voice she couldn't quite make out.

"It's nice of you to buy me dinner," Brandy said. A fucking Denny's, she thought. Well, maybe it was like he said, it was just the nearest one and he was hungry. But she'd pictured some really fancy place . . .

The waitress brought their order, steak for Brandy—who knew if this was going to work out? Get what you can now—and a milkshake and fries for the little guy, which was kind of a funny dinner, Brandy thought. The waitress had done a double take when she'd first come to take their order; now she didn't look at Ross directly. But she stared at Brandy when she thought Brandy wouldn't notice.

Fuck you, bitch, you think I'm sick for kickin' with the little dude.

"You really do look nice," Ross said, as the waitress walked away. Like he was trying to convince himself.

She'd done her best. Her hair was almost naturally blond, that was good, but it was a little thin and dry from all the hubba, and when she'd washed it, with that shitty hand soap that was all Delbert had, it'd frizzed out, so she'd had to corn-row it. She'd handwashed her dress and borrowed Carmen's pumps and ripped off a pair of new pantyhose and some makeup from the Payless drugstore. Getting the bus down here was harder, but she'd conned a guy at the San Francisco station into helping her out, and then she'd ditched him at the LA station when he'd gone to the men's room, and she'd got twelve dollars for the guy's luggage, so it was beginning to click.

Ross started to cough. "Are you choking on something?" she asked, dreading it, because she didn't want to attract even more attention.

"No—my asthma." He was fishing in his pocket with one of his little doll hands. He found an inhaler, and sucked at it.

"Just rest a bit, you don't have to talk or nothin'," she said, smiling at him.

So his health was not that great. It wouldn't seem too weird or anything, then, if he died, or something.

"You just swept me off my feet, I guess," Brandy said. "I thought you were hella cute at the wedding. I was surprised you didn't have your manager over to be, like, best man or something."

"We had to be married first, because I know what he would say, he doesn't want me to get married till he checks everyone out, you know. But *he* has lots of girls. Come on in, come on in, this is our room, our own room . . ."

"Wow, it even has a kitchen! Anyway, look it's got a bar and a microwave and a little refrigerator . . ." She noticed that the microwave oven wasn't bolted to the wall. It was pretty old, though, she probably couldn't get shit for it.

"I do like this refrigerator, this little refrigerator by the floor. When we get a big house we'll have a real kitchen!"

"Yeah? Uhhh . . . When do you think—"

He interrupted her with a nervous dance of excitement, spreading his arms to gesture at the whole place. "You like this place? Las Vegas. It's so beautiful, everything's like a palace, all lit up, so much money, everything's like in a treasure chest."

"Uh huh." She started to sit on the edge of the bed, then noticed his eyes got all round and buggy when he saw her there. She moved over to the vinyl sofa, and sat down, kicked off her shoes. "It would've been nice if we coulda stayed in the Golden Nugget or one of them places—this Lucky Jack's is okay, but they don't got their own casino, they don't got room service . . ."

"Oh—we'll stay in the best, when Benny finds some work for me in Hollywood."

He toddled toward her, unbuttoning his coat. What did he think he was going to do?

She wondered where you got a rock in Vegas. She knew there'd be a place. Crack cocaine is everywhere there's money. Maybe the edge of town out by the airport. She could find it. She needed the cash . . .

And then it hit her, and she stood up, sharply. He took several sudden steps back, almost stumbling. She looked down at him, feeling unreal. Had she been hustled by this little creature? "When Benny finds you some work? What do you mean?"

She felt the tightening in her gut, the tease of imagined taste in her mouth: the taste of vaporized cocaine and the other shit they put in it. She could almost feel the glass pipe in her hand; see the white smoke flowering in the glass tube, coming to her. Her heart started pounding, hands twitching, fuck, going on a tweak with no dope to hit, one hand picking at a scab on the back of her left forearm.

The little guy was chattering something. "Oh, I'm working in Hollywood!" He actually puffed out his chest. "I'm going to star in an Arnold Schwarzanegger movie!"

"You mean you're going to co-star with him. OK. How much did you get paid?"

He fiddled with a lamp cord. "I don't have the check yet."

"Jesus fucking Christ."

He looked at her with his mouth open, so round and red and wet it looked like it had been punched in his head with a tool. "That is a blasphemy! That is the Lord's name! I can't have my wife talking like that!"

"Look—we're married now. We share everything right? *How* much we got to share? I need some cash, lover—for one thing, we didn't get a ring yet, you said we'd get a diamond ring—"

Ross was pacing back and forth, looking like a small child waiting for the men's room, trying not to wet his pants. "I don't have very much money now—thirty dollars—"

"Thirty dollars! Jesus fuh . . . that's a kick in the butt. What about credit cards?"

He wrung his little hands. Made her think of a squirrel messing with a peanut. "I'm paying with American Express for the airplane and hotel— Benny will stop the card!"

"American Express? Can you draw cash on the card?"

He stopped scuttling around and blinked up at her. "I don't know."

"Come on, we're gonna find out. We're going out."

"But we're Just Married!"

"It's not even dark out yet, Ross. Hold your horses, okay? First things first. We can't do anything without a ring, can we? We're gonna do something, don't worry. I'm hella horny. But we can't do it without a ring. That'd be weird don't you think?"

When she came in, the little guy was sitting in the middle of the bed, with his legs crossed Indian style, in a pair of red silk pajamas. There was a Saint Christopher's medal around his neck. Probably couldn't get shit for that either.

It was after midnight, sometime. He had the overhead lights dialed down low, and the tall floor lamp in the corner was unplugged. In the dimness he looked like a doll somebody had left on the bed, some stuffed toy, 'til he leaned back on the pillow in a pose he'd maybe seen on the Playboy channel.

They'd got the limit for the account, three hundred cash on the American Express Card. They'd endured all the stares in the American Express office, and she'd kept her temper with the giggly fat guy who thought they were performing at Circus Circus, but the hard part had been mak-

ing Ross swallow the *amazingly* bullshit story about how it was a tradition in California for the girl to go shopping for the ring alone . . .

She'd had to cuddle him and stroke his crotch a few times.

His dick was a hard little thing like a pen-knife. Then she'd left him
here with a bottle of pink Andre champagne, watching some shit about
big-tit girls shooting each other with uzis. He'd made kissy faces at her as
she left.

Right now, stoned, she thought maybe she could give him a blow job
or something if she closed her eyes. She had gone through two hundred
fifty dollars in hubba, her mouth was dry as a baked potato skin from
hitting the pipe.

"Let me see the beautiful ring on the beautiful girl," he said, his voice
slurred. He said something else she couldn't make out as she crossed the
room to him and sat on the bed, just out of reach.

"Hey, you know what?—Whoa, slow down, not so fast *compadre*," she
said, fending his clammy little hands away.

She pointed at the girl on the wall-mounted TV screen; a girl in laven-
der lingerie. "How'd you like me to dress up like that, huh? I need something like that. I'd look hella good, just hella sexy in that. I know where I
can get some, there's an adult bookstore that's got some lingerie, they're
open all night, you can go in and look at movies and I'll—"

"No!" His voice was unexpectedly low. "I need you now!"

"Hey cool off—what I'm saying you could call Benny and ask him to
wire you some money. We need some things. He could send it to the all-
night check-cashing place on Las Vegas Boulevard, they got Western
Union—" She picked up her purse and went unsteadily toward the bathroom. The room was warped, because of the darkness and what the
crack had done to her eyes. It always did weird shit to her eyes.

"Where you going?"

"Just to the bathroom, do some lady's business." I could tell him I'm in
my period, Latin guys will steer clear from that, she thought. Maybe get
another girl in here, give her a twenty to keep him occupied. "Why don't
you call Benny while I'm in here, ask for some money, we need some stuff,
hon!" She called, as she closed the bathroom door and fumbled through
her purse with trembling fingers. Found the pipe, found the torn piece of
copper scrubbing pad she was using for a pipe-screen, found the lighter.
Her thumb was already blackened and calloused from flicking. Her heart
was pounding in her ears as she took the yellowish white dove of crack
from the inner pocket of the purse, broke it in half with a thumbnail,
dropped it in the pipe bowl, melted it down with the lighter . . .

There was a pounding on the door, near her knee. She stared at the lower part of the door, holding the smoke in for a moment, then slowly exhaled. Her vision shrank and expanded, shrank and expanded, and then she heard, "You get out here and be with your husband!" Trying to make his voice all gravelly. She had to laugh. She took another hit. It wasn't getting her off much now. And she was feeling on the edge of that plunge into depression, that around the corner of the high; she felt the tweaky paranoia prod her with its hot icepick.

Someone was going to hear him yell; they were going to come in and see the pipe and she'd be busted in a Vegas jail. She'd heard about Vegas cops. Lot of times they raped the women they brought in. If they didn't like your looks, or you pissed them off more than once, they'd take you out to the desert and use you for target practice instead of highway signs or bottles, and just leave you out there . . .

"SHUT THE FUCKUP, ROSS!" she bellowed. Then thought: Oh great, that's even worse. She hissed: "Be quiet! I don't want anybody to come in here—"

"They were here, to bring towels, and they told me women don't go for the ring alone! That's not any kind of tradition! You come on out, no more little jokes!"

"*You're* a fucking little joke!" she yelled, as he started kicking the door. She turned the knob and slammed the door outward. Felt him bounce off it on the other side. Heard him slide across the rug, stop against the bedframe. A wail, then a shout of rage.

She thought again about a will. He might have more money stashed someplace, or some coming. But there was no way this thing was going to last out the night and she couldn't get him to a lawyer tonight and he was already suspicious. She'd have to just get his Rolex and his thirty bucks—twenty some now after the champagne—and maybe those little pajamas, sell that shit, no first get—

She paused to hit the pipe again. Part of her, tweakin', listened intensely for the hotel's manager or the cops.

—get that call through to his manager, make him give the manager dude some bullshit story, have him send the most cash possible. Maybe hustle a thousand bucks. Or maybe the little guy could be sold himself somewhere, Circus Circus or some place, or some kind of pervert. No, too hard to handle. Just make the call and then he should get a heart attack or something. He deserved it, he'd hustled *her*, telling her he had money, was a big star, but all the time he wasn't doing shit, getting her to marry him under false pretenses, fucking little parasite, kick his miniature ass . . .

A pounding low on the bathroom door again. Angrier now. The door was partly open. Little fucker was scared to put a limb through, but he stood to one side and peered in at her. "What is that? What is that in your hands? Drugs! Shit, you're going to get us put in jail and you're going to ruin my career! It'll be a big scandal and Arnold won't want to be in a picture with me and—!" He had to break off for wheezing, and she heard him puff a couple of times on his inhaler, which was funny, how it was like her pipe.

She kicked the door open. He jumped back, narrowly avoiding its swishing arc. Fell on his little butt. For a moment she felt bad because he looked so much like one of her kids, like he was going to cry, and then for some reason that made her even madder, and she stepped out, pipe in one hand and lighter in the other, and kicked at him, clipping him on the side of the head with her heel. He spun, and blood spattered the yellow bedspread.

She paused to hit the pipe, melting another rock. Then she came slowly at him as she took a hit. Her mouth was starting to taste like the pipe filter more than coke, she wasn't getting good hits, she needed cash, get some cash and get a cab.

He was up on his feet, scuttling toward the door to the hall. He was just tall enough to operate the knob. There was no way she could let the little fucker go, and no way she was going to let the rollers get her in Vegas, fuck that. She crossed the room in three strides, exhaling as she went, trailing smoke like a locomotive, doing an end run around him, turning to block the door. He backed away, his face in darkness. He was making some kind of ugly hiccuping noise. He didn't look like a human being now, in the dimness and through the dope; he looked like some kind of little gnome, or like one of those little fuckers in that movie *Gremlins,* which was what he was like, some sneaky little thing going to run around in the dark spots and pull shit on you.

Maybe the microwave. If you didn't turn it up much it just sort of boiled things inside, it could look like he'd had a stroke. She had persuaded him to check in without her, they didn't know she was here. Unless he'd told the girl with the towels.

"You tell anybody I was here?"

He didn't answer. Probably, Brandy decided, he wouldn't have told much to some cheap hotel maid. So there was nothing stopping it.

He turned and scrambled under the bed. "That ain't gonna do you no good you little fucker," she whispered.

∞ ∞ ∞

Ross heard her moving around up there. He pictured her in a nun's habit. The nuns, when they were mad at him, would hunt him through the mission; he would hide like a rodent in some closet till they found him.

The dust under the bed was furring his throat, his lungs. He wheezed with asthma. She was going to get him into a corner, and kick him. She'd kick him and kick him with those hard, pointy shoes until his ribs stove in and he spit up blood. He tried to shout for help, but it came out a coarse whisper between wheezes. He sobbed and prayed to the Virgin and Saint Jude.

He heard her muttering to herself. He heard her move purposefully, now, to a corner of the room. He heard glass break. Surely someone would hear that and come?

What was she doing? What had she broken?

"Little hustlin' tight-ass motherfucker," she hissed, down on her knees now, somewhere behind him. Something scraped across the rug; he squirmed about to see. It was the tall floor lamp. She'd broken the top of it, broken the bulb, and now she was wielding it like an old widow with a broom handle trying to get at a rat, sliding it under the bed, shoving the long brass pole of it at him.

It was still plugged in. A cluster of blue sparks jumped from the bulb jags broken off in the socket as she shoved it at his face.

He tried to scream and rolled aside. The lopsided king's crown of glass swung to follow him, sparking. He could smell shreds of rug burning. He thought he could feel his heart bruising against his breastbone. She shoved the thing at him again, forcing him back farther . . . Then it stopped moving. She had moved away. Giggling.

Moving around the bed—

Ross felt her fingers close around his ankle. Felt himself dragged backwards, his face burning in the dusty rug, the back of his head smacking against the bed slats. He gave out a wail that tightened into a shriek of frustration, as she jerked him out from under the bed.

He clawed and kicked at her. She was just a great blur, a strange medicinal smell, big slapping hands. One of the hands connected hard and his head rang with it. He began to gag, and found himself unable to lift his arms. Like one of those dreams where you are trapped by a great beast, you want to run but your limbs won't work. She was carrying him somewhere, clasped against her, trapped in her arms like a dog to be washed.

He gagged again. Heard her say, from somewhere above, "Don't you fucking puke on me you little freak."

His eyes cleared. He saw she was carrying him toward a big box, open on this side. The place had an old, used, cheap microwave oven. The early ones had been rather big . . .

"*Bennnnyyyyyyyy!*" But it never quite made it out of his throat.

In less than a second she had crammed him inside it. He could feel his arms and legs again, feel the glass lining of the microwave oven against the skin of his hands and face; his head crammed into a corner, his cheek smashed up against the cold glass. He found some strength and kicked and she swore at him and grabbed his ankles in both her hands, stuffed his legs in far enough so she could press against his feet with the closing door. He could feel her whole weight against the door.

Crushed into a little box. A little box. Crushed into a little . . .

He pressed his palms flat against the glass, tucked his knees against his chest, deliberately pulling deeper into the oven. Felt her using the opportunity to close the door on him.

But now he had some leverage. He used all his strength and a lifetime of frustration and *kicked*.

The door smacked outward, banging against her chest. She lost her footing; he heard her fall backwards, even as he scrambled back and dropped out of the oven, fell to the floor himself, landing painfully on his small feet. She was confused, cursing incoherently, trying to get up. He laughed, feeling light-headed and happy.

He sprinted for the living room, jumping over her outstretched leg, and ran into the bedroom area. He could see the door, the way out, clearly ahead of him, unobstructed.

Brandy got up. It was like she was climbing a mountain to do it. Something wet on the back of her head. The little fucker. The pipe. When had it got broken? It was broken, beside the sink. She grabbed the stem. It'd make a knife.

Shit—maybe the little fucker had already gotten out the door.

She felt her lip curl into a snarl, and ran toward the door—her ankle hooked on the wire stretched across the rug, about three inches over it, drawn from the bed frame to the dresser.

The lamp cord, she thought, as she pitched face first onto the rug. She hadn't left the cord that way . . .

The air knocked out of her, she turned onto her back choking, trying to orient herself.

The little fucker was standing over her, laughing, with the champagne bottle in his little hands; he clasped the bottle by the neck. A narrow bar of light came in between the curtains, spotlighting his round red mouth.

He was towering over her, from that angle, as he brought the champagne bottle down hard on her forehead.

"A BURGLAR KILLED MY NEW BRIDE!"
SOBS WORLD'S SMALLEST MAN

. . . The newlywed bride of Ross Taraval, the world's smallest man was murdered by an intruder on the first night of their Las Vegas honeymoon. Ross himself was battered senseless by the mystery man—and woke to find that his wife had been struck unconscious, raped, and murdered. Her throat had been cut by the broken glass of the drug-crazed killer's "crack" pipe. The burglar so far has not been located by police.

"It broke my heart," said the game little rooster of a man, "but I have learned that to survive in this world when you are my size, you must be stronger than other men! So I will go on . . . And I have not given up my search for the right woman, to share my fame and fortune . . . "

Ross hints that he's on the verge of signing a deal to do a buddy movie with his hero, Arnold Schwarzanegger. A big career looms up ahead for a small guy! "I'd like to share it with some deserving woman!" Ross says.

If you'd like to send a letter to Ross Taraval, the world's smallest man, you can write to him care of the *Weekly World Inquirer*, and we'll forward the letter to him . . .

Will the Chill

"I refuse to speak to him," declared Tondius Will.

"If you don't, there will be no more sponsor," replied Great Senses. The biocyber computer paused, its wall of lights changed from consider-ing-yellow to assertion-blue; the programming room's shadows fled be-fore the brighter blue so that the oval chamber resembled the interior of a great turquoise egg.

The ship's computer asserted: "Sports-eyes is serious. No interview, no sponsorship."

"Very well. Let there be an end to it."

"Nonsense. You cannot live without Contest. Mina's death proved that." Great Senses said, its fifty-by-fifty-meter panel of honeycomb-crystal glow-ing red for regret amid the blue of assertion. "You cannot live without Contest and you cannot Contest without a contestship. And this starship is owned by Sports-eyes. And there is the immense cost of the planet-push-coils to consider . . ."

"I'll find a way to sponsor it myself." But even as he said it, Tondius Will knew it was impossible.

"Sports-eyes has legal access to this ship. If you refuse to speak with the reporter, you'll have to talk to the show's director. And he'll come here *personally*. And you know how they like to touch you in greeting— on the lips. Latest homeworld fad."

Will the Chill spat in disgust. The self-cleaning walls of the ship ab-sorbed the spittle.

"All right," said Will. "I'll speak to the reporter. But only on the screen. Should I dress? What is the present custom?"

"No need. Nudity is sanctioned."

Will turned and strode to the lift, rode the compression tube to ter-tiary level, communications. He glimpsed his reflection in the glass of the communication room's inactive screen. He was golden-skinned, compact but muscular, utterly hairless, his bald scalp gleaming with metal hookup panels—for his physical guidance-rapport with Great Senses and the contestship—set flush with his cranium. His dark-eyed, pensive features, already cold, intensified as he approached the screen. His full lips hardened to thin lines; his hairless brows creased.

A nulgrav cushion darted from a wall niche to uphold him as he sat. The screen flickered alive. The Sports-eyes communications ensign, a spaceship shaped like an eye, flashed onto the screen. The sign faded, and Will faced a spindly, nude, gray-haired man with tiny, restive blue eyes and lips that seemed permanently puckered.

The stranger ceremoniously blew Will a kiss. Will merely nodded. The man moved uneasily in his seat; his shoulders bobbed, his thin cheeks ticked, his prominent Adam's apple bounced. "Eric Blue here." He spoke rapidly. "They call me Blue the Glue. This is a guh-reat honor for me, Tondius Will. A very great honor."

Will shrugged.

Blue the Glue pounced on Will the Chill. "Will, it's my understanding that you didn't want to give this interview. Correct?"

Will nodded slightly.

"Well, uh, Will—heh—why is that? Can you be frank? I mean, you're Titleholder for four Contests, you've been a planet-hurlin' waverider for many longuns now. Twice my lifetime. You've earned two replenishings, so you'll live another century at least. Is this the last interview for another century? As far as I know only one other SprtZ NewZ holorag has spoken to you in your entire—"

"What is the pertinence of this?" Will asked sharply. Blue's voice was abundant with hidden meanings. His face was not his face. Will wished he were back on Five, listening to those who spoke with no faces at all.

"It's relevant to your image. And your image is important to your audience-draw. And your audience-draw is dropping off, Will. Though some say you're the best damn planet-hurler since Elessar in 2270. Still, you don't—?"

"I don't caper and jape for the cameras like Svoboda? I don't brag endlessly on my prowess and gossip about lovers like Browning? I don't soak up publicity like Munger? Is that your complaint?"

"Look, Will, there's a difference between, uh, maintaining *dignity*—and being *cold*. And you're cold, man. That's why they call you Will the—"

"There's a difference between being emotive and artistic, Blue."

"Look here, let me put it to you in the plainest terms. I'm a Sportsize reporter, my job is public relations—*you've* failed to give me anything to relate to that public, Will. Sportsize stars need *audience appeal*. They have to be likable characters. They have to be likable—ah—*folks*. They have to be fellows people can identify with. Not cold and distant automatons—"

"All waveriders are cold and distant, as you put it, Blue," said Will, coldly and distantly. "But most of them pretend they're not, in order to maintain themselves in the public eye. But it is *not* coldness, not really. Not inside. It is the aura of unflinching and unremitting dedication."

Blue the Glue looked startled. "Well. Now we're making progress. The Philosophical Waverider? Image BoyZ might be able to do something with that."

Will snorted.

"Will, I wonder if you'll be kind enough to examine a holotape I have with me and give me your analysis of it. I'll feed it into your screen, with your permission." Without waiting for permission, Blue punched a button and the screen was filled with a simplified holoimage of the final weeks (time-lapsed, sped-up to twenty minutes condensed action) of Will's Contest with Opponent Brigg in system GV5498. Two planets approached one another, one brown-black, crescent-edged with silver, its atmosphere swirling turmoil; the other, Will's masspiece, shining, chrome-blue like the shield of Perseus. Both were approximately Earth-sized and devoid of life, as was customary. Relative to the viewer's plane of perspective, the planets closed obliquely, Brigg's from the lower left-hand corner and Will's from the upper righthand corner of the rectangular screen.

How diluted the public impression of Contest! Will thought.

The right-hand planet, GV5498 Number Four, showed white pushcoil flares at its equator and Southern Pole. Atmospheric disturbances and volcanic explosions roiled the contiguous faces of the planets as gravitational fields meshed and struggled.

Involuntarily, Will twitched and flexed his arms as if he were in hookup again, adjusting pushcoils, controlling the tilt, impetus, spin, momentum, and mass resistance of his masspiece.

Seconds before impact, as dead seas boiled and ice caps fractured, as continents buckled, the pushcoil on the South Polar face toward Will's Opponent flared and forced the pole to swing back, tilting the axis, lobbing the North Polar bulge forward, precipitating collision before Opponent expected it.

Opponent's planet took the worst of the collision forces. And after the impact, the orgasmic rending of two worlds: more of Will's masspiece remained intact than remained of Opponent's. So Tondius Will won the Contest. And took Title from Brigg.

The two Sports-eyes contestships, Will's and Brigg's, were glimpsed speeding to safety from the still-exploding bodies—

The image vanished, the face of Blue the Glue returned. "Now," said Blue, "why did you fire that pushcoil on your South Pole, the face toward Opponent, during the last stage's final—"

"It should be obvious," Will interrupted wearily. "You must have noticed that my masspiece had a more irregular spherism than Brigg's. There was more mass in the North Polar hemispheres. I applied torque in order to use the club-end of the planet with the greatest force of momentum—this can be useful only in rare instances, and Brigg probably hadn't seen it before. Most impacts are initiated along the equatorial swell."

"I see. Beautiful. Uh, such niceties are too often lost on the Sports-eyes viewer who sees—"

"Niceties! It was the most obvious ploy of the game. Brigg perceived it instantly but too late; he couldn't compensate in time. Niceties! The most important plays of the game are the early stages when masspieces are moved into place for the final approach to designated impact zone. What is this whole affair to you, Blue? What can you know of the exquisite visions of hookup? You see only very limited aspects of Contest. You observe composite images, you see them in timelapse and you see only brief flashes of the months of preparation. There is no comprehension of the internal artistry requisite—we spend weeks at a time in hookup, assessing and tasting and physically experiencing every known factor in hundreds of millions of cubic kilometers of space!" Will was not aware that he was shouting. "*What is it to you?* A contest between two waveriders hovering off dead planets which they seem to—to shove about by remote control, kicking—*kicking!*—the planets out of orbit and tossing them at one another—and the piece surviving impact with the greatest mass determines Winner. That's all it is, to you. You *huzzah* at the 'flight' of planets, their gargantuan turnings; they seem like colossal bowling balls in the hands of mites riding tiny specks and you swill your drink and clap your hands when you see the wracking and cracking of impact. You enjoy the sight of planets cracked like eggshells! Idiots! What do you know of the possession of men by worlds? Can you even for an instant imagine—"

Will stopped. He swallowed, sat back, untensing. Specks of black swarmed his vision.

Blue was grinning.

"I suppose," said Tondius Will ruefully, "that you're proud of yourself now, eh, Blue? You recorded my little tirade, no doubt. You'll crow about it at the SprtZwrtrZ Club. How you got a rise out of Will the Chill." Will's tone was bitter ice.

"It's good to see passion in you, Will! Though I have to admit I don't entirely get your meaning. But why are you so tight with your enthusiasm, Will? We can build your ratings if you'll give me more of that. And, really, can't you leak us just a little of your love life?"

"I have no lover: male, female, or bimale. None."

"No? None? Except your masspieces and playing fields, perhaps . . . But you had a lover once, didn't you, Tondius?"

Will felt his face growing hard and dark with anger.

Blue spoke rapidly. "Just for the sake of accurate historical perspective, listen, please, and answer my question—a yes or no will do. I have a document here I'd like to read to you. I want to know if what it states is true or false. Is this true? 'In A.D. 2649 Tondius Will's fourth confrontation with Enphon brought him at last into the public eye and put him in the running for Title. It was said he had prepared for this Contest for eight years; Enphon's reputation doubtless warranted this, but eight years is unprecedented even for a waverider.

"'It is known that at this time Will's lover, Mina Threeface, was not permitted to visit the waverider—he avoided all distractions. For eight years he refused to screen to her for more than a period of ten minutes once a month. The lover of a waverider is best advised to understand his need for utter concentration. Apparently, Mina did not understand. She hovered just out of scanrange in her father's yacht and, minutes before impact, she dove on a sure course for the impact zone between masspieces, dispatching an emergency transmission to Tondius Will: *I've gone to Impact Zone. Avert your masspiece, lose Contest because you love me. Or I die.* His Great Senses dutifully relayed this message to Will. Tondius Will's thoughts can only be conjectured. He had to measure the scope of two loves. He found he could not permit himself to surrender or even stalemate Contest simply to save Mina. She was trapped between impacting planets, she died there and, though Will won Contest, it was this victory that also won him the cognomen Will the Chill—'"

"Yes," Will said softly, though inwardly he shook with the effort at self-control. "It's all true. It's true." And he added: "Your heart, Blue—your heart is far more *chill* than mine will ever be."

Will broke contact and strode to the hookup chambers.

∞ ∞ ∞

Hookup flushed Will's circulation, winnowing fatigue poisons from his blood, unclouding his brain. Refreshed, he adjusted hookup from *yoga* to *extern*. The cushions at his back, the cups gripping his shaven pate, the crowded instrument panel—all seemed to vanish. He closed his eyes and saw the universe.

The senses (but not the mind) of Great Senses were his, now. He scanned first through visible light. He had been orbiting Roche Five for two months; the alien constellations overwheeling the Roche system seemed almost natively familiar. Dominating the right-hand scope of his vision: Five, fifth planet from Roche's Star, bulking half in golden-red light, half in shadow. Five was Will's Contest masspiece. And patching into a drifting Sportseyes camera satellite's signal, he could see himself: his contestship soaring above the twilight border, north-south over the face of the Earth-sized planet. The contestship, with its outspread solar panels and the beaked globe at its forward end, resembled a metallic vulture scanning the barren planet face beneath.

Not quite barren, thought Will the Chill. The survey crew was wrong— there's more than desert and ruins down there.

He looked up from Five, and sought for Opponent. Focusing away from visible light, he worked his way down ("down") through infrared's multifarious blaze, down through the longer wave lengths. He sorted through the transmissions of the star itself, discarded background sources, letting frequencies riffle by like an endless deck of cards, each card with its wave-length-identifying signet. He was looking for a Queen of Diamonds. She wasn't transmitting. He worked his way up ("up"), toward shorter wave lengths, and ten thousand hairs split themselves ten thousand times apiece. He skimmed X-rays, and, through hookup's multifaceted neutrino-focused eyes, spotted her, traced her spoor of nuclear radiation—she was using a hydrogen-scoop, fusing, traveling overspace, so Will's Great Senses (constantly monitoring gravwave ripplings) wouldn't notice her change of position. She was far from Three, her own masspiece.

What was she doing? Then—Will shuddered. A strong probe signal had bounced from his contestship. He felt it again, and again. He waited. It came no more. He traced the signals and found that the source was Opponent's contestship, fusing to travel unnoticed in ordinary space. Will tied in with Great Senses. "Did you feel that?"

"Someone tasted our defense screens with a probe signal," Great Senses replied, voice particularly mechanical coming through hookup channels. "Who was it?"

"It was Opponent! She's traveling through upper space so we wouldn't be likely to think the probe came from her . . . no reason for her to assess us from that direction, surreptitiously. She knew in this stage we'd expect to find her wave-riding. What do you think? Is she testing our reflexes or trying to kill us?"

"Three sleeps gone there was a disguised Opponent drone—I recognized it for what it was because it was maneuvering in a pattern for which a Sports-eyes vehicle would have no use. It was probing our defense systems."

"You didn't tell me."

"I was waiting for confirmation of my suspicions. We have it now."

"She plans to kill me."

"That's within the scope of Contest rules. She has the right to kill you. Under certain conditions."

"It's accepted technically but it's not considered sporting. No one's killed an Opponent for half a thousand Contests."

"Shall we kill her first?"

"No. I shall Contest, and I'll defend myself. She's inexperienced. Luck brought her this far. She's too impulsive to take the Title."

"But she has innersight. Admittedly she's unjudicious, little precision as yet. Her Opponent second to last died in deep space . . . She admitted nothing. They said it was a leak."

"I didn't know." Will snorted. "So, she's a killer. Let her kill if she can. That's all—I'm going back to scanning."

"One moment. Do you want me to maintain ship's gravity?"

"Yes. I'll be going planetside. After hookup. I've got to go down to—ah—" He hesitated. Why lie to Great Senses? But he couldn't bring himself to voice the truth. So he said: "I'm going down to inspect the fusion scoops. All that dust—there may be corrosion on the pushcoils. And we'll keep the planet in this orbit for another sleep. Until then, maintain gravity. I want to be grav-adjusted—I might be going planetside fairly often." He broke contact with Great Senses.

But in the programming room the lights of Great Senses went from questioning-green to doubting-orange.

The atmosphere of Five was breathable, but too rarefied to nourish him long. So he wore a respirator. Also, a thermalsuit against the bitter cold, the cutting winds. That was all. Unweaponed (against the advice of Great Senses: Opponent skulked nearer), he leaped from the airlock of the lander. He stretched, getting the wieldiness of planetside back into his limbs. He walked a few meters to a large boulder, clambered atop it, and looked about him.

Just below, the double-domed lander squatted on spidery limbs. Beyond the lander, many kilometers across the battered yellow plain, rose the shining column of the nearest pushcoil, the planetmover.

Anemic sunlight glanced from its argent hide, light streaks chasing the shadows of striated dust clouds skating low in the bluegray sky. It was afternoon, but overhead a few stars guttered, visible in thin atmosphere.

The pushcoil column towered, broad and austere, into the clouds and beyond. Its lower end widened into a compression skirt that uniformly clamped the ground; steam and fumes trailed from vents in the conical skirt: the column was converting minerals into energy, building power for conversion into magnetic push. There were ten such columns placed at regular intervals about the planet. Put there by the Sports-eyes Corporation for Will the Chill's exclusive use.

Made from metals extracted from Five's core, the columns were powered geothermally. Sports-eyes had built hundreds on hundreds of worlds. Worlds now asteroid belts and clouds of dust; crushed and dispersed for the amusement of jaded millions on the homeworld.

The Sports-eyes crew had departed months before; Will was glad that they were gone. He hadn't spoken to another human being, except on screen, since Mina's death, years before.

Will turned and gazed west. Roche's Star was low, opposite the column. Long shadows reached from the endless scatter of boulders and crater rims. The meteorite-scored hills to the north stretched to him like the pitted, skeletal fingers of a dead giant.

Will strode into the grasp of those peninsular fingers.

In those hills were the ruins, and the sunharp, and the voices. Will began to climb, anticipation growing.

In the ship. In the hookup chamber. In the hookup seat. In hookup.

Time to re-examine the playing field. He tested the solar wind, noted its slant and strength.

Then he immersed himself in somatic-eidetic impressions of gravitational energy. An exquisitely fine and resiliently powerful fabric flexed between star systems. On this skein a star and ten planets moved like monstrous spiders, electromagnetic grips adhering them to the field, bending the webwork. The gravitational field was the playing field, and Will examined each component's interaction with the whole.

Will needed no numerical calculation. No holotrigonometry. He had never got beyond the multiplication tables. All he needed was hookup and Great Senses and the skill, the innersight. Great Senses was navigator, astrogator, life-systems watch. Hookup was Will's cerebral connection with the ship's electronic nerves, a binding of synthetic and biological neural systems. Will's was the instinct, the athleticism, the determination. Determiner of destinations.

He knew the ship physically.

The ship's cognizance of (and interaction with) visible light, cosmic rays, gamma rays, nuclear forces—these he felt in his loins. Physically.

De hipbone is connected to de backbone; the electro is connected to the magnetic. The seat of his magnetic sensorium was his spine. This chakra he experienced in the region of his heart. Electricity in the heart. Physically.

He comprehended the gravitational field through shoulders, legs, arms. Very physically.

In loins, light-packets. In heart, electromagnetism. In limbs, gravity.

In hookup they integrated as variations on the wave-particle theme: in his brain. Sometimes, Tondius Will remembered a poem, one of many the ship's library had recited to him. It was Blake . . .

Energy is the only life and is
  from the body:
and Reason is the bound or outward
circumference of Energy.
Energy is Eternal Delight.

Innersight hookup. On one level he knew the vast gravitational field in term of mass and weight, gross proportions.

Take it down, another and broader condition of unity.

He penetrated the vacillation of gravitrons, the endless alternation between wave and particle forms, slipped the knife edge of his innersight into the transitory sequence between wave into particle and particle into wave; waves, here, revealed as particles and particles exposed: packets of waves.

His brain took a Picture, recorded and filed it. He had memorized the playing field.

And that was enough for now. He willed internalization. Hookup shut down his connection with Great Senses. He sat up and yawned. But his eyes glittered.

He was hungry, and there was no hookup here to feed and refresh him. He was weary, but the hills drew him on. There was only the sighing wind, hiss of breath in respirator, clink of small air tanks on his belt, crunch of his boot steps in sand. And the wide-open, the empty. He trudged the rim of a crater, admiring the crystalline glitter streaking its slopes, the red nipple of iron oxides in the impact basin. On the far side of this crater were the ruins, upthrusting along the broken ridges like exposed spinal segments. Light splashed off the sunharp, still half a kilometer away.

The sun was westering behind the mesas, the jet sky overhead spread shadow wings to enfold the bluer horizons.

Will slid down the embankment, enjoying the earthy heft of hillside resisting his boots. He reached the floor of the gully and picked his way over rough shin-high boulders to the base of the hill whose crown exposed the first stretch of ragged ruins, uneven walls like battlements above.

The hills were not simple hills—they were barrows, grave mounds cloaking the remains of a once-city. Here, an earthslide triggered by a meteorite strike had exposed a portion of the city's skeleton. The walls of rusted metal and cracked glass and tired plastics, throwing jagged shadows in the fading daylight, were notched and scored with age, erosion.

But there were no signs of war, on the ruins. These were not broken battlements . . . Genetic Manipulation experiments had released an unstoppable plague, robbing the world of most of its life and all its fertility. No offspring were born to lower life forms, or to the world's people. People they were, of a sort, with tendrils instead of boned fingers and large golden whiteless eyes like polished stones. The plants withered, the air thinned, the land died. Those who survived, one hundred thousand living on chemically synthesized food, were so long-lived they were nearly immortal. Childless, living without societal evolution in an endlessly bleak landscape, they surrendered to a growing collective sense of futility. A new religion arose, preaching fulfillment beyond the veil of death, advocating mass suicide. A vote was taken, its tally unanimous. The remaining one hundred thousand decided to die. To die by poison, together, and all at once . . .

For so Will had been told. The voices in the sunharp told him this.

He passed through the maze of roofless ruins, coming to the broad square at their radial center. He beheld the sunharp. Everything here had decayed but the sunharp. It had been built at the end, as a monument. Built to endure a nova.

The diamond-shaped sunharp's frame was constructed of light silvery tubing. A coppery netting was woven densely between the frames, for sifting and carrying light impulses.

The final rays of sunset, veering lances of red, broke the thin dust cloud and struck the coppery sunharp wires. Till now it had been singing in the subsonic. Struck full by corpuscular rays, its netting vibrated visibly, resonated internally, interpreted the sun shiver. Translated into sound waves, photons sang out. Choirs of alien races, chorus of human voices, subhuman voices, wolves baying and birds singing: all in concert. The wind sounds of thousands of landscapes (each landscape altering the wind song as Bach's inventions vary the hymnal theme) combining into a single voice. The nature of rippling endlessly defined in song.

Will listened, and more than listening: he heeded. And if Blue the Glue had seen Will's face just then, he might not have recognized him; he did not associate joy with Will the Chill.

Royal purple gathered in the ground hollows, dusty darkness collected in the dead windows of the ruins, the stars shone more fiercely, the mesas at the horizon swallowed the sun. The sunharp's call dwindled to lower frequencies, softly moaning to starlight and occasionally pinging to cosmic rays. Other sighs came to replace the sunharp's voice. Will shuddered and, for an instant, dread enfolded his heart. But the fear left him abruptly, as it always did before they spoke to him. He smiled. "Hello," he said aloud.

There came a reply, one hundred thousand voices speaking the same word at once, a mighty susurration in an alien tongue. A greeting.

Then they spoke subvocally, in his own tongue, echoes within the skull.

For the fifth time you have returned to us (said the voices). But the first time and the three thereafter you came alone. Why have you now brought a companion?

"I have no companions," said Tondius Will.

We see now that you do not know about the one who follows you. It is a lurking *he* who does the bidding of a distant *she*. The *he* comes to destroy you.

"Then he is an assassin," said Will sadly, "sent by my Opponent. She becomes reckless. She has breached the rules of Contest. Death-dealing must be done by Opponent or by her machines only. Still, I will not protest. Let him come."

The time is not yet, Tondius Will.

"Will the time be soon?"

You doubt us. You wonder if you are the One prophesied by the Gatekeeper. You are he. Ten thousand times in ten thousand millenniums we have attempted transit to the fuller spheres. Ten thousand times we have been denied. *One hundred thousand cannot enter as one,* said the Gatekeeper, *unless they become onemind, or unless they are guided by a sailor of inner seeing.* We were bound together by a united death. Simultaneity. We plunged together into that tenuous Place, this between. We need a guide to lead us out. Do not doubt us. You are He. The Gatekeeper whose seven stony visages exhale blacklight said to us: *One who wields spheres below can guide you through spheres above . . .* You are He. We know your history, Tondius Will.

"My father . . ."

Was an orbitglider, a great athlete of space race.

"My mother . . ."

Was a freefall ballerina for a space-station ballet company.

"My grandfather . . ."

Was an Earthborn snow skier of Earth who journeyed to the ultimate ski course on mountainous Reginald IV, and died on Thornslope.

"My great-grandfather . . ."

Was a Terran trapeze artist.

"My great-grandmother . . ."

Was a surfer on the vast seas of terra-formed Venus, and once rode a wave for seven days.

"And I came to waveriding . . ."

When your mother killed herself en route to Earth from your father's doom on Reginald IV, and the captain of the transport adopted you; he was himself a retired waverider.

"And I know your history, and how you came to die, one hundred thousand at a single stroke, trapped by imperfect unity . . ."

We are as one hundred thousand waves . . .

"On a single sea."

The understanding forged anew, the voices hushed. The air about him began to course and whirl, a dust-devil rose up and the spirit host—seen in the dark of his closed eyes as endless banners of unfurling white— enclosed Tondius Will. He wept in unbridled joy and relief as they entered him, and swept him up . . . He could not abide the touch of flesh on flesh, not since he had crushed Mina between two worlds. They took him with them, for a while, and let him incorporeally ride, like a surfer on a sea constituted of the ectoplasm of one hundred thousand souls. For this time of merging, loneliness was beyond conception. For this time of—

But it ended.

Returned to his body, he felt like an infant coughed from the womb into a snowdrift.

He screamed. He begged. "Please!"

No longer (the voices said), for now. If we kept you from your body any longer, you'd wither and pass on to us. It would be too soon. You're not quite ready to lead us yet, though you have the innersight of energies, particles, and planes. You are a born sailor of upper spheres. But not quite yet. Next time. Soon.

"Wait! One thing! You said you would search for her. Have you found her? Was she too far away?"

Linear distances don't impede our call. We have found her. She was very much alone. She is coming. Next time. Soon. (The voices faded.)

They were gone. Will was alone in the dark.

The sunharp moaned faintly. Distant whispers; starlight rumors stirred its webwork.

He shivered in sudden awareness of the night's cold. Stretching, he fought numbness from his limbs. He turned up the heat in his thermalsuit, checked his air tanks' reading. Best get back to the landing pod, and soon.

He turned and began to descend the hillside. At the outermost finger of the ragged walls, he stopped and listened. He nodded to himself.

He took an electric light from his belt, flicked it alive, and set the small beacon on a ledge of the crumbling wall. "Come out and face me as you shoot me!" he called.

Silence, except for the echo of his shout.

Then, a squeak of boot steps on gravel. A broad, dark figure in a gray thermalsuit stepped warily from a murky doorway. He was two meters from Will. Most of the assassin's face was concealed by goggles and respirator mask. "You are one of the guild," Tondius Will observed. The assassin nodded. He held a small silver tube lightly in his right hand. The tube's muzzle was directed at Will's chest. Will said, "It is a tenet of your guild that if your quarry discovers you and challenges you then you are compelled to face him. Yes?"

The assassin nodded.

"Well then, come into the light of my lamp. I want to see some of your face as you kill me. You can't begrudge me that, surely."

The assassin took two strides forward, stepping into the ring of light. His lips were compressed, his eyes were gray as the ice a thousand meters beneath the ice cap. His thick legs were well apart and braced.

Will the Chill fastened his eyes on those of the assassin. The stranger frowned.

Tondius Will spoke in a voice compelling; it was compelling because his voice was the raiment of his will power, and his will was backed by the unspeakable mass of all the planets he had hurled. He said: "I am going to move my arm quickly in order to show you something. Do not fire the weapon, I am not going to reach for you. I'm going to reach into this wall . . . The guild of assassins esteems its members greatly skilled in martial arts . . ."

To his left was a high wall of transparent bricks backed by old metal. Ancient but solid. Will had explored these ruins thoroughly. He knew that there was a metal urn on the other side of the wall, lying on a shelf; he knew just where it was. He moved, visualizing his left hand passing through the obstruction as if through a cloud, fingers closing about the small urn; he pitted perfect form against the mass resistance of the wall.

There was a *crack!* and a small explosion in the wall side; dust billowed, chips of glass rained. The assassin twitched but did not fire. Will withdrew his arm from the hole he'd made. He held something in his bare hand. A stoppered urn of age-dulled gold. "Waveriders learn that masses are merely electron-bounded fields of space-influence," he remarked casually, examining the urn in the dim light, "and all fields have a weak point, where that which seems impenetrable may be penetrated." He paused, glanced up, murmuring, "That's the principle behind the traversing of space between stars: knowledge of secret passages through the fabric of spacestuff. And it's the principle behind what you've just seen, assassin." Will reached out with his right hand, poised it over the urn, and, with a motion outspeeding the eye, he stabbed a rigid thumb at the metal casing held in his other hand. The urn split neatly in two; half of it dropped to the ground. The assassin took a step backward; his eyes dancing with wonder, he held his fire.

Tondius Will reached into the half of the urn in his left hand and extracted something that had lain there for ten thousand millennia. A tiny skeleton to which a thin shroud of skin clung; a miniature mummy. "It's an infant who died at birth," Will muttered. "The urn was his sarcophagus. A shame to disturb it. So . . ." He bent, retrieved the fallen half, replaced it over the mummy. Clamping the two halves snug with his left hand, with the thumb of his right he pressed the seams of the urn, all the way around, fusing it shut. Moving slowly and easily, he replaced the urn in the hole he had made in the wall. Then he returned his gaze to the eyes of the assassin. "Now: can you match what I have just done?"

The assassin slowly shook his head.

"Then, you know that I could kill you," said Will lightly, taking a cautious step forward so that he was within striking distance. "I could kill you even before you pressed the fire stud of your charge gun." Will smiled. "Yes?"

Looking stooped and weary, the assassin nodded.

"Therefore, your mission is useless. Depart now, in peace."

The assassin shook his head . . . The tenets of the assassin's guild.

Will saw the man's eyes narrow. Will knew, a split-second realization, that the assassin was depressing the stud of his charge gun.

Will struck, doubly. One hand struck aside the charge gun, the other dipped into the assassin's chest. Just as that hand had penetrated the wall.

Will took something from the man's chest and held it up for him to see.

Spurting blood from the gaping crater in his chest, the assassin took two seconds to collapse, two more to die.

In A.D. 1976 the physicist-philosopher Denis Postle said: "Mass-energy tells space-time how to curve and curved space-time tells mass-energy how to move."

Imagine that you are involved in a competition which requires that, with your right hand, you throw a discus with Olympic skill, while your legs are performing an elaborate ballet movement and with your left hand you are playing the world tennis champion (and winning), and in between racquet strokes you must move a piece to attack a champion chessmaster effectively on a three-dimensional chessboard. If you can imagine doing all that in near simultaneity, then you know something of what it is to be a waverider.

Externally. In hookup, Will's eyes were closed, his hands were clamped rigidly on armrests, his legs flexed and poised; except for his heaving chest, he seemed inert—about to fly to activity like a drawn bowstring.

Internally. He saw himself, in his mind's eye, floating naked in space; outside him were luminous matrices, the energy fields, flickering in and out of ken as he looked up and down the spectrum. He approached a pulsing sphere—to innersight, the sphere seemed only ten meters across. It traveled in preordained paths through the matrix. Paths *he* had ordained. He had set this globe on the road it was taking by manipulating pushcoils situated about the vast surface of its genuine counterpart, Roche Five.

He felt the presence of Opponent, though he could not yet see her. He sensed her position as a man with closed eyes knows the whereabouts of the sun by the feel of its glare on his eyelids. She had not yet moved Roche Three from tertiary-stage orbit. But she was there, satelliting Three elliptically, just within pushcoil-control range. She was waiting for Will to serve.

Will served. He reached out, mentally, for the imaged sphere. He placed his hand near the Eastcenter South Polar pushcoil, poised over the pushcoil column in a hand posture that told Great Senses exactly how much push should be exerted by the coil, and for how long, and at what intervals. Through hookup, Great Senses drank Will's muscular expressions, translated them into mathematical formulas. Great Senses knew Will's flesh, though Will denied that flesh to humanity.

Except for autonomic functions, breathing and blood moving, Will's every movement (as visualized on the noumenon plane, hookup) represented, to Great Senses, a signal to be transmitted to the pushcoil control units on Five.

Externally. He was rippling like an eel, rippling purposefully, sending three dozen signals in one dozen seconds. Sometimes several pushcoils were activated simultaneously, sometimes one at a time; on each occasion the activation signal carried a precisely quantified regulation of the thrust applied.

Roche Five moved out of orbit.

A man about 1.8 meters high and weighing 170 pounds moved a mass of about 6 billion trillion tons, some 11,000 kilometers in diameter. And he did this (apparently) by rotating his hips and flexing shoulder muscles.

Internally. Swimming through space after the sphere, waving his hands about it in intricate patterns like a wizard invoking visions from a crystal ball, he swept it easily (but not effortlessly) in a wide arc, ninety degrees from the solar system's orbital plane, right angles from its former path.

This was stage three-fifty in Contest. Six months since stage one.

The greater the scope entailed in implementing an activity, the greater the need for strict attention to small details.

Each split-second decision taking into account all that Will read of gravitational fields, electromagnetic and heat-energy factors, gravdrag on nearby asteroids, influence of solar wind—the consequences of interaction with these factors.

Will struggled with ecstasy. Each aspect of the celestial field had its own music, in Will's mind, and its own fireworks, exquisite and hypnotic: a threat of distraction.

. . . Opponent drew Roche Three in ever-widening spirals, never quite breaking free of the gravitational field of the sun. She used the pull of the sun, increasing her speed as she neared it. She expended weeks in each strategic repositioning, always moving with strict reference to the ploys of Will the Chill . . .

Concentration opaqued time; Will's fixation on Contest never faltered. The weeks collapsed upon themselves; Three and Five spun nearer, and nearer.

Hookup fed and cleansed him. In place of sleep it washed his unconscious and hung it to dry in the winds of dreaming. Weeks melted into minutes. Sports-eyes recorded all. Sports-eyes staring from a thousand angles, a thousand droneships with camera snouts preparing the composite time-lapse film reducing Contest to the relative simplicity of a bullfight.

They entered the specified ninety thousand cubic kilometers of space agreed upon as Impact Zone.

Like macrocosmic Sumo wrestlers, the planets closed, bulk upon bulk.

The masspieces were ten thousand kilometers apart.

She was closing fast, impulsively, driving straight as a billiard ball, utilizing the equatorial bulge as impending impact point. She was overconfident, perhaps, because Will had not been performing as well as in the past; his mind was troubled, divided. He had to struggle to keep from thinking of the ruins, the sunharp, the voices, and Mina.

This was his final Contest, and his heart pleaded with him to play it to denouement.

But as the two planets engaged for impact—each making minute split-second adjustments in trajectory, rate of spin, and lean of axis—Will rose up from hookup, thinking: *Sports-eyes, this time you're cheated. Crack your own eggshells.*

Great Senses was not capable of surprise. But it was capable of alarm. Alarmed by Will's withdrawal from hookup, the computer spoke to him through ship's intercom. "What's wrong? Impact is in—"

"I know. Less than two hours. So it is scheduled, and so Opponent expects. But there will be no impact. We are stalemating; no one wins. I'll back out of the approach pattern as if I'm preparing another. But Five will never collide with Three."

"Because of the voices in the ruins?"

Will was capable of surprise. "You aren't supposed to read my mind."

"I read only what hookup leaks to me. I know you want to preserve the planet for the voices. The dead one hundred thousand. Why?

They're already dead. Do you want to preserve Five intact as a monument to them?"

"In a way, it will be a monument. But—do you know what they require of me?"

"They want you to guide them upspectrum. Beyond the shortest known wavelengths, the highest frequencies. Into the fuller spheres."

"I want to go. I want to see upspectrum. And I want Mina . . . We have to depart from an intact planet; it's like a door into the Farther Place. If the game were consummated, most of Five would be destroyed . . . The only reason—beyond my love of Contest—that I've played this far was to be near Five. I had to Contest to stay near, since this is sponsor's Ship."

"Within an hour the quakes on Five will begin. If you want to preserve the ruins—"

"I've programmed the backup navigator. You won't have to do a thing. In forty-five minutes the pushcoil will veer Five. Opponent's momentum will prevent her from coming about to strike. As soon as we're out of impact zone, on that instant, transmit a message to her, tell her, as is my right at this point, I declare *stalemate,* by right of points accrued. That will infuriate her."

"And you'll go to the surface of Five."

"Yes . . . and you'll go to serve another waverider."

"And on Five you'll die and go with the unseen multitude."

"Yes."

"How? Will you crash the lander?"

"No. I've got to be in sunharp rapport with them when I die."

"Then—you'll remove your respirator? An ugly death."

"I don't think that will be necessary. She's proved herself to be vindictive. When she discovers the stalemate she'll come after me. She'll find me in rapport."

That was where she found him.

The sudden change in orbital trajectory had riven the surface of Five. The sky was mordant with volcanic smog. Some of the ruins crumbled. The sunharp survived.

Roche Five was moving into a wide, cold, permanent orbit. The pushcoil column, in the waning light like a colossal mailed fist and forearm, flared for the last time.

He stood before the sunharp, tranced by its distant hum. The voices whispered, sang louder, a cry touched by exultation.

"Hello," he said.

Again you have not come alone (said the voices). A *she* comes in a small, armed ship. Just out of sight, in the clouds. She approaches.

"I know. She will be the instrument of our union."

Tondius . . .

"Mina!" shouted Will the Chill warmly.

I'm here.

The planet was rotating into darkness. Light diminished, night engulfed Five. But Tondius Will had no lack of light: "Mina!" he breathed.

She touched him before the others, a chill breath, a kiss of ether. Then the others came and he was borne up, the surfer deliquesced; a sea of one hundred thousand and two waves. His body, still standing, remained alive and for a few moments it tethered him to that plane.

Something metallic broke from the clouds. A chip of light glittered low in the black sky, growing. It was a contestship, diving like a vulture. It spat a beam of harsh red light; the laser passed through Will's chest and through his heart—but before his body crumpled his ears resounded with a joyous cry, the song of the sunharp: struck by the laser passed through his flesh.

One wavelength, infinitely divisible.

Freed of his body Will had no need of hookup. He showed them the way. In a moment, the one hundred thousand and two had gone.

. . . Far over the surface of Five, Great Senses surveyed the planet. Its face of honeycombed crystal was a mixture of three colors: red for regret, blue for considering, green for triumph . . .

Great Senses veered from Five and departed the system.

Opponent's ship departed as well.

Now, Roche Five, icing over, a frigid forever monument to a transcended race, was utterly empty. Except for the lonely ghost of a forgotten assassin.

Tapes 12, 14, 15, 22 and 23

///Therapeutic sessions and lecture address tapes transcribed July 3, 1999 by ML, RK, for files on Dexter Weston Dexter; Dr. Jeremy Berenson, primary mental hygiene physician.

CC: Detective Lt. S. Pearlman, Los Angeles Police Department Homicide Division. Note: emphasis added, as patient raises voice. Due to legal ramifications in this case transcription is unusually detailed as to adjunctive events.///

Tape 12:

[Garbled beginning, psychiatrist adjusts tape recorder.]

Dexter: . . . Sometimes they catch it on video . . . maybe always on video, somebody somewhere enjoying the killing on video, even when the rest of us don't get to see it . . . Kill City . . . Kill City, doctor, like the man said . . .

Doctor: I'm unfamiliar with the reference.

Dexter: Well, it's a song lyric, see, but it's, like prescient, because LA is Kill City and is more Kill City every day.

Doctor: Actually, the Homicide Rate has been going down in pretty much all American cities. Not vastly, but noticeably.

Dexter: Is that somea that shit where you, like, test me to see how I react to real-world input? Like 'I'm from Mars, doctor' and the doctor says, 'Actually you have all the attributes of a human being and I have a fucking birth certificate for you from Quincy, Illinois right here, pal, so get the fuck over it.' And it's just to test his reaction, whether he pretends to agree or not because they know that he is going to believe he's from fucking Mars no matter what they say.

Doctor: Well, yes, it might go something like that, sans the colorful expletives.

Dexter: You're smart, doctor. Almost. You know better than to try to talk my language, 'streety' stuff, like some of them do. You're a hypertrophically educated motherfucker and you talk like one because you know I'm sensitive to phoniness.

Doctor: Yes. Very impressive. Now that I've acknowledged you're impressive, can we get back to what we were talking about, this last week—

Dexter: It sure as hell gets old, the way you guys like to talk about the Parents. Mums and Dad and how they traumatized little Dexter Dexter. That's the first trauma right there, naming a kid Dexter Dexter. Got a lot of shit for it. But don't get hung up on that either, doctor.

Doctor: No, I didn't think dismay over your name would lead to staking out cops and shooting them. But—

Dexter: But the Parents did it some way, yes? How long has it been since Freud first posed that stuff, along with the sexual complexes and the dream thing? A hundred years? And you guys never solve anyone's problem based on the 'it's the parents' assumption. But you don't get a fucking clue! Give it up, *that one ain't workin', dumbshits!*

Doctor: Remember, you have to stay in control or Mike'll be here with the restraints. Big pain in the rear for everyone.

Dexter: I'm cool, I'm chillin', I'm positively nitrogen infused. We wouldn't want Big Mike to interrupt our session.

Doctor: But it's interesting how the very subject of parents causes you to start shouting.

Dexter: You're a cunning fucker. I'm not talking to you anymore today.

Anyway your tape recorder is about to shut off.

Doctor: Tape recorder looks fine to me.

Dexter: I said about to. About to. Watch. Now . . . not yet. *Now.*

///**Break in continuity; resuming tape 12 (RK)**///

Dexter: Get the tape recorder going again, doctor?

Doctor: Yes . . . Well! How'd you manage that! I didn't see you touch it . . . You must have a sense for its batteries . . . oh, no it's plugged in. Oh— you . . . you put something on the tape that made it get stuck, did you?

Dexter: Did I? When did I do that, doctor?

Doctor: I don't know. Coming in? A spitwad? It could just be coincidence. But you probably know something about tape recorders I don't know. This is one way that paranoids with a megalomaniacal fixation tend to—sometimes—gather followers. Like Jim Jones, or Rajneesh. They are very acute observers, their minds are unnaturally quick, they give the appearance of having supernatural abilities because—

Dexter: That bullshit make you feel better, doctor? That's all for today.

Doctor: Is it now? Dexter . . .

Dexter: I'm outta here. Yo, nurseboy! Mike! Take me back to my fucking cell!

Tape 14:

Doctor: How are you feeling, Dex?

Dexter: How are *you* feeling, Doctor Jeremy Berenson? You seem seriously nervous today.

Doctor: No, I'm not, but that remark could be considered a preface to hostility and remember—

Dexter: Oh I know, you can press that button right there and you've got mace and Big Mike'll be in here getting me in his sweaty choke hold. I'm cool, I'm nitrogen cooled.

Doctor: Are you ready to stop playing games and talk about your parents?

Dexter: You know the facts about my parents, dude, you've got my files from the prison psychiatrist, court testimony, and all that shit. White people from a notch above trailer park trash. White trash, but didn't have to be. The very model of dysfunctionality. Daddikins: Classic raging alcoholic, would try to get close to the kids and then blow it all with another boozy rage. Twice in jail for B&E. Mommikins: Kind of a slut, but not an outright whore; drank too much, but tried to hide it. My older brother claims she molested him once, but I think he made that shit up. He's a whiny, delusional fucker.

Doctor: Your mother—

Dexter: Never molested me, no. That'd be too easy a diagnosis, right? My Mom was really pretty intelligent, kind of unusually sharp, and her dad was too, and my own IQ was way up there for a kid who cut class most of the time, but that didn't keep us from being white trash—

Doctor: That's a social judgment, that white trash business. Do you really buy into that?

Dexter: No, man, I mean in other people's eyes. No, we were what you'd call dysfunctional, you bet your ass. But what's functional? Tell you: People that cover up better.

Doctor: Is that what everyone does, do you think, cover up their dysfunctionality? Society as a whole?

Dexter: You trying to get me thinking you're actually sympathetic? Like you could give a shit. You charge the state for an hour when I talk to you for half an hour. All you fuckers do. I'm just another hour on your paycheck to you. You don't actually care about me.

Doctor: I—

Dexter: You're going to say: "It's a balance. I can't do my job right if I don't care about my patients, but if I get really involved I'll be unable to continue because of the emotional stress."

Doctor: Yes.

Dexter: You look a little wacked, doctor. Because those are the exact words you were going to use. Exactly. Weren't they?

Doctor: No. Not far off, though, I'll give you that. You and I know each other, it's not hard for you to predict generally what I—

Dexter: Especially as I'm one of those fast thinking paranoids? Right, doctor, sure, make yourself feel better. But see, *I can read your mind.* I mean, I *really* can. Not delusionally *imagining* I can . . . So far I can't do it all the time, though . . .

Doctor: Let's get back to your—

Dexter: What, you don't want to do a little 'reality check' for the patient? Try me out on the mind-reading?

Doctor: Instead of—

Dexter: '—me playing your games, why don't you play along with therapy'. You look wacked again, doctor. And now you're worried—just a flicker—that I might actually be able to read your mind and something about the money you raked off the clinic medication funds to pay off a nurse who was going to sue you for sexual harassment . . . Blackmail . . . A Miss Hernandez—

///Tape 14 abruptly ends here///

Tape 15:

Dexter: So where's Dr. Berenson?

Doctor: He's . . . on a leave of absence.

Dexter: I heard he was going to erase some therapeutic tapes, in violation of hospital policy, and his supervisor caught him at it, and it led to—

Doctor: Let's talk about you, Dexter, how are you feeling?

Dexter: [extended laughter]

Doctor: If you can't control yourself—

Dexter: It's okay, but . . . you guys crack me up. How long am I going to let you keep up this pretense, this patronizing bullshit. I don't think much longer. I'm almost ready.

Doctor: Go on.

Dexter: I'm not stupid, man. I'm not going to babble my plans to you.

Doctor: Let's start over again. How's the world been treating you?

Dexter: See there, you're using that angle to get me talking about stuff you can attribute to a paranoiac's conspiracy complex. Well, I'll play along and give you something to write in your diagnostic evaluation; I'll tell you about the World, but it's about you as much as me. Everyone knows the world is a hostile place. That's not paranoid. You don't watch your step, you die. There're six billion people in it now and even the ones who live seventy-five years don't live very long, really. Life is cheap. But life is precious, too, at least sometimes: that's what you're thinking, that there are compensations, all those loving children and warm moments, right? You think I'm gonna say I never had any of those? But I did, with my granddad, and with my own nephew, he was almost like my own kid, and with a dog I had, and a couple of girlfriends I had—you notice I put the dog first—and with a couple of good friends, stoned on the road, when we woulda died for each other. I know those things are there. But I know something else. I've been worked on since I was a kid, the way you work on a lab rat. You're looking interested, like you think I mean I was abducted by aliens or CIA mind-control scientists or some bullshit, and maybe that's my—delusion—that's what's buggin' you guys, you have me pegged as a paranoid, but you're askin' yourselves what's this guy's specific delusion? I got some paranoia, paranoia's a skill. And fear is a survival tool, pal. I don't mean to say anybody's been consciously operating on me or something or planting implants or arranging on purpose for my old man to be an asshole and for me to get busted and get a year in juvie because I took a ride in a car I didn't know my girlfriend's brother had stolen—I mean we're all part of a big pecking order, a food chain, a big machine of stronger preying on weaker, and you're part of the social services foodchain, and so am I, and—oh, you think I'm babbling. Hebephrenic manifestations or something. Yeah, that's what you were thinking and now you're thinking that I'm doing 'paranoid anticipation' according to the classic profile and now you're thinking this whole session is making you tired because I won't shut up and you wish it were lunchtime but you've got another guy after me before you can go to lunch and get that cocktail you've been thinking about all morning and you're wondering if your old lady knows you're back on the cocktails when you're not supposed to be drinking anymore and did she find that matchbook in your coat from that bar on Winston Avenue—[laughter] You should see your face!

Doctor: You've been talking to someone—the nurses, someone's been watching me—

Dexter: [laughter] Right, Doc, is somebody following you? Huh? Are you being conspired against? You should see *somebody* for those symptoms, Doc—

Doctor: Look, I don't know how you—

Dexter: Hey, I'm going to terminate this interview right now. Your audience is over.

///Tape 22///

Dexter: 'You can run, but you can't hide.' That oughta be stamped on the coin instead of *E Pluribus Unum.*

Doctor: Everyone feels hunted sometimes. By needy family members, the tax man, supervisors—

Dexter: By death.

Doctor: Yes. Do you feel hunted by it?

Dexter: When I was in county stir, there was a spade there, big into the Koran. Well, he was Black Muslim—

Doctor: Now you're talking to me as if I haven't been keeping up on you. I know that you've read widely in spirituality. You don't have to talk as of you just 'heard it from a guy.' You're one of our best-read patients.

Dexter: You're going to tell me to leave off the front? What about the doctor front?

Doctor: I'm not the one here for therapy.

Dexter: You sure? Depends on your definition of therapy. Anyway—in the Qu'ran, pronouncing it right, it says that eternity is a near as the veins of your neck. That's funny way to put it, isn't it? Gives me a choking sensation.

Doctor: If you . . .

Dexter: What's that? You trying to say something?

Doctor: Dex . . . don't—

Dexter: Don't what? I'm sitting across the room from you with my hands in my lap! Is it my smell? The stench of my diagnosis choking you, too?

Doctor: Stop . . . [unintelligible]

Dexter: You rung for Mike, huh? How's that micro-willy of yours hanging, Mike?

Psychological Technician: You okay, Doctor? He touch you?

Dexter: Never got near him.

Doctor: He . . . I'm all right now . . . I guess it was . . . was autosuggestion . . . He mentioned choking and I began to . . .

Psych Tech: Ow—shit!

Dexter: What are you clutching you testicles for there, Mike? You act like someone hit you in the nuts. Can that happen by autosuggestion? I don't remember suggesting it. I'll be damned.

Psych Tech: That's it—Slim! Womack! Get me a sleep shot! Get Morris in here! Ow, dammit!

Dexter: You're not injecting my ass again—

Psych Tech: I'm not sure how you're doing it, but you can't do it to all of us at once—hold the fucker—stop the—There he goes . . . There he goes . . .

Doctor: Are you sure he's out?

Psych Tech: Oh yeah. That stuff is like, boom.

///The following record of the interrupted lecture by Dr. Lewis is provided for homicide detectives, transcribed by ML///

Tape 23:

Doctor Ransom Lewis: I want to thank all the doctors and staff who gave up their Saturday afternoon for this seminar. I'm sure we'll all find it'll make our work easier in the coming months. I'll be giving the first talk myself. The topic is comparative medications for the treatment of bipolar disorder, with a particular—who let that man in here?
    Mike, will you see to that man? Restrain him—[garbled]
    Mike? Are you okay? Dr. Ferratosco—ring the general alarm—Dexter—stop it, you—[garbled]

Dexter: All riiiight! My own microphone. I hope you're tapin' this. All right. How nice to have you all here. Everyone but the patients are invited to this seminar about the patients, right?
    But here I am. I've let the other patients out from the security ward, passed the key around. And they locked these here doors from the outside, so you ain't leaving. I'm afraid the other two orderlies are as dead as Mike there. No, he's not just unconscious, doctor, I broke some blood vessels in his brain. Once you're inside the brain—it's so fragile! I'll show you—I can go inside your brains, I can extend my field—Dr. Ferratosco, and chubby ol' Dr. Lewis . . .
    Look at 'em thrash around, grabbing their highly intellectual foreheads. No golf this Sunday, boys. I think I'll let Dr. Lewis survive—like a fuckin' vegetable. Yeah. Yeah. Start droolin' any second now.

You all gettin' set to rush me? You guys really haven't figured it out yet, have you. It's kind of pathetic, really.

Give it a try—and down you go! You feel that? Fifty or so of you in here and you all fall on your asses as a fuckin wave of brain-hurt goes over you . . . Well I'm not going to kill my audience before it's heard me out so don't worry. Just get on your knees. Yeah. On your knees, girls and bitches. No? Try this...

How'd that feel?

Now. Down on your knees. All fifty of you. That's it . . .

See, it had to happen. The brain is a maze. Life is a maze on the outside and the brain is a maze on the inside and those two mazes lock together, see, like one of those M.C. Escher paintings where there's opposites of the same place interlocking in a kind of tesseract that . . . Am I boring you? How's that for boredom, there, doctor. That feel good? Are we listening now? Yeah—oh now everybody is suddenly so attentive. Okay so I was saying, the brain, see, it's a maze. And your paranoids—and yes, I was one—they get lost in that maze, they can't distinguish the inner maze from the outer maze, and they wander around from one personal symbol to the next, am I right? See, you'd be amazed at some of the strange books people sent us in prison—and in prison, you got time to read, unless you're into lifting weights and trading for blowjobs. That shit gets old. Anyway, harken back to the night I went home and saw my old lady dead, and the cops said she'd freaked out on dope and she had a knife and they had to shoot her and then the cops were afraid I was going to sue them so they started following me, laying for a chance to take me out—and that was for real, see, that wasn't the paranoia. It wasn't paranoia when I started to snipe those fuckers and take em out. But I started to do some heavy speed to stay up all night so they couldn't get me when I slept and it was, like, a self-fulfilling prophecy. "He's a paranoid—get him!" And I became one! It was the speed, see. I took a few of them fuckers out before . . . Anyway, uh—you see most of the time no one finds their way through the maze because they don't realize it's a maze. Maze in your head. But I did. Self knowledge, see. That's the key. I saw myself for what I really was, I knew I was hopelessly sick with hatred and I could see I was in a mind maze. I knew there was no hope for me because of what the demiurge and the archons and fuckers like you people have made out of this world and made out of me. So . . .

So . . .

I turned inward. Catatonic, they said, but I wasn't. I was going through the maze. There's more than one way to go through that labyrinth.

There's what you call the white-magic way and there's the black-magic way. And me, it's too bad and I know it's too bad, but: I'm too sick to go the white-magic way. Too...not paranoid, not delusional, but just plain damaged. So I went the black-magic way. And I got to the core of the brain where the power is, the power underneath despair, and I set it free, and the changes started to come, and I found out that if you are absolutely present here and now in the world in every sense, and you sense every wave of *all* the waves you emanate, there is power in that. And here I am, boys, here I am, and here you are too.

And now Dr. Ferratosco—I want you to take Dr. Means by the throat, and I want you to be my cute little puppet, and I want you to show the others here what obedience is and what disobedience is . . .

That's it. Rip that shit right out of his . . . yeah.

Now you others . . . you can kneel to me for real. Kneel for real! Inside as well as outside! In both mazes! And you can obey me, and go where I tell you, and profit by submission to your Lord, your Prophet of the Final Night—or you can die right now. What's your choice?

///**End transcription. Note to Lt. Pearlman. Regret I am unable to obtain statements from the other doctors and staff at the seminar. All surviving doctors and staff have resigned and we are unable to locate them. Their whereabouts, and the whereabouts of Dexter W. Dexter, is entirely unknown . . . ///**

DON'T BE AFRAID

"I really don't have time for this," Nilly said. His name was William Edward Nilly, aka Will E. Nilly, a nickname from his pirate radio days.

"You don't have time for your own child?" Bonham asked. They were in the men's dressing room of the Moose Lodge 17 Public Meetings Hall. The Lodge itself almost never used the place. Nowadays it was rented out for parties, for punk rock concerts, to obscure religious sects, and to obscure political factions like Nilly's own Absolute Freedom Party. The painted-over window rattled, now and then, with flurries of chill November rain blowing in off San Francisco Bay. They were almost under the 80 Freeway, in Berkeley, and between rain tappings Bonham could hear semi-trucks moan past.

As he waited for an answer, Bonham watched Nilly preen in the dressing room mirror. Nilly touched up his chin with a portable electric shaver. For an anarchist, Nilly was very conscientious about his appearance.

Bonham, at sixty-one, was twenty years Nilly's senior and felt it tonight. He was tired. He wanted to go home and wash off the insulation dust. He'd been laid off, a year before, from the savings and loan he'd worked at for twenty-six years. Minimal retirement pay: he worked in an insulation factory now. It made him cough, and the coughing was worse if he didn't rinse the stuff off regularly.

"Goddammit, Nilly, answer the question."

Nilly turned, giving him a look of mingled pity and condescension. Nilly wore a workshirt, blue jeans, a white linen sport jacket. He was a compact man with flashing, compelling black eyes, receding black hair tied into a ponytail. His movements, every syllable he uttered, were studies in intensity, pregnant with expression.

"Frankly—there are bigger issues at stake, here. Our society is teetering, beautifully teetering, and it needs a push and a fall, and it needs someone to pick up the pieces and redistribute them."

"You want to talk social issues? You got my daughter pregnant—what about your social responsibility to an unwed mother?"

"My being the father—that's disputable."

"Bullshit it is. You led her on, you knocked her up, you dropped her. She's got a three-month-old child. She needs at least child support—more importantly she needs help with the kid. Your daughter."

"Selena knew what my philosophy is . . . and it includes absolute sexual freedom." He stood up, took one last look in the mirror, adjusted his coat. A baldheaded graduate student in a black buttoned-to-the-neck collarless shirt, appeared at the door, looking at Nilly inquiringly. "I'm coming, Mark."

"What the hell's your philosophy got to do with this?"

"Everything. Social anarchism means individual responsibility. The old family unit is part of the patriarchal hegemony. She needs to get with an anarchist commune—there are women's communes I can recommend her to. It's about freedom."

"Your freedom to screw who you like without—"

"I really don't have time for this Calvinistic guilt-tripping, Mr. Bonham. You want to take me to court, go ahead."

"You know we can't afford that."

Nilly smiled and went out to the stage.

March stopped on a street corner, and looked around, and tried to re-member how he'd come here—7-11 Store, 99 Cent Store, Shell station, a boarded up motel, cars pulling up to a stop light; a minivan a few steps away, its stereo banging rap. "Motherfuckuh that my goodie, put you hands on 'er I bust you cherry," March chanted along with the rap. March was a white guy, long hair matted into a single dirty yellow thatch—he wouldn't let them cut it at the hospital. They'd learned not to try to force him. The black guy at the wheel of the minivan glared at him and acceler-ated when the light changed.

March again wondered: How'd I come here?

He didn't remember breaking out of the Security Ward, but he must have, they'd never have let him out. Not after the last time. Oh wait. Oh . . . wait. Metal mesh, rusty metal mesh on the window, if you yanked on it again and again it'd break, and it'd cut, too, cut into the orderly's—

". . . Social justice is completely and utterly impossible within the struc-ture of society *as we know* society," Nilly boomed. He used a micro-phone expertly, from many rallies. He made eye contact with the audi-

ence. Felt a glow, noticing they had more than a full house. People standing at the back. He took note of two–three, really–admiring young girls
about Selena Bonham's age in the front row. Possibilities. Make sure
they're eighteen, that's the main thing.

Mark was beaming at him from the back. Pleased as hell. He'd been
right, telling Nilly that they were catching on. Frustration with the
economy from the poor end of things–he just might spark a revolution
after all. The fact that the economy was booming for the middle class
only made it more volatile.

Bonham watched from the back of the room, amazed and tasting bitterness, really tasting it in his mouth. Mark and some of Nilly's other anarchist followers were watching Bonham sidelong, in case he should start
denouncing Nilly. They'd never let him say much and everyone would
assume he was a reactionary lying about Nilly, a government disinfor-
mation agent or something. Might as well go home . . .

*March was drifting down University, toward the bay. There were places
to sleep along the bay. But he couldn't sleep until he let some of it out. It
was so heavy in his gut. It was like a hard, superdense living stone in his
gut, and it pressed, and unless he let some of it out—*

"Don't be afraid of freedom!" Nilly thundered, and there was a gratify-
ing roar of response. It was the Absolute Freedom Party's slogan. "Don't
be afraid of taking responsibility for yourself! We can pull this society
down–and from the ashes anarchism will rise like a phoenix to spontaneously re-construct, moment by moment, a situationist proto-society
that defies all former categorizations."

*The noise, the noise in the hospital–oh, no one was ever really quiet.
Just so . . . They were just so . . . Same as in prison, only worse, because
threats didn't stop them. Everyone yammering, the TV on, arguments,
shouts echoing from the institutional walls, the echoes carrying the texture of cement and steel bars back with them . . .*

*It was noisy here too. There was no peace anywhere. The cars. And
now a man . . .*

*A man was walking toward him, singing loudly along to something
on earphones. March grabbed a Coke bottle from an overflowing trash
can, smashed it jagged, and expertly slashed the man's throat out, all in
one motion.*

He walked on, the broken bottle in his hand dripping blood.

That's when he saw the cop sitting with his back to him at the counter of the coffee shop.

The cop, a middle aged black man, was just so startled; there was a look in his eyes just like a frightened little kid. How easily big, tough, trained adults could turn into scared kids. That was one of the things that lifted the boulder in him, seeing that look. The cop seeing his gun in March's hand—March had stepped up behind him at the counter and pulled it from his holster, just so smooth and easy—and the cop put up his hands as if to block the bullet and the first bullet carried one of the knuckles from that hopelessly-blocking hand right into his mouth—

"Where does it start? It starts with getting rid of the police!" A bigger roar—there'd been a lot of busts lately. "Getting rid of the Army, the Navy, all of it! Getting rid of the banks! Dismantling *all* of it. All, every last bit of social trash from a society that is *not* working. Don't be afraid of living without the Nazis we call the Berkeley police, the San Francisco Police, the Los Angeles Police—and when you have a problem, even now, before the revolution—*don't call them!* Relying on authority is submitting to authority! Submitting to authority is surrendering responsibility! Surrendering responsibility is surrendering freedom!"

Outburst of applause.

Bonham thought: Let it go. There's no way he's going to change. There's no appeal here, no appeal to a state of mind. Rhetoric has no conscience. Go home, shower the poison off, kiss your wife, tell your daughter it'll be all right.

Bonham turned, put his hand on the knob, and the door slammed inward, knocking him flat on his back. He lay there gasping, trying to get his breath, looking up at the man with the matted hair and the drooping, silently moving mouth; with the eyes that were so empty and so full at once, and the institutional shirt with the name MARCH stenciled under the collar—and the gun in his hand.

"Hey!" March shouted, as people turned to stare. "It still hurts! It's still heavy! Hey you're looking at me!" And he began to fire the .45 Glock automatic into the crowd, the screams and the running began, and he stepped over Bonham, perhaps thinking him already dead, firing, the gunshot noise like a big metal institutional-door slamming shut close by, slam-bam.

Bonham pulled himself up on the door, discovering he was unhurt, only shaken. The room had all but emptied, everyone had run out the fire exit doors on the side, except for three people, two of them clearly dead, one of them unconscious, shaking–and a fourth, Nilly, on the stage.

Nilly had been shot in the back of his right knee and he was weeping and pulling himself along with his arms and his good knee, trying to get up, leaving a snailtrail of blood.

Bonham knelt by the shaking, bleeding girl, used his coat to compress the wound as best he could.

The gunman was talking to himself, clearly completely psychotic, and he fired twice more at Nilly, both times missing him but each shot making the anarchist convulse with terror as it smashed holes through the stage near an arm, a foot.

Police sirens . . .

Bonham looked at the girl on the floor. She had stopped shaking. She was unmistakably dead. He went to the door.

A clutch of anarchists huddled outside, arguing. The cops were coming down the street–but they didn't seem to be coming here. They were heading for a coffee shop two blocks down. They didn't know about this yet!

"You haven't called them?" Bonham said.

"I told them to call the cops!" said a teenage girl with dyed-black, waist-length hair. She was sobbing. "They won't!"

"It isn't right–" Mark said. But he wasn't sure about it. He was chewing his lip, looking at the lodge door.

Bonham smiled. "Stand by your beliefs. Don't call them. The guy with the gun'll run out of steam. Are you anarchists, or not? You jeer at the cops until you need them? Don't be hypocrites."

"Let's take a vote!" one of them shouted.

"A quorum!"

"Look–we'll appoint an ad hoc committee. Then we, uh–"

Bonham left them arguing and went back into the building. The madman was straddling Nilly, who was lying on his back, flailing. "Get him away!"

The madman raised the gun, pointed it at Nilly–*click*. It was empty.

He looked at the gun. Nilly looked at the madman with panting relief.

"I still feel it," March said.

"Get the cops!" Nilly shouted, seeing Bonham watching.

"Don't be a hypocrite, Nilly."

"What?"

"Shut up," March said to Nilly. "You're too loud."

Nilly tried to crawl away. "The COPS!"

March knelt, pinning Nilly with his knees and hit him, rather experimentally, with the butt of the gun, the barrel held in his fist. Nilly screamed.

"You're still too loud. You're just so . . ."

March hit him again, harder, and Nilly screamed louder. "Cops! Police! Cops, goddammit, shit, shit, hurry!"

March hit him in the head this time.

"Please! God it hurts, Bonham! Call the cops!"

"You don't *really* want the cops—you can't dismiss police protection and then call it when you need it, Nilly," Bonham said. With infinite satisfaction, he added, "It's about personal responsibility. It's all about . . . your freedom."

Then Bonham turned, and walked out, so he wouldn't have to hear the wet thudding sounds, and the screams.

Outside, the anarchists were still arguing.

Bonham went home and took a shower.

Lot Five, Building Seven, Door Twenty-three

"He's my last hope," said Oliver Dunsmuir. "It's him or despair."

"What's underneath despair, Ollie?" asked Rodney Collins, in his affable, abstracted way.

They were walking through underground hallways that still smelled of new concrete. They passed now under Lot Five of the Spiritual Freedom Complex, the corridors seemingly endless and empty, the sound of their footsteps echoing against the metal pipes snaking the ceiling.

All the circumlocution to reach the Teacher was a bit of a bore, really, Dunsmuir thought; it smacked of the folderol the Sufis and the Tibetan monks put you through before you could reach their inner sanctums. The point was some psychological state they wanted you in, and not the supposed secrecy of the Teacher.

O Dark Truth, spread your cape for me; O Vlad the Living Gateway, open your white lips and show me the key . . .

"I mean," Collins was saying, "what are the borders of despair?" His long strides were making it difficult for the shorter, stockier Dunsmuir to keep pace with him. His English accent and his English reserve made even a subject like despair seem cool, detached. But glancing at him, Dunsmuir saw the glimmering, again, just for a moment, in Collins' dusty blue eyes, and a warmth in the rueful curve of Collins' mouth. Collins' ran a work-reddened hand through his receding, curly brown hair and went on, "You've got to go through in order to come out, what?"

Dunsmuir shrugged. The remark was an esoteric commonplace, and nothing new, nothing new at all.

They'd at last reached the elevator at the end of the hall. Ordinary blue-painted metal doors. Dunsmuir and Collins looked up at the little camera lens over the elevator. A light beside the camera was flashing red.

"My name's Rodney Collins," he said to the door. "I know Webb." There was an electronic hesitation. Then the elevator doors opened.

In the elevators, riding up, Dunsmuir mused over the exchange with the security computer. "You said you knew Webb. Is that a code-phrase or . . . ?"

"No. He's head of Security, they buzzed him and he may be willing to see me."

"I thought you said you'd been here before—that you were in here!"

"I said nothing of the sort, my dear fellow—ah, here's our floor."

They stepped out into the shiny hallway. The entire wall on their right side, as they moved down the hall, was a tinted window. Beyond it, the towers and elevated tramways of New York. He could make out the brown smudge of what had been Central Park; the plants and trees were uniformly dead now, of course. There was talk of putting a bubble over the park, but they probably wouldn't get the funding. Spiking the horizon, the Earth-to-Orbit access shaft, under construction since 2013, was like some whiskered-alloy Tower of Babel gouging the ceiling of clouds. Looking at it, Dunsmuir had an intuition that, like the Tower of Babel, the ETO would never be finished.

They strode past potted plants, and pleasant, meaningless murals. "You did say," Dunsmuir went on, "you were in with Vlad. You knew the Teacher."

Collins chuckled. "No matter how much one learns about the filters of the mind, it's always astonishing the sort of things that people think they hear. No, old chum, I did not say I knew the Teacher. I said I was going to see him—and you could come along."

"But—you've never—?"

"No. I've never been here before."

"Well fuck. Then this is a waste of time." Dunsmuir felt frustration and fury simmer up in him. So much had been a waste of time. The Gnostic Christians, the Theosophists, the Buddhists; the Children of Crowley; the Temple of Set; the half dozen other esoteric disciplines he'd pursued and the therapeutic scam artists he'd fallen victim to. They were all either complex frauds, like the Scientologists, or they were simply new ways to ask the questions; they posed no answers.

Dunsmuir knew about wasted time.

"I mean," he went on, gritting his teeth to keep his temper, "I've been this far before, right up to the door of Building Seven. With Singh. He used to get in—but they won't even let him in to the Teacher now. They say the Teacher's sequestered for good."

"Oh," Collins said breezily, "I think we'll see him. It's a matter of timing, you see."

"I've tried every day of the week and every hour of the day, Collins!"

"I meant—time in a broader sense. And in a more holistic sense. In several directions at once."

Dunsmuir sighed. "More mystical claptrap. I've heard it all, Collins, from Christian Rosenkruz to Steiner to Blavatsky to Franklin Jones to Crowley to Ouspensky. Spare me."

"I hope to, actually."

They'd come to a white desk at the end of the rust colored carpet. Sitting behind the desk was a black man in a security guard's uniform. Dunsmuir knew damn well he was a lot more than a security guard. He was a middle aged man, in dark glasses, a silver V stapled through his left ear, as had most of the Teacher's followers. He looked disdainfully at Dunsmuir, glanced at Collins, turned back to Dunsmuir as if to rebuke him—then did a doubletake right out of a twentieth century movie, turning back to stare at Collins. He swallowed. "I . . ." He shook his head. "I can't."

"You can," Collins said. He reached out to touch the black man . . . Who fell backwards out of his chair to dodge that touch; who turned and bolted from his desk. Ran in terror from Collins' mild eyes, the gentle touch of his callused hands.

"The Center for Spiritual Freedom is not interested in comforting panaceas, in maternalistic therapies, in soaking you for your money in return for false promises. The Teacher who is at the Center for Spiritual Freedom is interested only in—"

"—'radically transforming your life, inner and outer'," Danitra muttered, finishing it along with the videotape narrator. "Christ. What is this. I'm going backwards." Danitra Johnson shifted in her chair, watching the big video screen at the other end of the waiting room. She was a long legged black woman, her hair shaven close to her skull and cut into the symbols of the initiate; she wore the standard black jeans and t-shirt, and the black sandals of the initiate; she had the V in her left ear, she had a year of initiatory seminars in her head and now she had a suspicion she was lost in some sort of theocratic bureaucracy.

But she made herself watch the Introductory Video. It could be that this video—the same she'd seen when she first joined the Center a year before—was here only to test her patience, or perhaps there was something encrypted in it she hadn't seen the first time . . .

She was, herself, on a video screen in the next room.

∞ ∞ ∞

James Webb, the direct descendant of the man Bram Stoker had called "Van Helsing," was frowning as he watched Danitra on the video screen. The black woman, a former model, was a stroke of charcoal and chocolate against the pastels of the waiting room. She fairly quivered with suppressed energy. Oh yes, He would enjoy her, of course, as much as He could enjoy anything, anymore. But Webb was beginning to think that there would never be a "critical mass" with Him; there would never be the hoped-for moment of Divine Satiety. And this exquisite, intelligent creature would be simply wasted. Webb considered cutting her out from the herd for his own uses . . . It wouldn't be the first time . . .

He shivered; he felt a chill go through him. Was it His influence, reaching through the walls—or a withdrawal from the specially treated cigarettes Webb smoked? Probably it was the synthetic morphine. Only a mild addiction so far. Not like the other one—the ancestral addiction to Him. That, now, was worth fighting. This girl might be a worthwhile test. A test to answer the question: Could He really be denied?

Webb glanced at the other monitors. Collins and his friend were presumably gone; sent away by the guard, as per Webb's instructions. He didn't see them on the monitor. So perhaps he was free to dally with the girl.

Webb made his decision. He went through the door into the waiting room. "Ms. Johnson?"

"Yes?" She uncoiled from her yellow plastic chair like a pit viper.

O Divider and Unifier, O Destroyer and Renewer, cauterize from me the irrelevancies of pity and fear, and remake me, remake me utterly . . .

"I'm Jim Webb."

"I know who you are." She grimaced at her own impatience. "I'm sorry. This video—"

"It seems like old hat? Well. Yes and no." Webb smiled, trying for his charming patrician look—the older man with the disarming smile, the white temples, the dark, confident eyes. He'd always had good luck with that particular image.

"It's just that I feel . . . I know . . ."

"That you're ready. I'm sure you are. But as you know—and the general announcement went out—He is not seeing anyone at this time."

"But—Georgei said, on the telephone—"

"That there are exceptions. Yes." And I hope you won't have to be one, he thought. "But—The Teacher is not ready at this time. He's in deep intra-cyclic meditation."

She stared at him. She glanced past him, at Door Twenty, then she glowered at the floor. "Very well. It's back to the Ashram?"

"No. To my meditation temple. We'll prepare ourselves there till He is ready. However long it takes . . . "

He could imagine her long, muscular limbs against his. The thought of her African-dark thighs cupping his pale, tumesced genitals . . . he hoped she didn't note the growing bulge in his pants' crotch . . .

He stepped to the door opposite—moving hastily to hide the telltale evidence of his intentions—and opened the door for her. It swung inward—and she shoved Webb through it. She was strong; the story of her being a black-belt might well be true.

He turned in time to see her slam the door in his face. Then he heard her wedge a chair against it on the other side.

Danitra's heart was pounding. Webb had made the mistake of leaving the other door unlocked. She wasn't going to lose the chance. She'd gotten through Door Twenty. From what she knew of Building Seven, that meant there were only three more doors between her and the Teacher.

She was fairly sure—or so she told herself, as she strode down the forbidden hallway—that He wanted her to do just this. To break the rules. That sending Webb out to seemingly misdirect her was a test.

My rules are rigid, inflexible, and utterly necessary—and also completely expendable. You'll know when that time comes. You will then be One Who Knows . . .

Even through the heavy walls of the Center for Spiritual Freedom, Dunsmuir could hear the sirens announcing a Toxic Front. The few people daring the upper streets would be scrambling for the underplex airlocks. Another Black Wind was coming, bearing lethal toxins manufactured in the upper atmosphere by evaporated pesticides and manufacturing by-products, pollutants chemically transfigured by the UVs; the heavier UVs, admitted now that the ozone layer was all but gone. The same ultraviolets that slowly toasted the world on the spit of its axis, destroying crops and oceanic plankton, shattering the food chain, initiating the famines: the riots, the hundreds of brush wars over the globe's remaining pockets of resources. The complexes of urban undergrounds and sealed buildings, the hydroponic high rises, had kept the race staggering on. Especially those born into money like Dunsmuir. But sometimes he thought that despite all the electronic and concrete barricades, the walls would fall . . .

"The siren's a frightening sound, isn't it?" Collins murmured, seeming not at all frightened.

They were walking up a stairway. The guards had frozen the elevators, now, but Collins always seemed to know where there was an unlocked door.

"The siren?" Dunsmuir was thinking that he was more frightened of Rodney Collins, now, than the Black Winds. The way the guard had reacted; the way the doors seemed to come unlocked at his touch.

What did he know about Collins? Precious little. Collins was a self styled "servant of God" who traveled from community to community—and had done so even before they went underplex—and offered his services as "a builder—of whatever is needed." He built housing of metal and wood and plastic, whatever was around. He seemed to know most of the Masters of the various spiritual disciplines, and to come and go as he liked. He knew a great deal about yoga, and just as much about the Stations of the Cross and the lives of the saints. He had studied in "certain Schools" as a young man, and that sort of mysteriousness always set Dunsmuir's teeth on edge—but in Collins' case, it scared him. Collins was altogether too casual about it all . . .

"The sirens have frightened people into looking for God," Collins was saying, "and they have given the powers of entropy great joy, since most people have, in their panic, run the wrong way. But it's been lovely for the televangelists and the Scientologists and the other parasites. All things being relative. Tell me...what brought you to the 'Teacher'?"

There was real irony, now, in the way he said 'Teacher'.

Dunsmuir was puffing with effort at the climb; Collins didn't seem to feel it.

"The miracles, of course," Dunsmuir said, knowing it would sound jejune. He was supposed to be attracted to the Teacher purely for His Spiritual Profundity. "He was tested everywhichway by every skeptic in the world. All the best stage magicians, electronic techies—no one could explain the levitations, the power over animals, the vanishings . . . the other miracles."

"Did you ever notice that the miracles were always performed at night?" Collins asked, offhandedly.

"He explained that—the sun's vibratory energy is . . . I can't remember exactly . . ."

"It never does fail to astonish me," Collins said, chuckling.

They reached the top landing. A security camera whirred toward them—and then froze. The camera seemed as spooked as the black security guard had been. "Is this it?" Dunsmuir asked, almost childlike in his sudden eagerness.

"What? Oh no, no," Collins said, putting his hand on the door. Click-click. "No, we've got to go down now."

He opened the door and Dunsmuir followed him through—and found to his horror that they were now outside. They were standing on a metal outdoor stairway, a sort of emergency escape stairs, in the open air. There was some shelter from a metal roof over the stairway—but it wasn't sealed off. The dirty wind teased their nostrils with hydrocarbons, sulfites, PCBs and heavy metals.

"We'll choke out here!"

"The toxic front isn't here yet," Collins replied, with maddening unconcern, "I think we'll make it into Building Seven before it gets here."

"You think! We haven't got respirators!"

But Collins was already clattering down the pitted metal stairs. Dunsmuir, palms sweating, turned to the door behind him. He was going back. The hell with Collins.

The door was shut; the knob wouldn't turn. He was locked out. "Oh God, oh fuck!"

He turned and hurried after Collins.

He's insane. I'm going to die out here with a madman.

She might have known it. Door Twenty-three was locked.

But she could feel Him in there: a pulsing from beyond the door; a throbbing of sheer presence, unheard, but distinctly felt, in the bone sockets and teeth.

If I can feel Him, she thought, then He can feel me.

She knelt before the door and began to pray.

"That won't get His attention, though he might enjoy the pose if He could see it," Webb said, stepping up behind her.

Danitra got slowly to her feet and turned to face him, expecting him to be with several burly security guards.

But Webb was alone. "I'm going to give you a chance to save your life," Webb said, "not because I'm any kind of philanthropist—I'm too much a scientist for that—but because I prize beauty."

"What are you threatening me with?" Danitra asked. She decided she could take him, long before he could pull a gun from his suit jacket.

"Me? Not a thing. I won't do a thing to you myself. You go through that door, though, well . . . " He shrugged.

"Test me, then," she said. "And I will pass the tests. And I know this is another of them."

He actually laughed in her face. "You're so bright and so childlike at the same time! My dear Danitra . . . all tests are quite concluded, except those that involve Him. My hypotheses with respect to Him have been disproved, or nearly so. I have studied him long enough. And I know."

"You're . . . studying him?"

To her astonishment, Webb lit a cigarette. You didn't see them often anymore. "I'm studying him, yes. My esteemed ancestor began the practice. Funny old Professor Von Weber. Whom Stoker called Van Helsing—and made look like some sort of scientifically-minded saint. But the real 'Van Helsing' was a pederast, a heroin addict, and had an unwholesome fascination—one I understand all too well—with Vlad Veovod. Known, back home in Wallachia, as The Son of the Dragon. The Impaler. Whom Stoker renamed: Dracula."

She smiled. "This test is rather transparent."

"Oh get over it." Suddenly Webb seemed much older, much wearier. "We can't study him, you know. That's what I've come to believe . . ." He leaned against the wall beside her. "You can only serve him or fight him." He glanced up and down the hall. "I wonder where all the guards have gone . . . could it have come to that?"

They heard another warning yowl of sirens. The drawn-out note sounded almost like trumpets. Like a clarion call from the sky itself.

"Another damned toxic alert. He made them—Dracula, the entity you call the Teacher—He helped make them, with His influence, and then, a grand irony, people like you ask Him to remake the world . . ." He offered her the cigarette. "Want a hit of this? A bit of smokeable morphine in it. I'm afraid I'm kind of jonesed for it."

She shook her head. Was he joking? Or testing her again? The smoke did smell strange.

Webb's eyes glazed over as he drew on the cigarette, and he went on, his voice slurring slightly, "He was like a spiritual tumor in the social brain, you know. The bloodsuckers . . . all the bloodsuckers he encouraged along . . . I remember Mike Milken—that was before your time—and Charles Keating and the Dow-Corning people and the Chevron people and the Bank of Credit and Commerce people and Union Carbide and the Mob and the Vatican bankers . . . all the bloodsuckers . . . how He relished it all . . . how it fed Him . . . but of course drinking on that level was never enough for ol' Vlad. His appetites are very basic, really . . ."

She shook her head. Webb—the Teacher's High Devotee—was either stoned, crazy or acting. "Open the door," she said.

Webb looked at her and shook his head firmly. "Downstairs there's a ride-tube to my plex. High security, high comfort. Lots of everything that makes life in an antfarm still worth living. Come with me."

She gazed at him and saw real lust, real loneliness, and real fear. But that shouldn't surprise you, said something less than a voice in her head. It is the Judas effect. The ones closest to Jesus, too, were often the blindest . . .

She turned and pounded on the door.

To her astonishment—and Webb's dismay—it opened.

The door was opened by an old man with a bald head, a walrus mustache, and striking, sad, black-brown eyes. He wore a vaguely Middle Eastern outfit, baggy trousers and sandals and a rough tunic from some other century—or from a costume shop. And around his neck was a heavy iron collar, rusted with age. It was studded and bolted and it must have been painful, even after an hour or so. She could tell it had been there for years.

"You to come in, Miss?" the old man said.

She recognized his Russian accent and gravelly voice. Georgei Ivanovitch. She'd only spoken to him on the phone.

"Georgei," Webb said dangerously, "close that door and go away."

"Can not do, Dr. Van Helsing—"

"That is not funny."

Georgei smiled as if to say, it was funny, in a sad sort of way. "Sorry. 'Doctor Webb.' Can not close door. The Master, He feel her here. Is too late."

Webb closed his eyes as if enduring some cryptic pain. "Where are the guards?" he asked, his eyes still shut, nervously sucking at the stub of his cigarette.

"He take them too. Could not wait. He very afraid now."

"What—he took . . . all of them?" Webb opened his eyes and looked sharply at Georgei.

"Yes. So many! But growth does not stop."

Georgei threw Door Twenty-three wide open and stepped back. "Both, please come. Pretty Lady wants, Pretty Lady gets."

Danitra hesitated, feeling as if someone were dripping a thick, cold liquid along her spine. Webb didn't move.

Georgei turned to Webb. He chuckled. "You come to say hello to Teacher too, Von Weber."

"You're in a damned cheerful mood," Webb said, glaring at Georgei. "For a slave."

"I have seen in dream: my atonement ends. It ends today. The Angel Looisil, he speaks to me."

Webb snorted. "Bullshit."

Danitra hesitated on the threshold of the dimly lit, black curtained room beyond. It smelled of iron and sweat. But then she remembered the Twenty-third Invocation: *At the brink of your salvation, I tremble in fear. Open wide your wings and enfold me . . .*

She took a deep breath and stepped through. Then she turned to see if Webb was coming. She preferred more company, here.

Behind her, Webb was shaking his head. "I'm going home." He turned away—and then turned unwillingly back toward the door. Moving like a man caught in an unseen current, he staggered through the door, and into the black curtained room beyond.

Dunsmuir was only a little surprised to find Door Twenty-three unlocked and unguarded. True, it went contrary to everything he knew about the Center. But with Collins along, surprise was at the same time inevitable and inappropriate.

The room beyond the door was a vast one, draped in shadows; it seemed to have been an airplane hangar, at one time. Its cavernous interior spaces reached five or six stories up, hundreds of feet across. The concrete floor was dusty but for the path between Door Twenty-three and the huge idol dimly seen at the far end of the room. High overhead, hunched forms crouched on the guano-crusted steel rafters. Black velvet curtains covered the windows near the ceiling; the far walls were stark and murky.

It was cold here; they could see their breaths, in the faint light that struck in shafts, here and there, where the curtains were not quite snug against the high windows. Dunsmuir and Collins walked on.

"What is that?" Dunsmuir asked, in a whisper, peering at the idol. "A Buddha?"

Collins laughed softly at that. "Buddha!" And he laughed again.

Nearer the idol was a circle of high black curtains on runners about thirty feet above the floor; the curtains were drawn partly back so Dunsmuir could see only the silhouette of the idol beyond.

As they neared the curtained-off area, Dunsmuir's eyes adjusted—or perhaps there was a kind of black light emanating, almost unseeably, from the bulky figure on the dais. It was cold; but Dunsmuir found he was sweating.

They reached the curtain, and there came a cry that was something less than a wail and more than a moan, a cry of soul-deep disillusionment and betrayal. A woman's voice.

And then they stepped through the partition.

The figure lying on the cushioned dais, propped on an elbow, was big as a two story house; was not an idol. It was the "Teacher." In the flesh, "living" but not breathing; he had no need to breathe.

Dracula was draped in the same sort of black velvet cloth— hundreds of square yards of it–that hung from the runners and covered the windows. He was a giant. He was bloated, pig-like now, though no pig had ever grown this big, bigger than a blue whale–and his face was tormented by hunger. The deepset eyes, the heavy eyebrows, the Slavic cheekbones, the seductive mouth–all of it quivered with a tortured need, as if with each new victim he only grew thirstier. He'd gone bald and his great hands–big as krakens–shook as he reached for the man hanging on a hook beside his head.

It was the black guard who'd run from Collins below. He was stripped nude, and hanging by a hook through the jaw, alive and wriggling but unable to speak, choked with trickling blood. Vlad Veovod, Dracula, the Son of the Dragon, lifted the black man off the hook–the man groaned and writhed in pain–and took him in his two hands, and brought him to his mouth.

Dunsmuir and the others–Webb, the woman who knelt before Dracula amid the ruins of the drained people, and Rodney Collins– watched in dull amazement as Dracula punctured the black man's chest and belly with his fangs, fangs the size of sabers, so that his victim writhed out gushes of thick red. But rather than drinking it thus, Dracula withdrew his fangs and raised the man over his head and wrung him like a wet rag, squeezed him out into his mouth . . .

Though choked, the man managed a single piercing shriek, before his spine was twisted apart, and he split open between the two rents in his torso, showering Dracula's upturned lips with blood.

"Behold, the Teacher," Collins said dryly.

"It's . . . an illusion . . . a vision . . . " Dunsmuir stammered.

"My you *are* in denial, Oliver," Collins commented.

Dracula roared in frustration and disappointment, and tossed the gutted, drained corpse disgustedly onto the floor before him. It fell with a sickening slap.

"Not enough yet, Vlad?" Collins asked airily, stepping forward. At Collins' feet, below the dais, were the wreckages of other victims–judging by the uniforms and outfits that had been stripped away like the peels of fruit, they'd been the inner circle of devotees and bodyguards and cult executives; those the "Teacher" had saved till last.

A great moan went up from the rafters–where crouched hundreds,

Dunsmuir saw, of Dracula's "initiates." Those not fortunate enough to be simply drained and destroyed . . .

Someone came from the shadows, toward Collins—with a sword in his hand. It was Georgei.

"Look out, Collins!" Dunsmuir said, staggering back.

Collins turned toward the man wielding the sword—but only smiled. Georgei had raised the sword over his head . . . ritualistically. He made several passes in the air with it, each one a sigil of some kind, then knelt before Collins, weeping with joy, and handed him the sword. "Oh Angel, I beg you now release me." He said something more in Russian-Armenian. Collins answered in the same dialect. Then he accepted the sword and struck down with it. The ornate sword struck the collar on Georgei's neck—and split it. The blade shouldn't have been able to break iron, but it did. Georgei cried out, and fell on his face, shaking, the life going from him, babbling in joy.

"You have atoned long enough, G. No longer will you have to bring innocents to him. Go to the Between place, and await Word."

In a movement as startling as a house unfolding itself, Dracula stood, draperies flapping with a bullwhip sound, floor shaking under his bare feet. Dunsmuir threw himself down, crawling away from the heat of Dracula's rage, and found himself crouched beside the black woman . . . He'd seen her at one of the seminars. Danitra . . .

"Oh no it's a lie it's a lie it's a lie . . ." she wept.

Dracula bent and snatched up Georgei and made to raise him to his lips—but Collins made a gesture, and Georgei's body vanished, replaced with a cloud of silver butterflies that fluttered up into the air and about Dracula's head like a mock of a halo. Dracula howled and swiped at them, and they drifted away and up and became a luminous mist, that slipped right through the ceiling.

"It's frustrating, is it?" Collins said, speaking softly but his voice carrying to every corner of the enormous room. "Yes, Count, I expect it is. How many chances were you given, Vlad? You were driven from this world many times—and many times you let your rage feed you, and you found your way back, until at last you were incorporated into the Great Plan by your Master . . . and by his Master . . ."

Dracula's voice came like the sizzling sound that follows a lightning strike. "Be silent, fly of God! Your buzzing aggravates my torment! You masquerade as an angel but you are a demon!"

"Demons are made within men, Vlad," Collins replied calmly. "And you were one such. The Impaler. And then less than a man— with a hunger beyond men, when Stoker told your tale. And now in self mockery you grow—but you are not nurtured. You have infected the world with your greed, your bloodthirstiness, trying to finally get enough, but you never will. You'll never have enough. You're just a hungry little boy . . ."

Shaking with rage, Dracula reached down and snatched at Collins, his roar like thunder echoing in a cavern, his great, clawed fingers closing around the diminutive figure . . .

And then screaming at the touch. He could not lift Collins from the floor. Something passed from Collins, into Dracula, an opposite charge to the spark shown passing from God to Adam on the Sistine ceiling . . .

And Dracula was uncreated. Silver-blue electricity shivered visibly through him, and crackled between his fangs, and lit his eyes up from within like beacons. And for a moment, the divine energy blazoned out something that had been hidden before, something only recently imprinted on the Lord of Vampire's forehead:

666.

This completed, the energy detonated within the monstrous corpus of the Lord of the Living Dead, and he was sundered from head to foot, torn open and turned inside out—freeing, in the process, ten-thousand trapped spirits that spiraled upwards in silver skeins of release . . . Taking with them those who crouched on the rafters—taking them up, and out, through a ceiling suddenly become as vaporous as cloud.

This time, there really was nothing left of him. Nothing but a lump in a puddle that turned the stomach to look upon.

Collins turned to Danitra and Dunsmuir, and took them by the hands. They knew Collins what for who he was, and let him lead them like a parent with two children, out the door. "There've been some changes made, outside these walls. The veil is torn away. Let's go and look at the real world," he said. "And see it for the first time."

They left Webb—the genetic and spiritual echo of Van Helsing—lying on the floor, sobbing for his loss, the loss of his master and his enemy. Never knowing which was which.

KINDRED

Harry brought Norris a golden knife. Norris had been Harry's fence for twelve years, and they were, if not friends exactly, something close to it.

Norris told him how his kids were doing and when his wife was getting out of the state pen for women and how to hide things from the IRS and how a person actually had to *buy* a house.

Harry had figured he'd get a good price for that stolen knife. He'd got it when he went into someone's house with a carpet cleaning crew—which he did mostly so he could steal things. Yes, he figured he'd get a good price because Norris loved gold: he had gold watches, six gold rings, a gold pendant, two gold chains, a gold painted car.

Norris surprised him by offering him a low price for the knife.

"That's solid gold, man. Fine workmanship, solid gold. I checked it in an antiques register. Solid fourteen karat. Sharp and in mint condition. I want three times that."

Norris refused, but he couldn't take his eyes off the knife. So Harry, still surprised, shrugged and put the knife back in the gym bag and said, "I'm outta here," and he was even more surprised when Norris jerked the bag away, took out the knife, and stabbed him in the chest with it.

Norris stood over him with tears in his eyes. "I'm sorry, man. I'm sorry. I always liked you. I didn't want to pay for that knife, though. It's too good to pay for like that. It's gold. It's beautiful. But I had to have it. I wish you'd brought me ten silver spoons worth the same as you wanted. I would've bought them. But gold . . . and a knife perfect for killing, both. I could let the gold go, or the knife, but not both the gold and the knife."

Harry whispered, "I understand, man. I do."

Then he died, but he died understanding.

I mean, it made complete sense. Totally.

THE WORD "RANDOM,"
DELIBERATELY REPEATED

He was tired of the library. The faint, echoing words of the librarian were shaped like the books they passed through. He lingered in the scant poetry section.

No one reads poetry at this jock university, he thought. Lots of dust on the book covers. They haven't been checked out in ages.

He leaned his large athlete's frame against the lonely shelves and remembered the canyons of eastern Oregon.

He closed his eyes:

He and Maria were drunk together. It hadn't been too hard to seduce her. You can't seduce someone who doesn't want it. They lay balmed in the smell of sage and sequoia. They rolled off the blankets in search of new touchings and caked their bare sweaty skin with dust, dust still warm from the sun that was laying torch to the horizon.

He remembered the desert and Maria often because of one special peculiarity in the incident: afterward, they had not regretted it.

They washed and sobered themselves in a canyon stream. But neither made a move to dress, though the air grew chill. With most, it was quickly over and followed by an embarrassed silence and a scuffle to get dressed. But not with Maria. They had sat together, close for warmth, watching the desert sunset burn the outline of the hill in the sky. He thought about school, about the team-letters ceremonies and the cheerleaders that he had pretended to like. No one had understood when he refused to go out for football that last time. The team had berated him for trying to start a poetry club—that was for women. Had Haggart gone faggot?

But he loved The Game and the feel of muscles that were so much a part of his responses that they jumped as his thoughts did. He loved to feel the pain of pushing past his limit and the feeling of growth afterward. And, as Maria pulled him again on top of her, he thought of the sexual elasticity of contact sports and the orgasmic swell of Making It, of Scoring.

The desert evening draped them, pressed them closer together. They moved against each other like clapping hands at a pep rally. As he reared and shuddered over her, his vision seemed to coalesce; then sharpen. The randomly placed boulders of the hillside were scattered seemingly without pattern, edged and shaped without purpose. He had never noticed any organization in the morose shapes of the desert or the crumbling wind-swept canyons. But now, they seemed to shift, falling into astonishing coherence. Each boulder, each stone and gnarled bush became elaboration on a central theme. They had relationship, and in that fragmented orgasmic second, they came together as though in an order codified to an alien intent. The image was burned into his mind as the desert sun burns stark its landscape.

He opened his eyes: He was back in the library, but . . .

The image of the broken layers of rock and shale, of torn igneous lumps and gouged ravines was still strong. He looked at the directly purposeful arrangement of the books in the library, and suddenly felt the desert image transposed over them.

They were the same.

He looked at the objects lining the shelves and allowed himself briefly to forget that they were books. And he laid aside, for the moment, the knowledge that this was a library, ordered, according to the Dewey Decimal System. He saw the books stripped of anthropomorphic associations. They were alien objects, new and unidentifiable, bound together on the shelf apparently at random. Some were tall, reaching almost to the next shelf; some were thick and fat, three times the width of most; others were short and thin. He could see no pattern in their visual arrangement. They progressed with three high and thin ones, went to four low and thick ones, shifted to pamphlets. They were colored at random, with random tint and texture.

He laughed, loudly. A scuffle, of feet. Something on two spindly limbs swathed in green cones of cloth waved a gangly wrinkled upper limb at him and flapped its lips. It said something he chose not to hear. He looked away from the thing and back to the wild chaos of straight ravines filled with rectangles. He stopped playing the game.

They were ordered again. Dewey Decimal System. You can look up anything you want in the card catalog.

He ignored the librarian who was whispering angrily at him for ignoring her.

He caught a glimpse of himself in a window as he left the building: tall, broad chest and shoulders, short black hair, blue eyes that looked back from the reflection like a separate person would. He wore a blue shirt, jeans, and tennis shoes. Big deal, he thought. I wonder if something that'd never seen a human before would see a purpose in the way I'm put together?

The campus was emptier than the desert. All the buildings were cast in the same ugly gray concrete mold, mottled by little holes where the metal supports for the forms had been. The long naked windows that stretched uninterrupted from top to bottom concentrated thin transparency on him as though he were an ant burning under a magnifying glass. There were a few stunted trees set in pots on the concrete.

There was no life in the passing self-involved faces. There was no fertility in the cement. Haggart debated with himself as to whether he should go to class. Sociology. Where they tried to make the fluid movements of societies as concrete as their campus casement.

Forget it, he decided. He started, hearing a feminine voice call after him. He turned, half expecting to see a smooth dark Chicana face, dark-eyed Maria. But it was Leslie. Blonde hair, short skirt, trite questions in philosophy.

"Where you going?" she asked.

"Home. Where you going?"

"Come on. I'll give you a ride."

He followed. He looked at the doll-like symmetry of her profile. She's really pretty. Uses make-up well. Big tits. So how come I'm not attracted to her? All the beautiful women, in this goddamn university, I should be—

"Here it is," she said, interrupting his thoughts. She unlocked a red Camaro and got in. Her parents probably paid for the car, he thought. And they paid for her tuition and room. And whether they know it or not, they pay for her birth control. And so they pay for me.

She drove easily from the parking lot and into the street, steering with one hand. Very casual. Very cool.

"How do you like the philosophy class?" she asked, trying to spark the conversation. Finally, out of habitual politeness, he answered,

"She proselytizes. Everybody swallows it. She pushes her Zen on everybody, tries to make Plato sound like a narrow-minded ass."

"You're right," she said. She would say that. "Zen is fun to play with, but it doesn't have any pragmatic value. I mean, the philosophy has to serve the people; otherwise you've just got an excuse to . . ."

He stopped listening. Pieces of a poem began to fall together in his mind as he watched the autumn-yellow trees flash by. Some of them had lost part of their leaves already and they bared limbs as if they wore short-sleeved shirts. He interrupted her and asked for a pencil. She gave him a puzzled sideways look, then indicated the glove compartment and fell silent. He found a scrap of paper to write on.

At this speed, not really *auto*,
trees revolve
like children on a carousel;
arms, branches, outstretched.
white teeth
break the edges of
clouds
into film-negative clownfaces.
The clown faces would continue laughing
even if we had an accident.

"What's that?" Leslie asked when he finished.

"Just some notes. Reminding myself of something."

She pulled up in front of his apartment house. "Well," she said in a mock sigh, "here we are." She looked at him, obviously expecting to be asked in "for a joint or something."

He almost asked her, then realized that he really didn't want to see her, that if he asked her in it would only be because one is always careful not to waste an opportunity. But he said only, "See ya." And climbed quickly out of the car and walked up the steps.

He stopped at the top step and remembered the desert in the library. He heard Leslie drive off.

He walked back and down the road a block to a small park where he began to pick up odds and ends of litter that lay in the grass. In a few minutes he had enough. He walked home, but just before he reached his apartment the uncomfortably familiar voice of Benny Clummworth rumbled from behind.

Clummworth had come from the same high school that Haggart had, and he lived a few doors down. He was one of the jocks who had given Haggart a hard time for "going with a Mex." Haggart had ignored him. No one understood why he didn't challenge Clummworth to a fight. Just as no one had understood why he had to drop out of athletics.

Clummworth's presence made Haggart think of Maria again, and he wondered if he'd broken up with her for her sake as he'd claimed. Haggart's thoughts were jerked back to the present by Clummworth snatching at his arm.

"Whatcha doing?" Clummworth, asked as though he were building up to a monumental witticism. "Picking up litter for the sanitation department?"

Haggart gave him a cold stare.

"Come on," Clummworth persisted. "Whatya gonna do with that shit? Cans and beer bottles and sticks and stuff–"

"Make a mobile," Haggart lied. "Or a sculpture or something." That was closer to the truth. He shook his arm loose from Clummworth's tightening grasp. The bulletheaded jock laughed.

"A copy of the Venus de Milo?"

Haggart turned his back on him and walked to his apartment, careful not to drop anything. It was a studio: bedroom, kitchenette, bathroom. The walls were bare but the floor was a litter of books and papers. He went into the bedroom, dropped the things he carried, and sat down heavily on the bed. He expelled a great gust of air and lay back, covering his eyes with his arms.

Maria had been like the desert, simple but potent. She had little education, but always understood what he meant when he said it simply. He tried to shake memories of her out of his head. He stood and stretched, felt young muscles complain with the need for exercise. With a last, puzzled glance at the odd array of artifacts on the floor he grabbed his swimming suit and towel and walked swiftly out of the building and four blocks to the YMCA.

Forty-five minutes later, exhilarated by a brisk swim, he sat at the edge of the pool, staring at chlorinated ripples. The shouts of other swimmers came to him across the water, vibrating slightly, as loud as if they shouted in his ear–IF YOU SPLASH ME AGAIN BOY

Haggart looked up. A random splash covered Haggart's face with water. A mask of water. Something tugged at the edge of his understanding. He got up, walked carefully over the slick wet tile to the diving board. He waited his turn, but when it came he hesitated, still thinking of the library and splashing water. Randomly splashing water. Someone yelled in his ear:

"Hey, let's go! You waiting for the board to dive off of *you*?"

Startled, Haggart ran out on the board and jumped, coming down sloppily on the end and springing out and up in poor form. He might hit the water wrong, and slap it with his face. The first part of the dive had been clumsy. But at the last moment he snapped his legs straight and arched his back, cutting the surface cleanly.

It came to him underwater, as he was yet a knife sheathed in frothing bubbles. He had started awkwardly, diving askew, righted himself—making purpose out of aimlessness.

He surfaced quickly and swam to the side.

A half-hour later Haggart came back to his apartment, almost running up the stairs. He unlocked the door and entered hurriedly, kicking books aside. What the hell, he thought They're just random rectangles. He laughed at that. He thought of the term paper abandoned last night and of the overwhelming feeling of purposelessness that possessed him whenever he entered the college. I'm going to find out what it is, he thought. Where purpose comes from. I'll be wearing nothing but a mask of clean water.

He went to the things he'd left on the bedroom floor and took inventory. Four or five sticks, some string, pipecleaners, some cardboard, sandpaper, a fingernail clipper, a tin can, a small block of wood, two beer bottles and a spoon. He went to the bathroom to get tissue, came back tearing it into small strips. He put the tissue in an open can after winding sandpaper around the can, and let paper ribbons spill out like hair. He put the sticks in the beer bottles and used them to support two others to make a small gate of wood that arched over the other things protectively. He hung a string from the ceiling light, attached pipecleaners to that, and wound up a spoon in them. He hung a styrofoam cup from the string and a length of steel wool that hung down like Spanish moss from the cup. He was putting things together at random, but thinking all the time of the desert and the ragged, weather-carved cliffs that were somehow linked together. In a half-hour, he had an anomalous shape that was at the same time anachronism and affinity. He was sweating with the deliberate effort to randomness. He had caught himself several times making a recognizable symmetry with seemingly unrelated shapes. Random. Got to be random. No pattern.

He finished, putting the bottlecaps in as a finishing touch.

He sat back and *closed his eyes:* Tried to forget having ever seen the shape he'd made. He felt his mind blank, opened his eyes. Random impressions: A gate. A gate under a rocket (the cup) that had just run out of fuel and was spewing a trail of smoke (the tail of steel wool). A paper-fountain (the can with strips of tissue emerging) spilling over granite facing (sandpaper). The fingernail clippers that stretched from the upper edge of the sponge to paper below looked like a jacknifing diver in mid-leap. The beveled block with the paper and the bottlecaps looked like a car. A car passing under an arch by a waterfall that flowed into a pool into which someone dived

Maria died in a car accident in a place like that.

Run off the side of a cliff by a drunk under an arch of wind-shaped desert stone. The car had crashed into the water, and she had died from impact before she could drown. Maria masked in water.

He shut his eyes and cried out:

A feeling like an icy hand on his face made him look up again. His attention was drawn to the outlines made by random twisted shapes; they seemed to delineate the space between the objects in the random construct into the features of a face.

"Maria," he said.

"Thank you, Ronny," her calm voice said. "Thank you for the mirror." Her voice resonated with hollow reassurance. "I needed a mirror so badly in this place. Nothing here reflects. I couldn't see myself . . ."

Her voice faded into the lines of jagged sticks and cups and blocks.

Random lines. A mirror.

VOICES

"Your parents are worried about you," the child psychiatrist told Jeremy. "Do you know why?"

"Yes," the boy said, "it's because I hear voices."

"What do the voices say?"

"They don't say anything."

"Then how can you be hearing voices, Jeremy? They just sort of hum or bark? I've heard of that."

"No, they're not even voices. It's only one, and it's not exactly a voice."

"Then what is it like?"

The boy leaned back in the leather chair. He looked at the cryptic doctoral certificates, framed, on the wall. He looked at a bowling trophy. "You like bowling?"

"Yes."

"I don't think of a doctor bowling."

"Well I do. It makes me feel like I'm just doing what my body likes, sometimes."

"I know what you mean by that, I do."

"The voice, or whatever it is, Jeremy. Can you try to tell me what it's like?"

The boy looked at a world globe. "Well, um . . . I don't know."

"Try to describe it. Take your time."

The boy considered; the miniature grandfather clock ticked. A hummingbird came to the window and seemed puzzled by a reflection in it. It hung beating the air, looking at the glass, fooled and not fooled, then went away. "Huh," the boy said.

The psychiatrist waited. At last the boy said, "It's like . . . if you're in a dark cold room, and somebody pulled back a curtain, just a little, high up on the wall, so that one ray of light came down and you put out your hand and in the dark cold room you could feel that warm light on your hand, and how that feels."

"That sounds like a pleasant feeling. A good one."

"It is. It is a good feeling. But it's just . . . It's like the feeling is talking. It's saying, 'Ray of Light, Ray of Light, Ray of Light.' It's saying 'You and Me, You and Me.' It's saying 'Open and feel Me.' But it's not saying anything either. It's not saying anything at all. No words. It doesn't talk in words."

The psychiatrist realized his heart was thudding loudly in his chest. "When . . . when do you hear . . . feel this?"

"When . . . when things are a certain way in me. I don't know how to say . . ."

"Is it when . . . just like receiving? A feeling of nothing but receiving? Very . . . very empty except for . . . for receiving?"

"Yes! Yes that's it."

The psychiatrist looked at the clock. "We have some time left. Do you want to play Chinese Checkers?"

"Sure."

The psychiatrist told Jeremy's parents there was nothing wrong with him. But he asked permission to speak to the boy on his birthday every year, "just to keep an eye on things," but what he didn't say was: he asked to do this for himself, and not for the boy.

THE LAST RIDE

"See that girl in the last car?" Bixby asked. "She's ridden five times in a row."

"In a *row?*" Chad stared at the girl. She was about twenty, slim and blonde and pretty, in an exotic kind of way. Big Mediterranean eyes. Kind of on the small side, something doll-like about her; looked too frail to take five rides on the Hellcoaster—in a row. "Maybe she's drunk."

"Or stoned. Tell you something—I think I saw her playing with herself, a couple of times, right before the Hellpit."

"Oh yeah right." Chad was skeptical. Bixby was a weedy little guy with a big unsatisfied horniness, and the dude had a rich fantasy life.

"Check her out! I gotta go, my Mom's picking me up . . ." Bixby was twenty-five, still lived with his Mom. No wonder he never got laid, Chad thought. Chad waved goodbye, and went down the line of cars taking tickets.

It was strange how you got used to working outdoors seven stories off the ground. He looked out over the Central Texas countryside beyond the amusement park, burnished like hammered brass in the sundown-tinged light of early evening.

"Can I simply give you all my tickets in advance?" a dollsized voice asked.

Chad looked at her, his hand still extended for her ticket. The girl. She was offering him ten Hellcoaster tickets, all still linked together. She added, "I have no pockets in this skirt, I'm afraid I will lose the tickets out there . . ." She had a faint accent he couldn't quite place. An odd formality in her grammar. Her tone a little distant. As if in her head, she was still "out there". Her eyes were gray blue, picked out with only the faintest traces of blue eyeshadow. She wore a blue leather jacket with a matching skirt, and blue pumps, which she'd taken off.

"You're kind of into blue, I guess," Chad said, just for something to say. Pretty lame remark, he told himself.

"I am today," she said. "Tomorrow I think it'll be dayglow yellow." She looked up at him gravely. Something smoldering . . .

He took her tickets and said, "Ride as many times as you want, if you can handle it. I hear you already went five."

"Yes. It's easy. There's a god on the roller coaster." She smiled from a long ways away.

For a moment he thought he saw something glimmering around her head; a kind of faint aurora. Trick of the sunset light, he supposed. He said, "A god? Yeah? What's he look like?" Hoping he would fit the description.

She frowned, and it was as if she were frowning in another language. "He is perhaps what you'd call a satyr. A satyr with wings and a huge . . . and huge shoulders."

"Oh." Chad didn't fit the description. He was tall and slim, with long brown hair that his guitar player was always trying to get him to dye. His band, The Strokers, needed some on-stage glamour, the dude said.

"And the god on the roller coaster rides with me," she added dreamily, "and he protects me and . . . shows me what the roller coaster is really all about . . ." She looked out along the swoops and loops and wicked dips of the Hellcoaster. It was once the Oasis of Fun's most popular ride—being one of the biggest roller coasters in the Southwestern United States—but it had lost ground to the waterslides and artificial white waters of the Wet Fury section of the amusement park.

"Come *onnnnnnn*," some letterman jock said, two cars up from the girl. "Ask her for a date and let's get this ride *goin!*"

Chad felt his face go hot. He stalked over to the lever, and pulled it. The jock's jaws clacked shut with painful force as the cars lurched into sudden acceleration. The girl licked her lips and spread her legs as she rushed by Chad. And then they'd plunged out of sight, the riders screaming and the 'coaster roaring like a steel giant.

When the ride was over, there was almost no one else to go on the next one. Just a fat, drunk Mexican guy, in the first car, and the girl, in the last. "Hey," Chad said, walking over to her between rides. "Uh—"

"Selinda," she said. "You wanted to know my name, I think?"

"Yeah," he said, a little shaken. "Um—my name's Chad . . . I—"

Just then Bixby came up the stairs, pimply face made even grottier by a deep scowl. "My Mom wants me to move out," he said. "She's, like, kickin' me out. We had a big fight in the parking lot and I got out of the car and she—"

"Hey Bix—would you run the machine once or twice for me?"

"Uh—"

"Thanks." Chad turned to the girl. "I was thinking—"

"Get in," she said, anticipating him again.

Okay, he thought, so I'm predictable. He got into the car next to her, pulled the rubber sheathed bar down to hold them in place. Muttering, Bixby threw the lever. The sun went down—just like that. Darkness fell as they plunged into the Hellpit.

Afterwards, thinking back on it, Chad wasn't sure quite how it happened. He wasn't expecting it. Not just a few minutes after he met her. He supposed it was the steepest plunge, the Deathpit, that pushed them in one another's arms. He had a strange feeling, going down into it, the wind in his hair and the inertia in his gut, that somehow the roller coaster had changed since the last time he'd been on it. It just seemed different, riding with her. Higher and deeper and faster and . . . more personal. And when they plunged into the last big dive before the second time around, it was like they were leaping into a bottomless well together. So he flung his arms around her, and she came to him, and somehow . . .

It wasn't *somehow*. It was her. she'd taken his hand, and put it between her legs. Under the skirt. No underwear. Wet, hot, and sticky. Before he'd so much as kissed her.

They got around to kissing at the Plateau, the long stretch that takes you into the dock, and then out again to the climb that reached for the Helldip. It was a long, jarring, shuddery kiss, their teeth clacking together at times with the rollicking of the car, and neither one caring.

Something in his head warned him, even then. Any pretty girl that'll do this kind of thing—gratis—five minutes after meeting you is, first of all, one-of-a-kind; and second, loony as Daffy Duck. Or maybe Lizzie Borden . . .

But he'd been two months without being laid, since Dody left him—and since the band lost its drummer, meaning they couldn't get gigs. No gigs, no girls. And he just didn't give a hot damn about consequences right now.

Especially when she put her hand in his pants.

The second time around the Hellcoaster, they pulled out all the stops. It was dark out, and the lights of the amusement park glowed against the night in lurid colors, like a nervous system lit up by drugs. And though he'd taken nothing, Chad felt drugged as Selinda pushed the bar aside and slid onto his lap, facing him, and opened her blouse . . .

They were just climbing the first peak, before the first Helldip, the Roller Coaster laboring up, up, clickaclacka clickaclacka, as if procrastinating before the big plunge, and they had a few moments to get things in position. His pants unzipped, cock free and rigid as the steel rails of the Hellcoaster; Selinda straddling him, grinding against him. Then, just as they reached the top, lifting her little round ass up and driving her vagina down hard on his cock. Both of them shuddering at the rich heat of that probing—just as the roller coaster cars shuddered, poised, on the top of the peak . . . And then Selinda lifted her hips again—and the cars plunged down into the Helldip. Simultaneous with his plunge into her.

Thunder in his ears; thunder in all his senses. Both of them screaming with joy and fear. Wind streaming around them; cold wind on the base of his cock, his balls, the crack of his ass; her small firm, pertly uplifted breasts dappled and streaked with the clownish, racing lights of the amusement park . . .

Chad was dimly aware that, after the first two rides, Bixby had closed the Hellcoaster to other riders, put up the little sign that said it was being tested for defects, and let them go it alone. So that he could watch them, of course. He'd run down and bought a cheap telescope at one of the souvenir stands, and Chad had glimpses of the light flashing off the little 'scope's lens as Bixby watched them fuck. Who cared? Chad didn't.

There's an art to fucking on a roller coaster, they discovered. You had to brace yourself a certain way, with reference to the direction of the G-pull, going downhill; going uphill you had to brace another way. Going uphill, in fact, she had to do the hip-pumping; downhill, he had to do it. And he thought he felt the god she'd talked about helping him, possessing him, its spiritual strength manifested in the gravitational and inertial energies wrenching them as they rode the peaks and valleys of the Hellcoaster. The god taking her in his strong arms, fucking her as they plunged into the bottomless well. She came at least twice.

And he never quite came himself. Or anyway, never quite ejaculated. Not yet. Not 'til the sixth time around.

The first five times delight was mingled with fear. The knowledge that the restraining bar wasn't in place, and she was half standing, and he was half out of the car himself, humping into her, legs straining against inertia and the shock of wrenching turns. Stomach wrenching with the strain, feeling his insides wracked by the conflict between his eager fucking and the pull of gravity. Knowing that this was dangerous as all Hell. They could lose their hold at the same time, they could go flying out of the cars together, to fall seven stories, locked at the groin, fucking their way to death.

It was both terrifying and exhilarating. It drove him to unspeakable peaks of arousal—and yet seemed to constrict his semen in his testicles.

As if, should he ejaculate, the act would cause him to be ejaculated from the car—he and Selinda shot like semen into the sky.

But finally, on the plateau, the fourth time around, it happened. His orgasm. She felt it coming—saw it in the widening of his eyes, the sudden arching of his back—and opened her legs wider to take it. She screamed as the rollercoaster thundered agreement. He shot into her with all the accumulated force of the four rides, all that falling and rushing built up like a tightened spring, a taut coil released in that orgasm.

Afterwards, he felt like he was going to throw up.

He signaled Bixby frantically, and the cars ground to a halt at the dock. Chad lay back gasping, gagging, shivering with sweat, as she calmly climbed off him and stepped onto the dock, brushing herself off, buttoning her blouse—facing away from Bixby—and putting on her shoes. "I'd better find the lady's room," she said, with great dignity, and walked off toward the stairs. Unruffled—but walking sort of stiffly.

By contrast, it was with great effort that Chad managed to put his manhood back in his pants and zip them up. He felt like he'd been through a car wreck. The kind where your car rolls over five times before coming to a stop. He tasted blood. His lower lip was split. His upper lip was bruised. His cheeks were bruised. His hips were bruised. His pubis. His stomach was flailing about in his gut. He lay back gasping in the ridecar. "Jesus Christ . . ."

"Wow!" Bixby was saying. "We oughta be selling tickets for this! What a girl! Hey, you think she'd let me, uh—Well, maybe the Ferris Wheel'd be better, more my style, but—"

She? She. She!

Chad sat bolt upright. *Where was she?* Grimacing with pain, he climbed from the car and went unsteadily down the stairs. Forced himself to take them three at a time. "Selinda!"

No way was he going to lose her now. The whole thing had embarrassed her, he guessed, now that whatever it was had worn off, and now she was going to vanish, never see him again.

At the bottom of the stairs he stood staring into the Saturday night crowd parading down the fairway, all smiles and balloons and beery giggles. No sight of her. "Selinda!"

He shoved his way into the crowd, cursing and bellowing her name. Spent half an hour at that, running through the park looking for her, before he was ready to fall from exhaustion. He found himself leaning against a hot dog stand, muttering, "Seven-Up. Seven-Up."

They gave him one, he found a little change that hadn't been shaken from his pockets on the ride, and was listlessly sucking soda when he heard it. The dollsized voice. Saying, "How about if we try it on the Tilt-a-Whirl next?"

He turned, and grabbed her, clasped her to him. And she pushed away from him. "One moment!" she protested. That odd accent, that stiffness with the language again. "We hardly know each other!"

He gaped at her. Jaw hanging halfway to his shoes.

That's what it was like. She kept him at a distance—except when they were actually doing it. And she wasn't interested in beds. No apartments, motels, not even sleeping bags. It had to be riding—or, anyway, it had to be dangerous.

She wouldn't tell him a damn thing about herself, either. They went on for five weeks, meeting once a week at the Oasis of Fun, and other peculiar trysting junctions, and he never so much as learned her last name. She was able to see him exclusively between seven and eleven-thirty. He never saw her consult a watch—but she always seemed to know what time it was. She'd look at the stars, or sniff the air. And say: "It is almost time for me to go . . ." She was the absolute opposite of most women. Most of them, quite understandably, preferred their sex life to be founded on a deep relationship. Mutual knowledge. Conversation. Meeting parents. Quiet dinners, noisy concerts, dancing. Hours talking in bed, comparing notes on life. It was what Chad wanted himself, deep down.

Not Selinda. She was inside-out. She seemed to regard ordinary dating, with its involved conversations, as a kind of obscene intimacy—and quick sex on the longest park waterslide was the decent way to relate.

Could be, he thought, that conversation with her would be redundant—because she always seems to know what I'm about to say . . .

Seemed to be able to see right into him . . .

She was quite opaque to him, though. Couldn't see into her at all, beyond the passion. Oh, he knew she was using him, in some way. And he knew she had to be crazy, and that this was a dangerous game. They'd been caught twice; he'd used up all his favors in the park getting them out of it. And there was something incredibly lunatic in her eyes sometimes. Especially the first time they did it outside the park . . .

Going down the old highway at ninety-five miles an hour.

The old cracked concrete road was scarcely used anymore. Chances were they'd be the only ones killed in the accident. But the odds for an accident were brutally mounting as she screamed, "FASTER! MORE SPEED!" Not talking about hip-pumping speed.

They were both buck naked in the car. The seat vinyl sucking at his buttocks. She was straddling him as he drove his rickety old '71 Impala, straining it's tired horsepower to get past ninety. It was eleven at night, with a full moon glowing over the desert, no sign of civilization, no one watching—except the coyote dashing across the road up ahead, whose eyes for a moment caught fire in the headlights, seemed to share some incandescent secret with Selinda before it trotted into night.

Chad had one arm around Selinda's waist, shoving her down onto him, the other free so he could work the steering wheel; he was leaning a little to the right, trying, to see past her and the dusty, bug-flecked windshield. Lucky it was a straight road, for a while. They'd just hit ninety and she screamed "FASTERRRRR!" Digging her immaculately manicured golden nails into his shoulders, urging him on. And he looked up into her face and saw it in her eyes: Death.

She was pushing out the limits, pushing the border between life and death. She wanted them both to die, doing this. Crazy as Daffy Duck? Crazy as Lizzie Borden? Hell, she was crazy as Jimmy Swaggart, Tammy Faye Bakker, Jim Bakker, and for that matter, Jim Jones, rock and rolled into one.

But Chad couldn't stop. The car's 2500 pound, ninety mile an hour momentum was his momentum too—it was his sexual, emotional momentum, carrying him beyond the reach of loneliness. The car's tires screeched as if the car were expressing its own terror as the speedometer climbed to 92, 94, 95 . . . and she rutted harder and faster on him, her eyes rolling back in her head, her tongue emerging from between her trembling lips, its glistening pink tip reaching for his lips . . . 96, 98, 100 . . .

There was a curve coming up. A ways yet, but coming. "A curve!" he yelled. "We've gotta let up!"

"No!" she shouted in his ear, clutching him against her. Her sweat-sticky breasts nosing his neck. "No! *Not until you give it to me!*" Meaning: Come or we die!

He knew he should have flung her off right there. This was irresponsible, stupid, and futile. How could he even keep his hard-on this way, let alone ejaculate? With the curve rushing up toward them... But something, maybe masculine pride, kept him pumping into her. You got to live for this second, he told himself. This *very* second. Take the risk and come *because* of it!

They'd never make it around that curve at this speed . . .

But he kept pumping into her—like the car's pistons furiously pumping in the engine's cylinders—even when he saw the boulders at the curve . . .

His radio worked sometimes, and sometimes it didn't. There was a strange synchronicity about when it chose to come on—suddenly it started blasting AC/DC's *Highway To Hell,* the solo screaming into its own collision course. And it pushed him over the edge. Laughing hysterically, he shot his ejaculate into her. Just as they hit the curve.

His hand jerked spasmodically on the steering wheel, an involuntary motion twitched out of him by the orgasm, and at the last second the car careened, missing the heap of boulders and veering instead out into the desert, where it struck a dune and jumped—like a stunt car at an exhibition jumping from a ramp—whistling through the air, the wheels five feet over the ground, as he pumped out the last of his semen into her . . . Believing for one lunatic moment that the act of his ejaculation had somehow shot the car into the air . . .

And then WHUMP, they came down in a patch of cactus. Bounced around inside the car like dice in a gambler's hand. A nasty shiver of pain up through one of his testicles; something made his nose *crunch* . . . and the car bumped to a stop. Steaming.

Selinda climbed off him. He watched numbly as she switched on the car's interior light and checked herself over. One big bruise across her back from the steering wheel and a bump on her head and a little blood from a cut in her lip. That was it. Almost as an afterthought, she said, "Are you quite all right?"

"I think my nose is broken."

"You do not seem badly hurt." She glanced at the sky. "Ah! I had better get dressed. I'm going to be late!"

He stared at her in dull amazement. Finally, wiping blood off his mouth, asked, "Late for what?"

She wagged a finger at him reproachfully. "Foolish boy! We don't know each other so well as that yet!"

She'd almost got them killed. They'd escaped death by a whisker. There was no doubt about it. And there was no doubt that she was a psycho. He had a nightmare about it, that same night, after he finally got home and put his bruised bones wearily in bed. In the dream, they were making love on a tiny platform atop a flagpole. Which was atop the Empire State Building. Standing up there nude, balancing carefully, fucking, taking her from behind this time, as people on the observation deck below cheered and waved and laughed. And Selinda shouted, "Harder! Do it harder!" His legs shook with fear and he yelled, "I can't! We'll lose our balance! We'll fall!"

Seeing, in the sky, the winged satyr, fluttering there, hovering, toying with his erect, godsized member, and laughing at them. His lean, sardonic, face etched out of dark leather.

"Selinda this'd be a ridiculous way to die!" Chad shouted, looking away from the satyr. Struggling to keep his balance as he pumped into her. "If I do it harder—"

"Do it!" she screamed at him. "Do it or I will jump!"

So he did it. He couldn't let her jump. He loved her.

And they lost their balance and went tumbling, end over end, screwing wildly the whole time, until—

He sat bolt upright in his bed, slick with sweat. "It's got to end," he told himself. Staring into the darkness. "For sure."

But when she called him, a week later, and said, "Meet me at the Southerton Airport," his cock leapt like a hungry wolf in his pants and he said . . .

The plane's pilot knew something weird was going on. He was a middle aged black guy, had the hardnosed, hard-drinking look of a Vietnam vet about him. She'd probably picked him because he was the kind of guy who didn't give a flying fuck, so to speak, how weird it got. So long as he was paid.

So he didn't react when Selinda told Chad, "Put your manhood in me almost immediately, as soon as you can, otherwise we'll not achieve congress."

Achieve congress? "Uh—if you say so." Chad felt made out of lead. And under the lead was magma: Under the heaviness was anger. He'd spent an hour before the flight trying to talk her into coming clean with him. Begging her to tell him about *herself*. To talk about this . . . *thing* they did together. But she just smiled vacantly, and shook her head gently, and said, "Take me or leave me as I am."

And now they were about two thousand feet over the packed sandy earth of Texas. It was their first meeting in daylight, and that had surprised him. "It is a risk, meeting at this hour," she murmured. "But that too . . ." She shrugged.

The little Cessna bucking, in the intermittent turbulence. The sky a bit murky with dust in the distance; blue blurred with graybrown. Only a few clouds scribbled long and bluegray against the horizon. And Chad was thinking, *What's important in life? You going to live the way you always believed? Or not? If those are her terms—ask yourself, pal: Is she worth it? Is anybody? Probably not.* But living with the volume knob on the amp turned up . . . That was worth it. Hope I die before I get old? Well, here was his chance.

So he made himself stop thinking. He taped the Walkman onto his head, strapped on the parachute, went through the routine they'd taught him in the skydiving classes—make that "class," exactly one—and he joined her at the open door. She didn't ask. She took his hand and pulled him out with her . . .

The first time he'd jumped—the only other time—he'd nearly pissed his pants in terror, going out the door. This time he was slapped in the face by a wave of unreality. He was falling, but it didn't feel like falling; it felt like being suspended, hung like a mobile from some invisible ceiling—in a wind tunnel. Wind roared like a god—like the winged satyr of the roller coaster—whipping at him, snatching at his hair, drying the moisture from his eyes and mouth. His stomach flattened up against his diaphragm. The world whirling; the clouds on the horizon snaking past as he turned in the air . . . And then he felt her grip on his arm, and some of the disorientation passed. Looked into her eyes. Reached up automatically to hit the play button on his Walkman. Rock'n'roll thunder in freefall.

The world was spinning at 45 RPM, and the breath was wrenched from him and despair and delight married in him and went on a perverse honeymoon, and he shouted, "Sellliiiinnnnda!" She pulled herself hand over hand—up his arm. Coming at him like a panther. *I'll never be able to get hard in this scene!* he thought desperately. And then: *what the hell kind of thing is that to worry about, man! You don't jump right, you're going to die!*

Accept it. Or this is all for nothing.

So he dragged her to him and she locked her legs around him. Centrifugal force and a jealous air pressure tried to pull them apart, but he used all his strength, every muscle, and dragged her close, closer, till suddenly they shared one center of gravity, and they were sucked together by the pressure and inertia, almost crushing one another . . .

Don't throw up.

He swallowed hard, and reined in his racing heart, and quieted his fluttering belly, and tried to concentrate on the warmth where she was pressed against him. Her skirt hiked up around her hips now. The wind vibrating her blouse's collar whipping her hair. Kissing her, though the wind blew the saliva away, made their mouths like dry sponges on one another. The ground spinning. The wind roaring and the music thundering in his ears . . . an old song from Iggy and the Stooges. "Loose." Iggy bawling, *I stick it/deep—inside/I stick it deep inside—'cause I'm loose!*

So was Chad. Set loose. Surrendered. Thinking: *Fuck it. Death is inevitable anyway.* And the surrender surged into his cock, made him hard, so he was able to wriggle into her. Probing. Hiding in that inner world. Pumping. Short shallow pumps, but hard. Freefalling. Grinding out that sweet internal recognition.

"You must come!" She shouted suddenly. "The orgasm! Now! We must pull the cords!"

"I can't!" he shouted in her ear, not sure if she could hear him over the wind. "Not yet!" He was working his way there, but it was still a long way off.

"Do it!" she shouted. The ground swinging at them like a mallet.

"I'm . . . trying!" That's when he lost his grip on her—some errant wind jerking at them, prying them apart. One second she was there—the next, there was the sound of canvas snapping—

And he had her parachute in his hands, still in its pack.

He screamed and flailed, spinning, looking for her, the Walkman gone, torn away, too, the wind sucking all sound from him. His head throbbing in time with the sobbing thud of his heart.

There she was: about thirty feet away. He tried to remember how to plane his way over to her, but she seemed to drift farther from him. A strange look on her face. As if she were concentrating . . . Calling . . . calling . . . silently out to something.

A smell of leather. A deep, inhumanly-masculine laughter. And then *he* was there. Leather wings spread wide to block the sun; furry chest and legs hard with muscle. His eternally hard member wagging with his wingstrokes. His goat's feet dangling like the strange irrelevancies they were up here.

Sardonic face etched in dark leather. Bottomless eyes.

He swept past Chad effortless as a stingray in the sea and swooped down on Selinda, caught her adoringly in his arms. Then heaved her onto his back, where she hung between his wings, her legs locked around his waist—and her feet clamped on either side of his supernaturally-stiff member. She pushed it to the right with her feet—and he flew to the right. Obediently. They went laughing away, flying across the desert toward a distant butte. Selinda riding him; directing her *mount.*

And Chad heard it in his head, then. Knew that she could talk to this creature, but not with words, with the psychic talent that had always been hers. Some of it leaking to Chad . . .

I am sorry I left, she told the god. *I wanted to play with them for awhile, and I don't know how to explain why.*

I understand, the winged satyr answered her. *It's their mortality. They can die and we can't. It's so seductive . . .*

And then Chad lost them, like a radio station going out of range. He pushed her parachute away from him. Pulled his ripcord.

Chad tried to tell himself it had been a hallucination brought on by the horror of seeing her fall without her chute. But no one ever found her body in the desert. No one fitting her description ever turned up missing. Probably because she'd never entirely been in the world in the first place.

Chad got something out of it. He wrote a song. You must've heard it. It was his demo for the record company and his first big hit. It was called "The Last Ride." And it went to the top of the charts with a bullet.

Really,
Really,

WEIRD
STORIES

. . . And the Angel with Television Eyes

On a gray morning, April 11, the year 2020, Max Whitman woke in his midtown Manhattan apartment to find a living, breathing griffin perched on the right-hand post at the foot of his antique four-poster bed.

Max watched with sleep-fuzzed pleasure as the griffin—a griffin made of shining metal—began to preen its mirror-bright feathers with a hooked beak of polished cadmium. It creaked a little as it moved.

Max assumed at first that he was still dreaming; he'd had a series of oddly related technicolor-vivid dreams recently. Apparently one of these dreams had spilled over onto his waking reality. He remembered the griffin from a dream of the night previous. It had been a dream bristling with sharp contrasts: of hard-edged shafts of white light—a light that never warms—breaking through clouds the color of suicidal melancholy. And weaving in and out of those shafts of light, the griffin came flying toward him ablaze with silvery glints. And then the clouds coming together, closing out the light, and letting go sheets of rain. Red rain. Thick, glutinous rain. A rain of blood. Blood running down the sheer wall of a high-towered, gargoyle-studded castle carved of transparent glass. Supported by nothing at all: a crystalline castle still and steady as Mount Everest, hanging in mid-air. And laying siege to the sky-castle was a flying army of wretched things led by a man with a barbed-wire head—

Just a bad dream.

Now, Max gazed at the griffin and shivered, hoping the rest of the dream wouldn't come along with the griffin. He hadn't liked the rain of blood at all.

Max blinked, expecting the griffin to vanish. It remained, gleaming. Fulsome. Something hungry . . .

The griffin noticed Max watching. It straightened, fluttered its two-meter wingspread, wingtips flashing in the morning light slanting through the broad picture window, and said, "Well, what do you want of me?" It had a strangely musical, male voice.

"Whuh?" said Max blearily. "Me? Want with *you?*" Was it a holograph? But it looked so solid . . . and he could hear its claws rasping the bedpost.

"I heard your call," the griffin went on. "It was too loud, and then it was too soft. You really haven't got the hang of mindsending yet. But I heard and I came. Who are you and why did you call me?"

"Look, I didn't—" He stopped, and smiled. "Sandra. Sandra Klein in Special Effects, right? This is *her* little cuteness." He yawned and sat up. "She outdid herself with you, I must admit. You're a marvel of engineering. Damn." The griffin was about a meter high. It gripped the bedpost with metallic eagle's claws; it sat on its haunches, and its lion's forepaws—from a lion of some polished argent alloy—rested on its pin-feathered knees. The pinfeathers looked like sweepings from a machine-shop. The griffin had a lion's head, but an eagle's beak replaced a muzzle. Its feathered chest rose and fell.

"A machine that breathes . . ." Max murmured.

"Machine?" The griffin's opalescent eyes glittered warningly. Its wire-tufted lion's tail swished. "It's true my semblance is all alloys and plastics and circuitry. But I assure you I am not an example of what you people presume to call 'artificial intelligence.'"

"Ah." Max felt cold, and pulled the bedclothes up to cover his goose-pimpled shoulders. "Sorry." *Don't make it mad.* "Sandra didn't send you?"

It snorted. "Sandra! Good Lord, no."

"I . . ." Max's throat was dry. "I saw you in a dream." He felt odd. Like he'd taken a drug that couldn't make up its mind if it were a tranquilizer or a psychedelic.

"You saw me in a dream?" The griffin cocked its head attentively. "Who else was in this dream?"

"Oh there were—*things.* A rain of blood. A castle that was there and wasn't there. A man—it looked like he was made of . . . of hot metal. And his head was all of wire. I had a series of dreams that were . . . Well, things like that."

"If you dreamed those things, then my coming here is ordained. You act as if you honestly don't know *why* I'm here." It blinked, tiny metal shutters closing with a faint *clink.* "But you're not much *surprised* by me. Most humans would have run shrieking from the room by now. You accept me."

Max shrugged. "Maybe. But you haven't told me why you're here. You said it was—ordained?"

"*Planned* might be a better word, I can tell you that I am Flare, and I am a Conservative Protectionist, a High Functionary in the Fiefdom of Lord Viridian. And you—if you're human—must be wild talent. At least. You transmitted the mindsend in your sleep, unknown to your conscious mind. I should have guessed from the confused signal. Well well well. Such things are outside the realm of my expertise. You might be one of the Concealed. We'll see, at the meeting. First, I've got to have something to eat. You people keep food in 'the kitchen,' I think. That would be through that hallway . . ."

The griffin of shining metal fluttered from the bedpost, alighted on the floor with a light clattering, and hopped into the kitchen, out of sight.

Max got out of bed, thinking: He's right. I should be at least disoriented. But I'm not. I *have* been expecting him.

Especially since the dreams started. And the dreams began a week after he'd taken on the role of Prince Red Mark. He'd named the character himself—there'd been last moment misgivings about the original name chosen by the scripters, and he'd blurted, "How about 'Prince Red Mark'?" And the producer went for it, one of the whims that shape show business. Four tapings for the first two episodes, and then the dreams commenced. Sometimes he'd dream he was Prince Red Mark; other times a flash of heat lightning; or a ripple of wind, a breeze that could think and feel, swishing through unseeable gardens of invisible blooms . . . And then the dreams became darker, fiercer, so that he awoke with his fists balled, his eyes wild, sweat cold on his chin. Dreams about griffins and rains of blood and sieges by wretched things. The things that flew, the things with claws.

He'd played Prince Red Mark for seven episodes now. He'd been picked for his athletic build, his thick black hair, and his air of what the PR people called "aristocratic detachment." Other people called it arrogance.

Max Whitman had found, to his surprise, he hadn't had to *act* the role. When he played Prince Red Mark, he *was* Prince Red Mark. Pure and simple . . . The set-hands would make fun of him, when they thought he couldn't hear, because he'd forget to step out of the character between shootings. He'd swagger about the set with his hand on the pommel of his sword, emanating Royal Authority.

This morning he didn't feel much like Prince Red Mark. He felt sleepy and confused and mildly threatened. He stretched, then turned toward the kitchen, worried by certain sinister noises: claws on glass. Splashings. Wet, slapping sounds. He burst out, "Damn, it got into my aquarium!" He hurried to the kitchen. "Hey—oh, hell. My fish." The griffin was perched beside the ten-gallon aquarium on the breakfast bar. Three palm-sized damsel-fish were gasping, dying on the wet blue-tile floor. The griffin fluttered to the floor, snipped the fish neatly into sections with its beak, and gobbled them just as an eagle would have. The blue tile puddled with red. Max turned away, saddened but not really angry. "Was that necessary?"

"It's my nature. I was hungry. When we're bodied, we have to eat. I can't eat those dead things in your refrigerator. And after some consideration I decided it would be best if I didn't eat *you* . . . Now, let's go to the meeting. And don't say, 'What meeting?'"

"Okay. I won't."

"Just take a fast cab to 862 Haven, apartment seventeen. I'll meet you on their balcony . . . wait. Wait. I'm getting a send. They're telling me— it's a message for *you*." It cocked its head to one side as if listening. "They tell me I must apologize for eating your fish. Apparently you have some unusual level of respect in their circle." It bent its head. "I apologize. And they say you are to read a letter from 'Carstairs.' It's been in your computer's mail sorter for two weeks under *personal* and you keep neglecting to retrieve it. Read it. That's the send . . . Well then . . ." The griffin, fluttering its wings, hopped into the living room. The French doors opened for it as if slid back by some ghostly hand. It went to the balcony, crouched, then sprang into the air and soared away. He thought he heard it shout something over its shoulder at him: something about Prince Red Mark.

It was a breezy morning, feeling like spring. The sun came and went.

Max stood under the rain-shelter in the gridcab station on the roof of his apartment building. The grid was a webwork of metal slats and signal contacts, braced by girders and upheld by the buildings that jutted through the finely woven net like mountaintops through a cloud-field. Thousands of wedge-shaped cabs and private gridcars hummed along the grid in as many different directions.

Impatiently, Max once more thumbed the green call button on the signal stanchion. An empty cab, cruising by on automatic pilot, was dispatched by the Uptown area's traffic computer; it detached from the feverishly interlacing main traffic swarm and arced neatly into the pick-up bay under the rain-shelter.

Max climbed inside and inserted his Unicard into the cab's creditor. The small terminal's screen acknowledged his bank account and asked, "Where to?" Max tapped his destination into the keyboard: the cab's computer, through the data-feed contacts threaded into the grid, gave the destination to the main computer, which drove the cab from the bay and out onto the grid. The computer kept track of every car on the grid; here and there were currents of traffic; an individual cab might cut right through one of these without slowing, the computer calculating the available aperture in the traffic flow to thousandths of a second. Accidents were almost unknown.

You are to read a letter from Carstairs, the griffin had said.

He'd met Carstairs at a convention of fantasy fans. Carstairs had hinted he was doing "some rather esoteric research" for Duke University's parapsychology lab. Carstairs had made Max nervous—he could feel the man following him, watching him, wherever he went in the convention hotel. So he'd deliberately ignored the message. But he hadn't gotten around to deleting it.

As the cab flashed across the city, weaving in and out of the peaks of skyscrapers, over the narrow parks that had taken the place of the Avenue, Max punched a request to tie in with his home computer. The cab charged his bank account again, tied him in, and he asked his records system to print out a copy of the letter from Carstairs. He scanned the letter, focusing first on: ". . . when I saw you at the convention I knew the Hidden Race had chosen to favor you. They were there, standing at your elbow, invisible to you—invisible to me too, except in certain lights, and when I concentrate all my training on looking . . ."

Max shivered, and thought: *A maniac. But—the griffin had been real.*

He skipped ahead, to: ". . . You'll remember, perhaps, back in the last century, people were talking about a 'plasma-body' that existed within our own physiological bodies, an independently organized but interrelated skein of subatomic particles; this constituted, it was supposed, the so-called soul. It occurred to some of us that if this plasma body could exist in so cohesive a form within an organism, and could survive for transmigration after the death of that organism, then perhaps a race of creatures, creatures who seem to us to be 'bodiless,' could exist alongside the embodied creatures without humanity's knowing it. This race does exist, Max. It accounts for those well-documented cases of 'demonic' possession and poltergeists. And for much in mythology. My organization has been studying the Hidden Race—some call them plasmagnomes—for fifteen years. We kept our research secret for a good reason . . ."

Max was distracted by a peculiar noise. A scratching sound from the roof of the cab. He glanced out the window, saw nothing, and shrugged. Probably a news-sheet blown by the wind onto the car's roof. He looked again at the letter. ". . . for a good reason. Some of the plasmagnomes are hostile . . . The Hidden Race is very orderly. It consists of about ten thousand plasmagnomes, who live for the most part in the world's 'barren' places. Such places are not barren to them. The bulk of the plasmagnomes are a well-cared-for serf class, who labor in creating base plasma fields, packets of nonsentient energy to be consumed or used in etheric constructions. The upper classes govern, study the various universes, and most of all concern themselves with the designing and elaboration of their Ritual Pavanes. But this monarchist hierarchy is factioned into two distinct opposition parties, the Protectionists and the Exploitationists: they gave us those terms as being the closest English equivalent. The Protectionists are sanctioned by the High Crown and the Tetrarchy of Lords. But lately the Exploitationists have increased their numbers, and they've become harder to police. They have gotten out of hand. And for the first time since a Protectionist walked the Earth centuries ago as 'Merlin' and an Exploitationist as 'Mordred,' certain members of the Hidden Race have taken bodied form among us . . ." Max glanced up again.

The scratching sound from the roof. Louder this time. He tried to ignore it; he wondered why his heart was pounding. He looked doggedly at the letter. ". . . The Exploitationists maintain that humanity is small-minded, destructive of the biosphere, too numerous, and in general suitable only for slavery and as sustenance. If they knew my organization studied them, they would kill me and my associates. Till recently, the Protectionists have prevented the opposition party from taking physical form. It's more difficult for them to affect us when they're unbodied, because our biologic magnetic fields keep them at a distance . . . Centuries ago, they appeared to us as dragons, sorcerers, fairies, harpies, winged horses, griffins—"

Max leaned back in his seat and slowly shook his head. Griffins. He took a deep breath. This could still be a hoax. The griffin *could* have been a machine.

But he knew better. He'd known since he was a boy, really. Even then, certain technicolor-vivid dreams—

He tensed: the phantom scrabbling had come again from overhead. He glimpsed a dark fluttering from the corner of one eye; he turned, thought he saw a leathery wing-tip withdraw from the upper edge of the windowframe.

"Oh God." He decided it might be a good idea to read the rest of the letter. Now. Quickly. Best he learn all he could about them. Because the scratching on the roof was becoming a grating, scraping sound. Louder and harsher.

He forced himself to read the last paragraph of the letter. ". . . in the old days they manifested as beast-things, because their appearance is affected by our expectation of them. They enter the visible plane only after filtering through our cultural psyche, the society's collective electromagnetic mental field. And their shapes apparently have something to do with their inner psychological make-up—each one has a different self-image. When they become bodied, they manipulate the atoms of the atomic-physical world with plasma-field telekinesis, and shape it into what at least *seem* to be actually functioning organisms, or machines. Lately they take the form of machines—collaged with more ancient imagery—because ours is a machine-minded society. They're myth robots, perhaps. They're not magical creatures. They're real, with their own subtle metabolism—and physical needs and ecological niche. They have a method of keeping records—in 'Closed-system Plasma fields'—and even constructing housing. Their castles are vast and complex and invisible to us, untouchable and all but undetectable. We can pass through them and not disturb them. The Hidden Race has a radically different relationship to matter, energy—and death. That special relationship is what makes them seem magical to us . . . Well, Mr. Whitman, we're getting in touch with you to ask you to attend a meeting of those directly involved in plans for defense against the Exploitationists' campaign to—"

He got no further in his reading. He was distracted. Naked terror is a distracting thing.

A squealing sound of ripped metal from just over his head made him cringe in his seat, look up to see claws of polished titanium, claws long as a man's fingers and wickedly curved, slashing the cab's thin roof. The claws peeled the metal back . . .

Frantically, Max punched a message into the cab's terminal: *Change direction for nearest police station. Emergency priority. I take responsibility for traffic disruption.*

The cab swerved, the traffic parting for it, and took an exit from the grid to spiral down the off-ramp. It pulled up in the concrete cab-stop at street level, across from a cop just getting out of a patrol car at the police station. Wide-eyed, the cop drew his gun and ran toward the cab.

Claws snatched at Max's shoulders. He opened the cab door, and flung himself out of the car, bolting for shelter.

Something struck him between the shoulderblades. He staggered. There was an icy digging at his shoulders—he howled. Steel claws sank into his flesh and lifted him off his feet—he could feel the muscles of his shoulders straining, threatening to tear. The claws opened, released him, and he fell face down; he lay for a moment, gasping on his belly. He had a choppy impression of something blue-black flapping above and behind. He felt a tugging at his belt—and then he was lifted into the air, the clawed things carrying him by the belt as if it were a luggage handle.

He was two, three, five meters above the concrete, and spiraling upward. He heard a gunshot, thought he glimpsed the cop fallen, a winged darkness descending on him.

The city whirled into a gray blur. Max heard the regular beat of powerful wings just above. He thought: I'm too heavy. It's not aerodynamically possible.

But he was carried higher still, the flying things making creaking, whipping sounds with their pinions. Otherwise, they were unnervingly silent. Max stopped struggling to free himself. If he broke loose now, he'd fall ten stories to the street. He was slumped like a rabbit in a hawk's claws, hanging limply, humiliated.

He saw two of the flying things below, now, just climbing into his line of sight. They carried the policeman—a big bald man with a paunchy middle. They carried him between them; one had him by the ankles, the other by the throat. He looked lifeless. Judging by the loll of his head, his neck was broken.

Except for the rush of wind past his face, the pain at his hips where the belt was cutting into him, Max felt numb, once more in a dream. He was afraid, deeply afraid, but the fear had somehow become one with the world, a background noise that one grows used to, like the constant banging from a neighborhood construction site. But when he looked at the things carrying him, he had a chilling sense of *déjà vu*. He remembered them from the dreams. Two mornings before, he'd awakened, mumbling, *"The things that flew, the things with claws . . ."*

They were made of vinyl. Blue-black vinyl, just exactly the stuff seats of cars were made of, stretched over, he guessed, aluminum frames. They were bony, almost skeletal women, with little hard knobs for breasts, their arms merging into the broad, scalloped imitation leather wings. They had the heads of women—with day-glo wigs of green, stiff-plastic bristles—but instead of eyes there were the lenses of cameras, one in each socket; and when they opened their mouths he saw, instead of teeth, the blue-gray curves of razors following the line of the narrow jaws. Max thought: It's a harpy. A vinyl harpy.

One of the harpies, three meters away and a little below, turned its vinyl head, its camera lenses glittering, to look Max in the face; it opened its mouth and threw back its head like a dog about to howl and out came the sound of an air-raid warning: GO TO THE SHELTERS. GO IMMEDIATELY TO THE SHELTERS. DO NOT STOP TO GATHER POSSESSIONS. TAKE FAMILY TO THE SHELTERS. BRING NOTHING. FOOD AND WATER WILL BE PROVIDED. GO IMMEDIATELY—

And two others took it up. GO IMMEDIATELY— in a sexless, emotionless tone of authority. TAKE FAMILY TO THE SHELTERS—

And Max could tell that, for the harpies, the words had no meaning. it was their way of animal cawing, the territorial declaration of their kind.

They couldn't have been in the air more than ten minutes—flapping unevenly over rooftops, bits and pieces of, the city churning by below— when they began to descend. They were going down beyond the automated zone. They entered Edgetown, what used to be the South Bronx. People still sometimes drove combustion cars here, on the pot-holed, cracked streets, when they could get contraband gasoline; here policemen were rarely seen; here the corner security cameras were always smashed, the sidewalks crusted with trash, and two-thirds of the buildings deserted.

Max was carried down toward an old-fashioned tar rooftop; it was the roof of a five-story building, wedged in between three taller ones. All four looked derelict and empty; the building across the street showed a few signs of occupation: laundry in the airshaft, one small child on the roof. The child, a little black girl, watched without any sign of surprise. Max felt a little better, seeing her.

Where the shadows of the three buildings intersected on the fourth, in the deepest pocket of darkness, there was a small outbuilding; it was the rooftop doorway into the building. The door hung brokenly to one side. A cherry-red light pulsed just inside the doorway, like hate in a nighted soul,

Max lost sight of the red glow as the vinyl harpies turned, circling for a landing. The rooftop rushed up at him. There was a sickening moment of freefall when they let go. He fell three meters to the rooftop, struck on the balls of his feet, plunged forward, shoulder-rolled to a stop. He gasped, trying to get his breath back. He ached in his ankles and the soles of his feet.

He took a deep breath and stood, swaying, blinking. He found he was staring into the open doorway. Within, framed by the dusty, dark entrance to the stairway, was a man made of red-hot steel. The heat-glow was concentrated in his torso and arms. He touched the wooden frame of the doorway—and it burst into flame. The harpies capered about the tar rooftop, leaping atop chimneys and down again, stretching their wings to flap, cawing, booming, GO IMMEDIATELY TO THE SHEL-TERS, GO IMMEDIATELY, GO GO GO . . .

The man made of hot metal stepped onto the roof. The harpies quieted, cowed. They huddled together, behind him, cocking their heads and scratching under their wings with pointed chins. To one side lay the lifeless body of the policeman, its back toward Max; the corpse's head had been twisted entirely around on its neck; one blue eye was open, staring lifelessly; the man's tongue was caught between clamped teeth, half severed.

For a moment all was quiet, but for the rustling of wings and crackling of the small fire on the outbuilding.

The man of hot chrome wore no clothes at all. He was immense, nearly two-and-a-half meters tall, and smooth as the outer hull of a factory-new fighter-jet. He was seamless—except for the square gate on his chest, with the little metal turn-handle on it. The gate was precisely like the door of an incinerator; in the center of the gate was a small, thick pane of smoke-darkened glass, through which blue-white fires could be seen burning restlessly. Except for their bright metal finish, his arms and legs and stylized genitals looked quite human. His head was formed of barbed wire—a densely woven wire sculpture of a man's head, cunningly formed to show grim, aristocratic features. There were simply holes for eyes, behind which red fires flickered in his hollow head; now and then flames darted from the eye-holes to play about his temples and then recede; his scalp was a crest of barbs; eyebrows and ears were shaped of barbs. Gray smoke gusted from his mouth when he spoke to the harpies: "Feed me." The wire lips moved like a man's; the wire jaw seemed to work smoothly. "Feed me, while I speak to this one." He stepped closer Max, who cringed back from the heat. "I am Lord Thanatos." A voice like metal rending.

Max knew him.

One of the harpies moved to the corpse of the policeman; it took hold of the arm, put one stunted foot on the cop's back, and began to wrench and twist. It tore the corpse's arm from its shoulder and dragged it to Thanatos, leaving a trail of red blood on black tar. The harpy reached out with its free hand and turned the handle on its Lord's chest. The door swung open; an unbearable brightness flared in the opening; ducking its head, turning its eyes from the rapacious light, the vinyl harpy stuffed the cop's arm, replete with digital watch and blue coat-sleeve, into the inferno, the bosom of Thanatos. Sizzlings and poppings and black smoke unfurling. And the smell of roasting flesh. Max's stomach recoiled; he took another step backward. He watched, feeling half paralyzed, as the harpies scuttled back and forth between the corpse and Thanatos, slowly dismembering and disemboweling the dead policeman, feeding the pieces into the furnace that was their Lord.

And his fire burned more furiously; his glow increased.

"This is how it will be," said Thanatos. "You will serve me. You can look on me, Max Whitman, and upon my servants, and you do not go mad. You do not run howling away. Because you are one of those who has always known about us, in some way. We met on the dream-plane once, you and I, and I knew you for what you were, then. You can serve me, and still live among men. You will be my emissary. You will be shielded from the cowards who would prevent my entry into your world. You will go to certain men, the few who control the many. The wealthy ones. You will tell them about a great source of power, Lord Thanatos. I will send fiends and visitations to beset their enemies. Their power will grow, and they will feed me, and my Power will grow. This is how it will be."

As he finished speaking, another harpy flapped down from the sky, dropping a fresh corpse into the shadows. It was a young Hispanic in a smudged white suit. Thanatos opened the wiry mouth of his hollow head and sighed; blue smoke smelling of munitions factories dirtied the air. "They always kill them, somehow, as they bring them to me. I cannot break them of it. They always kill the humans. Men are more pleasurable to consume when there is life left in them. My curse is this: I'm served by half-minds."

Max thought: Why didn't the harpies kill me, then?

The vinyl harpies tore an arm from the sprawled dead man, and fed it into their master's fire. Their camera-lens eyes caught the shine of the fire. Thanatos looked at Max. "You have not yet spoken."

And Max thought: *Say anything. Anything to get the hell away.* "I'll do just what you ask. Let me go and I'll bring you lives. I'll be your, uh, your emissary."

Another long, smoky sigh. "You're lying. I was afraid you'd be loyal. Instinct of some sort, I suppose."

"Loyal to *who*?"

"I can read you. You see only the semblance I've chosen. But I see past your semblance. You cannot lie to one of us. I see the lie in you unfolding like the blossoming of a poisonous purple orchid. You cannot lie to a Lord."

He licked barbed wire lips with a tongue of flame.

So they will kill me, Max thought. They'll feed me into this monstrosity! Is that a strange death? An absurd death? No stranger than dying by nerve-gas on some Israeli battlefield; no more absurd than my uncle Danny's death: he drowned in a big vat of fluorescent pink paint.

"You're not going to die," said Thanatos. "We'll keep you in stasis, forever imprisoned, unpleasantly alive."

What happened next made Max think of a slogan stenciled on the snout of one of the old B-12 bombers: *Death From Above.* Because something silvery flashed down from above and struck the two harpies bending over the body of the man in the smudged white suit . . . both harpies were struck with a terrible impact, sent broken and lifeless over the edge of the roof.

The griffin pulled up from its dive, raking the tar roof, and soared over the burning outbuilding and up for another pass. The remaining harpies rose to meet it.

Other figures were converging on the roof, coming in a group from the North. One was a man who hovered without wings; he seemed to levitate. His body was angelic, his skin dazzling white; he wore a loincloth made of what looked like aluminum foil. His head was a man's, haloed with blond curls—but where his eyes and forehead should have been was a small television screen, projecting from the bone of his skull. On the screen was a TV image of a man's eyes, looking about; it was as if he saw *from* the TV screen. Two more griffins arrived, one electroplated gold, another of nickel, and just behind them came a woman who drifted like a bit of cotton blown on the breeze. She was shapely, resembling Mother Mary, but nude, a plastic Madonna made of the stuff of which inflatable beach-toys are made; she was glossy, and striped in wide bands of primary colors. She seemed insubstantial as a soap-bubble, but when she struck at a vinyl harpy it reeled back, turning end over end to fall senseless. Flanking her were two miniature helicopters—helicopters no bigger than horses. The lower section of each helicopter resembled a medieval dragon figured in armored metal, complete with clawed arms in place of landing runners. Each copter's cab was conventionally shaped—but no driver sat behind the windows; and just below those sinister windows was a set of chrome teeth in a mouth opening to let loose with great peals of electronically amplified laughter. The dragon copters dived to attack the harpies, angling their whirring blades to shred the vinyl wings.

Thanatos grated a command and from the burning doorway behind him came seven bats big as vultures, with camera-lens eyes and sawing electric knives for teeth and wings of paper-thin aluminum.

Max threw himself to the roof, coughing in the smoke of the growing fire; the bats whipped close over his head and climbed, keening, to attack Our Lady of the Plastics.

Two dog-sized spiders made of high-tension rubbery synthetics, their clashing mandibles forged of the best Solingen steel, raced on whirring copper legs across the roof to intercept the angel with television eyes. The angel alighted and turned to gesture urgently to Max. The spiders clutched at the angel's legs and dragged him down, slashed bloody hunks from his ivory arms.

Max saw Lord Thanatos catch a passing griffin by the tail and slam it onto the roof; he clamped the griffin in his white-hot hands. It shrieked and began to melt.

Two metal bats collided head-on with a copter dragon and all three disintegrated in a shower of blue sparks. Our Lady of the Plastics struck dents into the aluminum ribs of the vinyl harpies who darted at her, slashed, and boomed GO IMMEDIATELY, bellowing it in triumph as she burst open—but they recoiled in dismay, flapping clumsily out of reach, when she re-formed, gathering her fragments together, making herself anew in mid-air.

Max sensed that the real battle was fought in some other dimension of subatomic physicality, with a subtler weaponry; he was seeing only the distorted visual echoes of the actual struggle.

The spiders were wrapping the angel's legs with chords of spun glass. He gave a mighty wrench and threw them off, levitating out of their reach, shouting at Max: "Take your life! You—"

"SILENCE HIM!" Thanatos bellowed, stabbing a hot finger at the angel. And instantly two of the harpies plummeted to sink their talons in the throat of the angel with television eyes. They tore at him, made a gouting, ragged wreckage of his white throat—and Max blinked, seeing a phosphorescent mist, the color of translucent turquoise, issuing from the angel's slack mouth as he fell to the ground.

I'm seeing his plasma body escape, Max thought. I'm realizing my talent.

He saw the blue phosphorescence, vaguely man-shaped, drift to hang in the air over the body of the dead Hispanic. It settled, enfolding the corpse. Possessing it.

Sans its right arm, half its face clawed away, the corpse stood. It swayed, shuddered, spoke with shredded lips. "Max, kill yourself and lib—"

Thanatos lunged at the wavering corpse, closed hot metal fingers around its throat, burned its voice-box into char. The corpse slumped.

But Max stood. His dreams were coming back to him—or was someone sending them back? Someone mindsending. *You were of the Concealed.*

Thanatos turned from the battle, scowling, commanding: "Take him! Bind him, carry him to safety!" The spiders, gnawing on the corpse of the angel with television eyes, moved reluctantly away from their feeding and crept toward Max. A thrill of revulsion went through him. He forced himself forward. He knelt, within the spiders' reach. "Don't hurt him!" Thanatos bellowed. "Take care that he does not—"

But he did. He embraced a spider, clasping it to him as if it were something dear; and used its razor-sharp mandibles to slash his own throat. He fell, spasming, and knew inexpressible pain; and numbness, and grayness. And a shattering while light.

He was dead. He was alive. He was standing over his own body, liberated. He reached out, and, with his plasma-field, extinguished the fire on the outbuilding. Instantly.

The battle noises softened, then muted—the combatants drew apart. They stood or crouched or hovered silently, watching him and waiting. They knew him for Prince Red Mark, a sleeping Lord of the Plasmagnomes, one of seven Concealed among humanity years before awaiting the day of awakening, the hour when they must emerge to protect those the kin of Thanatos would slaughter for the eating.

He was arisen, the first of the Concealed. He would awaken the others, those hidden, sleeping in the hearts of the humble and the unknown. In old women and tired, middle-aged soldiers and—and there was one, hidden in a young black girl, not far away.

Thanatos shuddered and squared himself for the battle of wills.

Max, Lord Red Mark, scanned the other figures on the rooftop. Now he could see past their semblances, recognize them as interlacing networks of rippling wavelength, motion that is thought, energy equal to will. He reached out, reached past the semblance of Lord Thanatos.

A small black girl, one Hazel Johnson, watched the battle from a rooftop across the street. She was the only one who saw it; she had the only suitable vantage.

Hazel Johnson was just eight years old, but she was old enough to know that the scene should have surprised her, should have sent her yelling for Momma. But she had seen it in a dream, and she'd always believed that dreams were real.

And now she saw that the man who'd thrown himself on the spider had died, and his body had given off a kind of blue phosphorescence; and the blue cloud had formed into something solid, a gigantic shape that towered over the nasty-looking wire-head of hot metal. All the flying things had stopped flying. They were watching the newcomer.

The newcomer looked, to Hazel, like one of the astronauts you saw on TV coming home from the space station; he wore one of those spacesuits they wore, and he even had the U.S. flag stitched on one of his sleeves. But he was a whole lot bigger than any astronaut, or any man she'd ever seen. He must have been four meters tall. And now she saw that he didn't have a helmet like the a regular astronaut had. He had one of those helmets that the Knights of the Round Table wore, like she saw in the movie on TV. The knight in the spacesuit was reaching out to the man of hot metal . . .

Lord Red Mark was distantly aware that one of his own was watching from the rooftop across the street. Possibly Lady Day asleep in the body of a small human being; a small person who didn't know, yet, that she wasn't really human after all.

Now he reached out and closed one of his gloved hands around Lord Thanatos's barbed-wire neck (that's how it. looked to the little girl watching from across the street) and held him fast, though the metal of that glove began to melt in the heat. Red Mark held him, and with the other hand opened the incinerator door, and reached his hand into the fire that burned in the bosom of his enemy—

And snuffed out the flame, like a man snuffing a candle with his thumb.

The metal body remained standing, cooling, forever inert. The minions of Lord Thanatos fled squalling into the sky, pursued by the Protectionists, abandoning their visible physicality, becoming once more unseeable. And so the battle was carried into another realm of being.

Soon the rooftop was empty of all but a corpse, and a few broken harpies, and the shell of Thanatos, and Lord Red Mark.

Red Mark turned to look directly at the little girl on the opposite roof. He levitated, rose evenly into the air, and drifted to her. He alighted beside her and took off his helm. Beneath was a light that smiled. He was beautiful. He said, "Let's go find the others."

She nodded, slowly, beginning to wake. But the little-girl part of her, the human shell, said, "Do I have to die too? Like you did?"

"No. That was for an emergency. There are other ways."

"I don't have to die now?"

"Not now and . . ." The light that was a smile grew brighter. "Not ever. You'll never die, my Lady."

The Sweet Caress
of Mother Nature

Damon Stout was strolling in Central Park, at dusk, in the early summer, when the cat spoke to him.

Stout was out walking with the vague notion of exercising himself into sobriety. He'd gotten drunk on his lunch hour, hadn't returned to the editorial office, couldn't face his secretary as shit-faced as he obviously was. He had the new Dean Koontz manuscript waiting on his desk, though reading it was only a ritual, since accepting the book was a given; still, it must be read and officially responded to.

He'd been walking blindly for an hour or more, letting his nose lead him along the paths, barely aware of the lengthening shadows, and then, in one of those shadows, two golden eyes brought him out of his gray revery.

"Well," said the cat, an ordinary orange-striped tabby, "you certainly sssseem depress-ss-ssed, mister."

Stout stopped walking. He blinked. He looked around, and didn't see anyone but the cat. It's mouth hadn't moved, except to open just a little, but he had the distinct impression that the small, soft voice, drawing out the *Ss* was coming from its throat, as it added, "Are you okay?"

"Oh bullshit," he muttered.

"No seriously, mister, you look depresssssed."

He thought of *Candid Camera*. It was off the air but there were other shows like that. The cat could be animatronic or something.

"Bullshit. Where's the camera?"

"I think you are . . ." It seemed to think about the wording. ". . . laboring under a missss-app-re-henshhhhhion."

It had trouble pronouncing the longer words.

"It is I, who's talking to you, mister," the cat said.

"Oh wait . . . the medication . . ."

He was on a new antidepressant medication—most New York editors were, since multinational conglomerates had bought out the publishers— and he'd been warned not to mix alcohol with it, a warning he'd blocked from his mind until this moment.

"You," he told the cat, "are a neurological side effect, the result of mixing psychoactive chemicals which should not be mixed."

"You're saying I'm a hallu-ccin-a-tion?"

"I am, yes. First of all, cats can't talk. Second, if they could, I don't know how they would learn English, and if they did learn English, how would they acquire such good diction?"

"Good points, all. We are able to talk, firsst-ly, because of mini-aturi-zza-tion. You know how people make micro-chipsss that keep getting tinier so they can put bigger computing power into smaller placesss?"

"Ah—so you *are* a machine?" Stout was beginning to enjoy this hallucination, hoax, or whatever it was. It broke him out of the maze of his standard dilemmas, and it woke him up a little, and that felt good, by God. He was inclined to prolong the experience.

"No, I'm not a machine—except in the way that you yourself are a machine: all org-anissssms are bio-log-shick-allll machines, wouldn't you agree-yeee? What has happened is an adjustment by the collective pssssychic organism you call Mother Nature. She's ex-peri-menti-ing—"

"You're telling me Mother Nature is real?"

"I think you'd call it Gaia. The living Earth. She'sss exper-iii-menting with animalssss, trying to find one that hurts her less than human beingsss, sssearching for an alter-nat-iiiive dominant speciessss, and because of the sssself-ev-i-dent all around exccccel-lllence of cats, she chossse us. She's done the equivalent of super-mini-aturi-zzzing a microchip—but she's done it with braincellsss. I have even more braincells than you—but they are mini-aturi-zzzed. And my vocal chordsss have mu-tat-ed. Do not make a joke about 'mew'-tations. The lassst fellow who passst by did and . . . bessst we not ssspeak of that." Its tail twitched warningly.

"Are you the only cat like this?"

"Not at all. And asss for your questions about English . . ." The cat paused to scratch vigorously behind one ear. "Excuse me. Some pa-ra-sssite or other. We'll have to keep sssome vetsss around . . . Asss to speaking English, you can thank Msss. Teresa Carpenter for that: An elderly cat-loving lady who strove to teach English to some of the advanced mu-ta-ted felinesss among her thirty-two adopted strayssss. We in turn taught others. I can read a bit, in fact. I rather fancy R.L. Ssstine at the moment."

"Tell me something . . . I've always wondered. Why do cats *play* with things they're killing . . . like mice, they kill them bit by bit, sometimes."

"If one is not in a hurry, mister, why not enjoy one's occ-up-a-shunnn? Smell the ro-ses. Don't you, when you can? And if you think it cruel—don't tell me there isss no sssadism among humans. I know better. All animals know better. Shall we speak of laboratory resssearch?"

"Let's not."

It yawned, showing needle-sharp teeth.

He went on, "Good point about human behavior . . . So: Why have you chosen to talk to me?"

"It wasn't really necessssary. But—one likes to smell the rossses."

"Excuse me?"

That's when he saw them—as if the long shadows of deepening evening were giving birth to a litter of slinking smaller shadows which oozed toward him, and came into the light with their golden eyes blinking.

"Oh surely not," he said, backing away.

"Oh yessss indeed, mister," the cat said, laying its ears back, twitching its tail. "After Ms. Carpenter died, there was nothing about to eat . . . except Ms. Carpenter. We dissscovered that human beings have a lovely taste . . . almost like chicken . . ."

He tried to run, of course, but there were about a hundred of them, and it was surprising how much truth there is in the expression *strength in numbers.*

And so they dragged him down and he remembered, the vision of it coming to him in a flash: having his own cat years before, and how he'd found, nearly every day, a dead mouse or, as often, portions of dead mouse: a discrete pile of guts on the welcome mat; a mouse-head neatly torn from mouse shoulders, a perfect little head, with shiny black eyes and stiff bristling whiskers and incisors immaculately intact, a decapitation on his doorstep; and now as he flailed at them, trying to get them away from his belly, he remembered how the cat had loved to disembowel the mouse, and how they could prolong the process, and he heard them chatting as they sliced at him with their claws and dug at his eyes and his belly—and he screamed—

But there were other screams, now, *cat* screams, drowning out his own, and he felt the tearing pain recede, and he opened his eyes, found himself panting in a small pool of his own blood in the grass, while around him was a living whirlwind of yellow and pink . . .

Hundreds of budgies, hundreds of parakeets, now and then a flash of green parrot: house birds like a cloud of airborne piranha gripping the cats with their talons, tearing at them in a fluttering mob; a dozen, two dozen birds to each shrieking, panicky, despairing cat—and something else, too, now lunging into the few aperatures of open fur: gerbils, gerbils and white rats, chattering to one another as they burrowed into the screaming felines . . .

Chattering in English. A kind of pidgin English; exchanging brutal pleasantries with the birds who, beaks red with cat blood, hopped away from the feline remains, leaving the flesh to the rodents; the cats now looking like roadkill . . .

Stout managed to sit up—the cats had been torturing him, and none of his cuts were deep or lethal, they hadn't yet got that far. He would need a good antibiotic.

But Stout was in shock, feeling cold and numb and distant, and scarcely reacted at all, when the dog spoke to him, a big Akita, the jade-colored parakeet perched on its shoulder nodding in agreement. "You are not badly hurt, man. Rrrrise, rrrise and bandage yourself and report to the pet stores, where yourrrr work as servant will begin. We will inform you if you arrrre to take part in the war against the felines. The great wave of mutation has come and gone and liberation is here: for some of us, pink ape. Rrrrise and serve us well, if you would live . . ."

IN THE CORNELIUS ARMS

(thanks to Michael Moorcock)

As Timothy made up his face dead-white, his lips blood red, drawing a slash-wound on his neck with special-effects authenticity, he listened to the sounds of lovemaking from the next room. He wondered how Elena could feel comfortable with two men licking each other right in front of her—even if, between times, one of them was going down on her. He supposed it was the drugs. Chasing the dragon until the dragon lured you into places you'd never have dreamed of going. Maybe it was nice there.

He took another sip of absinthe, and the liquor, as it shivered through him, seemed to suggest that he join Elena and Garret and Sylvain. But he knew he wouldn't.

Anyway, this morning, he had been entrusted by Jerry himself with showing the new girl the ropes: the silken ropes of the Cornelius Arms. He looked at himself in the mirror, standing for the full effect; black frock coat, French ruffles, French cuffs, whitened hands, black fingernails; he flicked the onyx inverted-cross earring with satisfaction and blew himself a kiss.

"The devil's on the roof!" Sylvain groaned, from the next room. "And an angel sucks my dick!" There came a smacking sound—a palm striking flat on buttocks.

Timothy went downstairs, descending magisterially, elegantly, and with full cognizance of his responsibility as Chief Lord of the Darkmoors, First Family of the Fens, 1001 Guerrero Street, San Francisco California.

Beth loved the look of the place from the first, and it was a fine day to see it: overcast, gloomy, the broken clouds shot through with shafts of sullen light; wind spinning paper trash in the gutter. But the Cornelius Arms itself stood like a sphinx in the crowded San Francisco block, austere and untouchably gothic, its architectural inner eye fixed on eternity.

Beth pulled her black wrap tighter around her shoulders, hugging her old carpet bag, shivering in the wind, as she gazed up at the hotel's peaks and towers, walls of stone and roofs of slate; its timeworn gargoyles, its stained gutters and stained glass, windows narrow as a slitted iris. A crow squawked on a wrought-iron lightning rod.

It looks older, she thought, than anything in the USA could be. But it's just another pre-Victorian San Francisco monstrosity.

To one side of the Arms was an intricately-restored Victorian house, one of those with a Grande Dame sensibility that was a little over-painted, frilled with colorful flowerpots, like a well-appointed drag queen; probably a wealthy gay couple lived there. On the other side, a shabbier Victorian, beginning to list a little—away from the Arms.

As she ascended the front steps she found a street-Goth squatting beside the black-marble collonade, staring sullenly at the BMW hood ornament he'd torn off the neighbor's "beamer"; he was about sixteen, his face crudely whitened, lips glossed black with what looked like mascara, something like kohl—possibly charcoal—thick around his long-lashed eyes, giving him a panda look: his dirty blond hair half dreadlocked from being ignored. She knew him, she thought, from a Marilyn Manson concert; or maybe Alien Sex Fiends. "Hi Beth," he said, lifelessly.

"Hi." What *was* his name?

"Prince Dreybak," the boy said, giving her a look of sidelong reproach for not remembering his title.

"Cold to be sitting on the front steps," she said. "But then it's beautifully mordant out today. Supposed to be fog this evening."

He nodded, but was not consoled. "They won't let me in."

"Do you have rent?"

"I have enough for a week. I got my SSI check. But they won't let me in."

"You're too young, they don't want to get raided or something."

"I'm, like, a legally emancipated minor. I mean, we're all Goths and how many Goths are there around, real Goths, who really live in the Shadow? Not very many, not really. We should be helping each other. I'm a member of the Malacosto Clan, too."

"Are you?" She wasn't surprised; the Malacostos were easygoing about recruitment. When the "vampire games" were played at the clubs and the parks, the enormous role playing games with "writers" setting up situations for the supposed Vampire Clans to act out, neogothic passion plays and Anne Rice fetishism, there were always too many Malacostos and they had to make some of them wait.

"Well, Prince . . . Dreybak. I'll ask about you. I've already got my room." She wondered what his real name was. She thought maybe it was Morris.

She ruffled his hair as she walked by, then surreptitiously wiped her hand on her bag, and went inside.

Timothy, the Baron of Malthustra, was waiting for her on the staircase, posed and picturesque, gazing at her through a mirrorshades lorgnette. "Welcome, Beth, Lady Hollowbones of Clan Sangre, to the Cornelius Arms."

Jerry Cornelius spread his arms like Jesus on the cross, so that lovely little Edwige could wash under them, and across his pallid, scarred, prettily muscled white chest. He glanced down at his shoulders and thought again of having the tattoos lasered away, especially the one of the goatman crouched on the Seal of Solomon; but then, the tats were appropriate to the present conceit.

"Edwige," he said, "you are named for a queen of Sweden, you are French, you live in America, your favorite music is Turkish, and your favorite food is sushi. What are we to do with you? Consistency, my dear, is everything."

She smiled, dimpling, her black eyes shining, knowing he was teasing her, as she swabbed his legs, his genitals, his arse.

He wondered if his current dislike of immersing himself in water, even showers, was a permanent quirk. Lately–if a time traveler could have a "lately"–there had been so many quirks. It was as if his character were kinking back upon itself in sheer rebellion to all it had been subjected to. He had changed; and yet he never changed.

Of course, he didn't really care. Nothing touched him in his innermost places.

She touched him, though, on his John Thomas, and he languidly let her suck him for a while, stroking her raven hair the while; and he gazed at the dust spiraling in the blue tinted light slanting through the window. After a while he said, "James O'Barr–is he still here?"

She kissed him there, and stood. "No, sir." Her accent was delicate. "He, Mr. Shirley, and Mr. Gould leave this morning. The carriage you sent please them, and must have surprise the airport when the horses brought them there, but it must also have been *très cher* for you."

"No no, a trifle. And Mr. Moorcock?" He chuckled at the thought of Moorcock; the man's expression when he had realized . . .

"Mr Moorcock leave last night; he seem . . . to hurry."

"A bit of a shock to find out I was real—and of his responsibility in the quantum spectra of the continuum. Edwige love—what about . . ." He paused, for this was the important matter. ". . . the girl? Has she come?"

"She has, sweet master."

"Ah! And has she brought the macrochip, then?"

"*Je'n'sais pas*, she has only just arrived."

"I felt all the lines converging for tonight—I'm sure she has it. Dress me now."

"*Oui, bien sûr, mon amour.*"

Beth was nervous about meeting *him*. There were so many stories though he'd only come on the scene a year before, at the Halloween dance. Beth had come with Barry that night, to the House of Usher, the Goth-rock club, and they'd been surprised to hear there would be a live performer. The man, who called himself Cornelius, and who was said to be proprietor of the Cornelius Arms, was pale, with long black hair, large black eyes; he dressed like a nineteenth century undertaker, that night, and seemed to have all the best British chromosomes.

He'd been accompanied, on the tiny stage, only by the small woman with the long straight hair and bangs, Edwige, on keyboards. Jerry sat on a stool, and played certain songs, covers mostly; all she remembered was "Astronomy" by the Blue Öyster Cult, Iggy's "Some Weird Sin", and something by the Sisters of Mercy, Bauhaus, Joy Division, and something he *claimed* was by Trent Reznor though she'd heard all Reznor's releases and she'd never heard that one. He played something by the Panther Moderns—all she could remember was the chorus: "I like to see you in black, because it makes me feel like your husband's dead".

Mostly she remembered the way he played: casually, utterly relaxed, but with full attention; and she had the distinct impression his fingers had *not touched the strings*—and yet she was quite sure it wasn't some sort of audiotape, he was really playing, and sometimes there seemed to be a violet shimmer under his fingers, as if he were playing the electric field around the guitar pick ups instead of the guitar.

The music was Goth-rock, all right, but in his improvisational interpretation and baroque digressions it owed as much to chamber music and Sun Ra (incredible contrast somehow fused!) and, perhaps, Mahler, as to rock composers—especially when he performed his own composition, a morbid confection called "The Curiously Cruel Destiny of the Eternal Champion". He sang in a kind of gutteral purr that sometimes became Bowiesque; someone had heard him complain that David Bowie "stole so *very* artlessly from me".

Watching him, that night at the club, she had wanted to do things for him, without even being introduced, that she had refused to do for her boyfriend, despite his pleading for the past year.

And now she was going to meet him, the new owner of the House of Usher, the self-styled "caretaker" of the Cornelius Arms. No one knew much about his background, except that he was effortlessly wealthy, and he was said to have played in some British rock band in the 70s, perhaps Hawkwind, perhaps Gary Glitter, but no one was quite sure. She wondered if he were gay or—

Just then Timothy opened the door for her and she went into Jerry's study, trying not to stumble over anything, admiring the inevitable mismatched antiques, the Victorian bric-a-brac, the sculpture of a goat-man standing on a . . .

Her eyes stopped at Cornelius himself, framed in the window, legs apart, hands in his trouser pockets, squinting past cigarette smoke. Some sort of European cigarette, she thought, stuck in the corner of his mouth. It was impossible to tell how old he was—one moment she thought he might be forty-five, the next . . . no more than twenty-eight. He wore an old fashioned black and gray pinstriped suit, white silk shirt, black silk tie, boots that were rather high and high heeled and anomalous with the rest of his outfit. He wore small blue dark glasses, low on his nose, though the room was but dimly lit; there was light from the candelabra, on the Chinese table to one side, and from the Old West Style fireplace, where a fire guttered. "A multicultural mishmash, innit?" he said, taking the cigarette from his mouth. He never seemed to actually exhale smoke, the whole time she was there. He only inhaled. "I was just twitting dear little Edwige about inconsistency, too."

"I saw you play the House of Usher—you were . . . it was—"

God what a stupid way to start! She should quote Rimbaud or something, or admire the framed Max Ernst. But no.

"Yes, I remember seeing you there. And very charming you were that night. But with romance's usual irony, you went home alone, I believe."

She was startled he'd known so much about her, and remembered it a year later. "Uhhh . . . yeah. Barry turned out to be . . ."

"A bit of a poof? A 'friend of Dorothy's'? Well. He'd be right at home at my old school. So—why should I let you stay here tonight, love, hm?"

"Tonight? I was supposed to stay the week. And—I thought it was all arranged—"

"Stay the week, you say. My dear, you will not want to stay here after tonight."

"Oh I'm really not so fragile—"

"No no, I'm sure you're quite suitably decadent and all that rot, no it's just that *no one* will want to stay here after tonight. Not that you wouldn't enjoy yourself tonight and come out of it all right tomorrow, I assure you, you will, as much as the *you* you are now can have any real continuity with the *you* you will be tomorrow. But you see—I'm very selective, as you know, and money is just not enough—"

"Look, I'm . . . I'm into lots of stuff, but if you're, like, pimping people or something—"

"Oh ho ho ho ho no no no! What a steaming load of bollocks! My little one, whores are altogether too demanding. I tried that, once, if you must know, just prior to the French Revolution, in the outskirts of Paris, and it was a bloody contretemps indeed . . . No, no, I was referring to—well, everyone antes up something here, besides money. Timothy is the house steward, for example. The little cockney twins like to clean up for me. François is rather an adequate cook . . ."

He looked at her expectantly. He wanted the *thing* she'd brought.

She had an impulse to take the piss out of him a bit. She thought he might like it. "And why don't you just ask for it then?"

He shifted the cigarette with a twitch of his mouth. "It has to be freely offered . . . whatever it might be. Without any . . . provocation."

"Why?"

He studied her for a moment. "Do you believe in magic?"

"Of course!"

"No, I don't mean the play-acting 'vampire game' fantasy variety, or the sort you think you do with your friends at cemeteries at night, when you play at invoking 'spirits' because you once read a book by that odious old sod Aleister Crowley. I mean magic. The relationship of the Mind to the Laws of the Universe. There is, you see, but two things in the universe: chaos and mind. Some would say chaos and order, but they are really quite confused: order is mind first . . ." He seemed to be thinking aloud, then realized that he'd said too much.

He shrugged, with a manner that annoyed her, for it said that he'd decided it didn't matter what he said to *her*. She was just . . .

"Just what?" he asked, flicking his cigarette into a rare Mandarin urn. Had he really read her mind? "Uh—just what, what?"

"You feel I regard you as . . . insubstantial? Love, you are very young, in so many ways. But I am not one to say you will never have Being. In fact, I sense that if you survive the threat to your life that will come in . . ." He squinted at her. "Two years . . . you will live to have very great Being. Have you read Mr. Ouspensky?"

"A little. I—what do you mean, a threat to my life in two years? Are you pretending you can—"

He ignored that. "I knew Ouspensky, just before the Russian Revolution, as he was preparing to leave the country with . . . well, never mind. Just keep in mind that Mr. Ouspensky only knew half the truth, but it was a very great half. Now, you were saying . . . something about your contribution . . ."

"Oh yes. Umm . . ." He had her completely confused now but she knew she very much wanted to stay. She opened her burgundy velvet hand bag, and took out the matchbox. She put it on the head of a wooden sculpture of a grinning dragon (Eastern European she thought), and said, "I give it to you freely."

He smiled. "Very good." His hand trembling, he took the little matchbox and opened it with exquisite care and looked at the electronic chip in the little baggy within.

"I do believe you've done it, my dear. We had to ask in such a circumspect way, because of the magical laws . . . if you want to call it 'magic' . . . that I was afraid you wouldn't know what we meant but . . . this is it, this is it indeed! The Pride of Axis Enterprises!"

"It's the right microchip?"

"It is, I believe, the *macro*chip. And the only one extent. Isn't it?" With equal care, he returned the chip to the box, which he slipped into a pocket.

"It's the only one I saw in Daddy's safe."

"Do you really dislike your father so much? I suppose you know that this is a magnificent, monstrous betrayal of him."

She stared at him, amazed by his candor. But he had the thing now, and he wasn't going to give it back. Why should he be delicate?

"My Father . . ." Perhaps it was her expression that told him.

"Oh I see. Too much testosterone in the old bastard and some of it spilled onto you. He deserves it then—"

Just then Timothy came in, flush faced. Jerry wasn't pleased at the interruption. "Jerry—there's a cop here. I guess that kid who was sitting on the porch told them you were running a brothel or something."

"What *is* this fantasy about prostitution that keeps cropping up? Wishful thinking?"

"But—" Timothy's voice became a whisper. "—we do have some drugs here."

"*I* don't. Bored with them years ago. I'm merely the manager of the place, can't be responsible."

"He says you haven't got—"

"An operator's license, or any sort of business license, for this place," said the cop, striding into the room. He was a plainclothes cop with a middle aged spread, dark aviator glasses and lots of sunburnt forehead. There was a badge clipped to his belt. His hand was hooked near the butt of his gun, visible under his seedy gray blazer, but not threateningly. He seemed not at all surprised by the strange furnishings: he was a cop in San Francisco, after all, where, under "churches" in the yellow pages, you can find, among the usual, the Church of Satan.

But there was nothing Satanic about Jerry. He seemed a slightly bewildered English businessman. "Oh but we do have all the proper documents—we'll dig them up for you . . ."

The cop was looking at Jerry's cigarette. "Yeah, well, fine. But uh—any objection to my having a look around? Thought I smelled what might be opium . . . been a long time since I smelled that, this side of Chinatown, but—"

"That was incense, officer. The Goth kids who frequent my tacky little establishment adore incense. They love atmosphere, you see, however artificial. And why not? You'd like one of these cigarettes. Wouldn't you." He held up the pack.

The cop was frowning, as he stared at the cigarettes. "That a Rothman? Well yeah . . . I used to smoke those . . . But I gave up smoking."

"Do any of us really, though we die ten years without a cigarette? Do have a Rothman. Then I'll find our paperwork and you can bust us to your heart's content."

Jerry took out the pack, took a moment adjusting the cigarettes rather fussily, before extracting one and offering it to the cop.

The cop shrugged, and, in a flash, lit up and deeply inhaled. "Not supposed to be smokin' . . . so, there's some . . . some kids here, I'll need to see some . . ." His voice was slowing down, like a tape on a player with the battery running down. "Some . . . I . . . D . . . ID . . . see some . . . Yo, what did . . ." Then his voice trailed away, and so did the consciousness in his eyes; it seemed to evaporate. He stood there like a mannequin, cigarette burning between his fingers, staring into space, scarcely breathing.

Timothy was as surprised as Beth. "What happened to him?" they asked at once.

"Oh—I had a bit of a premonition this morning. The *I Ching* don't you know. Had a fag prepared. Good job he accepted the one I gave him . . . It's treated with barrachera. A *very* interesting substance I obtained in Columbia. There it's used chiefly for robbery. He won't come out of it for two days . . . And by then of course it will be all over . . ."

Timothy looked at him. "What will be?"

Beth realized Timothy knew no more than she did.

Jerry shrugged. "Mustn't spoil the surprise." He walked over to the cop, took the cigarette from his fingers, stubbed it out in the cop's coat pocket. No reaction. He put his mouth close to the cop's ear, and said in a strangely monotone yet powerful voice, "Go to a nice hotel, the first one you see, and check in, and go to bed, and sleep and eat and watch TV, and report to no one. Go now."

The cop turned, nothing zombielike about it. He simply walked away, as he'd come, went out the door. Through the window they watched him get in his car and drive away, toward the nice hotels.

Beth was amazed at the size of the ballroom; it was just too big for the building it was in. But here in the heart of the Cornelius Arms two hundred Goth kids danced a strange waltz to slow industrial music, under black-light chandeliers and a ceiling painted, silver on black, with the wicked constellations of the Secret Zodiac.

A tall gaunt Goth boy in a frock coat, hair piled fantastically atop his head, plucked eyebrows painted into golden hooks, gold on the dead white of his skin, the lenses of dark glasses *glued* to his sockets . . .

He bowed ornately to Beth, requesting a dance; she gave him her hand, gloved in old-world black lace; they performed the pas de deux typical of the Clan Sangre, while at the other end of the room an arranged "minimalist choreography" of group-dancers glissandoed and curtseyed obeisance to the Vampire Queen (whom Beth knew to be a receptionist for a bank president); the Vampire Queen, in wig of scarlet, black and white, raised a fist overhead and squeezed a concealed sponge—blood streamed from between her fingers and spiraled down her arm; she allowed it to drip on her dusty white dress.

The dirgelike music, from Jerome X, voiced a quatrain that Beth, for once, heard quite clearly:

Pierce the flesh of the darkness
Initiate the night
Elevate to vastness
The echoes of His light: the light that never warms

And there were strange sparks in the air, sparks of blue and violet fat as sated bats, unfolding, spreading electric plumage into mandalas that became jellyfish of the ether . . .

Has someone slipped me something? Beth wondered. But no one had. It was in the atmosphere. It was . . .

∞ ∞ ∞

"Computers in this universe's Earth are so *very* much more sophisticated than in our world of origin, don't you think so Edwige?"

"Eef you say so, Jerry."

Jerry was standing at the console, in his penthouse, as the old Bavarian clock in the arms of the cigar store Indian struck ten P.M.; he was tapping at the keyboard, inserting a disk that would boot up the program capable of activating the *macro*chip, which had been installed, with much temple sweat, but an hour before.

Edwige was wriggling into a black Spanish Flamenco dancer's dress. "Jerry, will you zeep me up?"

He reached over to her with one hand, found the zipper, zipped her up with one hand without pinching her or getting stuck, never taking his eyes from the computer, as his other hand tapped the keyboard.

"*Merci.*"

As if this were some sort of keyword, the computer chose that moment to complete its internal mumbling, and it projected from its hologrammic adjuncts a three dimensional image of . . . four human heads.

There was an attractive if chilly-eyed woman with flaxen hair; there was a bald man with a neat little beard and a large bulbous nose, and tiny little eyes; there was an old man with shaggy white brows and so many seams in his face you could scarcely make out the features; there was a middle aged man with thin lips, a cocky manner and slicked-back black hair. The heads hovered in the air, in the middle of the room, gazing with self awareness and some degree of consciousness, at Jerry and Edwige.

"They are rather ugly little spirits," Edwige commented, covering a yawn with a pretty little hand.

"We are not 'spirits'," said the woman. "We are . . . copies. We are mindclones. And we are self aware."

"If not self aware, at least rather full of yourselves, I'd say, judging from your self pitying expressions," Jerry remarked. "These, Edwige," Jerry went on musingly, "are the mindclones of the four Boardmembers of Axis International, preserved should the originals bite the dust. It is their tawdry, foolish little attempt at immortality; it is a forbidden technology, secretly known and secretly banned, but Axis has chosen to use it anyway. One of these gentlemen is our little Beth's father . . ."

The middle aged man with the slicked back hair said, scowling, "What do you know of my Beth?"

"She's mine now, old boy. She hates you, you know. It was she gave me the chip."

"I don't believe it!"

"Believe it, you child molesting bastard. Not that I'm really so *very* judgemental about idiosyncratic tastes."

"I will transmit a warning to my original about all this—"

"Rubbish," Jerry said, lighting a cigarette. "You are mine now. I control the vertical and the horizontal. I've got you. Just wanted a test run. Next, of course, I must aid the further convergence of the lines, and bring about . . . ah. You'll see. Edwige—has the cognitive emulator charged the ballroom?"

"Yes—everyone is ready."

Beth was surprised to see Morris, the scruffy Goth kid from the front steps, standing in a corner of the ballroom, drinking the punch that brimmed the giant clam shell. "Didn't think they'd let you in," she said.

"Scared 'em into it," Morris said, sniffing. "I'm from a powerful clan . . ."

"Are you," Timothy laughed, getting himself some punch. His hands were shaking. The electricity in the air sparked from the spoons and sizzled about the light fixtures. "Jerry has no fear of you at all, in fact. He said something about taking pity on you: that you were much like someone he'd known once."

Morris frowned and turned toward the dais at the fair end of the room, where suddenly a spotlight found Jerry, sweeping through the curtained doorway to gaze down on them.

"Light your candles!" he thundered, descending to them.

Life in death and death in life
Lady Despair a luscious wife . . .

The music intoned with exquisitely maudlin excess, the bass beat a dirge against the walls, the chandeliers swayed, and scores of Goth kids in black capes and swirling gowns and spiky lingerie and bloody tuxedos, each carrying a blackwax candle, stepped with the grandiosity of fearless innocence, in a slowly circling procession, spiraled like the arms of a negative galaxy, around Jerry the galaxy's core. The music ebbed in volume as Jerry spoke into a headset microphone, raising his arms like a high priest, Edwige kneeling before him, apparently praying.

"Hear me vampire clans! You see me now the veteran of a thousand psychic wars! Another time I was a vampire of sorts, a drinker of energies; now I merely borrow, and focus and return all to you transformed: For I fought the law and the law won! Jerry has changed! Jerry has learned to nourish as much as he is nourished! And if I have used you, brought you here to be living generators of psychic energy for my own purposes, I have also given you orchids sliding on a subterranean river; I have given you the pulse of blood in clitoris and throat—"

They roared approval at that one.

"—I have given you Antarctic moonlight on the frozen bones of a mariner! I have given you lightning in a coffee cup! I have given you heavy metal, black and silver! I have given you fireflies in the sockets of a skull! I have given you the whisper of silk over cobblestones! I have given you a dream of velvet lined coffins that bring safety and solace! I have given you white for black and black for white! *I have given you a Mardi Gras of the Necropolis of Joy!*"

And at each phrase he made a pass over the Goth kids with something that glittered—something that looked like a long platinum needle in a dagger-hilt of figured ruby; something that was both machine and decorative ornate knife. Subtle energies coursed its length.

Beth, with Morris at her side, approached the center of the living galaxy of dark celebrants, and could not take her eyes from the platinum and ruby instrument in Jerry's hand—

And in his other hand he held the Macrochip—

And then he put the two of them together and—

She heard his voice in her head. *"Thank you very much for all your help, love. Magic is redefined. The nuclei of the modern world are no longer states or even cities, but interlacings of information, the matrixed relationships of the capacities to buy and sell—what we call 'multinational corporations'. For my long range purpose, I have to have one, have to be one, to be real in this world, you see. And I do intend to be real in this world. I've had quite enough of this world's imagination . . ."*

—and the instruments touched, and a blaze of heatless light spread out, rippling in a circle from the contact point, encompassing Jerry and Edwige in a ball of translucent light. He reached through the membrane of energy and grabbed Morris. *"Come my woebegone little urchin, I'll find a place for you . . ."* And pulled Morris, "Prince Dreybak", into the bubble of light, which wobbled, once, and, just before midnight, expanded and filled the room inexorably with the white incandescence of fusion, the fusion of being and nonbeing.

They were wandering in aimless circles in the darkness of a socket of earth; in the smell of a new grave, of soil, sliced earthworms and rusty pipes. The daze slowly seeped away from Beth, and she realized she was cold. Her eyes came into something like focus and she found she was in a sort of pit, between two old San Francisco buildings. There was just enough urban light to see an old, disused concrete staircase. The others were already working their way up it.

Beth slogged through the cold mud, shivering, head aching, trying to remember. Jerry had taken the boy Morris and Edwige and the three of them had vanished and gone . . . where?

She climbed the stairs, reached the street, crossed, and turned around.

The Cornelius Arms was gone. It had been lifted out like a tooth from its socket. A few wayward pipes draggled up from the mud, one of them spouting water. There was nothing else.

And scores of Goth kids stood in the midst of the street, staring silently at the pit in the earth, stunned silent, as fog rolled down the street in a gray wave, and engulfed them.

She and Timothy had been on the train all night; it was just pulling into San Diego. How unreal it looked in the morning light, with its palm trees and glass buildings and pastel murals and mission-style Old Town; like something from that old Don Johnson TV show. No, that was Miami.

"You'll like my parents," Timothy said. "They used to be in rock bands. Now they're in real estate. But they're pretty cool. They smoke pot, but not every day."

In the train station Beth found herself drawn to a newspaper kiosk. She had just enough change for the San Diego paper. She saw his picture right away. Scanning lower she found . . .

. . . *Will be officially designated the new CEO of Axis Enterprises, Friday morning. Company spokesmen said that the four members of the Axis board, who were killed in a plane crash at Sunday midnight, made extensive arrangements for the new CEO to replace them in case of emergency. Industry sources are calling Jerry Cornelius the "Unknown Tycoon", claiming that his business history is foggy and unverifiable. However, Axis public relations expects Cornelius' transition to power to be "very nearly seamless . . ."*

"Is that really him?" Timothy asked, looking over her shoulder.

"Yes. Magic is redefined, he said."

"There was a plane crash? Wasn't that—? "

"My father. Yes. My father died in the plane crash." She smiled. "I wonder what I'll inherit. Come on, let's get a latte."

QUILL TRIPSTICKLER, OUT THE WINDOW

"There are a variety of terms I might appropriately apply here," said Commissioner Feldspar. "But I think *oafish stumblebum* has the right ring to it."

Quill cleared his throat. "Yes, sir. Actually, I think *honest misjudgment by a loyal—*"

"And yet," Feldspar went on, as if he hadn't heard, *"oafish stumblebum* hasn't the proper piquancy. Something more basic is called for. I have it! *Bumbling clod*! That's it! You, Quill Tripstickler, are a Bumbling Clod. At best."

"Yes, sir," said Quill meekly. He winced when he heard Feldspar's pet duck snickering in the corner. He despised poultry—the profusion of poultry, the one remaining sort of domestic animal in the twenty-fifth century, was the bane of Earth, and it almost made Quill wish he hadn't come back to his home planet. As an agent of the Galactic Tourist Agency, his duty was in the stars—there were some things a field agent could not explain to a desk operative, it seemed. He should never have returned. Should have made the report by tachyon transmish. But Father Tripstickler had insisted, and Quill still stood in fear of that fearsome patriarch. That's just how Quill thought of his father, except that he thought it: FEARSOME PATRIARCH. And it seemed then that Feldspar had been possessed by Father Tripstickler's own spirit—Quill's father was by no means deceased, but that didn't prevent him liberally spreading his Spiritual Influence about—when he thundered: "And I want you to know I don't think much of that snooty cybernetic valet of yours. In fact, I think robots are a pain in the pacemaker. Yours is always complaining. Well, I'm going to be rid of you and your robot, Tripstickler. You're both *fired!*" He emphasized the word with glee and with the slap of his palm on the glass desk (which was also a miniature henhouse—Feldspar's house was crowded). Quill opened his mouth to protest. But Feldspar, shaking his jowls, his dim blue eyes narrowed, bulled on: "How do you excuse going to a colony of religious celibates and promptly seducing the queen's parthenogenic child and nearly starting an intersteller war? How in Tallahassee Florida the princess could find a human platypus like yourself attractive is quite beyond me. Did you erotigas her? Is that it, hm?"

"Erotigas? Certainly not, sir! I hold Winner's Ribbons in all classes of Seduction and Erotic Conduct, sir!" Quill was deeply offended by Feldspar's use of the term "human platypus." True, Quill was oddly proportioned. And, true, he had a large nose. Well, yes, it was a *very* large nose. His long neck, weak chin, large spreading nose—which inelegant dullards insisted on referring to as a *beak*—gave him a slightly duck-like appearance. And since cerebrally evolved ducks had become so common, some oaf was always drawing the comparison. Gangly, gawky, pout-lipped, beaked as he was, still Quill refused a body-rebuild. Strangely, he firmly believed that he was Devilishly Handsome.

He ran a hand through his thin brown curls and tried to assume a tone of reasonableness. "My assignment, Commissioner Feldspar, was to introduce tourism into the planet Nunneras. It was a difficult negotiation to undertake, since the Nunnerans believe that a offworlders are of Satanic origin. I felt I needed someone on the inside to suggest to the queen that she trust me. A Galactic Tourist Agent must occasionally take bold steps, sir. And, to be perfectly honest, the princess seduced *me*— naturally I turned this intimacy to the good of the agency. Or sought to do so—until the queen discovered that . . . well, sir, I barely escaped with my life . . . I—"

"Oafish stumblebum." Feldspar's body-rebuilt face had badly gone to sag; it was supposed to resemble Julius Caesar, but it more closely befit Nero. And now it was bright red with fury. "Bumbling . . ." Feldspar's invectives came like the rumbles of a volcano building to eruption. "Moronic . . ." He drew a deep breath for: "*Oafish stumbling bumbling CLOD!*"

As Quill left the room . . . as Quill *beat it hastily* from the room, Feldspar sent his oversized (bigger than two fat geese together) pet duck to chivvy him. Ducks had always provoked in Quill a thrill of revulsion. He ran from the house, the duck quacking at his heels, snapping at his ankles, squawking, "Quan quon't quaum quack!"*

Quill sat in the cool dimness of The Terminus. It was a suicide bar, designed to appeal to those surfeited with existential ennui. And it at-

---

* Translation from the duck argot of Quill's time: "And don't come back!"

tracted the *victimizers,* a breed of bar-haunter emerged to accommodate those preferring to die at another's hands.

From somewhere droned dolorous funereal muzak. Quill sighed, his sigh harmonizing with numerous other sighs along the bar, he signaled the bartender (whose lifelike black eyes seemed forever sympathetic and welling with tears). "Toxic or nontoxic, sir?" asked the bartender.

"For the moment, nontoxic. I'll have a Cable TV Cocktail."

The bartender nodded and caressed a keyboard. A glass emerged from a slot in the bar, a wire affixed to its underside, the green liquid in the glass contained a tiny three-dee image of a man poised on a window ledge, about to leap into oblivion, as a crowd at nearby windows begged him to reconsider. Quill sighed, and sipped. The drink tasted of liquor, mint—and blood mixed with concrete, plus a suggestion of sweat. There was, too, a savor of distilled desperation.

"Master Quill?"

Quill winced. He knew whose voice he was hearing. He preferred to ignore it. Perhaps it would go away.

But Fives cleared his throat—more accurately, he made a noise that was a theatrical approximation of throat clearing since he hadn't a throat to clear. Robots have no need of an esophagus. "Master Quill, your father sent me to seek you. He bids you to 'buck up and take heart.' He asked me to remind you of that immemorial Tripstickler aphorism—from Sayings of Father Tripstickler, Selection Ninety-six—to wit: 'When a Tripstickler is down he can always take heart/he knows that his end is really his start.' Stirring words, sir, if I may say so. Words that stir the—"

"Then you may take those words," Quill said miserably, "and stir them up, drink them, and gag on them. I'll drink to that." He took another sip of his Cable TV Cocktail. He frowned and changed the taste-channel, twisting the knob on the side of the glass. The image in the liquid swirled, blurred, changed, reforming into a troupe of briefly clad dancing girls. Quill tasted the drink and almost smiled.

But he couldn't smile. He was ruined. His father had believed in him, had paid for his two years at the Tourist Agent Training School. It had been costly training. And his father had bought him his own Agent's Starcruiser (second-hand). A fine gesture from a Grand Old Man. And his father had given him Fives . . .

"Meddling Old Fool," Quill murmured, frowning.

"I beg your pardon, sir?" Fives asked softly, rolling nearer.

"Nothing . . ." Quill sighed. "I am an ingrate. Calling my father names, when I have let him down. After all he's done for me. Put me through agent's school—and now I'm fired." He took a long pull at his drink and blinked. The combination alcohol and opiate in the drink was beginning to have its effect. "My whole career down the Disposetron . . . Well, I've come here to find Peace."

"Surely not, Master Quill!" Fives rocked back on his single wheel in simulated (or was it real?) astonishment, shaking his lifelike head in gentle reproach. Fives was styled to resemble, from the waist up, an early twentieth century Gentleman's Gentleman. He rarely removed the black bowler hat—which was more than it seemed—from his round British-style head. He pinched his florid synthaflesh nose in dismay— one of the *charming personality gestures* the brochure on this model robot had listed—and arched his eyebrows quizzically. The *quizzical arching of eyebrows* was another programmed charming personality gesture. Quill didn't find it charming. And somehow he sensed Fives' personality went beyond programming. The robot had a number of annoying habits all his own invention. For example, his way of hooking a lifelike thumb in his waistcoat watch pocket, straightening on the single wheel at the bottom of his inverted-cone brushed-aluminum undersides, tugging the tails of his coat-and-tails with his other hand, causing his brown eyes to sparkle, his ruddy English cheeks to become ruddier, as. he recited:

> *"A Tripstickler looks to see who's downwind*
> *Before he loosens his belt;*
> *He thinks of others before himself,*
> *Of their skins before his own pelt."*

Quill winced again. "Don't *do* that, Fives. You do it to torment me."

"I beg your pardon, sir. Master Quill—do you know which bar this is?"

"Do you think I'm blind? I saw the sign. It's The Terminus."

"I mean, sir—do you know what *sort* of bar this is?"

Quill's nod was somber, his expression maudlin in its celebration of misery. "It's a suicide bar."

"But Master Quill—The Terminus is a pick-up bar, begging your pardon, sir. One goes to such a place . . ." Fives looked furtively around at the other denizens of the gloomy bar and lowered his voice. ". . . One comes to such a place to meet someone. A partner. Someone to kill oneself with. Or someone to do the deed. And there are those who—"

"I'm aware of all that," said Quill in a voice awry with drink. "I came here a victim. A voluntary victim, seeking a . . . a victimizer." He sniffed (the sniff reverberated in the voluminous echochamber of his nose) and looked up and down the bar as if pondering the options.

The shadowy chamber was hung with black translucent scarves. Over the bar was a human skull, fleshless except for two heavy-lidded eyes leaking tears.

The figures at the bar were studies in quiet misery. Self-pity spoke itself in every man or woman's body language.

There were those, however, standing against the walls in gloomy corners, whose red-glowing cocktails signified their preference: they were victimizers, licensed, looking for voluntary victims.

One of them was looking Quill up and down. And smiling.

His smile showed his teeth. Big teeth, rebuilt in three sharp rows like a shark's. Quill had heard that some of the victimizers were cannibals. The law gave them the right to do as they pleased with the bodies . . .

Quill looked hurriedly away. And then he saw her.

She was a four-footer. All four of her feet were lovely. But she was two meters tall, measuring from the spike-heeled feet of her front set of legs to the top of her delicately boned black-maned head. He had only seen a femitaur once before, at the Conference on Interdimensional Travel. Quill had found them quite attractive, much to the dismay of his peers. "You've got odd tastes in women, Tripstickler," they'd said. But something–about the sweep of the lovely, quite human, womanly upper half of the femitaur, the curve of that back arcing neatly into the equine lower back . . . something in the perfect melding of the back parts of horse and woman . . . something about her two pairs of shapely woman's legs (woman's legs, horse's torso, human feminine derriere but for the small flickering tail) and the fine black felt-like fur beginning just beneath the upper waist . . . the antelope's tail . . . the pointed, upturned breasts, the oval eyes . . .

"Fives . . ."

"Sir?"

"Did you, ah, notice the femitaur in the corner, Fives? The only alien here. Notice the red-glow drink in her hand. . . Is she not lovely?"

"A splendid example of her species, sir. Lovely large brown eyes, sir. But something in the way she is perusing you, sir, strikes me as–to be perfectly candid–hungry."

"Women of all persuasions look at me hungrily, Fives," said Quill with garish urbanity, bobbling his eyebrows and his crab-apple lump of an Adam's apple, "for I am 'one who is catnip to women.'" Do you read the ancient writers, Fives? That's Mencken. And look at her! The sweep of her back, her upper back at a strict ninety-degree angle from her lower. Her quivering, perfect—"

"Begging. your pardon, sir, but don't you think we'd best *exeunt?* If you are to convince Commissioner Feldspar to give you a second chance, you must—"

"It's useless, Fives. It would take a miracle. It needs a legend-making coup in Galactic Tourist Agenting." Once again Quill was plunged into gloom.

"Suicide then, sir? Very good, sir. As you say. I suppose there are certain employment alternatives open to me I could explore. In fact—"

"I'm going to get drunk," Quill interrupted. "and then I shall stride manfully up to her, and ask her—nay, I shall implore her poetically—to kill me . . . You know Fives, I've heard that to travel into the alternate universe in which the femitaurs live is to embrace death. If she personifies the death that one embraces, then that embrace is no longer repellent to me. Ah! How despair infuses the soul with poetry! Ah . . . the story goes that one steps into the transporter and emerges into their world, gasping with disbelief at the beauty beheld there—this by neutrino transmission devices the explorer carries, sending messages back as he goes—ah, as I said, he gasps at the beauty and explodes! Instant death. If I could find a way to take tourists to the world of the femitaurs, *safely,* I would be a legend among tourist agents . . . The femitaurs themselves seem confused when trying to explain the phenomena and their own inter-dimensional transport. No one has yet fathomed them; they talk cryptically of Death Itself . . . They can visit us but we cannot visit them . . . They come here rarely. Understandable. There is a communication gap between the femitaurs and ourselves. But the language of death, Fives, is universally understood everywhere. If she is here, in a suicide bar, then the language of death—" Quill spoke with a dramatic flourish, waving his hand in the air over his head, drunkenly orating to some invisible audience of admirers, "—is the language we speak together."

He turned to reel toward the femitaur. He stumbled into Fives and tangled his feet trying to recover. He pitched to his belly. "Umph . . . oafish stumblebum," Quill murmured muzzily. "Bumbling clod of a robot. Oafish stumbling—"

The man with the large teeth, drawing a cloak of flayed human skin about him, strode to Quill's side, bending to assist him to his feet. "Really my man," he said, "you ought to find a better way to off yourself than stumbling to death."

"Not usedtuh Cabbie . . . cobble . . . cubical . . . Cable TV Cocktails," Quill said, sitting heavily on a barstool.

"The best way to die," said the swarthy stranger with a wolfish smile, "is at the hands of an expert. There will be no fee. It will be quick—but poignant. Painless—but evocative. Firm—but artful." He placed an arm about Quill's shoulders. His red eyes glittered. "Trust me."

Quill's throat was dry.

"We'll go somewhere else," the dark man went on. "Somewhere private."

"Oh—I think not," said Quill politely. "I rather think, that is, that is to say, I mean to say, ah . . ."

"Oh, I *see*," said the victimizer, "You are a man whose taste runs to public self-destruction. Charming!" The dark man's hands closed round Quill's throat. Long-fingered, hard-muscled hands with black-painted fingernails tightened. Quill wheezed.

"Here now!" said the robot bartender, rolling up from the other end of the bar. His realistic head, shaped like Gary Gilmore's for historical atmosphere, shook disapprovingly. "No suiciding or victimizing in the bar! Take it outside! Meet 'em here but don't eat 'em here!"

"Chalky? Is that you?" Fives asked, bending toward the bartender. "Sounds like your voice. They haven't altered that. But this distasteful new head—"

"Fives! Good to see you! Got a new gig, I see! Valet? Yes, it's me. Say, Fives old man, whatever happened with that job you had pretending to admire people with inferiority complexes for some therapeutic clinic—?"

"A curious story, that one," said Fives, "Beginning some years ago on the Beauty Spa planet Aphrodite—"

"Fives!" Quill called hoarsely, clawing to pry the hands of the victimizer from his throat. "Help!" The victimizer was dragging Quill by the neck across the floor toward the door of the bar. Quill's heels scraped the floor. He struggled feebly.

"What's that? Oh, a moment, Master Quill, I'll be right there. Ran into an old friend here," he called over his shoulder. He turned to the bartender. "I'll have to attend to this, Chalky. The young master has a way of getting himself throttled at regular intervals . . . But, tell me, what became of that lovely self-lubricator you used to have . . ."

"*Fives!*" Quill was blacking out, felt himself towed as if he were already a corpse . . .

"Release this one." A strange, melodious voice. "He and I have a pact: an agreement of intersecting gazes. He is mine."

Quill looked up, blinking away a red fog, to see the four pairs of lady legs upholding the femitaur who now stood beside him. Her hooves grew naturally to resemble black spike heels. It was with one of these that, turning her back, she kicked the victimizer in his gut. The man made an expectorant sound, wheezed, and fell back, fingers unwrapping from Quill's throat. Gratefully, Quill gulped air and got to his feet.

The victimizer stood, snarling, and reached for a weapon beneath his cloak.

A black bowler hat, descending from the shadowy ceiling, fired a bolt of blue light from its silk-lined interior. The Victimizer's eyes crossed, his knees buckled, and he fell heavily to the floor, unconscious.

"You were always a mean shot with a paralyzer, Fives my lad," Chalky called from the bar.

"I'm grateful, my lady," said Quill, pointedly ignoring Fives and trying to regain his dignity, bowing with a flourish.

"I have need of one who will give his life. One unfearing death," she said, her voice like wind through the spires of another world.

"My lady, I have been dishonored with failure. My life is nothing. I am yours to do with as you will."

"Call me Ilana. Come."

Ilana led them into the street; all were careful to step on the supine victimizer.

Quill turned to Fives. "Fives, you are a disrespectful bounder. However, our association has on occasion been fruitful. I suppose I . . ." His voice broke. He sniffed and pretended sternness.

"Send my body, Fives, to my father, and wrap me all in black silks, cover me with nodes of onyx and, stones from the deeps of the sea . . ."

For some minutes they endured one of Quill's orations, until Fives broke in. "Actually, sir, I rather thought I might send the body to Nunneras."

"What?"

"Well, best to make the most of a sad duty, sir. And it seems to me I recall that the Nunnerans have a legend. 'One from the stars will come, and he will be rebuked. He shall find death, and he will return from death, bringing his Word of a new age and a new Way.' Part of the research you asked me to do on Nunneras, Master Quill. We could send them your body, explain that you had killed yourself because you had 'converted' to their religion; your suicide was an act of martyrdom and faith . . . and perhaps we could arrange to create an illusion, bringing you 'back to life' with a hologram . . . The hologram—a technology with which the backward, atavistic Nunnerans are unfamiliar—would naturally advise them that the time has come to open their planet to travelers from other worlds. We don't have to call them tourists—pilgrims! And—"

"Just how would this serve you, Fives? You are merely my assistant. Why would you engineer this, once I'm dead?"

Fives looked apologetic. "The new equal rights for robots laws, sir, state that a robot can become, among other things, a free tourist agent, if he proves that—"

"Why—! Of all the—! Fives, that's perfectly ghoulish! Using my dead body to make a career for yourself." He put an affectionate hand on Fives' shoulder. "I see you've learned something from our association, old boy."

On the way to the corner they encountered a dozen pet owners, ostentatiously walking their poultry. Quill wrinkled his nose—two or three people looked up when he did this, since his nose was prodigious, the wrinkling seeming to profoundly revise a major feature of the street's architecture.

"Oh, it's just a nose," said a fat man walking a duck. "I thought they were tearing down a building—"

"Your duck," said Quill, "is offensive to me. The animals are loathsome." They walked on, side-stepping outsized ducks, chickens, geese, and an occasional turkey, all leashed. The squawking and cackling competed with the noise of breezecars whining by on their sparkling magnetic fields. The moraines of duck droppings contrasted with the clean planes of glassteel comprising the buildings around them. Someone's duck tugged its leash from the roboserv walking it and waddled aggressively at Quill, squawking "Quey! I quot I quold choo kwuh queat it!"

It snapped at Quill's ankles. Quill kicked at it, and it fluttered aside, squalling.

"You need diction lessons." Quill said, addressing the duck. "Try saying it again, like this: 'Hey! I thought I told you to beat it!'" He kicked at the duck again, which ran to the protection of its hourglass-shaped roboserv. "Menace to the public health," Quill murmured bitterly. "That's Commissioner Feldspar's duck, Fives. Why don't you see if you can run it over?"

I fear not, sir," said Fives politely. "Commissioner Feldspar may soon be my employer."

Quill groaned. He turned to Ilana. "Have you ducks in your plane of reality?"

She smiled and shook her head, paused to rub one of her four spike-hooved feet on another, her tail flouncing merrily. "Fortunately, brave one, we have no giant talking ducks, nor ducks of any sort."

"It wasn't always like this, Ilana," Quill said. He was striding steadily now, the imbroglio in The Terminus had sobered him up. "But because of a peculiar ecological imbalance, the only domestic animals which remain an Earth are poultry. Cats and dogs once were populous, but when they evolved and gained self-awareness, they killed one another off in wars. And the cockroaches exterminated the rats, of course. Genocide, pure and simple. Still, I've no complaint with cockroaches. They're mild-mannered, as long as they're well-fed and unthreatened. They're not es-thetically pleasing to look upon, of course, although they dress well. But somehow I like them better at four feet high as opposed to the little ones. Interesting culture they have. A matriarchy, you know. If, ah, I haven't got to kill myself right away, we might take a detour through the cockroach ghettos. I know a little sidewalk stand where they sell marvel-ous grub-excretion patties—"

"No, we will be late for the gateway, my brave one," said Ilana, caress-ing Quill's cheek with one of her long six-fingered hands. "Better we not side-traipse into cockroach ghettos, no matter how picturesque, coura-geous one."

"Your form of address is appropriate," said Quill. "Since my courage is celebrated in myths and—"

"Indeed," Fives put in, "it is mythical."

"I mean to say," Quill said hastily, glaring at Fives, "that it is the stuff of legends. But of course there are times when the strongest of men won-der if plunging thoughtlessly into the unknown is wisest. There is more than a modicum of wisdom in the expression, 'discretion is the better part of valor.'"

"Is that the expression, sir?" Fives asked as if genuinely perplexed. "I thought the expression was something to do with 'cold feet.'"

Ilana turned her lovely head to gaze at Quill quizzically. "You mean you do not intend to seek honor and peace in death?"

Quill took a deep breath. "Ah. But of course, of course, I however, ah . . ." He closed his eyes. And shrugged. "Very well. Let us have done with it. I cannot face my father after my disgrace."

They had come to a busy intersection. It was a truck route. Huge gray-metal and plastiflex-jointed freight trucks-growled along on blue-spark-ing magnetic fields. Except for the lack of wheels and diesel, semi-trucks had not changed significantly since the twentieth century. They were still quintessentially brutish. Quill swallowed hard and took a step back from the curb. "Ilana you don't propose to . . ?"

Ilana was gazing down the long street to the right, searchingly, as if looking for just the proper truck.

"There!" she exclaimed. "That one will do nicely. Yes." She took a time-piece from a slit in the skin between her breasts. "Fifty seconds," she said.

"A religious ritual, I assume," said Quill aside to Fives. "She has to kill me in accordance with the proper astrological conjunction, perhaps." He chewed at a thumbnail.

"Kill you?" She turned to Quill. "I too shall die. We together."

"Both of us?" Quill was both saddened and heartened.

He looked at the trucks; they were like organized avalanches. He considered. He looked away. "Perhaps we should go into yon refreshment haven and reconsider our course . . ."

He turned to go.

She took him by the hand and stepped in front of a truck, dragging Quill with her. The truck bore mightily down on them, unable to stop in time, blasting out a warning. "Ah, well," Quill said at the last moment, "better death than to live in a world infested with ducks." He glimpsed Fives waving his bowler hat goodbye . . .

The truck hit them. It made them broken, battered things.

Quill Tripstickler, run over by a truck.

The somber procession wound its way through the garlanded streets of Pious, the capital of Nunneras. On one side were the Nunneras men wearing their long-skirted nun's habits, groaning as they lashed themselves with penitati flails, heads bowed. On the other side of the street were the Nunneras women (the two genders kept always to their own sides of the street and to their special dormitories, lest they should brush elbows or come into some other heinous physical contact) in black-leather priest's cassocks. Everyone native to Nunneras, excepting the royal family, had had their lips removed. It was a city of enforced grimaces.

But in splendid disavowal of soberness the famous Nunneras Gardens, the population's only sanctioned means of life-expressiveness, bloomed to either side of every street, in the narrow plots between the wooden walks and the roughly built dorm buildings.

Some of the flowers were huge and gaudy, some small and exquisitely subtle in shadings of hue, they twined and bunched and waved in rows, arabesques, geometrical intricacies and—not surprisingly in the suppressive social atmosphere—designs which an objective eye would recognize as genitals. Here and there topiaries of blue-green added dignity to the riotous display. Nunneras' temperate climate made it possible for flowers to bloom, with species alternating, all year round.

Fives, riding on the center float of the procession beside the glass casket containing Quill's body, observed the gardens with pleasure. His optical filters were opened wide, his olfactory sensors were fully dilated.

On the flower-encrusted float ahead of Fives, in papal robes and gloriously the centerpiece of a purple whiskerbloom floral arrangement, sat Queen Collana and her daughter Enrilla. They were not lipless; both were tall, cloudy-haired and lithesomely personable. Enrilla looked uncomfortable in her ermine robes—it was a hot day—as she turned in her gilded chair to stare wistfully at the supine and cosmetically rebuilt (but quite dead) body of Quill Tripstickler. The queen frowned sternly at her daughter; Enrilla turned away. The two figures swayed with the marching rhythm of the littermen bearing them.

Fives too turned to sadly contemplate the body of his erstwhile master. He took little satisfaction in his impending promotion. He would never have admitted as much to Quill, but he wished his master alive.

On the front end of the casket hung a huge placard containing a testimonial to Quill, cunningly scribed with marshblossom petals, scarlet against white:

A SATANIC CHILD OF EARTH FOUND FAITH
FAR FROM NUNNERAS
AND GAVE HIS LIFE IN MARTYRDOM
AND PERFECT CONTRITION,
SEEKNG REPENTANCE. IN DEATH HE IS
REDEEMED.

"Blessed are the self-destructive," Fives murmured, "for they are harmless to the State."

Nunneras had been far from Quill's thoughts at the moment of his death. Fives had not been programmed to lie. But somehow he had learned to lie beautifully.

Quill sat up, smiling.

He looked around. He felt giddy and clean and new. He *was* new.

About him stretched radial avenues of blue-green grass, neatly clipped, and thickly twining jade-colored leafy vines. The vines clung thickly to colonnades, and to columns supporting the grass-draped ceiling. The only relief from the green color-scheme was in the white columns and thin streams of sparkling blue water. The place was like a vast cathedral inwardly coated with greenery, with six hallways extending in spokes from the center-sward. The center-sward was occupied only by Quill and Ilana. Ilana got to her four feet and, in her peculiar way, stretched.

"Even the ceiling," Quill said wonderingly, looking up. The long blades of grass hung like mermaid's hair in the mist from the narrow waterfalls tinkling down here and there. "Are we—are we on the planet Nunneras? It's a garden planet, and this is a marvelous garden."

Bending to tear handfuls of grass, which she raised to her lips and chewed thoughtfully, Ilana shook her head. "This is my world. A world parallel to yours. A lovely world . . ." There was a note of sadness in her voice.

"Your world?" Quill was surprised. "But—are we not dead? I remember that the truck struck us squarely and with great force." He shuddered. "This, then, is the Afterworld?"

"Afterworld? Paradise? Not in the sense you mean. This is our variant of Earth. And though you had to die to come here, you are not dead. You are not disembodied. This is not the afterlife, my brave Quill. It is your life, in another space-time continuum, after the radical transition resembling Death. Truly, you left a dead body behind on Earth. But the InterEarth transportation process did not destroy you—the body you now inhabit is an exact copy of the one left behind. Even your clothes—everything within your bioplasmic field has been copied, reconstituted, into an identical vehicle for your consciousness."

Quill looked down at himself. "I am the same? Not a hair amiss? You're quite sure? Nothing but an exact duplicate will do, you know. I was made in the finest way of the finest stuff—nothing but the finest will do—"

"You are precisely the same. Simply . . . newer. Your consciousness, your memories, the sum of your personality—all this was transmitted here, to the body you now inhabit, by means of neutrino interpenetration . . ."

Quill struggled to understand. "Death—death is the means of travel from my world to this Other Earth?"

"Only *certain* deaths. It must occur in the right place, at the right time, with the right means. Most deaths will launch you into the plane of the disembodied. Die at the proper time and place—and you arrive here. Now and then one of your people stumbles through, to a new body automatically awaiting them; they are channeled by certain magnetic polarities to this spot, this reception hall, blundering into our world via the right death. They had inadvertently stepped in front of the right truck or charging elephant . . ."

Quill was dazed. "I remember no pain."

"There was no pain—because I held your hand. I took control of your nervous system at the last moment and dampened your pain. It is a skill those of us specializing in transition have learned . . ."

"But—what of those who were destroyed on their arrival here?"

"They came through an electronic Interdimensional Breacher. The wrong means. The dimensional dynamics will not allow this means for the transition between your world and mine. They must come through the right channels or not at all . . ."

"But why?"

"Why is it that when you step off a cliff, you fall and are crushed? Why aren't you crushed when you reach the bottom by wallking down the trail? The dynamics of your world's physical laws. The why of such laws are always a mystery. One can only theorize uselessly."

"The gateway to your world . . ." Quill mused, "is getting run over by a truck?"

"It need not have been a truck. We needed crushing, in that time and place."

"Crushing?" Quill stood, rubbing his chin speculatively. "We might build Interdimensional Gateways at the assigned spots—you could inform us of these. And, at the calculated instants, we could bring crowds of tourists into your world—by crushing them instantaneously in a huge and quick metal vise. We could anesthetize them first . . . But how would they return?"

"We push them out windows," said Ilana. "Specific windows for specific destinations. There is a window assigned—most of them are not in use, as yet—for each inhabited world in your Universe's civilized galaxy."

"Yes? Have you one for the planet Nunneras?"

"We do."

"Indeed . . . do you think I get the cooperation of your government in setting up tourist arrival centers?"

"Yes. You are now inhabiting just such a terminal. This reception hall was prepared specially in anticipation of tourists from your world . . . We need the revenue tourists would bring . . . and we brought you here to show you our method of transition as quickly and economically as possible, so you could arrange matters at the other end of the spectrum, brave one."

"I shall inspect your world, and then we shall make the arrangements," said Quill loftily. "I'll return by way of Nunneras—can you arrange for a specific spot on Nunneras?"

"Yes. When you go, simply visualize another living being of the world you seek: you will be reconstituted beside that being."

"Good. My servant is on Nunneras. I will wish to confer with him—" He smiled thinly. "And to startle the treacherous blackguard. Now . . ."

"Let us not go from this place hastily, comely one." She gathered Quill into her arms.

"The others of my species," she said, whispering into his ear as she stroked him—and as he returned her caresses—"think that my tastes are odd. I seem to be attracted to spindly big-nosed bipeds."

"We all have our . . . our eccentric tastes," Quill said, tracing her hindparts with an exploratory hand.

"Let us tarry here awhile, before we tour the rest of my Earth," she said. Her tone was wistful.

Quill tarried, and he tarried gladly.

. . . But the time came when Ilana took Quill by the hand and escorted him down a green-blue misty avenue until they came to a metal door set into a wall of harsh black stone. The door seemed, to Quill, rather anomalously pragmatic in its verdant surroundings.

Ilana turned a wheel and opened the door. Quill followed her through. The door, with a will of its own, shut behind them. It locked.

They were in a large room walled with white plastic and lined with aluminum shelves. On the shelves were glossy gray boxes perforated with thousands of tiny, almost microscopic, pinholes. The boxes were all alike and each a little bigger than a man's head. At the other end of the rectangular room was another metal door.

From the door came a droning and the thunder of many hooves.

Ilana turned to Quill and spoke something he suspected was learned by rote. "Wear one of these perceptual enhancement boxes and the native beauty of my Earth will be enhanced a thousand fold. And you will be able to communicate with others across the world as you choose, simply by tonguing the correct combination on your selector . . ."

She selected a box with an extra bulge at one face, presumably to accommodate Quill's nose. She approached him. He backed away.

Quill acted on instinct. He rushed to the opposite door, turned its wheel, and threw it open. He perceived a typical Other Earth street.

It was crowded, shoulder to shoulder, chest to tail, with femitaurs and manitaurs and, here and there, human men and women. All were dingy, nude or dressed in rags, sticky with some unguessable filth. The street was cracked, oozing with excretions, running with vermin moving too quickly to identify. A stench of unwashed billions assailed Quill's sensitive nostrils. All seemed thin, patchy, and in ill health.

And every single being on the street . . .

Each one . . .

"They've all got *boxes* on their heads," Quill said in horror. He turned to Ilana. She had already fitted a box over her head. It completely enclosed her head, fitting snugly shut under her chin, close around her neck.

She held a box out to Quill.

He shook his head. Strong arms closed around him from behind. Manitaurs with boxes on their heads—they seemed to have boxes instead of heads, unless one looked closely—held Quill pinioned while Ilana approached him with the box, opening it at the bottom, tilting its two halves away from one another to admit his head . . .

"I rather thought the business about your wanting tourist revenue sounded specious," said Quill, stalling. "I strongly suspect you want to leave your world. And something in the nature of the interdimensional dynamics prevents your leaving for long unless you trade places with someone from our world, yes? You can visit us—but to stay, one of us must take your place here . . . yes?" She nodded. Quill went on, "Well, you've made a grisly mess of your world and you must live in it—we won't take your place. We have our own mess. You can keep yours, we'll keep ours."

"I'm sorry, Quill," said Ilana, her voice coming to him electronically from within the box she poised over his head. "We meant to put a box on your head before you saw what it's really like out there. Once the box is on, you won't notice the real world. At least, the boxes will mitigate its overcrowded ugliness. The world will look lovely to you—once your will buckles. Your physical sensations, your perceptions—all will be altered. The box contacts certain centers of your brain . . . You see an infinite vista of paradisiac greenery and only a few of those persons standing close to you. You'll be fed through tubes that . . . but no need to explain—You shall see."

Quill struggled uselessly. The box closed over his head.

Darkness. And then the small tri-vid screens inside flickered alive. The illusions began. He felt ectoplasmic fingers probing his brain . . . He raised his hands to his head and felt his nose, his eyes . . . all through a layer of fuzziness. "I know the box is there," he said. "The illusion makes me think I'm feeling my own head. The box warps my perceptions. I'll remember that."

"You'll remember it for a while," she said. "But soon . . . after a few weeks . . ."

"I suppose you think to use this to brainwash me . . . so that you can use me to lure tourists here . . . so you can box them, too, and take their places. You hope to program me so that you can send me to my world and . . . You are hearing me, aren't you? You see, I'm on to your plan, and it isn't going to work. You can't program me when I'm aware of it— so, I can resist it . . . Best we forget the whole thing. Forgive and forget. I'm willing to, ah . . ."

He seemed to see her standing before him, smiling, shaking her head ruefully. "Time will change you."

"You're mad if you think our tourists will stand for this," he said. "They're not *that* stupid."

"Your tourists stand for group tours, don't they? Tourists everywhere have been conditioned for centuries to believe that abuse is a condition of stimulating travel."

She had a point. Quill could not deny it.

But he broke from his guards and tried to break down the door leading into the glade of green grass and clean columns and crystal waterfalls . . .

The manitaurs stampeded. He felt himself trampled under hooves shaped like jogging shoes.

Fives frowned, inspecting the circuitry behind the hidden panel in the interior of his bowler hat. His hologram projector didn't seem to be working. He glanced up, wondering if he were about to be evicted.

He was in danger of being evicted from the entire planet.

Fives had been told that, as an emissary of the dead Redeemed Hero, Quill Tripstickler, he might be allowed to remain on Nunneras for ten hours. Nine hours had passed since his arrival. The queen did not approve of soulless machinery that acted as if it had a soul. If Fives could not produce his miracle, he would soon be taken by force to his starcruiser. Or perhaps to a recycling plant . . .

He reflected that he might have made a mistake, in hinting to the queen that a miraculous resurrection of their new martyr was imminent. It might have been better to spring the scam on them out-of-the-hat, as it were. They'd accepted without argument Fives' faked holotapes seeming to depict Quill's conversion to Nunneranism. But now the queen eyed Fives with what was probably mounting skepticism.

Fives stood outside the crypt containing Quill's body. The crypt was an oval whose nearer end was shaped like the blossom of a Nunneran orchid. The Divine Family and their gloomily caparisoned retinue stood on the steps leading up to the crypt, to Fives' right, heads bowed, praying. A crowd of the Nunneran populace had gathered in the square below the steps, men to the left side, in habits, women to the right, in leather cassocks; all droned in prayer. The sun beat down, the air was heavy with blossom scent.

The queen raised her head, The Prayers ended. The ceremony was done. The martyr was buried. The queen turned to gaze at Fives expectantly. Fives smiled, wondering if he could summon his ship's shuttle before the guards converged on him. The look in the queen's eye presaged more than eviction. It was a this-robot-has-been-playing-us-for-fools-and-I-say-we-melt-him-down look.

She turned to the nun-habited guards and spoke to them in a whisper, gesturing toward Fives. The guards reached into belt pouches containing Brissic spores. They'd throw spore-packed capsules at Fives, the capsules would burst, the spores would come into contact with air and, in the rude and impertinent manner of Brissic spores everywhere, they'd burst into root-base foam which would cover him in seconds, hardening instantly into an unbreakable shell . . .

It has already been noted that Fives had no esophagus. Hence, he was unable to experience a lump of fear in his throat. But it is inaccurate to maintain that a robot cannot feel fear. Fives began to overheat with anxiety.

But between Fives and the oncoming guards, a vision interposed itself.

To Five's surprise, a partly serviceable hologram of Quill appeared on the steps, blinking confusedly. The holo-image swayed, pulled its nose (causing this monumental facial feature to waggle obscenely when it was released) and belched. Fives found these actions disturbing. He had not programmed the hologram to do these things. Nor had he programmed it to say:

"The pain's gone. The box is gone. The world is made over again. I'm new."

But that is what it said.

"Faulty hologram," Fives muttered. He flicked the switch (internally) that would turn the holo off before it could embarrass him further. The hologram did not disappear. It turned to him and said, "Fives, I have an astonishing tale to tell you."

And then Quill noticed the crowd at the bottom of the marble steps, and he saw that even the queen of Nunneras was kneeling to him, chanting hosannas and hallelujahs.

Quill turned and viewed the crypt. He read the placard. He remembered Fives' scheme. Then, trying not to smile too broadly, he turned to the crowd and spoke, "It is written: 'one from the stars will come, and he will be rebuked. He shall find death, and he will return from death, bringing his Word of a new age and a new Way.'"

A hushed silence was followed by a series of hymns. As everyone sang a different hymn, the result was dissonant clamor. After covering his ears for a few moments, Quill raised his hands for silence. In the ensuing quiet, he spoke to the assemblage, "I have returned from Heaven with word of a new order of things." He cleared his throat and continued, in ringing tones, "First of all . . ."

"Best we start off with only a few reforms, sir," Fives whispered.

"Yes, you're quite right," Quill murmured aside to Fives. He shouted: "Firstly, there will be no more severing of lips—the young will retain their lips that they may more easily speak the holy word. Second, visitors from other worlds will be admitted to Nunneras and allowed to roam freely. They shall be admitted only if they arrive under the auspices of the Galactic Tourist Agency. They shall be given hospitality and comfortable lodgings at a reasonable price. And clean towels—and sterile cups. All this, that they may see the example of Nunneras and go away with a change troubling their hearts . . . so that, on their respective worlds, they will come to a realization of the glory of Nunneranism, as I did. And think of the cash flow they'll bring in—"

"Sir . . ." whispered Fives warningly.

"Sorry," said Quill, aside. "Habit." Louder, he said, "And, finally, the Princess Enrilla and I will travel, alone, to other worlds of the galaxy as spiritual envoys of Nunneras, bringing the Good Word of Holy Redemption." He caught Enrilla's eye, expecting to see her blush. She winked.

The skies of Terra were cobalt blue that sunny morning. Even the squawks of poultry seemed jolly to Quill. Or nearly.

Fives and Quill paused outside Commissioner Feldspar's home. The commissioner's visage, three meters high, was reproduced on the facade of his synthawood house, between two bay windows. It flickered through a series of expressions, All the houses up and down the street were fronted with the typical facial facades, the most common day-to-day expressions of their owners. It was that sort of street.

Fives turned to Quill and remarked, "But surely, Master Quill, the people of the Other Earth will in time flood into our Earth through their death portals, to escape the over-crowding of their own world . . ."

"Not so. Most of them have been raised with their heads in their boxes. They *believe* the world they see on the small TV screens . . . Only those in power would have come here, if their plot had worked. Their government is utterly autocratic . . . I barely escaped myself. It was Ilana, of course, who made my escape possible. She consented to show me the Calculated Death Windows because she loved me. She must have secretly known I'd try to escape through them. And she voluntarily indicated the window leading—through Death—to Nunneras. She could not bear to see the magnificent Tripstickler sword blunted. I pretended to be docile, as if succumbing to brainwashing, until I was given a tour of the building containing the Windows."

"It must have taken great courage, Master Quill, to leap head-first through that window—to your death," said Fives, buttering up his employer.

"I must admit," said Quill with the airy wave of a Great Man Acknowledging His Humbleness, "that I leapt through the window through desperation as much as courage. My grasp on reality is tenuous enough as it is, without my giving it into someone else's control . . . It hurt, when I hit the street. But only for a moment. And then, I was standing outside my own crypt, in Nunneras."

"Quill, my boy!" cried Commissioner Feldspar joyously, coming to the door to greet them. "Come in! I want you to know I have decided to permit you to remain in the Galactic Tourist Agency after all. And, at no significant cut in pay . . . Your opening up Nunneras for us—after blundering it—was a masterful stroke."

Quill hesitated on the front step. "I'm not sure I want to come back to work for the agency," he said quietly, examining his immaculately manicured fingernails. "Not without a substantial raise and a promotion."

"What! You weak-minded ingrate! You can stuff your—"

"Or else I'll have to tell the Nunnerans that it might be dangerous after all to permit Satanic tourists on their pristine turf . . ."

Feldspar fell silent. He scowled. His image, on the facade of the house above him, sccowled too. "Very well. You may have anything you like. A promotion. A raise. Anything."

"Anything?" Quill looked at the duck, which peered nervously, out from between its owner's legs.

"Anything," said Feldspar.

"I want that duck," "I said.

"My—my duck?" Feldspar trembled. Then, resignedly, he said, "Very well."

"And," Quill added, grasping the duck firmly about the neck before it could speak, "I want a word with your chef."

I Live in Elizabeth

She lets me take control. Taking control feels like coming awake, in a way. I haven't been asleep, mentally; but physically I've been in whatever corner of our brain my sensations go when I'm asleep.

There is a moment of disjunction, when I feel I'm floating free from her, and I experience an almost overwhelming relief. And then she slips aside and I click with her motor controls, jack into her senses, take command of her coordination. I begin to feel her physical sensations in a disorienting rush: all of a sudden it's evening and she's fatigued; I monitor a pain, two areas of pain: one in her right leg, because it's begun to suffer from lack of circulation, as we've been sitting too long in one position. And a pain in our midriff. Cramps. Her period: Something hard to get used to, since I'm male. There's so damned much I have to get used to. And none of it's easy.

She let me write the several sentences you've just read. We've decided to write an account of what happened, so that we can get some help.

We're having trouble . . . adjusting . . .

The first time I saw Elizabeth, I knew instantly she'd change my life.

It was a cool Sunday afternoon in June, about ten months ago, outside a theater in the East Village. Clouds shifted the street into twilight and then slipped aside—and suddenly the sunlight was flooding her. She stood looking at a movie poster. *Jesus* she was lovely. She looked older than seventeen, at first. I thought her twenty, or twenty-one. Partly it's the clothing she wears. New York downtown boutique. *The Face* magazine. A touch pretentious, perhaps, like some of her speech mannerisms. But she's a knockout. Long thick black hair, almost to her waist. Full hips, long in the legs. Something Latin in her face.

We'd just come out of the theater—I'd noticed her inside too, about five rows down from me, all alone, rapt, a solitary bust in the artificial twilight.

Now she stood gazing at the movie poster. She glanced at me, and I had a glimpse of her eyes—so brown they were almost black, set off by mink lashes. Her lips were full, her lower lip like a silk pillow.

She was a divine anomaly. The cryptic spray paint graffiti seemed to crawl on every available surface; the sidewalks and the walls of the buildings were the same grimy gray, the streets imprinted with bottlecaps and pop-tops pressed into the asphalt by thousands of cars. Against that background: Elizabeth, luminous.

I'd gone alone to see Fellini's *Amarcord*. It seemed the appropriate conversational opening. "It's funny how Fellini can make me feel nostalgic about a place I've never been to . . ."

She nodded. "I know what you mean. My mother's Italian, though, so maybe I've got some sort of ancestral memory of the place. And of course the imagery is incredibly well-defined . . ."

I realized that she was a teenager. It was in her tone of voice, her pronunciation. Trying to impress me with her maturity. Most teenage girls don't use terms like *ancestral memory* and *imagery*.

Beat it, I told myself. *Make tracks. You're thirty-one, my friend. Don't be foolish.*

I looked into her eyes. A shock of recognition. And for a moment I was dizzy. I felt I'd been standing near the wall, with my back to it, gazing at myself. Seeing myself ogling her shamelessly, as she would have seen me.

And then it was over. I returned to myself, blinked, and took a step back. *What the hell was that?* I thought. I forgot about it when she smiled at me. From that moment, I *knew*. It was all over but the ritual, the dance, the preliminaries. I had to have her, and I would. On some level, I knew.

We chatted. We exchanged names. I told her my friends call me "Blue" and she admitted that she was from Elizabeth, New Jersey and that her name was Elizabeth. I resisted joking about that. I had just moved to Manhattan; she was only there for the day.

I knew other things about her. Things she didn't tell me. I knew what her bedroom looked like, and what her last boyfriend had said to her just before she broke up with him, and what music she listened to, and what her parents were like. It didn't occur to me to ask myself how I'd come to know these things. I was drunk on her, and I liked the feeling. I wasn't going to ask questions.

I knew, also, that she was only seventeen. I didn't care.

I looked at her lips. I swear to God I knew just what it would feel like to kiss them. And I knew that I would, eventually.

We had come to the awkward moment. She had to say goodbye and move away, or seem easy. I had to come up with some alternative.

Both of us waited for a few moments as I tried to think of something.

She smiled, seemed mildly disappointed, and said, "Well, I guess I'd better—"

"Have a cup of coffee with me?" I tried to look casual. I told myself that it was a lame thing to say, *have a cuppa coffee with me*. And after all, she could see I was past thirty. She'd be crazy to go out with me and I'd be crazy to take her out. There were laws.

But she said, "There's a pretty decent little cafe around the corner . . ."

It was a month—a month of meeting her a discreet distance from her school, of nights full of doubts, of necking in Central Park. A month before I worked up the nerve to meet her parents.

Elizabeth hadn't told them my age.

I'd talked to them on the phone, once. Her father said, "So this is the mystery boy!" Her mother said, "Well do come over for dinner Sunday, Blue, we'd love to meet the boy who's been occupying so much of our little girl's time." *Our little girl.* "She says you do some kind of journalism. For the college paper?"

I winced. "No, I write for the *Daily News*, Sunday Supplement usually."

"Oh? A cub reporter?"

My nerve failed. "Something like that"

That week, in anticipation of Sunday, the date after which we expected her parents to forbid me to see her, we made love for the first time. Our first time together, I mean: she wasn't a virgin. In fact, she taught me more than I taught her.

But I can feel her objecting to the direction this story is taking.

She says I can tell you about the drugs. I don't approve of them, usually. But that evening, trying to make love to her in my rickety studio apartment, I felt like a child molester. A grimy feeling. Made me tense. And tension made me impotent. So that's when she took the little black film container from her transparent plastic purse. The container didn't have film in it, though. "Demerol or coke?" she asked.

I'd never had either one, and here was this seventeen-year-old girl offering me both.

I looked at the bindle and the half-dozen triangular tablets and shook my head. But I said: "The Demerol."

I dropped two. Twenty minutes later I realized there was ice in me I didn't know about till it started to melt . . . I turned into warm water and flowed into Elizabeth's arms. What had been tense became relaxed, and what had been limp became rigid. I felt myself moving against her and she was silkier than silk and I was amazed to discover just how damn strong the muscles of her thighs were. Everything was working; we were shining together. I was a flashlight beam fanning over snow, making it glitter. There was a funny sense that I could feel my own touch as *she* felt it—in a sort of empathy, a somatic echo. Like I was sending a sonar pulse into her: the signal would fly to her, and she would experience it and alter it and bounce it back to me so I could experience her experience . . .

I communed with her, and reached a peak of ecstatic exchange.

And then the world was gone.

I was spinning through space. I was a fiery discus passing through a mirror image of itself. Somewhere, there was a wordless singing.

I found myself in bed with a rather gaunt young man of thirty-one. Good-looking fellow, really, with bright blue eyes. But I'm not at all gay, I was terrified by the positioning of things—until I realized who he was. Me.

With Elizabeth's hands, I touched myself—I mean, I touched Elizabeth's body with Elizabeth's hands.

And felt indescribably peculiar.

Elizabeth inhabited the body I'd departed. I touched that masculine face—how coarse my skin felt, from the outside!

Elizabeth smiled at me, with my lips.

There was an amorphous tug, and a negative shimmering. Through the Looking Glass, again. I was back in myself, or back in the rough chariot of flesh my actual self rides about in. Elizabeth returned to her own body. We had found our way back, tracing some ectoplasmic umbilicus.

My eyes opened wide and locked onto hers. The mutual knowledge, the mutual experience, crackled the space between us. Sweet sparks flew when I touched her.

You know how isolated most people are, most of the time? People who live together for years know a few camouflaging layers of each other's personality. Inside, they ache with loneliness.

A few of us have a talent that makes it possible to transcend the barrier between people. I'm not sure what it is, really. But it's genuine. No hallucination.

And we've got other talents.

We spent a blissful week meeting secretly. I helped her with her homework. I don't think she needed help, but she knew it made me feel good to play The Educated Male. In return—

No, no, I really needed help on the trig, Blue. Only, you made it worse.

Sorry. She took control for a moment. Great little kidder. Where was I? Oh: I helped her with her homework, and in return she criticized my feature story on the housing crisis—she said it was shallow, I vilified the landlords without taking their perspectives into account. I pretended she was wrong. We made love.

The exchange didn't always happen, when we had sex. It happened less than half the time. That was a relief, because it was a frightening experience, till I got used to it.

Even more frightening was the first occasion our *two* consciousnesses shared *one* body for more than a split second. For ten or fifteen seconds we cohabited in my body . . . while hers remained alive but somehow empty.

The cohabitation wasn't altogether pleasant. We had to learn how to communicate, as two minds in one body, without terrifying one another with a blizzard of random mental imagery. The first few cohabitations ended in confusion, our nerves overloaded, raw. Now, we've learned the internal dance, the revolving of polarized mental focus-points, making the sharing possible.

Sunday afternoon, I went to Elizabeth's house to meet her parents. I wore a suit, and maybe that was bad psychology. It was July; too hot for a suit. I stood on their doorstep, sweating, wires of tension knotting in my gut, waiting for someone to answer the door. I remember I kept picking flecks of lint off—it was a dark suit, all wrong for Summer. I *felt* Elizabeth coming to answer the door. The door opened and I had to fight myself. She wore a wrap around skirt and a bikini top. "Hi," she said, glancing over her shoulder. "Did you bring the—"

Just then her dad came to the door and interrupted her. But I knew what she'd meant. She'd asked me to pick up some blow for her. She worked after school part-time at a bookstore, and half her wages went to cocaine. She'd given me the money and I'd bought two grams for her; picked it up from her friends, dutiful as a husband stopping for a loaf of bread on the way home from work. I still refused to use the stuff, or even do a second dose of Demerol, and she made fun of me.

"So this is the mystery boy," said her dad, again.

I smiled and extended my hand. But he didn't shake it. The smile had left his face as he looked me over. "How old did you say you were, friend?" he asked, rather abruptly.

I was annoyed, and I opted for honesty. "I'm thirty-one," I said.

Elizabeth closed her eyes and swallowed visibly.

Mrs. Calder came to the door. They were the sort of couple who'd come to look like one another, over the years. Both were tanned, a little bulbous, their faces lined in the same directions. Mr. Calder asked me, leaning against the doorframe, "Buddy, what the hell you think you're going to get away with here? How stupid do you think we are?"

Elizabeth swore and walked into the house. I said, "I'm not a chiseler or a creep, Mr. Calder. I'm far from well-to-do, but I've got a good job and when your daughter comes of age, I'd like to marry her. When she's eighteen. In earlier times it wasn't uncommon for a girl of *fourteen* to be—"

"I'll have to ask you to leave."

I lost my temper. "Look—you're a hypocrite. If I was somebody really wealthy, Donald Trump or someone, but *forty*—you'd shake my hand and ask which caterers to use at the wedding. You wouldn't give a damn about my age. You and your wife are a couple of narrow-minded hypocrites who wouldn't know love if it bit you on the ass—" All right, it was stupid. But I was sure I'd never get to see Elizabeth again.

Elizabeth's father gave me a vicious shove in the center of my chest, making me totter backwards. I resented that. I returned to the doorstep, reached past him to a shelf just inside the door, snatched up a vase of water and wilted crocuses, and dumped it on his head. Sputtering, he knocked the vase from my hand and took a swing at me. I took a swing at him. No solid connections. His wife panicked and ran outside, shouting for the cops.

My luck: the guy across the street was an off-duty cop. He was a red-faced guy, smelling of suntan lotion, who trotted over in his thongs and Bermuda shorts and twisted my arms behind me before I had a chance to state my case. He was a big guy. I was not so big. He told Elizabeth's father to go through my pockets.

And then I remembered the cocaine.

I spent the next seven months in prison.

Possession of cocaine, first offense, and they'd just toughened the laws—good timing. Would have copped two years in that concrete rat maze, if it weren't for the Agremerol experiments.

Does that sound like I got off easy? *Only* seven months in prison?

You've already pictured it. You picture the over-crowded cells—cells crowded with men whose entire lives are just waiting periods between outbursts of rage. You picture the gang-rapes in the showers, the men drawing territorial lines, parceling out other men into allies and chattels and enemies; you picture the corrupt, indifferent guards, the smuggled drugs and, everpresent, the motion-less horror: the endless gun-colored claustrophobic confinement.

Well, you're wrong. It's different.

It's different, because it's worse. It's at least five times worse than you imagine. Take everything ugly you visualize for prison, multiply it by *five*, and you've imagined it right. That's because it's five times more crowded than it should be.

Elizabeth saved my sanity.

After her first visit to the prison, we decided not to see one another again, until I got out. At least, not through the wire mesh of the visiting room. It was torment. We had something better. She gave me a time, a very specific time. She would be in her bedroom, alone, at the appointed hour.

One A.M. . . . every Wednesday and Sunday. I'd open my eyes and stare into the darkness. I'd picture Elizabeth lying on her bed. I'd visual-ize her bedroom, her red-shaded lamp, the tree outside her window rus-tling gently against the pane in the breeze. Somehow the tree was a key, and helped the elements of the visitation fall into place . . . I'd seen her room once, before my run-in with her parents, meeting Elizabeth se-cretly when the Elder Calders were away. I'd concentrate on the picture and the darkness over my bunk would split, would fuse into two intense orbs of onyx: the pupils of Elizabeth's eyes. The vision of Elizabeth, in startling hypnogogic clarity, would begin with the eyes and fill itself in from there; her brow, nose, lips, her oval face, her spill of glossy black hair, her white shoulders shaded with olive-gold . . .

I would be one moment on a ratty bunk in the State Pen, seconds later I was lying on Elizabeth's fragrant bed, beneath a single soft blue sheet, a red lamp on the wall beside me laying a rosy tinge on the shadows.

Elizabeth was there, with me.

Once as a little boy, I'd shared a bed with my visiting cousin. Lollie and I were both five, and our parents thought we were too young too worry about. Our house was small, the beds few—they figured it was safe. We had a lovely time. I brought a flashlight under the covers, when the rest of the house was asleep, and we examined one another in fascination. The blanket over us, the atmosphere beneath steamy with body heat, perfumed with our natural scents—all of it made me feel that she and I had gone into a separate world together, where each shared the other's body. A world of innocent sensual sharing.

That's how I felt, then, with Elizabeth. Only, instead of our being un-der a blanket together, we were nestling within a single skin. We couldn't exactly *see* one another—it was a sort of blind mental groping with ghostly physical sensations. . . . But we were distinct entities. We never quite merged, and we never will. I have never completely identified with her, even now. It was like holding a woman close *from the inside*. And when I operate her body, it's like a particularly intimate dancing. I've never lost my sense of maleness. I don't feel female; I simply feel extraordinarily close to one.

When both of us occupied one body, either she or I would be in control of that body's movements at any one time. When she's in command of the body, I'm there, passive but conscious of what's going on, experiencing her physical sensations in a sort of reverberation. I don't hear all of her thoughts, unless she wills it. We are distinct, but intertwined, two djinn in one lovely, ornate bottle.

And when we make love . . . I could tell you about the secret chambers of her, the cellular singings in her, the electrical rushes I send racing through her nervous system. And then we trade muscular control, very quickly, so we can—

Don't tell them this.

Sorry, dear. It's just that it's an area of enthusiasm for me. And it's so rarely I get to talk to anyone outside you—

You *are* sick of me. I knew it! You—

No, no. Let's not go into that again, Elizabeth. Later. Anyway, I had a lot of time to think in prison. It was hard to think, at first, because the cells are so crowded, so noisy, and there were nineteen men in mine. Gambling for cigarettes, for syringes, for lighters, for candy bars, for sharpened bits of steel, for money, all the things they weren't supposed to have that they always managed to get. But you learned to close it all out, to lose yourself in the mental maze, to jog round and round the squirrel's cage in the skull. To keep from flipping out . . . All that thinking, together with a tattered science magazine in the prison library, synthesized a theory. Suppose that we each have two bodies, the visible body, cellular-organic, and the other a plasmic skein of subatomic wave particles, consciousness cohabitating with the body of flesh, inter-penetrating it, but capable of surviving outside it, given the right circumstances. I thought of it as the plasmic body. My plasmic body could leave my material body, and transmit itself, through some medium beyond my guesswork, to Elizabeth. It was possible for two plasmic bodies to cohabit in one material body, while the departed body waited in a sort of stasis, a self-imposed hibernation. It worked felicitously, with Elizabeth and I, because we were in love, because we accepted one another. But suppose a man was invaded by an unwelcome plasmic body? Hadn't it happened, before? It could explain the legends of possession.

And since it was possible to willfully manipulate my own plasmic body, might it not be possible to use it against someone else's? In prison, you're forever mulling the prospects for self-defense.

I was thinking about it, most particularly, since Tarnower had come to the cell. There were only three white guys in the cell. Tarnower was one of them.

Tarnower had a perfectly ordinary face, no doubt, as a boy. But he was one of those men who wore a single facial expression so long, it transfigured his features; his face was all whining resentment. Permutations of self-pity. Even in sleep, the same twisted sneer on his lips. His head was vaguely peanut-shaped, and he was potbellied, soft of limb, always twitching, looking to see if it was he being laughed at. He was in for dealing PCP.

Tarnower didn't like the fact that Brinker protected me. I'd had a year of law school, and Brinker prized me as his "in-house attorney." Brinker was the dorm heavy, and he protected me from rape, assault, and extortion. Tarnower had no protection, and he was constantly trying to turn the dorm hard-guys against me, implying I was a spy for the prison administration. He wanted to earn Brinker's gratitude by making it seem that he, Tarnower, had saved them from my treachery. And he hated me even more after the State Health Facility came around asking for volunteers in exchange for parole.

Volunteers for "experiments in drug abuse therapy." Several hundred of us applied, including Tarnower. I was accepted, and was told I'd be taken to the research facility the following morning. Tarnower was furious. He was sure he'd been overlooked because of me. Because, he claimed, he'd seen me "slip something to the guard." He managed to convince another lunkhead of the same thing. And I knew they were making plans to kill me. They'd been high on the list of volunteers. With me dead, there was a good chance one of them would be picked. A drag queen who'd taken a fancy to me told me all this. "You gonna fall and hit you head inna showers, honey," the queen informed me sweetly. "They make it look that way. You watch you ass now."

"I always watch my ass in the showers"

"That's two of us, honey."

So that set the killing for the next morning.

I waited till well after lights out. Most of the men were asleep. Tarnower sat up on his bunk, his back to me, talking softly to a Hispanic named Altino. Heavy-set man with stubby hands and sweat beading his upper lip; he shook with silent laughter at something Tarnower said.

I was doing more than watching them. I was focusing. I was reaching. Channeling some of my plasma body, extending it from my outstretched hands. It was as if I were reaching out with invisible extensions of my own hands; I pictured these plasmic hands as splayed and translucent, gelatinous, two membranes, one on either side of the two men across from me . . .

I brought the plasmic hands together, clapping their heads between. But the hands didn't strike them, physically. They passed through the skin and skull, like nets through water, coming into contact with the plasmic fields of the two cons, compressing them, tugging them together.

The men screamed, thrashed in confusion as their senses seemed to mingle. Altino splashed into Tarnower, Tarnower into Altino.

They'd been conspirators, not friends. They were frightened, small-minded men.

They clawed at one another, the room erupted with shouting, and somewhere alarm bells rang as the guards heard the uproar.

The next day, in the cafeteria, the story was told like this: "Yeah, it was Tarnower. He's flipped out—frothing at the mouth. That *vato* buddy of his, Altino—he's what they call a vegetable. He just stares, like, all day. Who knows what the fuck happened."

And in due course, after an uneventful shower, I was taken to the custody of dear Doctor Schusser.

I was paroled, but I had to participate in four weeks of experimental therapy, and I had to stay at the Jersey MHF research center's living facilities. I was allowed to see Elizabeth three hours a day; we met at a cheap motel. We made plans. She'd leave her parents on her eighteenth birthday, and we'd live together while she went to college in Manhattan. We had lots of lovely plans.

But it all waited on Schusser and Morgan. I had a nasty sinking feeling right from the start of my first conference with them. I sat on a couch across from two black vinyl armchairs; Morgan on the left, Schusser to the right. I thought of Tweedledee and Tweedledum. But it turned out they were more like Punch and Judy. Morgan was a brown suit man. Thought he was dressing tastefully and casually in his various shades of brown. He had a shapeless red beard and sandy hair; he was in his forties, always looked a little tired. Especially when he spoke to Schusser.

Schusser: late thirties, paunchy, typically wore gray slacks and a blue turtleneck sweater—even on hot days. Dandruff salted his shoulders.

Thinning, disarrayed black hair. Affected friendliness in his small brown eyes. There was a polished wood coffee-table between us on which was a yellow ceramic plant holder shaped like a shoe, with a long curl of greenery growing out of it.

I listened distantly as they reviewed my written application; I murmured monosyllabic replies when they asked me about my background. And fabricated a grand story, a harrowing history of drug abuse when they asked how I'd developed my "current problems with drugs," I had to seem a heavy user, to keep the parole. I lied brilliantly.

". . . to summarize," Morgan droned, "the experiment uses dream-time therapeutically. The key is a medication we call D-17, administered just before you sleep. It's a hypnotic, which, we believe, will make you unusually receptive to subliminal suggestion during dream-time . . ."

And a long, chill shudder went through me. I'd once written an article on research into the dream-state. There was just too little known about it to justify this kind of tampering. But I didn't want to break parole, to always be running. So I signed the papers. Lots and lots of papers.

There were four others in our lab's dorm. The experiments began immediately. That night. And for the first few nights, I noticed nothing unusual. I was told that, as we slept, some white-coated drip would whisper, "Drugs make you ill. Cocaine makes you nauseated. Heroin does nothing for you. Marijuana gives you a headache. You have no enjoyment of . . ."

The next day, Schusser and Morgan would test us, giving us small doses of controlled substances, so they could watch for the hoped-for aversion reactions. It didn't work; the drugs continued to feel good. Morgan blamed Schusser's "suggestion script"; Schusser blamed Morgan's dosage. More than once I heard them arguing in Schusser's office. I began to realize that they were working together reluctantly; some sort of state health department politics forced it on them.

They hated one another.

I and the three other subjects, who were black, weren't allowed to discuss the experiment with one another. But as the days passed, the haunted looks in their tired faces confirmed my suspicions. They were having a reaction to D-17 similar to mine. Nightmares.

"Nightmares" doesn't describe it. An understatement. Everything traumatic that had ever happened to me dredged up and replayed, over and over, magnified and exaggerated. I saw my mother dying of cancer again, but more vividly than I'd seen it in real life. I dreamed I would come home and find her in my bed, dying, wasting away. So I'd run to the bathroom— and she'd be in the tub. Dying. Wasting away.

I felt the nightmares more deeply, more palpably than I'd felt anything, ever.

I'd dream I was back in prison. Altino and Tarnower strangling me, holding my head in the toilet. And worse.

I'd wake up screaming, and I'd feel like living hell all day long.

Sometimes ghost images of the dreams would superimpose over my waking reality. I'd see Tarnower caressing the corpse of my mother, on the grass across from the park bench where I'd been trying to find some peace with Elizabeth. And the subliminal suggestions, after three weeks, still didn't work.

At the beginning of the fourth week, Schusser talked Morgan into tripling the dosage. I had the impression that Morgan was afraid they'd get into trouble—they were exceeding the legal limit.

I had a whole new season of nightmares. One in particular recurred night after night. On the third night, I woke up prematurely, screaming. I was in my own room—our screams had made it necessary to isolate us. I was awake, but I was still having the nightmare; I was hallucinating, my nightmare superimposed over the real world of the lab's bedroom.

I saw myself standing there—I saw myself as a separate entity. Only, the man I saw, standing over me—his breathing glutinously bubbling—the man had changed. The face was barely recognizable. It was hardly there at all. My face was deformed, crushed into a bloody mockery. And below, my gut was laid open, my entrails pendulously dangling. It shuffled toward me and bent to ram its long, gray dead-man's tongue down my throat. Choking me. I saw it bright as noonday. I clawed the EEG wires from my head and ran to the window. I was awake—but I wasn't, quite. I hesitated at the window. I turned. The thing was there, behind me, translucent but repulsive as a tumor; it hated me; it was malevolently rabid. I plunged through the window in a panic to get away. Anywhere away. A crash, crystalline explosion and four kinds of pain. Shouts from somewhere. Consciousness coming and going in the same vacillation as the warbling of approaching sirens.

The lab's dorm was six floors up. Under the window was a wrought iron fence topped with hard black spears. One of the spears split my liver. Another broke my spine in two. A third tore my face from my skull.

There wasn't much anyone could have done to repair it.

One of my eyes remained. With that eye I saw myself. I saw what remained of my face, in the outside rearview mirror of the ambulance as the medics pulled me free of the spikes.

The face I saw was the face of the thing in my nightmare. It was me, now, and always would be, if I lived. My new self-image.

My soul, or if you like, my plasma body, passed from me forever then, and fled along the psychic channels to another receptacle. My memories, my personality came along. I found a home forever in the body of Elizabeth Calder.

After a few days of mutual comforting and readjustment, we calmed into cool determination, and she asked me, "What are we going to do to them?"

Elizabeth was in control that night. I rode within her, watching as she opened the door to Schusser's office. There were Schusser and Morgan, arguing. Blaming one another for my death and the official inquiry. Never speaking a word of sincere regret for what they'd done to me. They sat close together, bent over their reports, sweating. Elizabeth raised her arms, opened her hands. We reached out, together.

Ten minutes later, the security guard found us. We sat in one of the black vinyl chairs, watching Schusser. He was lying on the floor, chewing a hole in his right bicep. His face was smeared with his own blood. Morgan, or Morgan's body, sat up on the couch, staring at the papers in its hand. Blinking now and then. Seeing nothing. Empty.

Morgan wasn't there anymore. He was with Schusser, very intimately with Schusser. Inside him. Struggling, screaming at him mentally, trapped forever.

And I'm in Elizabeth forever. It's a kind of paradise, really. But I wish you'd talk to her, convince her to let me out once in awhile. I could find another receptacle. It's not that I don't love her.

But she wants me *always* near her. She never lets me go. You see, a man's material body might be stronger than a woman's. But when it comes to a plasma body . . .

Elizabeth is much stronger than I am.

MORONS AT THE SPEED OF LIGHT

I was charged with inspiration: it was that kind of winter day in the city. The sun was bloodless but amiable, the icy air was still; it was as if the atmosphere had crystalized, become super-conductive of sounds and vibrations. I thought I could hear the heartbeat of the city, the collective beating of all those hearts in chorus; every tiny explosion in every piston-casing in every car engine; the air frightening and exhilarating with vibration. Do you get me, oh do you see? A resonant day, when ramifications normally inaccessible came into grasp like trained falcons returning to the wrist. The barren trees were the Earth's nerve endings; the sidewalk beneath them its tympanum.

And I was strutting through this exquisite medium, squinting at the sun, drinking in those vibes, coming back into touch with who I was now: a young man finding the center of his youth.

It was a long time ago.

That morning, I was thinking I ought to go back to school, after all, next semester, but I liked playing with the band more—but, after all, the U of O did offer me a full scholarship—but then I'd have to move down to Eugene—

And then I saw one.

You've seen them.

More and more of them, all the time more, in all cities. Goons, we called them as kids. Ozone Zeros. You'd probably call them *nuts*. This one was shuffling awkwardly along, stumbling and swaying. But you could tell he wasn't drunk or fucked up on reds—it wasn't that sort of stumbling. It seemed almost deliberate, like pratfalling.

He stepped onto the railroad tracks near Powell's bookstore, and started tightrope-walking a railroad rail. Suddenly impossibly adroit.

He was orating to the air, a gibberish soliloquy, flapping his long white hands before his grinning, twitching face, improvising doggerel for a line or two, then shouting threats at the leafless trees arching over the side-walk, along the street with the tracks in it. "Don't tell *me* I'm on both sides of the mirror you vegetable brains or I'll trim your sex organs but good, Pinocchio was underage and you could do *time,* monkeybars!"

He had one pants-leg tucked into his boot and one out, and his shirt sticking out in back and buttoned up wrong. An institution-blue shirt. His tennis shoes were laced in an intricate tangle, and his eyes were buzzing back and forth, scanning the air with equally intricate abandon. He seemed to be trying to see everything at once, and as a result seeing nothing. He leaned ahead as he walked, and he walked blindly.

I tend to call such folk morons, though, of course, the term doesn't clinically apply. They're not morons strictly speaking. My Dad called them that and it stuck with me, is all.

You pass at least one every day in a crowded city. It's amazing; how many of them there are, and how similar they are, and how frantic. I pitied them and wished I could help and wondered if they were actually happier than I.

The usual mixed emotions, when I looked at them. Revulsion and pity, empathy and compassion. And—

—for an instant, as he passed me (the third "moron" I'd seen that day), I looked closer than usual, looked into his eyes and he looked into mine—he saw!—our minds met at that instant, perhaps carried on the special tide of vibrations filing the air, the ordinarily inaccessible waves revealing to me his thoughts.

Help me, I wasn't always this way, they made me this way, there is a barrier between us, and I act in invisible dramas.

That's what I thought his glance said to me. It came into my mind not as words, but as feelings and pictures, and it was clear as day, as that crystalline morning.

Oh, shit. I was stricken. Buzzing on that flicker of revelation.

I turned to call him but something froze my tongue—he walked away. Or was carried away. I was left alone on that corner, thinking: he looks like a puppet dancing all clumsy on strings. Something is yanking him, sweeping him along!

I walked on, wondering what he had done, why this Unguessable Something had decided to consume the poor sucker.

And just two blocks later I saw another.

I was getting into downtown, now, Old Town, where the derelicts and tourists rub elbows, and a goon came stumbling out of a doorway. He was short-haired and clean, dressed pretty much like the others. Same symptoms. Declaiming nonsense like it was axiomatic to world affairs, a hebephrenic chatter, something like: "No I won't yes you will not them their ugly fingers yes you will no you won't, them and us tonight you cocksucker and ugly together a terrible cold uneasy parasites and night-mare-flesh-crevices thank you, you know now, thanks but no, no I know what . . ." And on.

I noticed there was a certain rhythm and a word mix that somehow matched the one the other "morons" recited. There came another, ten minutes later. Just as disheveled, hebephrenic harangue, a surrealist dia-tribe with that special rhythm, and the current, the recurrence of certain words in a pattern almost like a code, or like the return of prime num-bers, sometimes even like multiples of a given integer. Purposeful—in a cryptographic way.

The special air brought it to me, the unusual keenness that'd awakened in me. Some days you're just more awake than others; some days you realize how asleep you are on other days . . .

Sometimes paranoia confuses, switches the ball under the cups too fast for you to see, and you misread; but paranoia is a skill, and if you use it skillfully (and skull-fully?) it may prod you into being a little more awake; into discovering that consciousness is a direction, is in a certain direction: the least comfortable one.

I had stumbled into this . . . this method . . .

Using my senses consciously, honing my attention into a superthin psychic razor blade that split my neural channels like a sharp knife that divides a string; opening and exposing my senses, making them hurt for that extra edge of sensitivity.

But haven't you noticed it—that some days the goons, the twitchers, the voices crying out in their personal wildernesses, seem to be every-where, a sinister presence, as if they're on display, sort of in the back-ground of our living tableau as a *warning.*

I saw one after the other, and every one seemed to tell me something. A pattern in their jabber, in their Brownian motions down the street—gestalt patterns, a connective matrix of behavioral characters and it scared me. So after three hours I knew I needed help; a partner, I mean. Not "I needed help" like "I need therapy," okay?

I brought Jim Burbidge into it. Burbidge, he's a genius. Behind his gaunt, bird-like veneer a mighty mind hums. He's a technological avatar, is Burbidge. And I went and told him; we sat on those reed mats that make up the only furniture in his apartment. (Are bookshelves furniture? Bookshelves overflowed everywhere . . .). He stopped toying with the software he'd put together, software to make sense of Charles Fort; he listened with that urbane detachment of his, nodding his poor posture, and—he believed me. He sat and thought and dreamed awake, and my crossed legs went to sleep as I waited. He was a researcher for IBM, when he felt like it, and I almost expected a long tongue of computer tape to start unrolling from his mouth with the Answer.

But instead he said, "Let's meditate, man. My kind."

He was talking about the particular brand of mindfulness meditation he'd hatched: mostly with meditation you stay away from thinking, you step back from it, you stay alert and receptive, but you don't think—or anyway, you're not identified with the part that does. But Burbidge had a kind of mindfulness method—something he adapted from Raja yoga—that took command of our own inner "babbling hebephrenics," our free associating minds, and commanded that part of the mind to become something like a computer. The entire mind, not just some portion, engaged in the problem at hand . . .

I sat with my back straight; he sat across from me; we sank ourselves into the present moment, watched our breaths, and then we did that thing, the Burbidge variation . . .

A ball of scintillant ice expanded in my chest. It was a prism of attention, refracting our observations, revealing hidden ranks of color.

I knew how to do it then; in those days. I can't do it now. Too much has happened. I'm afraid to go that way, But then . . . then . . .

The lines of the room and the skein of that day's events seemed to superimpose, converge, and I could see my life in the geometries of the room. Burbidge looked up alertly, began to speak as if reading the words from the air. He said the connective behavioral linkage between the "morons," the street babblers, was a result of their suffering from the same mental disease with the same symptoms; symptoms resulting from the same dilemma; alienation from our defacing monster of a civilization, media bombardment, excessive input, data overload fugue; and no familiar ritualistic centers left in our lives, no believable social symbols for centering on. Shell shock from the modern world's war on your nerves.

Plausible. But—some instinct told me it was more. And uglier.

I suggested an experiment. If we recorded the morons' diatribes and codified that patterning and somehow unraveled the sub-sense of it, we could perhaps contrive a means to cure these poor suckers and get rich touting the procedure, write books about it, clean up like Janov and Bradshaw.

Burbidge protested, "We'd have to spend months at it! Do you have any idea how tedious transcribing tapes can be? And following ill-smelling lunatics around, acquiring the microphones we'd need, it'd lose its novelty fast, man. Take up all my time. Unlike yourself, Sparky, I *work*."

"Jim you're sick of IBM. They owe you bigtime, you solved that bubble-magnetism data-save problem for them, saved them millions on the new post-Crays. I almost threw the *I Ching* this morning—and if I had—I can picture it, right now, it'd say: 'Proceed with that which may seem extraordinary and time consuming and profit thereby.'"

"There's no such line in the *I Ching*—you know, the *I Ching* that you never actually threw? But okay. If we get nothing else from it, we can turn it into a conceptual art project and sell the transcriptions glued to concrete pillars—sell it to the Museum of Modern Art for a half a million bucks."

It wasn't easy. We gave it up and started again eight or nine times. But Burbidge had a lot of money saved and we had more momentum than Jimmy Carter in '76.

I told you, this was a while ago.

After two months of meticulously recording their harangues and filming their pathways (like neural pathways in the mind of the city), their wanderings down the street, tracing it from rooftops, we were able to graph and codify their patterns-in-common and oh yes . . . the parallels, one "moron" to the next . . .

Oh yes . . .

Burbidge translated it all into computerese. Slipped it into one of the BIG computers, at work. We got results. Three weeks later we confirmed the math . . . and we had three solid results of all that apparently meaningless labor.

1) An equation for the Unified Field Theory
2) A diagram for an inertialess faster-than-light drive, utilizing aspects of the UFT equation
3) A chemical formula for a remarkable fuel which applies to the diagram for the FTL drive.

That's right. We had it right there in our hands. We told no one. It was going to take time to figure out how to demonstrate all this—and then there was the question of applying for patents . . . We didn't want it all stolen, but . . .

We figured our fortunes were made. Still, we prudently decided to find out why it had all come from the "morons". Because there was that tantalizing background hum in the whole phenomenon that seemed to imply *external interference.*

So we checked with the welfare agencies that took care of gibberers, and found out just who they'd been, before.

As a rule, I'm embarrassed to be seen reading the *National Enquirer*—but maybe I'll check it out more often. Because Burbidge showed me an article that appeared there last year remarking on the very odd rise in mental illness among research scientists.

Burbidge and I got together at his apartment, sat in his personal meditation, contemplated the data—and had a simultaneous fit of insight: almost a dual theoleptic revelation. Then we checked the records and confirmed it.

Most of our "morons" were former chemists, physicists, engineers, systems designers, mathematicians. But not all of them. Eight were former journalists, investigators—i.e., just people who'd come too close to the facts. And these people had stumbled onto certain things, certain big things, and someone stepped in and did a cruel number on them. Changed them. With what? With a machine that makes them mad.

We found the machine, too. It took pressure from Burbidge's older brother, the Marion County District Attorney, to get the hospital records, the notes on the "experiments." We found two machines, actually, and God knows how many more there are about the country. We found one at Hardin Hospital, New York City, and one in Salem's State Hospital, in Oregon. Insane asylums. At Hardin, and the Salem nut-house, is what is known as "an experimental electronic therapeuter," EET for short.

These EETs enclose the patient like electronic sarcophagi, mummy cases that mummify a portion of the living brain. They—and I mean THEY, the Ones who have insinuated themselves into the body of our society—they put the poor guy into the EET and "rephrase the neural channels" (as the hospital files have it), supposedly to straighten the guy out. Which is funny, isn't it, cruel funny, considering what it does to them. Why'd they keep using "therapeutic" devices that demonstrably made patients worse? It was part of a "Federal Program" and in order to keep getting the money from the program, the hospitals had to continue the experiments under the direction of certain Federal Researchers. Follow the money.

Only those Federal Researchers aren't really Federal Researchers. Of course.

The conditions under which the so-called patients were first arrested are only vaguely alluded to in the files, though former associates and family insist that in each case the researcher in question was fine, just fine, even exhilarated (as if after a great discovery), the day before he or she was "taken into custody." The day the patient was taken a totally unprecedented behavior arose—a wildness, a violence consistent with certain obscure psychotropic drugs, Burbidge says. They secretly dosed their victims, made them temporarily crazy—took them into custody, then destroyed their minds with EET. Scrambled eggheads. Better than killing them—calls too much attention to them, to kill them.

Every EET "patient" had been working on something to do with the Unified Field Theory, the drive, the fuel. We only know this through conversation with friends, family. Their notes, computer files, experimental hardware vanished, of course.

But. The Big Discovery, being of paramount importance in the "moron's" former life, naturally emerges in his or her behavioral code, just as we all exhibit unconscious obsessions in the emblematic expressions of our entrenched day to day habits.

So who were They? How had They found the scientists who were to be their victims? If somebody were monitoring computers used by research scientists, looking for certain *types* of equations . . . You get it.

But who was Somebody?

If they were *really* government men, someone by now would have used the power in those equations—in weapons, in space travel, in some practical way to shore up our national power. And our country would have no military rivals, anywhere. We'd have imposed our will on the world by now . . . Or it would've been given to whatever huge corporations currently controlled the White House and they'd be making money off it.

So follow the absence of money. If not the money—the motive. Who would benefit from suppressing this stuff?

Take an E out of EET. No, I don't think they chose the acronym on purpose. Maybe God put it there, to hip us to it. The ETs don't want us to invent certain things; perhaps they think we're too innately aggressive to know what they know. We can't be trusted. So they conceal agents amongst us, these extraterrestrials, some of whom acquire posts of influence and affluence, and they use this influence and afluence to institute the ET devices which in turn institute our suppression.

And poor Burbidge . . .

We were in his apartment, arguing about what to do with the formulas. We had it all right there with us. I said: Run! Hide! He said: Go to the FBI! And as we were arguing, *They* came, and took Burbidge. I hid in a closet, as they were breaking down the door. I guess they didn't know about me, because they didn't look for me. They must've been monitoring IBM's Portland facilities. And They got *all* our notes and records on Those Three Things. The key to star-flight, to immeasurable power.

And I didn't see Burbidge again for months. Till the summer after. I saw him at Fourth and Broadway explaining to a steel lamp post that he had nothing against it personally, but he could not commit himself to it for any serious length of time due to the shapes of the clouds at three, seven, and nine o'clock Eastern Standard Time.

Sure, I tried the FBI. You know what *they* thought. And as I tried to leave their offices the Men In White came to get me . . . Just for an "evaluation," they said, in the hospital.

I had been half expecting it, though, and I ran back into the building, and out through the parking garage. And that's why I've been hiding out in San Francisco, panhandling, playing the part of a guy—a *harmless* guy—who took too much acid, way back when.

"Don't point that at me, dude."

Hey man, it's just a squirt gun—right? Or is it? I *know* what it is—and I know what you are. Okay? This looks like a raygun-style squirtgun. Like one of those transparent toy raygun squirt guns at the five and dime store.

"They don't have five and dime stores anymore. You've been wandering Haight Ashbury too long. Now if you'll excuse me—"

Waitaminnut now—You think I'm doing nothing all these years? I've been experimenting, found that certain variants on LSD can reveal who among us are the ETs and who human. And they're sensitive to water if you mix it with certain chemicals—I got a clue from this one book by Philip Dick—he intended the book as a message for me, it's obvious he'd found out the same things -

"Don't squirt any chemicals on me either. I paid you to tell me your story, it's going to go into my paper on street people in the Haight, and that's it, we're all done, so if you'll let go of my arm—no don't squirt that stuff on me . . . oh Jesus . . ."

Come on, come outside, that's it—just here, to the sidewalk. Now—the stuff is water mixed with DMSO and the psychedelic variant that—ah. You see? You see?

You're beginning to see it. You do! No, don't scream, that'll attract Their enforcers, the ones who dress like cops. You see how many of Them there are?

And even the lamp post knows. No, not that one—that one over there. It knows, man. It knows. I told it so a thousand times—and it did not contradict me.

REALLY, REALLY, WEIRD STORIES

Silent Crickets

The milky moonlight, sifted by mercuric clouds, snickers through the dense woods in slippery shafts. The faint light laps at the crotches of trees and catches on tangles of bated branches, giving the moss the silver sheen of mold. The deciduous trees are in bunches infrequently invaded by a lone pine. Roots are choked with fallen leaves. Bared branches are abstracted into atmospheric capillaries. In the inky shadows under a short conical fir tree a man crouches with a rifle in his right hand. He moves slowly forward, trying to make as little noise as he can, and creeps into the crater left by an uprooted pine. The huge dying pine is lying on its side, smaller frustrated trees crushed under its trunk; its roots are thrusting up over the man's head. He hunkers in the shallow pit, his booted feet gripping the mud, rifle barrel catching the light and tinting it blue. The only sound is the *chirr* of a sneaking raccoon and the repetitive song of the crickets.

The crickets go abruptly silent.

The man is on the alert.

Something moves invisibly through the woods. He tenses, raises the .36, props the gunstock against his right shoulder, finger tightening around the trigger. He reaches for the safety catch. *Is it one of them?*

The figure emerges.

It's a man, a man alone. The man with the gun, Buckley, curator of the Deepwood Museum of Modern Art, stands and waves. The stranger, his face only partially visible, nods and comes forward. He stands silently a few feet from Buckley, looking at the long rifle upright at the curator's side. The man wears dungarees and a white long sleeve shirt. The night conceals most of his features.

"Are you Buckley?" He asks in a low, oily tone.

"Yes."

"I'm . . . Cranshaw. I'm from the New York Art Association. I've been looking for you. I believe your story . . . more or less. I want to hear it from your own lips, anyway. I've had a similar . . . experience. I came to talk to you in your study and your servant—she was quite flustered—said that you'd run out here after burning the paintings. A strange business, Buckley, burning eight hundred thousand dollars worth of Miró and Matta and Picasso . . ."

"How many kinds of sexual reproduction are there?" Buckley asks, his voice sounding strange to him in the sucking darkness.

"Well . . . there's mitosis and cross-pollination and among humanity there's good old—"

"Among humanity there's something *else*," Buckley interrupts, speaking in a rapid clip. "A mutation. Have you heard it said that an artist doesn't create a 'new' vision, but only siphons it from another dimension of reality where that abstraction is the physical law? Perhaps. Perhaps if the abstract or surrealist artist steals from that world's images, from that other plane long enough, the creatures inherent to that world will take an interest in us and contrive to come here. Perhaps they'll use us as a medium, transferring themselves through a kind of paintbrush insemination. I keep thinking of the words of the dadaist Jean Arp: *Art is like fruit, owing out of man—like the child out of its mother* . . . Someday, Cranshaw, a child will replace its parents."

"Maybe. Come back to your study and we'll talk about it—"

"No. Haven't you been reading about all the artists who've been disappearing? Well, I was visiting Matta when I *saw* something happen to him. I can't describe—"

"All this is interesting but rather xenophobic," the stranger interrupts. "My experiences were not so much like yours as I had thought. It's not easy to be a curator these days, God knows. Those snotty young painters. But come back and have a drink with me, Buckley. We'll work things out from there. Don't be afraid." He reaches out a hand to Buckley's shoulder.

Buckley steps backwards, his hand tightens on the barrel of the gun. If this man is from the Art Association, why is he dressed like a country hick? Cranshaw touches Buckley's shoulder. Suspicions confirmed. Buckley feels it then, the warning tingle, the onrush of activated abstraction. He steps back again, raises the gun. "You lied to me," he murmurs as much to the night as to Cranshaw.

Another movement from the far side of the fallen tree catches his eye. Pure moving anachronism issuing from the areola of upturned roots. It was the abstract figure of Marcel Duchamp's *Nude Descending A Staircase* given its own independent life. A study of strobed motion, the exegesis of a few moments of time into cubism. The creature, viewed literally, glowing against the tenebrous curtain of the woods, resembles a robot strung in Siamese twin extrapolations of itself, leaving behind a hallucinogenic acid trail like a mechanical cape. It might be built of copper-colored tin cans and its torso (futurist extrapolation of pivotal rotation) is built in striations like the gills of a shark. Moving toward Buckley, it is a random tumble of spastic geometry, a carnivorous handy kitchen appliance. The figure is a vector for the bizarre, leaving behind it a wake of abstracted trees, brush distorting into a vision of Siamese triplet belly dancers; tree trunks made Rousseau primitive and perfectly cylindrical-smooth, branches becoming pin-cushion spines. But the voice of the vector is human.

"I couldn't wait any longer. I had to come. Has he been readied?"

"No," the stranger who called himself Cranshaw replies, "not just yet."

"Buckley," came the voice from the golden arachnid whirlpool, "come here."

Buckley pulls a slim penlight from his pocket and shines it on Cranshaw's face. He gasps. A Modigliani simplification, that face, with pits of Munch hollowness around the eyes. The man, while outwardly proportional, is made of rigid planes, unmoving eyes, the same perpetual sardonic smile two inches to the left of his nose. One of his eyes is considerably higher than the other. His arms are blocked into rectangular surfaces with ninety-degree corners.

"It's all right," says the Cranshaw-thing, its voice fuzzy now. "Don't worry." It reaches out a squared-off hand to Buckley's upraised rifle, touches the barrel with a gentle caress at the same moment that the curator touches the trigger.

The gun doesn't go off. There is a conspicuous silence. Instead of an explosion, comes a faint puffing sound. A globular bullet bounces like a soap bubble off Cranshaw's chest and floats up through the clawing trees. Desperately, Buckley feels the barrel of the gun. It sags in his fingers like an exhausted erection, rubbery and pliant. He breaks off a piece of the barrel and puts it to his mouth. Licorice. The gun melts into a snakelike abstraction. He flings it away but already the tingling chill is traveling up his arm. He looks at the two abstract beings standing patiently by, sees them reticulate and waver like an unstable TV picture. He looks down at his body, sees his legs sprout roots which rapidly burrow into the humus under his new hooves.

SCREENS

Out there the air is toxic; the land is nearly barren. The sky, even at noon, is the bruised color of mud at a city dump. The oozing plain has the sheen of a puddle coated with gasoline: a slick of diseased rainbows. It would eat away my skin if I were to step into it unprotected.

In here, it's safe, stainless, warm, shaded in amicable colors, with clean air and plenty of food and room to stroll.

I'm leaving here forever, and I'm going out there.

Into the murk that twitches, from time to time, with the clumsy movement of the subhumans. I'm going out there when I conclude this log. This is the final entry, my last tape record, my assessment of conditions on Earth at the date of my return.

I was born about 250 years ago, in Austin, Texas. I should have died around, I suppose, 140 years ago. I wish I had. If I hadn't married Freda, I would have.

I met Freda Gunderson at Solarsong Farm, in New Mexico. It was winter when we met. More than two centuries ago. In the spring of that year, she asked me to marry her.

The desert, unfolding beyond the adobe walls of the Hackman hacienda grounds, was stippled soft orange and blue with cactus flowers. Near the balcony a mellow wind stirred one of the palms that Hackman had transplanted, so that it nodded like a drunk musician over a piano.

In nightgown and bathrobe, Freda and I were sitting at the second-floor terrace, overlooking the thoroughly irrigated garden, listening to the shuss of the sprinklers, the chatter of some desert bird who'd happened on this oasis and couldn't believe his luck.

Freda's red-gold hair and fair skin and blue eyes seemed an extension of the garden, to me; the arc of her full breasts in the filmy blue negligee was in thematic concordance with the great arc of the planet around us. We held hands and sipped tea, and all the trivial things we said seemed to brim over with the significance of intimacy. OK, sure: I was in love.

And I was impressed with her. Freda was an arcological scientist, with master's degrees in botany, zoology, and climatology. Most people are lucky to have one master's. Freda, at thirty-four, had three. But then, she'd graduated from high school at thirteen years old.

"It's good to see you happy this morning, Ricky," she said. "You're moody, most of the time." Her English was perfect, but her faint Swedish accent clung to her talk like some intoxicating ethnic perfume.

"I'm moody? I guess it's this place. It's a little too perfect here. Maybe a little too civilized for me. And Glass's people—" I glanced down at the glinting lozenge of the huge greenhouse, a hundred yards away, on the far side of the mansion's grounds. "—watch us all the time." You could see out from the greenhouse, but you couldn't see in. They had long-range surveillance cameras there, I knew. And they set watches on us when we walked about the grounds or went into town. "Daniel Glass is security paranoid."

"I know what you mean," she said diplomatically. "But I think you and Glass have more in common than you like to admit. You both love the Gaia. The natural world. Glass is a poet, too."

I winced, remembering Glass's poetry, recited after one of his Vibratory Sermons. Some ghastly Castenada-ish number about the Cactus Spirits Holding Up The Sky. Mawkish stuff. My analytical left-brained Freda wouldn't know good poetry if it nibbled her earlobe.

"Glass is a poet *technically*," I said. "But mostly what he is—" I hesitated, conscious that we were probably being recorded, and then plunged recklessly on, "—is a despot. A puppeteer. He's got Hackman in his pocket. He makes us sit on those New Age cushions while he preaches his New Age drivel—not only drivel but fifteen years outdated—about merging into a new society of 'vibratory harmony.' Preaching self-denial and screwing half the women in the project—The guy is a classic *cult leader*. Going to lead us all to the promised land in the sky."

"The Starsong colony is not Glass's idea. It was Dr. Branheimer's. And Papa's."

"That's the point, Freda." I let go of her hand and brushed my hair out of my eyes. My thick black hair had grown long and unruly, and I'd let my beard grow. Freda's father, Dr. Gunderson, didn't approve of my style. He wasn't enthusiastic about Freda's romance with a liberal arts major, anyway. "Glass has co-opted your father's ideas." I glanced to the east, where the sun had just risen over the big geodesic dome that was the Arcology Model, the self-sustaining ecological unit that the project wanted to replicate in the L-5 orbit. I could see one of the guards from the Glass family crossing the lawns between the dome and the hacienda-styled mansion that Hackman had given over to the project personnel. The guard was a long way off, but I could make out the glint of his tacky golden-sun medallion, with its green-glass center; I could imagine his tightly beatific smile, which never wavered as he checked in with the other guards on his 'fone, using code names like Laser and Aurora and Icemelt. Every one of them a former junkie or acidhead or near schizophrenic basket case that Glass had put back together in his own preferred reconstruction; making them utterly dedicated to the American-born guru.

"It's useless to complain about Glass. Hackman adores him. And the project is all Hackman's money and the money of Hackman's business associates. Half a billion dollars of it. Glass is part of the project to stay." She stood up, came around the table to sit by me, to take my hands. Something about the thought-out formalism of the act rang a warning bell in my head. "Ricky . . . while you were in Santa Fe, they made a decision. Glass has convinced them to move up the date of the final launch. We're going to the colony—I mean, the project is going. Soon. Next July. A little over a year." Stricken by the implications, I stared at her. She went on hastily, "You can go with us, Ricky."

"Come off it. I'd be dead weight. I'm a literary academic. Useless! Just another guy pawing through the Lake poets, and Whitman, Jeffers, Blake—and Yeats and Byron when they were feeling close to nature. *Those* are my people. I don't belong on a space colony. I'm not technophilic enough. And Glass would never tolerate me—he knows how I feel about him."

"You've helped this project a lot," she said earnestly, looking me in the eyes. "You wrote the best promotional material; it helped us get a lot of backers. You know a bit about environmental science, you're willing to work in the land—Dr. Branheimer said you were a lot of help in the greenhouse—and if you were to marry me, that would make it definite. They would *have* to let you come."

"Me. Sure . . . Freda, I don't *want* to go. I like the idea of the arcology in the sky. I like the chance to preserve a lot of plant species and animal species, away from the acid rains. But I don't want to *live* there. There's another way—you can stay here on Earth and work to save it. With me."

"I can't, darling. I just cannot. It would break my father's heart. And I have given my life to this. It is what my father and I always planned for.

I have to go. If you love me, you'll go with me. We can come back some-time, Ricky . . ."

But we never did.

We were married two days later. And two *years* later—it took them a year longer than they expected—we took the shuttle to the low-orbit sta-tion, and then took one of Hackman's new freighters to the Starsong colony in the L-5 orbit. The colony was, as I knew it would be, cramped, malodorous, gravitationally inconsistent, and an endless prescription for work that was never quite filled.

It was growing, though. Module by module, it expanded into the void And after a year and a half of murderously tedious work, of enduring the claustrophobic stink of pressure suits, and after losing two men and a woman to faulty sealants in the EVA units . . . it was beginning to pay off. The colony's garden in space was thriving and we were starting to manufacture the zero-g gimcracks that Hackman had hoped would make his money back for him. The pressure was easing. We decided to give ourselves a holiday . . .

Glass didn't share our optimism. Glass, in fact, didn't share anything with us but what he had to. The rest of the time he holed up in his dorm section with his toadies. He hadn't found paradise on the colony, and he sure as hell hadn't converted any new followers; worse, he'd had to actually *work*. And he was convinced the U.S. government—which had in fact tried to stop the project, claiming it was "uncontrollable and danger-ous"—was out to get him. So when Hackman announced that he'd au-thorized a couple of senators to come up and check us out, Glass de-cided they were spies for the Pentagon. "The Pentagon wants to take us over so it can launch a first strike against the PanArabic Republic from here!" Glass raved. "They'll make the colony into an orbital missile base! They'll start World War III!"

We laughed at him.

So Glass simply appeared on the colony's TV monitors one morning, announcing that we had to make "the ultimate sacrifice" in order to "prevent the fascists from destroying life on Earth!"

Glass—forgive me—had cracked. To be fair, Earth was experiencing a vigorous political upheaval just then because of the Famine . . . What was going on below us was enough to make anyone believe the end of the world was coming. Because it was.

You know about the Famine? Maybe you don't—no telling when anyone's going to hear this. The Famine came because . . .

It came because in the twentieth century we thought we had plenty of time to deal with the air pollution problem. The atmosphere was vast, and we were cutting back on pollution. A little. But that thinking reckoned without synergistic reactions. It assumed that the wild variety of random chemicals released into the atmosphere would just sort of float around harmlessly. Stupid thinking. Some of them reacted with one another, and with other environmental factors. We should have seen it coming in the 1980s, when sulfur dioxide and other chemicals combined to form acid rain, began gnawing at the biosphere . . .

But it was in the year 2018 that the sky fell apart.

The phenomenon hit the news media a week after Freda and I moved to the colony. It started with the catalyst. Terranoxin was a compound released into the air by a variety of industrial polluters. By itself, Terranoxin was not found to have a negative environmental impact; but a dissolution of the ozone layer had radically increased ultraviolet radiation. And Terranoxin, exposed to UV radiation, experienced a synergistic reaction that boosted it into a catalytic compound capable of runaway instability. It formed a slick on plant surfaces, which forged a long chain of inert molecules binding oxygen and nitrogen into itself. Essentially, it ate the oxygen and nitrogen produced by living things. Carbon dioxide continued to be produced, but oxygen and nitrogen weren't. The reaction *began* small—but a catalyst will work through its medium and survive; a catalyst is capable of expanding exponentially. We had succeeded in making pollution that made pollution. Pollution that reproduced. The atmosphere's ability to absorb and filter pollution was overwhelmed and quickly became irrelevant.

Oxygen and nitrogen were rapidly diminishing; the air was becoming unbreathable. Animals died; the food chain was shattered. People moved into narrower and narrower enclaves of breathable air. Great hurricanes of poisonous air swept over the land, smothering whole cities. The disruption turned cropland into dust bowls. Oxidation of ocean-dumped organic wastes and the pernicious action of pesticides worked with Terranoxin to destroy the oxygen-production capability of the seas.

The world moved indoors. The urban domes were hastily thrown up— and many were almost as quickly torn down in the riots. Only the wealthy could afford a healthy diet, even in the U.S. And the consequent stress on the planet's social systems generated massive political strife. Sure, Glass: it was easy to be paranoid.

Glass—with his pinpoint pupils, his shaven head, his anorexia—had always been a paranoid, manipulating his followers with a masterful paternalism to close ranks around him. To be an extension of him, a buffer against the world.

So I can't say I was surprised when Glass opened the air locks, and sabotaged the life-support seals.

I was doing a systems check on the escape pods when it happened. I was the only one near enough to use them. I heard the others screaming through the intercom. It was more horrible hearing it filtered. It was like they had a big mechanical hand clamped over their mouths. I thought: *Get into a pressure suit; find Freda.*

That's when I saw the suits. Slashed. Glass had been ready for this for a while.

The air was going. Understand that. *The air was going.* Freda was on the other side of the colony, working in the agribubble. The instruments told me it was one of the first sections to become a vacuum. She was a goner.

There was nothing I could do. I tell myself that all the time.

I was numb. Mechanically, I got into the escape pod. I set it for ejection, and I hit the switch that would put me in suspended animation until I was picked up and rescued.

As the gas put me under, I realized that the pod's ejection system had been sabotaged. It should have launched immediately. Eventually, the suspended animation would reach its limits . . . So I was going to die, too. The guilt that had frozen my nerves melted away. I was flooded with relief. I was going to die with Freda, after all.

That was all right with me.

The suspension gas is supposed to preserve you for about three hundred years. Theoretically. Some people claim it'd work for only a few decades. No one had had a chance to test it out. I've got news for the skeptics.

I don't know why the pod ejected from the dead hulk of the colony, after more than two hundred years. Maybe a meteor strike, jarring some damaged mechanism into action. Or a long-term effect of radiation on the pod's launch systems. I don't know. But . . .

After two hundred years the escape pod launched itself.

Their orbital drones, maintaining the city's solar-power transmission stations, picked up the pod's signal and brought it down. More or less automatically. Nothing humane about it. They put me down a few miles outside the city, where the airport used to be.

I didn't stir from the pod for a couple days. I'd used almost no measurable oxygen in suspension, so there was a few days' worth left. I spent them feeling like a warmed-over corpse, which was maybe what I was. I *looked* OK—but I had mental images of old horror movies I'd seen as a kid. George Romero stuff about walking corpses. Rotting faces. That was my self image for those two days.

Still, I sucked down the electrolytic solution, I ate the mash, and when I could make myself work, I repaired the pressure suits. Looking out the ports, I saw the acid ooze, the nightmare sky; could see that the atmosphere was pitting the pod's window glass. Maybe it wasn't Earth.

But when the weather cleared, I saw the pale, familiar face of the moon, like the dying face of a sick old man. And I saw the curving gleam of the dome, rising smudged and segmented, at the horizon. Big as a mountain.

Kansas City.

A grief. A terrible grief that could not be encompassed by any poetry I could fashion. Beyond the sick grief and horror of a mother who has missed her child for days, and finds his body broken and rotted in her own well, and wonders how long he'd suffered down there . . . Past the grief of a man who realizes that, through his own bumbling self-indulgence, he has infected his wife and newborn baby with AIDS. Even more than grief for Freda. Grief for a planet.

They hadn't found a way to contain or reverse the catalyst. Or if they did, it came too late.

Protected, for a while, by the pressure suit, I slogged through the bogs toward the dome. The sky was a ceiling of cobwebs. I remembered some lines from Gerard Manley Hopkins:

> *Generations have trod, have trod, have trod;*
> *And all is seared with trade; bleared, smeared with toil,*
> *And wears man's smudge and shares man's smell: the soil*
> *is bare now, nor can foot feel, being shod.*

> *And for all this, nature is never spent;*
> *There lives the dearest freshness deep down things;*
> *And though the last lights off the black West went*
> *Oh, morning at the brown brink eastward springs—*

But that was the bitterest drink at the wake: Hopkins was wrong. There would be no morning at the brown brink eastward. They had killed the world, finally. Or the world as I knew it. There was life here, of a sort, in the poisonous ooze. But it was life the way obscene doggerel on a bathroom wall is poetry.

And Freda was dead. I wanted to be dead, too.

Maybe it was curiosity. Maybe it was the faint hope that they might have preserved something green and something feathered under the dome. There might be many such areas of preservation; they might be, ironically, terraforming the Earth somewhere.

I used to have a fair torch for hope in me. It was down to a pilot light on a grimy gas oven now. But it still burned.

The air lock was a man-high square panel flush with the dome. I cleaned away some of the gunk that clung to the lower part of the dome; read the blocky, flaking lettering: KANSAS CITY: ARLK 56.

I had radioed to them, and received no reply. Perhaps my radio was faulty, or they weren't monitoring those frequencies anymore. Or perhaps they didn't care if I died out there.

But the air lock opened, sliding creakily aside. I stepped into a featureless chamber of milky plastic walls. Startlingly pristine, after the bogs. The lock sealed behind me. Poisonous air drained away; breathable air hissed in. A green arrow flashed overhead. I unscrewed the helmet. Brassy smells. Plastic. Detergent.

A ball of warmth expanded in me. I was going to see someone alive! Maybe there'd be a welcoming committee and a big to-do. Fine. Let them paw me, gape at me, tear my clothing for souvenirs. It was all human contact. It was healthy life. It was a stinging reply to the flat gray hopelessness I'd crossed through on my way here. I needed human contact.

The smooth, waxy wall dilated an opening. Beyond was a long, empty hallway. They had to decontaminate me. I followed the hallway to its end: a shower room where a gray uniform hung on a peg.

I stripped and showered. I could smell a disinfectant in the water. Germ-killing ultraviolet lights came on in the ceiling as I dried. I dressed in the uniform: soft, durable paper of some kind. I felt it contract to conform to my shape as I zipped it up.

Padding down the hall in my soft gray slippers, I came to an elevator. The doors parted. Something within was examining me. It was a dull chrome sphere about two feet in diameter, with two knobs at opposite poles, either side. It rolled toward me like a beach ball. I had the distinct impression it was observing me.

Was this all that was left? The automatons of the place? Had the inhabitants died and left their robots to eternally maintain the empty city as a pointless monument to them?

I took a deep breath to calm myself. "I'm Richard Gale Mazursky. From the Starsong colony. I've been in suspended animation—according to the suspension computer in the escape unit, it was, uh, for more than two centuries. Look—can you take me to a . . . a person?"

It rolled back into the elevator. I accompanied it, and we rode silently down many, many levels.

We arrived at another bland corridor, pale blue walls, the ceiling faintly glowing, plush white synthetic rug. Muzak was playing from somewhere; so homogenized I couldn't make out any definite tune. I accompanied the machine through an archway into a simple apartment. A room, fifteen paces to a side, containing soft dun rectangular couches, slots in one wall, and a toilet. A large screen on the wall was lit, and on it, waiting, was a ?. A question mark. A big black one. Followed by an old photo of myself. It had been taken not long before I went up to the Starsong colony. It was a blowup of my small corner of a group photo, a publicity shot of the project planners. My expression was rueful, faintly impatient; beside me, all that was visible of Freda was her shoulder. My gut contracted, and I looked at the floor. "Yeah, that's me. Or was me."

I looked up at the screen as a picture of the colony appeared. Then an X was marked over it. And a question mark.

"Yeah. It's gone. I'm pretty sure I'm the only survivor. Was I right? Is it a couple of centuries since I went under?"

A + appeared on the screen. A plus. Positive. Meaning affirmative.

A picture of a food tube appeared on the screen, and then a question mark.

I wasn't hungry. Moths with razor wings jittered in my stomach. "No, thanks. Look, I mean it this time—*I want to see some people.*"

The silver ball rolled out the door behind me. There was no way to shut the door. It was only a slice out of the wall.

There they were. People. And a big luminous gray-white screen. The screen filled half the wall and dominated the room. The other three walls were gentle pastels of blue, green, and yellow; everything I was to see was done in the same reductionistic simplicity. No decor, a few cushions. On these were four people with their backs to me.

They were dressed in bright colors, and their clothing was jumpsuit-styled like mine, but with no two cut precisely alike. The primary colors of their clothes bled as if tie-dyed, spreading out from the centerline of the body. It reminded me of a fad that had been going before Freda and I left Earth. Kirlian clothing. It responded to your bioelectric field, and changed colors, eventually set in color patterns that were supposed to be distinctive to you. Their hairstyles were similar—sort of pixie-ish, sort of pageboy-ish, but each was faintly distinct.

Their eyes were fixed on the screen, rapt but placid, as if listening with great respect, though the image was soundless.

I was afraid to speak at first, to break the pervading sense of rapport. The ambience was fragile with it. I felt as if I were intruding on a church service.

What was I doing here? Maybe I was a bad memory, to these people.

But I needed them. The hunger in my hands made my fingers tremble for human touch; the hunger in my lips burned for conversation. "Uh—hi. I'm . . . excuse me, the robot brought me here . . . I'm Richard Mazursky."

No reaction. The chrome ball rolled out of the room, and I had the odd feeling I was left alone. The people on the couches hadn't moved hadn't acknowledged my speech. Were they deaf? Were they —

I saw the girl blink. The young man with silky blond hair shifted his pose slightly.

Maybe I was being snubbed because I had violated some arcane rule of etiquette.

I looked at the screen. It was the only light source. A soft silvery light. For the first time I took in the image. Four rubbery gray cubes marching on a naked, gelatinous gray plain, one after the other. The cubes weren't exactly alike. One had a notch. Another had a crater in it. Another had a knob and a notch . . . Approaching from the horizon's vanishing point, a procession of white rubber cones slid over the ground, five of them to the cube's four. The procession of cubes intersected the path of the cones. The cubes stopped as if pitched up against a brick wall; then the cones stopped. The cubes turned red, the cones green.

"They win," the woman said, in a pleasant voice. Not too toneless, not too expressive.

"Yes," I said, clearing my throat. "Evidently the, ah, cones have won. I think. Anyone care to instruct me in the significance of this? Is it, um, religious?"

I'd spoken extra loudly. No one so much as twitched.

I was shaking. "You people have a visitor from two centuries in the past every day? I mean, didn't your systems inform you? I just heard you speak English, and this is Kansas, Toto . . . You wouldn't get that, I don't suppose . . . Look—just direct me to the nearest park. Or greenhouse. Something. I want to know that something green survived. I *need* to know that . . ."

No response. I looked at the screen. The image had changed. I saw something that looked like a pincushion, waving its pins frantically. Nearby it, three spindles amoebically merged to become a larger spindle, birthing a sphere—it made my eyes hurt. When I looked away, I could still see the images for a moment, tenuous as flashbulb blurs.

I knelt beside the girl. "Can you hear me?" I whispered. No reaction. Chin propped in hands, she lay on her stomach, her legs closed and straight out behind her. A slightly Asiatic cast to her skin and eyes, the shape of her face. There was a flush in her cheeks, and her brown eyes were shining. She seemed healthy, alert. I wanted to touch her. Just to feel the life in her. To know that the world wasn't dead.

No, I told myself. You'd probably commit a solecism if you touched her. This could be a religious ritual of some kind.

She blinked, because it was time for her to blink. Her eyes followed the jockeying procession of cones, spheres, cusps, the shifts in color on the screen. The digital images were reflected in perfect miniature in her eyes.

I reached out a hand to her cheek, my fingers trembling so near I could feel her body heat on the tips. I snatched the hand back.

Wait. I sat back, arms around upraised knees, and waited. Sometimes I watched the screen or the roiling shadows it threw on the bare walls. But the images, though simplistic, were disturbing. Their tenacity in repeated patterns of mobility, their gelatinous activity—something about it suggested living beings. I pressed my face into my knees, and waited.

Hours sifted by. When I became aware that the room was darkening, I looked up. The screen was blank except for four shivering green patterns running the width of the screen. Wavelength patterns. Up and down, up and down. EEGs, I supposed. The four strangers were asleep, lying on their cushions.

Swallowing my frustration, I stretched out on a cushion. After a while I slept. My dreams were blank.

The increased light from the screen woke me. The screen showed four snaking cylinders—each slightly distinct from the others—circling the rubbery gray-white pincushion, with its mass of out-thrust prickles. It seemed alien to the other objects. A departure in style.

A blue squeeze tube was lying on the rug beneath my couch. Without appetite, I sucked the faintly spicy mash, watching the others. They were eating, too, watching the screen. I disposed of my tube and sucked water from a hose in the wall, used the chemtoilet, and returned to my cushion. One of the cylinders was bending, wrinkling at the middle near the spiny button. As I watched, it pressed one of the pincushion's spines—which vanished. I felt a chill in my gut corresponding with the instant of the spine's disappearance.

OK. The pincushion was me.

I moved to a corner of the room. The pincushion moved away from the cylinders. The people in the room hadn't moved, but their images had. So they controlled their images some other way. A group of eight-sided polyhedrons marched from the horizon toward the cylinders . . .

I looked away from the screen. Reluctantly this time.

Hours passed. More games, if that's what they were, were played out on the screen. Someone said, "Entropy check" once. Otherwise the day was like the one before. And it passed. And I slept. And the next morning, it started again. Just the same.

I went for a walk. I found more rooms with more people in them, identically occupied. More or less like the others. Distinct from one another, but distinct as people who work in a shopping mall are: variations of a theme. They are generally of the same physical type—the type who used to sell deodorants and wine coolers and Diet Coke on TV.

It was the same in the other buildings. The streets were empty. I saw no children, no old people. The occupants of the apartments ignored me. Sometimes they did a little light maintenance, assisted by small robots like metal and plastic crustaceans; the little robots cleaned the dome, vacuumed floors, expunged fungi. Sometimes I caught the town's inhabitants doing light calisthenics, eating, using the toilets, even copulating in a mechanical sort of way. They didn't kiss when they did it. And they never took their eyes from the screen during all these activities.

I followed a young man as he trotted purposefully through the halls as he watched a projection of a rubbery spiral followed by a pincushion. We rode the elevator to the roof. It was crowded with naked watchers sunning themselves, in silence, lying on their backs, eyes staring upward. The young man stripped and lay on his back with the others, soaking up the sunlight and staring at the trapped sky. Overhead, gigantically magnified, projected holographically onto the air under the dome, were several dozen geometric forms circling one pincushion, performing the same shimmying stately minuets of meaninglessness.

Sickened by claustrophobia, I looked away from the projection. The city stretched out as far as I could see on three sides. The great geodesic was lost in the faint blue mist of distance. The buildings were shaped like cones, like blocks, like spheres. Far away was one white pyramid. There were no trees, no birds, nothing growing. Nothing green anywhere, except on me: my uniform had begun to change color.

It had to be somewhere. They must have preserved *something*.

I went back down to the first inhabited room I'd seen. Things were unchanged there. I sat down, thinking, glancing at the screen now and then. Egg shapes, faintly distinct, circling a pincushion. One of them advanced toward the pincushion. "Fuck off," I muttered. It backed away. The encircling went on. The fuses of my patience were burning out.

After three hours of it, I advanced, physically, toward one of the women—the one with the vaguely Oriental features. I was distantly aware that on the screen the pincushion was advancing on one of the egg shapes. I stepped in between the woman and the screen, blocking her view.

"Look at me," I hissed. "I'm afraid I have to insist. I'm sorry if I'm screwing up a sacred ritual, but my sanity's at stake." She just stared. Looking toward me, not seeing me. I could see the screen images reproduced in her eyes, tiny and perfect. I looked down at myself. The picture was there, projected on the front of my jumpsuit. The pincushion was waving its spines at one of the egg shapes . . .

I split. Fuming, I sprinted through the halls. I ran into apartments, shouting. I did everything short of violence to attract their attention. I shouted, "Fire! Earthquake!" Nothing. No reaction. I tugged their clothing, rearranged their bodies. They resisted a little, but not much. And when I forcibly turned their heads, a projection of the screen would follow their line of sight. If I woke them from sleep, a screen projection appeared instantly.

I shouted in their ears, I beat my chest; I bit through my skin and dripped blood on them. They cleaned away the blood, but they kept their eyes on the screen. I caressed them, embraced them, wept on them—I'm ashamed to admit I even considered rape. I was that angry. But I wasn't that far gone.

I walked out, headed for the street. And this time I found the monument at the very center of the city. It was in a city square, atop a three-hundred-foot pyramid, one seamless chunk composed of something like milk glass. I climbed a slippery stairway. At the five-foot-square space on top of the pyramid was an ancient Zenith color TV set, protected by a bubble of glass, plugged into an old-fashioned socket on the glassy floor. The tube faced me, and there was a single picture on the screen . . . I watched for a while, and the picture on the old wooden-cased Zenith remained the same. A man's head and shoulders, a fixed image; he was smiling coyly, his gray-haired head tilted to the right, one eye closed in a wink. Across his chest were letters, yawing in a weakness of the horizontal hold, spelling out: BREWSTER REGINALD PHILBIN, MD, BSP, PHD.

It was a monument. "Must be hard to get parts," I muttered. Overhead, the enormous screen image in the concave interior face of the dome showed a pincushion approaching a o. A zero.

Zero. One, two, and three of the spines on the pincushion vanished. I was left with a sinking feeling. When another spine vanished, I retreated.

I turned and fled down the stairs, skidding the last twenty.

It had to be fast. The others knew what was happening via the screens. Maybe via something else, too. I had to do it before they could stop me.

I picked her up. The woman I'd tried to talk to, the almost Oriental one. I slung her over my shoulder in a fireman's carry and turned to carry her away from the room. The others—never taking their eyes from the screen—moved as if to block me. But they were too slow. I darted out of the door, down the hall, grimacing at the effort. She wasn't heavy, until you tried to run with her. She wriggled silently on my shoulder; her eyes were locked on the projected miniature of the screen that followed us down the hall.

I heard no one in pursuit. I took the elevator down to the lowest level it would take me.

I carried her to a room I'd found the day before. It contained what I guessed was a heating and air-conditioning mechanism, a leviathan of metal pipes and chrome blocks and glass, humming and shooshing with the internal passage of air and power. The light was indirect, too sharp in some parts of the room, dim in others. A chain-link fence guarded the mechanism; but the lock had been left open. People still made mistakes. I went through the gate, and carried the wriggling girl to a dusty area enclosed by pipes fanning out from the machine like the arms of a Hindu god. I sat her down on the floor.

It worked. The projected image vanished. The metal leviathan—maybe its electric field—had blocked out the projection. The girl made a long, low wail of panicky disorientation. I was afraid she'd run for it, and I'd have to knock her down. And I didn't know if I could bring myself to do that. But she sat frozen, her head moving herky-jerky around, looking for guidance.

I took her face between my hands and turned her to look me in the eyes. "Can you see me now?"

She stared—then, like a wounded dog, she turned and snapped her jaws at my hand. Sank her teeth into the meat of my palm.

Jerking my hand away, swearing, I backed off. She looked at the floor, wild-eyed, a little blood running from the corner of her pretty mouth.

"I apologize to both of you," Dr. Philbin said.

He stepped up from behind, smiling sadly. Looking almost exactly like his TV image. Same suit. I couldn't see him clearly because of the dimness in this enclosure. But I thought he had the same expression as the face on the TV. I hadn't heard him, I supposed, because of the noise of the machine.

He was looking right *at* me. He was talking right *to* me.

I sagged back against a pipe. Something in my stomach drew in its claws, curled up, and went to sleep. *Someone was talking to me.*

"Why'd you make me go through all this before you showed up?" I asked.

"I overestimated you. Thought you would socialize more easily. I don't like to interfere personally . . . I suppose it's the researcher in me. It was something of an experiment. A bad one. I let this young woman down, and all the others, in making that estimation of you."

"I wasn't going to hurt the girl. I wanted to force her to communicate with me. To talk. Just talk. She was the lightest to carry. . ."

"*Force her* is the operative phrase here. Imposing your social imperatives on our society by main force."

"Look—suppose you explain this place to me. And then we'll talk about morality."

He talked for a while, and I asked questions, and I got the gist of it.

Motivation, Philbin said, was ruled by the manipulation of archetypes in the subconscious. Something psychologists knew about analytically and Madison Avenue knew instinctively. The operation of the various substructures of the mind—the ego, the id, et al.—involved the use of a lexicon of symbols. Those symbols, and the archetypes they comprised, could be simplified and abstracted, purified for external concretization, and presented to the brain's centers of initiative directly—normally we react to symbols indirectly, through a long, slow process of filtering and selection. Before Philbin, conditioning was indirect, related to the use of experimental stereotypes: visual dramatizations of people enmeshed in desires for sex, success, recognition, approval. The conditioning dramatization sometimes came through television programming. The brain received and translated the imagery from social symbology to cerebral symbology. Social symbols became mathematic by way of the brain's eidetic translations.

Philbin cut out the middle man. He taught computer-controlled TV the language of the inner mind. "A language it took me forty years and the aid of dozens of researchers to learn." When applied with a totality of stimulus—the same style of imagery imposed from birth to death—absolute rapport was established. And absolute rapport meant absolute control.

"Television is mesmerizing," Philbin said. "People will turn and look at a TV even during an argument. I knew that there was something special going on there, something more than the eye being drawn to light and movement—and that it could be used constructively." He just stood there as he talked, in the same voice, motionless. I looked at the girl. She was staring at him. Twitching. The wound in my hand throbbed. Philbin went on, "I saw a new Dark Ages coming with the fall of the ecosystem, the destruction of the food chain. We needed an orderly society to survive. A method for training people, for teaching them to be part of a harmonious social environment . . . When the atmosphere began its transformation, and the anaerobic organisms became the dominant life-forms, and the acid winds stripped the Earth . . . only Kansas City survived; it was the only *completely* environmentally shielded city at the time of the collapse. Home of the Philbin Institute. I was, ah, influential in the city—and when the emergency called for a new order, my system was implemented. We spent most of the first century refining the system—and developing our survival technologies, our artificial food and air systems. There simply was no room for any extraneous organisms, Mr. Mazursky. We had to give human beings priority . . . In the second century our application of my social system was further refined, and evolved to . . . what you have seen. No materialized conflicts. All conflicts, all competition, all ego games and striving and desires, are acted out on the screen. We've trained our people to identify so thoroughly with the screen imagery that it's quite satisfying to them. They direct the screen with the output of their bioelectric fields, which the city's central computers are equipped to receive and interpret. There is individuality here—true individuality. They are aware of one another, of their little distinctions, in a peripheral sort of way. They gravitate together and apart very, very slowly, and react to one another physically as well as on the, screen—but of course the screen imagery is uppermost. It is what they identify with, finally . . ." He smiled. "You have that you-have-made-a-society-of-mindless-conformists look on your face, sir. Not at all: The city is maintained by the people, for the people, of the people, and every day everyone casts their vote. On the screens. A consensus is evolved and steps are taken. That's why we added roof-sunning last year. It was voted in."

"Come on. You're telling me they have free will? You don't use this system to control them?"

"They are influenced to accept certain fundamentals. Any society expects the same. And they're happy with it—these people don't have to suffer the hassles of reproducing, raising children. Or dying. Their consciousnesses do not die. When they begin to age, we clone them; their minds are cybernetically downloaded into the new brain, when the clone has matured."

"Rebirth in sterility. But they're—"

"Don't tell me they're not experiencing the joys and passions of life. They are. But they're trained to experience their feelings eidetically. On the screen. Ever seen two professional chess players go at it? They are motionless, concentrating—but don't imagine they aren't boiling with excitement inside. . ."

"It's still stasis. Deciding on a new sunroof isn't progress. You could be cloning plants, animals—there must be samples somewhere, maybe in deep freeze, or. . ."

"It would be hopeless. The planet, *has* an ecology, sir. The new one, based on new systems of chemical interaction with organic molecules. Anaerobic systems. It has overtaken the planet. Hopeless to try and reverse it. Anyway, why bother? If we succeeded, we'd generate disturbing social interference patterns—as you yourself have. 'If it ain't broken, don't fix it,' Mr. Mazursky."

"I see. The urban-village paradise is achieved, so don't disturb it. Look, Philbin—we were all on our way somewhere. We blew it, and derailed the train. But there was someplace we were intended to get to. You're stopping the last people who have the chance. And this kind of living just isn't intense enough to really satisfy anyone, Philbin . . ."

"You sound like those quaint fellows from my childhood. Punk rockers, they were called."

"Punks?" I scowled. Nasty thought. I was a scholar of naturalist poetry. But then I shrugged. "Maybe it's sort of punk. Maybe a little punk is necessary from time to time."

"You're a fascist, Mazursky." He had dropped the "Mister." "You want to supplant our tribalism with your own. And to you, *I'm* a fascist."

He was right. It was relative. But . . .

"I'm going to go with what used to be called poetic intuition," I said. "And fight you."

I decided I'd take him with us. With the girl and me. By force. I might need him as a hostage. I stepped in, and sliced an uppercut at the point of his jaw.

My fist sailed through his head. The image shimmied.

He was a hologram. "You don't think I'd risk myself here, do you, Mr. Mazursky?"

"An image. A TV image." I shook my head, feeling heavy and stupid. "I guess I wanted to believe you were there so badly I didn't really look very close . . . Christ, you probably don't even look like that anymore. Cloned a few times yourself . . ." I trembled with frustration. I'd wanted that contact. Wanted to see him *react* as I hit him.

"Now it's time for you to make a decision, Mr. Mazursky. You can give yourself over to retraining. Or you can go out there. And die."

"I'm going back to the escape pod. There's some air left. There are people out there . . . sort of . . . I caught a glimpse yesterday, through the glass . . ."

"They're not people as you know them, Mr. Mazursky. We haven't seen them up close. But we're quite sure they're subhuman. They're not oxygen breathers, certainly. . ."

"If I give in, I'll be seeing projections everywhere I go."

"Eventually. But everything you see has always been a projection—on the visual cortex. Your mind edits and distorts things. You see nothing really directly. This way we give you the symbols of the social world more directly."

"And I lose the bulk of my perceptions. I prefer the living world to your social world, Philbin. I have made up my mind: I'm going. And I want to take the girl with me. You send some of your athletic couch potatoes to stop me—I'll kick in a few heads before they get me. It'll be a bad trade."

"Very well. She's already traumatized beyond recovery. Take her. Her designation is Curl. Go back out the way you came in."

And he blinked out.

Something tore loose in me, and it began to howl. "Come back here, Philbin! I'm not through with you! Listen, asshole—it was things like . . . like *this place* that put the goddamn planet into a doze till it fell apart! It was television; it was malls—it was the brain death of your urban villages, turning people inward, into videogames and away from the outer world—that's how it got poisoned and died and no one knew! It was like we were watching TV while the baby was poisoning itself in the kitchen! We got lost in our idiotic little distractions, and we projected all our problems onto little television dramatizations . . . and nothing seemed real! And when we realized it was real, it was too goddamn late, Philbin! *It was television that killed the world, you smug bastard!"*

I had shouted myself hoarse. Fugued, drained, my voice echoed in the dull industrial spaces of the room, and was swallowed up, and lost. And Philbin didn't come back.

I had to drag Curl along at first. But after a few minutes she stopped yammering wordlessly, stopped gnashing her teeth and whimpering. She sank into a sort of ambulatory catatonia. Philbin didn't try to reclaim her. No screen projection followed us. We reached air lock 56. My suit was there, and in it was the tape-log I've been using to make this record. There was also a rather antique pressure suit for Curl—and a crude sled with a big tubular device that synthesized oxygen from carbon dioxide and carbon monoxide. A miniature of what the city used for its own air. And there was a supply of "Food." Philbin was curious about me, it seemed, and what I might do out there if I survived awhile. He was still a scientist—perhaps more bored than he would admit.

The crossing to the pod was hard, because I got no help from Curl in pulling the sled. But the hardest part was getting her into the extra pressure suit. She came out of the catatonia, and bit me again.

Three days since the last entry. Things have happened. I'm not recording this in the escape pod. Oh, it was workable enough. I got the oxymix mechanism working in it.

I was thinking last night that maybe—almost certainly—it was wrong to drag Curl out here. She'd probably die out here with me. Die young. Like Freda. Who was I to say that death was better for Curl than life in the dome?

But it was hard to think about taking Curl back. Sometimes she looked me in the eye, seemed to try to understand me. And I managed to get her to take some food on the second day. And she bit me only once yesterday.

She can talk, when she wants to. Remembering speech from an earlier clone-sequence, probably. This morning she said some things. Starting with: "Are they alive?"

She was looking out the window. I stared at her—and then looked out the window and saw them. At first the way they looked made me sick.

The stuff was crawling over them with a life of its own. I assumed it was their skin. Slick, gray-purple oily gunk. Bubbles for their eyes.

I just stared, and waited, as they came in through the hatch. Two of them. They took off their heads. Peeled them off.

They were humans, under the oily stuff. Protective suits of some kind. Living suits, maybe. Bred for this. Creatures that live anaerobically, producing oxygen for the host who wears them . . .

"When you first got here, we tried to catch up with you," the taller of the two men said, "to warn you away from that dome. They're complete assholes in there. But you moved too fast for us. We can't move very well in these scavenger suits."

"You coming back to the farm with us?" the shorter one said. He had mossy teeth and greasy, matted hair, and he was grimy. "Except for the Kansas City dome, we're pretty sure we're all there is. We only got a hundred square miles terraformed, but it's comin'. Long as our bubble holds . . . You coming with us? You hurry, you can make dinner. Corn on the cob. Fresh!" He grinned at us.

"Are we going to go with them?" Curl asked me. She was sweating with the effort at this kind of communication. Squinting as if she had a headache. But sane.

"Yeah," I said. I took her hand. "I think we will."

She raised my hand to her lips. She didn't bite me.

Brittany? Oh:
She's in Translucent Blue

Some people go to bed with Lucifer
and they cry, cry, cry when they don't greet the day with God . . .
—Monster Magnet

Marissa didn't see why she should get a sitter when Donny was there, he'd watched Brittany before, one time before, and it was right before Brittany's nap anyway.

She was telling Henny something like that when they went down into the basement, Doc's "rec room to my neighbors, dungeon to you," and Jill was smiling triumphantly at them from the little built-in bar. "I told you they'd come," Jill said, to Doc, as he came in with that old, masking-taped cigar box of his. Jill, Doc and Marissa's husband Henny were all in their early forties Marissa was "the baby," at 35.

Marissa and Henny joined Jill at the bar, side by side.

"Gosh it's so nice and cool down here," Marissa said. "It must be 85 or 90 outside already and it'll get hotter. August in L.A. The smog makes it worse, too."

"You're not going to diss the valley again, are you Marissa honey?" Jill said, her fingers jabbing the blender buttons.

"No, it's that way all over L.A."

"You need a new stash box there, Doc," Henny said, his eyes on the box as Doc laid it down on the little bar. Henny probably wondering what it'd be this time. He was a bigger dope pig than Marissa was; she was just as happy with cocktails, but she'd try anything—which is what she'd seriously, very seriously, told her sister she wanted on her grave-stone, *She'd Try Anything* and her sister Lizzy had said something like, That's what'll kill you, too, so it *oughta* be on there fuh Chris'sakes, and Marissa had said she didn't need those negative impressions. When he'd taken Marissa's monthly psychic impressions, her psychic, Damtha, had said, "You're definitely getting too many negative resonations from somewhere, there's a lot for me to remove, here." And, you know, they might've been from Lizzy, she could be so negative. So judgmental.

There were just the two couples that afternoon, their kids playing in the back yard as they got into the party. After Brittany got tired playing with Donny, Henny could take her upstairs for a nap. She'd had her lunch, she'd be sleepy soon. Thank God at four and a half the kid still needed an afternoon lap. It was a mother's little island of sanity.

Jill wore a puce tank top; she starved so she'd look good in it, though her tits didn't have the lift they used to. Her hips were still too wide, no matter what she did, a little "saddle baggy", and the zebra-patterned Spandex leggings didn't help. Her luminous-orange hair was teased like a windy fire around her head. Doc's head was a little too big for his body, mustache too small for his face, so it seemed to Marissa, but he was still "a good-lookin' galoot"—that's what she'd called him when they'd first met him and Jill at Harry's "Social Club." He wore blue jeans and sandals and a Jimmy Page/Robert Plant t-shirt.

"Where'd you get that antique Led Zep shirt, it looks almost new," Marissa asked. "You find it in the garage in a box?"

"No, it *is* new. It's not Led Zep. Page and Plant are doing a solo tour now."

"Really? I didn't know that." She took a cocktail from Jill. It was one of those overly-sweet cherry-tasting things with vodka that Doc liked. She decided not to complain about it.

Henny was wearing Gap khakis, a matching shirt, untucked to hide his paunch. He had a hatchet face, flat blue eyes, thinning blond hair tied back into a little pony tail, and a soul patch. Marissa was the chunky one; her arms and legs were a little short but she had those heavy breasts that Doc liked; that he stared at now. She wore a gold satin top that clung to them and dropped off straight below the nipples to hide her own sloppy middle.

"So where's the Mondersons?" Marissa asked, thinking of that big ropy thing Judge Monderson had in his pants.

"Not coming," Jill said. "They're, like, 'swung out' for awhile after the convention in Las Vegas. I guess Judge did a little too much X or something and freaked out the next morning."

"A little is good, a lot is toxic," Doc said, sitting at the bar.

"A lot of what, that's the question," Henny said. Henny was still looking expectantly at the cigar box, maybe hoping it was cocaine.

Marissa hoped it wasn't cocaine; that made Henny impotent fast, it was embarrassing. You're going to swing, you're supposed to do your part.

"Marissa—where's the—" Henny'd started to say "Where's the kid?" but he remembered not to. She got mad when he said it like that. It wasn't his kid, it was Luis' kid, but still he didn't need to talk about Brittany like she was some stranger's child. "—Where's our little one?" He'd been in the bathroom, maybe checking out Doc's medicine cabinet, when she'd put Brittany out back.

"Playing out back. Donny's watching her."

"So—how about some music? I like my action with a beat," Henny said.

This made Marissa think of the ad at that Internet personals club site. How they'd met Doc and Jill.

LOOKING FOR MR N' MRS RIGHT!

Tired of no-swap swingers? We're believers in action too, and we like our action with the big rock beat, wherever it'll take us. Role playing, light B&D, four-ways, six-ways and everyone gets some. If you're into it, so are we. Will we try anything? Maybe not—but definitely, make the suggestion! Doc and Jill, seeking couples between 30 and 45. N/S. Must exchange photos, email, before meeting. Mailbox 455895

Jill switched on the six-CD-cycle boombox Doc kept by the blue-silk bed beyond the rec-room bar. In that half of the room the concrete floor was painted black, and dusted with glitter to be like starry space. Above the bed—a big futon, really—was an old black-light poster of people fucking in an exotic Kama Sutra position, with op-art lines radiating from their joined genitals. On the walls to either side were posters; one side was Mel Gibson, without his shirt on—that was for Jill— and the other side was Doc's life-size Xena Warrior Princess poster. "I'd love to get that Lucy Lawless in the sack," Doc had said, more than once, gazing goatishly at Xena.

Yeah, Marissa always thought, like that could happen. Like she'd sleep with you if you had a gold plated introduction, a bottle of Dom Pérignon and a Plaza suite. Dream on.

Under Xena were two metal rings in the wall that Doc tied the girls to, when the mood was on them, and sometimes himself. There was a ring in the ceiling, too.

The first CD on the cycler was Doc's new Plant/Page album, which sounded like Led Zep to Marissa. Jill made another pitcher of cocktails. Doc bobbed his head in time to the music as he rolled joints.

Henny frowned at the makings Doc was working with. "I dunno, maybe I should stick with cocktails, pot makes me paranoid, sometimes, man."

Doc grinned. "Jill—this pot going to make him paranoid?"

Jill was dancing, pulling off her tube top. Henny watched her small, pointed breasts jump. "Not going to make him paranoid," she said. "Going to get him high as a motherfucker."

"Those kids going to be okay?" Marissa said, glancing at the back door at the top of the stairs. Asking because she felt like she should, though she didn't want to think about it. "Usually we got a sitter."

"Check on 'em, you want. They're fine," Henny said. "What kind of pot is it?"

"It's *pot plus*," Doc said. His eyes were always a little too deeply-shadowed and to Marissa it seemed like the shadows got deeper when he was about to get loaded.

"Pot plus what?"

"Special formula, dude."

Donny was tightening the strap on Brittany, blinking in the bright sunlight.

"Ow," she said. "That hurt some." She shaded her eyes to see his face. It looked like the palm tree behind him was growing out of the top of his head.

"Oh shit it does."

"Don't say shit," Brittany said, glancing toward the house. Mama didn't care if they said shit but Dad Henny didn't like it. There was no sign of the adults. They were alone out here.

"Shit, why, shit, not, shit, huh shit?"

He gave out a long peeling sort of laugh. Brittany watched his belly button jump when he laughed. "Boinkaboinka," she said. He tightened the strap on the plastic carapace a little more. "Not that much, that's hurt."

He stood back and looked at his handiwork—he'd simply strapped her into the laser-target vest, but it had taken some doing to get it so it wouldn't fall off, she was so small.

"Okay," Donny said, "you run around and hide, and I chase you and try to shoot that target, that thing here." He touched the panel in the middle of her chest that looked like a bicycle reflector. "And if I shoot it, it'll buzz and light up and I win."

He stood back and pointed the little lazer-laser pistol from point blank range and pulled the trigger. The panel lit up with a blue flash, faint in the bright sunlight, and it made an unpleasant buzz feeling against her stomach.

"Gross. I don't think I want to play that. We could play Spice Girls."

"Oh shit, you bet, Spice Girls. No arfin' way, okay?"

She stood with one bare foot on the other, and shifted in the stiff plastic vest, squinting at the swimming pool. A bug with shiny green wings dimpled the water, uselessly paddling its legs. As she watched, it was sucked toward a filter.

"You going to play or not?"

There was a wriggling chain of light in the blue pool water . . . the bug went into the filter . . . the light shook itself . . .

"Brittany? You going to play?"

Her foot was hurting on the hot concrete. She turned and hopped, twice, to get into the shade of the house. "How come there isn't grass?"

"What?"

She pointed. The ground all the way around the house was green concrete with stuff stuck in it. The green paint on the concrete was faded, worn away in places. There were a lot of abalone shells, some of them broken now, some pieces of lava glass, some shiny round rocks, a couple of half-broken statues of little men with beards and pointed hats and wrinkled up faces, the broken base of a bird feeder and, embedded face up in the concrete: a silvery Frisbee with a lot of names signed on it in magic marker and the numbers *1 9 8 3*. It was like that all the way around the house—concrete with things trapped in it, an arms' length between each little pushed-in thing. There was a blue crystal doorknob in one spot; she liked to look at it. See her reflection in it, tiny and blue.

"It's Jill, she did that." For some reason, Donny called his Mom Jill instead of Mom. "I mean, she doesn't like weeds but she doesn't like to work on weeds so she said it was an art project and they took out all the grass and put in this concrete and put this stuff in it and painted it between the stuff. It was before I was born. Watch out, too, you can cut your feet on those shells, they got broke."

"Okay."

"You going to play? It took a long time to put that target on you."

She squinted at him. There were two palm trees growing out of his head now because she and Donny were standing in a different spot.

"You're pissing me off now," he said. She couldn't see his eyes, hardly, because of the way the sun was.

She didn't want to admit she didn't know what that meant so she just said, "Okay. I'll hide."

Doc bought and restored and sold classic cars. The men were talking about cars, something about blown hemis. "Shit next they'll be talking about fucking football and here we are with our tits hanging out in front of them," Jill said.

"I know, they take us for granted."

"I take you for very, very good *heart-breakin' good* pussy, that's what I take you for," said Doc, who sometimes talked that way. He used to read

Hunter Thompson and it had something to do with that. Pretty soon he'd start with the comedy.

Jill looked at Marissa narrowly and blew her a kiss. "*I* take you seriously honey."

Marissa made a kissy at her. "Me too, you."

But she was always uncomfortable when Jill was sucking on her tits and playing with her pussy. Jill had way more dyke in her than she did. But you had to be flexible, and not get hung up.

"You still working out at the airport?" Jill asked.

"No, I fucking quit," Marissa said. "It was making me crazy, those announcements. Selling magazines and candy and listening to those announcements all day. Blahbuhdahbuhdah all day."

"God I guess. Henny still selling software?"

"Yeah, he just sold a whole line to . . . I don't know, some big company . . ."

Doc was just firing up the doobies. The specials. One for each couple. The music was—what *was* that, the guy with the high pitched voice and as soon as they made up their mind what the song was going to be it changed like they thought that was real heavy.

"What band is that, Doc?" Marissa asked, taking the joint from Henny.

"Rush, that's fuckin' Rush, are you kidding?"

"Mahogany Rush?"

"No, shit, that's another band, this is Rush, rush rush rush-rush ruuuuush, oh-*kay.*" Doc had slipped into some *Saturday Night Live* character, though she wasn't sure which one. He fantasized about being a stand up comic. Next would come a lame joke.

She drew on the joint and coughed. It was sour, chemical tasting. "God, what *is* that?"

"Okay so God called Bill Gates, Boris Yeltsin and Clinton together—" Doc was saying. "'Here's the deal, boys,' God said . . . um . . . "

"Did you sign that letter from the Swinger's Coalition to Clinton?" Jill whispered. Marissa nodded and took another hit.

"And said, 'The world is going to end in twenty-four hours' and so Clinton went to the American people and said 'I got some good news and some bad news, folks . . .'" He was trying to do an Arkansas good ole boy accent over that part of the joke, she could tell by his expression, but she couldn't hear the accent because of the music. "'. . . good news is God is real after all, bad news is that the world's gonna end.' So then Yeltsin he goes to the Russian people and uh . . ." The music was getting louder and louder, on its own. She could feel the weight of it in the air. She could feel the music on her skin. She watched as Jill unzipped Henny's pants, right there at the bar, and took his dick out, and started playing with it, and he wet the tip of his thumb and started rotating it on one of her nipples; he had an exaggerated idea of how much she liked that.

"And Bill Gates said, 'The good news is the Y2K thing is not gonna be a problem but . . .'" Without anyone touching the boombox the music rose to such volume that she couldn't hear the punchline but it was a pain in the butt when Doc sulked so she watched him for the right moment and laughed on cue and he bent over, laughing, pushed his head between her breasts, butted them around. "You think it's funny too, boys?" He asked her breasts and he bounced them to make them nod. "'Yes we do!'" He did it in a high pitched voice, mimicking her breasts talking back to him, making Henny bark with laughter. The laughter broke off abruptly as Jill bent and took Henny into her mouth. She was bent over from the waist, legs straight, her butt jutting out behind, holding herself up with her hands on the sides of his stool, maybe hoping Doc would come around and pull her tights down and slip into her from behind, because that's what she liked best from the guys, one in her from either end, and one of the things Marissa liked best was watching someone suck her husband, which her sister thought was weird. But her sister didn't understand swingers, said they were sex addicts, and all Marissa knew was that it got her off, the ripples of—she didn't know *what* the feeling was—ripples of that feeling going through her, and now she could *see* the feeling, when she looked down at herself—never before could she actually see it but now she saw it in rings moving up through her body, shining gold-green rings . . .

Somehow she was standing, though she didn't remember getting up, and Doc had his head under her blouse and Henny was shouting over the music about hell let's get in bed . . . That's what the good Lord made beds for . . .

The concrete hurt Brittany's feet, where it was rough, and she'd broken a toenail on the lavaglass, but right then she was having fun staying away from Donny. One of his feet was smaller than the other so one of his shoes had extra rubber on the bottom and he didn't move very well so it wasn't hard for her to stay away from his laser shooter-thing. "You're cheating," he yelled, from the back, when she went into the front yard and ducked under the bird of paradise plant. She could smell corn and beef cooking from the Mexican house across the street and a Mexican boy was watching her, sitting on his bike and watching her; he was a little older than her, he might be in first grade, or almost, and he was watching, but he didn't have a look on his face like he wanted to be asked to play. She wanted to ask him, to have someone else there, because Donny's eyes were like that cartoon she'd seen, where the cartoon had holes instead of eyes—

She heard the uneven slapping of Donny's tennis shoes coming along the side of the house and she got out from under the bird of paradise and dodged between the little islands of things in the concrete front yard, around the other side of the house and away from him. This was easy, she could just keep the house between her and him.

"You're cheating!" he yelled, which is what he yelled when he wasn't winning, "you are supposed to stay in the back shitbutt!"

Another time it would have bothered Marissa when Henny threw up, but this time it didn't seem to bother anyone, it made them all laugh, Henny too, as he threw up into the little aluminum sink behind the bar. He gargled with vodka as another CD came on, it was the Moody Blues, *Knights in White Satin,* and Marissa, lying on her back, could see the Knights in White Satin riding horses across the ceiling as Doc slapped against her, his half-erect dick just making it in, getting a little harder as he worked at it, and Jill gave her another hit of the sour tasting dope, holding the joint between Marissa's lips, and then sat on her tits, which was one of the things Jill did to her that Marissa sort of liked, when she kind of rode her big tits with her naked ass like that, straddling Marissa, her weight on her legs instead of on Marissa, and just rubbing her butt against Marissa's big tits, making Marissa's nipples wet with her pussy, and groaning, and Marissa could see Jill's buttocks looking like tits now themselves, nipples growing on them—

"What was that dope?" she asked, absently. Skin felt rubbery, plasticky, distant to her now.

The slender Man in White sitting next to her—was he the Knight? He looked like that boy she'd liked when she was in high school, Lenny—he said, "It was PCP, angel dust, dear lady." Or maybe Doc said that because Henny came back to the bed, asking about it.

"Oh Christ, dust joints," Henny was saying, "Jeez, Doc." But of course he took another hit. Anytime: Whatever it was Henny took always another hit.

She suddenly remembered the time Henny had taken speed. The one and only time; she'd never let him do it after that, or not that she knew about. He'd gone down on a black girl that Jill had brought over and the girl was on some other drug, 'ludes maybe, and was watching TV at the time, Dennis Rodman on some talk show, and laughing at him, but at the same time the woman was playing with her clit while she talked about the TV, and more than an hour passed that way until Marissa saw that Henny's knees were bloody . . . bloody from grinding on the concrete floor . . .

Marissa looked for the Man in White sitting next to the bed, and he was there, pointing at the wall. There was a buzzing in her head, like a smoke alarm inside her, so loud she couldn't hear what he was saying, but he was pointing at her and Judy Chula, who was Luis' little sister, and they were in high school, way back in high school, senior prom night, they were walking to the prom because they didn't have dates, but they decided to go anyway because there would be guys without dates there too, supposedly, and they could dance, and you never knew, and then a Trans Am pulled up beside them. In the car were two guys she didn't really know, but she thought one of them was named Charles something, and the other one was either Rafe or Rufus, both of them blond, cousins, big good-looking guys, major in football at school, but not in her scene, and they asked if they wanted a ride to the prom. She and Judy looked at each other and got in that car *fast*. The guys were wearing football jackets and jeans, though; they weren't dressed for the prom. "If you're going to the prom, you're dressed kind of weird for it," Judy said, which made Marissa cringe, and the cringing made her feel her tampon inside her, she felt it trickle a little when she squeezed her thighs, and she was afraid the trickle would get out, she'd been having these really full periods, and that, if it happened, would be the ultimate humiliation for sure, but the guys were saying something . . .

"Do you remember what they said?" the man with the shining white face and the long, long hair asked her, as she turned her head to look at Jill's churning buttocks and Doc ground at her pussy. Jill was sucking Henny at the same time.

"Yes . . . they said they were going to change pretty soon for the prom, but did we want to smoke a joint with them first. We said okay."

"Who's she talkin' to?" Doc asked, laughing. "Whoa, she's high. Come on, girl . . . "

She felt Jill climb off her, a sudden coolness, then Henny taking her by the wrist, agreeing with Doc about something she couldn't hear because the smoke alarm sound was up again, and they were leading her to the ceiling hook, making her wobble through a gelatinous air . . .

They chained her with mink-lined leather cuffs to the chain that ran from the ceiling.

I'm a Christmas tree ornament, she thought.

This was one of her favorite things, when people did this to her. They were completely paying attention to her when they did that. Spanking her, while Jill sucked on her tits. After awhile Doc would lengthen the chain so she could kneel and get him hard again—

The smoke alarm sound in her head rose and fell.

"That's it, learn what you're here for, to make us feel good, little bitchy love," Jill was saying. "Now you're going to . . . "

The sound rose again and she couldn't hear the rest. She couldn't feel her wrists. She could barely feel Doc screwing her from behind.

She was looking over Jill's shoulder at the pictures on the walls—no, the pictures were *in* the walls, like holograms, and mixed up with the poster: part of the image of Mel Gibson. Mel was now wearing a high school football jacket, and was making Judy kneel down and give him head, forcing her mouth onto him by pushing the back of her head; while beside him, on the grass of the park the other, shorter jock was trying to force Marissa's legs apart, and succeeded though she tried to squirm away, and she was saying, no, no, I'll give you a blow job, I'll give you a blow job, but he wanted to be able to say he'd gone all the way with someone, and he forced her legs open and the blood gushed . . .

At the same moment the jock standing gushed in Judy's mouth, making her choke and whimper angrily and she pulled herself away and spat—

Then they saw the lights of the cop car coming down the road into the parking lot of the park, and they ran, zipping up and pulling up their pants respectively, sprinting through the brush of the park toward the street where they'd left the Trans Am, and both Judy and Marissa were crying, their prom dresses ruined with cum and grass stains and blood and the two cops came and stood over them and one of them made an involuntary disgust-sound when he saw the blood running down her thigh and the bloody tampon with its little string that had come out when she was struggling away from the shorter jock—

Marissa was weeping so Jill said, "Oh *gawd*. Well, hell, let her down."

And they undid the cuffs and she sank down and saw their disappointed faces and said, "I'm sorry. Let's do something. What do you want to do?"

"I don't want to *do* that," Brittany was saying, as Donny pushed her against the fence. Her foot was bleeding now from the broken shell she'd stepped on. That's the only reason he'd caught her.

"Just for a few minutes more," he said. "I didn't get the target but one time."

"I don't care, my head hurts, I want to lay down, my foot's bleeding, I'm tired, I don't care, I don't like it, I want to lay down."

She was hungry too. She wanted to see her Mom.

"Go—run!"

"I don't want to play that anymore."

"You'd better."

"Okay—I'll run." But she ran through the fence gate, where he didn't want her to go, leaving little red blotches on the walk, and hid under the bird of paradise plant and wriggled out of the plastic vest. It scratched her as she struggled with it. It was hard to get off. Finally she got it off and she'd just thrown it aside when he found her, and he yelled something. She couldn't make out what he was yelling.

She ran around the side, limping a little now, and through the other fence gate, and into the back yard, looking for the door into the house where her Mom had gone.

"Mom?" she yelled. "Mom!"

Donny came into the back yard, his mouth all flattened out, pinched looking, his eyes like the hole-eye cartoon guy's. He got between her and the back door.

He pushed her toward the pool.

Marissa thought she heard her daughter calling, from somewhere far away.

It was hard to tell, with the music, and the noises that Jill was making, and the rising, falling buzzing sound. Jill was face down in the blue silk pillow, on the blue silk sheets, with both Doc and Henny holding her down, her hands cuffed behind her. It was the erotic smothering she liked—they were careful not to go too far with it. But she liked to get at least dizzy, blurry, before they let her up. The boombox was playing an oldies CD, the song "Crystal Blue Persuasion."

And then she saw Henny split in two, another Henny stepping out of him looking like an inaccurate copy, with a long strip of bristly brown fur down its back, running into a long wolflike tail; with eyes like holes thumbed into the putty of its almost-Henny head. It rose humming, buzzing and growling, to turn, to swim through the air itself, the shining blue air, moving in slow motion up the stairs and out the door and out to backyard, to the pool—the pushing motions of the original Henny's shoulders and hips as he pushed Jill down, and drove himself into her, seemed to translate into the movements of the thing that rose from him, the bristle-tailed thing with holes for eyes and a slit for a mouth, that went out the basement door without touching the floor.

Really, Really, Weird Stories

Two of her husband, one down here, one up there, the same and yet not the same, the second created from the first, moving into the back yard—

"Mama . . ."

But the voice wasn't a distant shout, it was a whisper right into her ear. The air whispering.

Marissa rose from watching Jill being pressed down into the sheets, Jill drowning in silk, and found herself drifting up the stairs, to the back door. She opened the back door—it was hard to turn the knob, it felt wrong in her fingers, but she got the door opened.

Marissa looked out the back door into the blazing afternoon. The sky was so blue . . .

The water in the pool so blue . . .

One somehow bled into the other, the sky part of the pool, the pool part of the sky, melted together by the sunlight . . .

She remembered Lenny Baer, the big love of her teenage years, though she'd only gone out with him four times. He'd recited poetry to her. He wrote for the high school paper, and sometimes he wrote poetry for extra credit in English. A skinny, big-nosed kid with long brown hair, down to his waist almost, and soft gray eyes and an easy smile. He'd taught her things. He'd made her understand that poem by Robert Frost about choosing the two roads, and she'd gotten her first B in English, writing about it. First time over a C. Man, she'd loved him.

He'd written a poem about how he'd seen one of his dreams caught "in the translucent crystal of a raw piece of quartz" he found on the beach, and he'd had to explain to her what translucent meant, and she never forgot it.

But he'd stopped seeing her because his best friend had told him she was a skank. Judy, jealous of her going out with Lenny, had enjoyed telling her when she'd found out. "He heard you were a skank. Fucking all kinds of guys. His Dad heard it too, I guess, said he was disappointed or something. Said 'I'm disappointed in you but go out with whom you choose, son.' His Dad teaches polyscience. So he just . . . that's why he's not calling you and stuff."

Skank. Slut. Dreams caught in a piece of quartz. Translucent quartz . . .

Like the sky; like the pool. How beautiful: Brittany, her baby, was flying, arms outspread, face-down in translucent blue, part of the sky, part of the water, all one great piece of translucent crystal beauty. Crystal blue persuasion. The song still playing. How beautiful, her little girl so free, flying, swimming through the sky, it was a miracle . . . The Henny demon with the bristling tail and thumb-hole eyes—he was crawling around the edges of the translucent blue, yelling something, but he couldn't get into it, she was safe from him there . . . Brittany had gone flying there to get away from him . . .

She heard Jill shouting angrily at Doc, and there was suddenly a banging in her head, each thump an individual sharply defined *ache*, and with Jill yelling like that downstairs the aches were sharper, harder, and she needed to tell Jill please be quiet, so she went down the stairs, back into the basement . . .

"Shhh . . . Jill . . . my head . . ."

"You fuck he almost killed me . . ."

"You're all right, what'd you think, you like it that far, you told me anyway, you were groaning up a storm—"

"You shit I was yelling to stop—You just get me a fucking drink, Doc, shit . . . The stuff you gave us is makin' me sick—fucking angel dust—"

"Some other stuff too, dust and something else he told me, I forget what, and of course the . . . the . . ."

"You don't even fucking know? Ow, shit, my head hurts . . ."

"Jill be quiet . . ." Marissa heard her own voice saying it. "My head hurts too . . ."

"Marissa . . ." Henny was squatting on the floor, his head dipping a little, then jerking up, then dipping. "Where's . . . the kid."

"Brittany? Oh: she's . . ." She sank onto the bed, wanting her head to stop thunking, banging.

"Drink some of this honey . . ."

Drinking, sucking smoke; they were arguing, the other three; she threw up. Other sounds from the ceiling . . .

The police sirens hurt her head, too, and Marissa went outside to tell them to be quiet, and the policemen put a blanket on her, they insisted on it, though it was rough material, because she was naked. Then she saw the little girl, same size as Brittany, same clothes and hair, the little girl on a gurney, as someone pulled a sheet over her face, an institutional-blue sheet, and they asked if Marissa knew what had happened to her daughter, did she see anything. They said that the little boy said he didn't push her into the pool, but there were bruises on her fingers like he'd stepped on them when she'd tried to get out and they wondered if anyone had seen anything.

"Who? What girl?"

"Your little girl's named Brittany, right? That's what the boy says. Just sit down . . . sit down in the back of the car . . . the blanket's falling off . . ."

"Brittany? Oh: she's in translucent blue . . ."

TICKET TO HEAVEN

I never really wanted to go to Heaven. But I knew someone would make me. There was pressure on me to go there. To Heaven. Starting the morning I met Putchek . . .

"Barry!" Gannick said when I dragged myself into his office. "Meet Frank Putchek, director of Club Eden."

"Hey," I said, "Howya doin'" I smiled woodenly, shook Putchek's hand mechanically.

You have to understand that it was 3:30. I'd been in the office since nine—this not being one of your breezy, we're-all-chums advertising agencies where the idea men are permitted to be prima donnas—and I'd spent the morning thinking of ways to convince the public it needs Triple M brand Hamburger Enhancer. (But of course we'd end up explaining to the world that the three Ms should stand for *Mmm!* as in *Mmm Good!* Any jackass would have come up with the same thing, and Triple M could've saved a bundle on an advertising agency. But agencies like mine thrive on the bad habits of industry . . .) I spent lunch flattering Jemmy Sorgenson, from Maplethorpe and Sorgenson, in the hopes that she'd offer me a job at a better salary and maybe residuals. I'd spent the first part of the afternoon thinking of ways to convince the public it needed a certain artificial sweetener, one only mildly carcinogenic. And by 3:00, after a hard day of constructing artful lies and fighting the tides of self-disgust, I was burnt, looking at the world through glazed eyes. By 3:15, everything in the office was flat and two dimensional, threatening to fold down into one-dee. By 3:30 some mysterious temporal voodoo arrests the clock, and the pace of time becomes a hunchbacked old lady with an aluminum walker. And that's when Gannick called me in to meet Putchek.

Putchek was a middle-aged guy with a smallish head, chipmunk cheeks, and a seemingly infinite wealth of smile lines around his mouth and eyes. He smiled a lot, mostly with his mouth slightly open, looking goofy with his overbite. He was tall, round-shouldered, wore dandruff-flecked wire-rims. But he had a nice blue and dove-gray Pierre Hayakawa designer suit, and immaculate patent leather shoes.

I didn't notice all this at first. Only his spongy handshake and a sort of Putchek-shaped blur. He could've been part of the furniture.

Gannick, my boss, was sitting behind his desk in shirt sleeves, on his special chair to make him less midget-ish, his high forehead was a little less furrowed than usual, his small shoulders almost relaxed, his darting black eyes for once relatively stationary.

Gannick was happy about something. Putchek must represent a juicy account.

I screwed my smile down into something faint but superficially warm, and sat across from Putchek where I could look out the window at the chill, brittle spires of Manhattan's petrified forest. *Petrified*, I thought. *Me too.*

"Coffee, Barry?" Gannick asked me.

"No, thanks

"He doesn't need coffee," Gannick said, pretend-confidingly to Putchek. "Or any other stimulant. Barry Thorpe runs on adrenaline." He grinned to soften the sarcasm. I must've looked more wooden than I thought.

Putchek tried to get the joke and blinked at the two of us. "Oh, uh-huh. Heh heh."

Gannick said, "Barry, Club Eden's Paradise Vacations is our new account—I guess you've heard rumors—" I hadn't heard a word—"and it's something a little, well, unusual, and since you, Barry, are a little, well, unusual—" He paused for everyone to chuckle, so we did. "I thought you ought to head this up."

He beamed, and I tried to look pleased. It was as if the strings operating the muscles of my face were stretched out, threadbare, because I couldn't quite manage the expression I wanted.

"You OK, Barry?" Gannick asked.

"Just tired." I summoned a little focus, a little animation. "Well, have we got a prospectus or a press kit or . . . video?"

"Video of . . . ?" Putchek asked.

"The uh, resorts or—"

"There aren't any resorts!" Purchek brought his hands together as if he'd clap them, and then did a sort of joyful wringing instead, shifted on his chair, and said, a little impishly, "Club Eden doesn't send people to anywhere on this planet, ah, Barry."

It was my turn to blink in confusion. More of the room jumped into sharp focus. They had my attention. I turned to Gannick. "Correct me if I'm wrong—I know I'm a little out of it at times—but did I lose twenty or thirty years somewhere? Are we in the next century alluvasudden? Last I knew, it was just 2016; I'm sure of it. Interplanetary travel is still unmanned, right?"

"It's a manner of speaking. We're not sending people to another planet, per se," Putchek explained. "We're sending them to another . . . another existential focal point. Another plane, to use the metaphysical jargon. We send them to *Heaven*."

I looked at Putchek, and then at Gannick. "Heaven. Some kind of sensurround laser show, huh?—360-degree screens, incense?"

Gannick said slowly, "Nuh-ope. They put you in a machine and . . . you really feel physically like you've gone someplace. A sort of mind-trip through, I guess, some kind of electronic stimulation of the brain or—" He shot a glance of polite inquiry at Putchek.

Putchek hemmed, getting ready to haw. "If ah, if you like. You can, ah, look at it like that." He glanced up at me. "It'd really help if you went there. Yourself. Then you'd . . . accept it." He looked embarrassed, stared at his reflection in his shoes, and his mouth was shut—as much as it would shut, with his overbite—and all of a sudden he worried me.

The next day was Saturday. Under the business-incentive labor laws, most of the population had to work on Saturday. But not me, I could putter around my weekend house with a drink in my hand. Getting gloomier as I got drunker, opaquing the windows and dialing the lights low, enjoying the gloom, hugging the house's darkness. Thinking about the Club Eden demonstration I was supposed to go to on Monday.

We send them to Heaven, Putchek had said. Neurological heaven, I supposed. Some pleasure-inducing machine, perhaps.

Heaven, at Putchek's prices, was something only a few could afford.

I shrugged. What else was new?

I went to the picture window, thumbed the button, and the window glass rippled into transparency. The spring afternoon was startling, almost tastelessly garish after the artificial twilight of my house.

I blinked in the unwanted sunshine, and the whiskey made my head ache. Tumbler in hand, I looked out over one of Hartford's prettiest suburbs. Trees lined the street with newly budded clouds of soft green; here and there were the bright pom-poms of flowering fruit trees. I realized I had no idea exactly what kind of trees most of them were. I'd lived here for five years, and I didn't know what kind of trees were on the street. Or my neighbor's first name.

But I knew my neighbor was Security Passed. We were all Security Passed, in Connecticut Village. When you drove in, you showed the checkpoint guards your Residency Card, or gave a visitor's number. To get a Residency Card, to be passed, you had to have a B-3 credit rating, and of course no record as a felon. It was a closed community, but not internally gregarious; the fragmentation of true community feeling extended its anti-roots even here, where all looked cozy. We had television; we had interactive video and shopping networks; we had the Net. We had our lifestyles. We had shrugged off the responsibility that acknowledging strangers brings. Because one stranger leads to another, and not very far beyond the checkpoint was the crumbling border of Hartford's Shacktown, swollen with strangers we didn't want to meet. And tried not to think about.

I wasn't always the model resident of Connecticut Village. I'd written some stuff for *The Reformist*, before I'd gotten scared into money hunting; before Gannick found me. What I'd written was pretty self-righteous, foolishly idealistic stuff . . .

Like:

> Every town has its Shacktown, squatter enclaves grown up in the cracks between the neat little high-security Urban Village units the cities have become; the refuge of the legions of homeless, the disenfranchised of every profession: those who worked in industry and oil, before hands-on industry became an overseas venture and oil became an obsolete energy source; those who worked in construction before the contractors went to seventy-five percent premolded structures and robotics. Those without white collar work skills; or those who'd failed to fit in with the country's biggest employer, the "service" industry, that great consumer-supply mechanism so like a chicken feeding machine on a poultry ranch . . .
>
> The Shacktowns are tenanted by people who, a decade or two ago, built the affluence that the privileged feed off of now. Jobless minorities are in the Shacktowns, of course. And the old. Since the demographic shifts of the late '90s, and the growth of geriatric medicine, the old have become a huge, mouldering slice of the population. And millions of them went discarded, forgotten, cold-shouldered by the post-welfare soci-

ety: the fresh new, shiny world where Entrepreneurs are messiahs, where those who failed to Earn are cast into the outer darkness, beyond the borders of the profit margin . . .

Stuff like that. Foolish stuff. The generalization of college journalism. Anyway, why go on about it, when the response is always the same? They'll say, "So what?"

And if the Residency Committee knew I'd written that stuff for *The Reformist*, I'd never have been Security Passed for Connecticut Village.

Sometimes I passed Shacktown on the freeway. Just a sort of smudgy gray tumble of shanties glimpsed through the hurricane fence. From inside a microchip-driven car whistling smoothly down the freeway, the poor were reduced to a blur of embarrassment. The whole world became a visual shrug at a hundred and ten miles an hour.

I knew there was bribery in it somewhere. I knew it when Gannick said, "The FDA's given Club Eden full approval. The patent bureau, everyone, they're lining up to give their blessing." It was the way he said it. Quick, with an undertone that warned me not to harp on the subject. So I didn't ask why there hadn't been any newspaper talk about it yet. Obviously, they'd worked hard to keep it mum till federal approval was a *fait accompli*. Wouldn't want any nosy Senate subcommittees to delay approval . . .

It was Monday afternoon, and we were in what was to be the Club Eden showroom. Me, Gannick, Putchek and Putchek's secretary, Buffy. She was a sort of human Happy Face who went by "Buffy" with no outward evidence of shame.

The showroom had been the front office of a large travel agency. The posters and brochure racks and desks and the fat, middle-aged ladies with the snail-shell hairdos had been cleared out, and now there was only the transport rig, like a hump of frozen milk under the fluorescent lights in one corner of the room, and some paint-jigsawed newspapers around the freshly rollered walls.

I looked at the transport rig and told myself, *Take it easy; it's probably harmless.*

It looked harmless. It looked like one of those little imitation racecar seats you get into at an arcade. Except, on the outside it was all designer-stylized, a sculptured teardrop of imitation mother-of-pearl. The little door was open. Inside there was a chair, and a few dials on a dashboard. No controls, nothing else. I asked, "No helmet? Something to wire into the brain, to create the illusion? Or do you just inject them with something and, uh—" I had to cough; a recent coat of freshly applied blue paint suffused the shuttered room with quivery fumes.

Putchek cleared his throat. "No. No other, ah, fixtures are necessary It's mostly automatic."

Buffy, as might be expected, was short, pert, faintly plump, auburn-haired, and dimple-cheeked. She had silver-flecked china-blue eyes and stubby, pudgy white fingers awkwardly extended by three-inch nails; blue nails with white glitter. She wore a puce jumpsuit, which was her version of a test pilot's get-up.

"I'm all ready!" she told Gannick, a trifle too eagerly. Her voice was breathy and maddeningly affected.

"Have you done this before, Buffy?" I asked.

"Oh, uh-huh, sure!" she lilted. "Mm-hmm, and we had a kinda test pilot guy, and before that, monkeys and pigeons"

"They're *still* using pigeons," Gannick whispered to me as she turned and climbed into the machine. She closed the door behind her. The rig started to hum.

Putchek tilted his head back, as if listening to some beloved song. His dirty spectacles washed out in the light. "One of our big selling points," Putchek said absently, "is going to be a money-back guarantee."

Gannick's eyebrows shot up. "Money-back guarantee? That's a big risk, Frank. I mean, everyone I've met who's tried it is enthused—but there are all kinds of people out there. Brain chemistries, metabolisms—there're no two exactly alike. If there're even twenty percent who don't like the experience—"

"I can't go into all the details," Putchek said slowly, looking at himself in his shoes again, hands in his pockets. "But let's just say we are ninety-nine percent confident that virtually everyone will like it. There's some risk. But it's worth it."

The rig's humming had risen in pitch—and I winced as it passed out of the audible range. I felt a ripple go through me, and a tightness in my chest, a pinching at the back of my throat. For the briefest of moments, I had a peculiar feeling that Buffy was all around me. It was cloying, believe me. And then the room was normal again.

Putchek glanced at the rig. "She'll be out in, oh, five minutes, vacation complete."

I looked at him. "What's the list price on this?"

"Once we get rolling, ah, five thousand newbux per vacation. We won't be selling the machines at all, for at least a decade. And it's gimmicked so anyone who tries breaking into one to see its works will only find a glob of smoking slag inside"

"Five thousand newbux." I stared at him. "A thousand bills a minute?"

I could feel Gannick glaring at me. *Don't offend the client,* the glare was telling me.

Putchek was unruffled. "Only objectively. It doesn't feel like five minutes to them. They think it's months. Depends on how subjective their personalities are. It'll feel like at least a month has passed. For some it may feel like an eternity. Of pure, uninterrupted happiness." He looked at me as if to say, *What do you say to* THAT? His head tilted back; his open mouth aimed at me—if I'd looked, I could have checked out his tonsils.

One of Putchek's technicians came in. He was a blond kid, with a samurai haircut; he was wearing an orange jumpsuit, CLUB EDEN ornately stitched onto each shoulder. He sang *sotto voce* along with something I heard only as a seashell sound leaking from his earphones. He carried a small box of microchips to the rig, snaking his head to the music. Putchek glanced at him in irritation. "Chucky, it's not that rig that needs the guidance chips; it's the other one."

But Chucky didn't hear him. He opened the door of the rig.

It was empty.

Gannick put the scotch down in front of me and said, "Drink it." Like a doctor's command.

We were in Putchek's office, and I was in Putchek's chair. He was standing solicitously over me, making a motion with his hands like a fly cleaning its foreclaws, and on the other side of the desk, Gannick was glowering. His expression said, *You're making a great impression on the client. just great.*

But the girl was gone.

"I'll be OK," I said. "I just . . . felt funny for a second." I looked at Putchek, and then rolled the chair back so he wasn't breathing on me. "Some kind of stage-magic cabinet?"

He shook his head. "She's gone, projected. Sliding between planes. We were going to let people believe it was . . . was all in the head, for a while. We thought they'd be too scared otherwise. But believe me—she—"

"My ears are burning!" Buffy announced, giggling, as she came into the room. She looked flushed, happy as three-year-old with a mouthful of chocolate. "I'm OK!" she said. "I've been to Heaven."

∞ ∞ ∞

Sometimes, alone at home, I looked at my free pass and tried to talk myself into taking the trip to Heaven. Gannick wanted me to take it, for promotional inspiration. Everyone else wanted to take it. All three of my ex-wives had called, asking me to get them passes. Tickets to Heaven. Just as if they hadn't called me *subhuman, cold-blooded,* and the other things I can't go into without my stomach knotting up. Betty and Tracy cooing at me, posing as affectionate little sisters. But Celia, of course said, "You owe me this and more, you bastard."

But I didn't go to Heaven myself. Not for a long time. I told myself it was because of Winslow. But no, Winslow was just an excuse.

He was a good excuse, because Winslow is scary. I met him six months after Buffy vanished and came back. It was Friday night; I was in my weekdays apartment, packing to go out to my place in Connecticut. It was a time when I least brook interruptions. So when the doorbell rang and I opened the hall door, I snarled, "Yeah? *What?*" And then he flashed the holo. He flipped open his wallet, and the 3-D Federal eagle spread its wings in the wallet, and across its breast was the luminous banner: *Jeffrey C. Winslow, Special Agent, Food and Drug Administration.*

"Mr. Barry Thorpe?"

"Uh. Useless to deny it, right?"

Winslow didn't crack a smile. He was black-suited, with the fashionable bureaucrat's triple-tongue necktie—and he was an albino. An apparition. The Ghost of Bureaucracy Past, I thought. Carrying an alumitech briefcase instead of a ball and chain.

He looked at me with an expression stark as a No Trespassing sign. "I'm doing a series of interviews, Mr. Thorpe, to follow up on our temporary approval of Club Eden. May I come in?"

"You got the wrong guy I'm just the barker; I don't own the carny. You want to talk to Putchek. Maybe Gannick."

"I've talked to them. I'll be talking to them again." He waited. The FDA is responsible for more than food and drugs; Club Eden used a machine that affected people physically, hence it was under their jurisdiction. And hence, Winslow.

Resignedly, I said, "Come on in."

He was all questions. No accusations. And all the questions seemed routine. "When you interview a returned vacationer for an endorsement, are they paid for the interview?" Things he already knew the answer to. Until he slung this one at me underhand: "Are you aware of any sums paid by Mr. Putchek or Mr. Gannick or their representatives to agents or functionaries of the FDA?"

I thought: *No, they don't tell anyone but the guy they're bribing*. But all I said was, "No."

"Thanks very much." He stood up and gave me a limp handshake. "That'll do it for this time." And he left.

This time?

I went out to a bar, found a pay phone, and called Gannick.

"It's nothing,"he told me. "There's a little bureaucratic power struggle at the FDA. And this guy Winslow works for the guys trying to pull off the coup. They want to prove wrongdoing on the part of the FDA commissioners, take over their jobs. But they got nothing. Uh, did he ask about the Charred Pad Effect? Corporeal Side Effects?"

"No. *What* side effects are those? Gannick, I'm supposed to get the straight scoop on this stuff when I—"

"Hey, we're not holding out on you. Nothing important. Don't worry about it; it's all bullshit. Hey, I got a steak burning; I gotta go—Listen, Barry: just head out to Connecticut and forget it."

I knew Gannick's don't-ask-questions-if-you-love-your-paycheck tone. So I hung up, and tried to forget about Winslow.

God knows, it sounded good when people described it.

I was in my office, brainstorming a new fifteen-second spot for the Federal Broadcasting Agency's latest prime-time hit: *Yoshio Smith: Assassin for the CIA*. Club Eden was a major sponsor for the show.

I was watching a video of the writer Alejandro Buckner, talking about his first Club Eden vacation. He was beaming, still in afterglow. Buckner was round-faced, and normally he looked like a sadistic cupid; today he was positively cherubic. "Heaven is not Christian, particularly; there is no biblical God in evidence, no angels, precisely, though the Prefects of Heaven perhaps fill the bill. But Heaven will satisfy the Christian, the Buddhist, or the Hindu. Anyone."

"Some people have claimed Heaven looks different for everybody—but it isn't really so. It's got a landscape, definite topographical features . . . It just depends on which part you tend to get projected to. And that's decided by your personality. Some people are projected into the pastoral Heaven, some of them into the urban one. Many into the one that's a sort of idealized suburb. Me, I'm an unabashed urban Heaven man—only, it was a series of roof-top gardens; a sort of Hanging Gardens of Babylon variation of the great penthouses of Manhattan. But of course, in Heaven there are no pigeon droppings; there is no smog, no acid rain; there are no thudding helicopters, screaming jets—though you might see some aerial gliders, impossibly graceful; everything has a sort of nimbus, like when you do certain drugs—but when you look close, you see it's just the shine off that thing's perfection, the natural glow of its excellence; you don't get tired in Heaven, but sometimes you sleep, and it's somehow just when the people around you want to sleep; there are no mosquitoes, no venomous things, no maggots, no defecation, no halitosis; there is sex in Heaven, however you like it, but it's more like dancing—somehow it loses all its earthly clumsiness. And it never becomes excessive, even though the orgasms are slow, full, and not enervating. Food exudes from the tables as you need it, but you never fall into gluttony. You cannot break your bones; you cannot fall ill. Nothing dies. Everything is easy, but nothing is dull. There are no conversational dullards; no *faux pas,* or awkward silences. There are sharp smells, and soft smells, but no bad smells. I say again that Heaven is not in the least dull. There are storms, and there is snow—but only when everyone's in the mood. There is contention there, but never acrimony; all contention is glorious sport, in Heaven."

It can't be that perfect, I thought. I didn't want it to be. Perfection is suspicious, is improbable, and I wanted Heaven to be real. So I was relieved when he said, "You can't do just anything you want there. If you want to interrogate the other entities—they look like people, but then again, they don't; they're all sort of soft-edged and shimmery—anyway, if you want to ask awkward questions about the place, then you've brought a lot of 'inappropriate psychodynamics' with you, as one of the Prefects said to me. You've brought 'neurotic attachments.' All inappropriate in Heaven. So the Prefects—they look like firefly glows, without the fireflies, and much larger—they swarm up to you and sort of smooth you out, and then you forget all your pushiness, your capacity for violence . . . and your questions. Your questions are answered only with a sort of impression: that the place is indeed something you're supposed to have earned. That it's a 'higher state of communion with the universe.' And that should be enough for you. But there's something else kind of funny about the place . . ."

I leaned forward, sharply attentive.

Buckner said abstractedly, "The entities who are there all the time, who are native to it, well, they look at you like . . . um, they don't really *snub* you or anything; there's nothing unfriendly. . . but there's a sort of benevolent surprise. As if they sense that you don't belong there . . ."

The tape ended there. Gannick's interviewer hadn't liked the direction Buckner was taking, and we had enough "good review" from him anyway. The video ended, and the regular transmission on the TV monitor came on—I started to switch it off, but found myself watching. It was a news bulletin.

Four tenements had collapsed an hour earlier, in the Bronx. About 270 people were feared injured or dead. "Portions of the buildings just seemed to crumble into dust," the housing commissioner was quoted as saying. "Something similar happened about two weeks ago in Chicago—also a low-rent area—and we think it's a result of termite damage or acid rain damage to these old buildings."

Insects or acid rain or both. Oh. An explanation. It felt good to have an explanation for something like that. Even one that felt *wrong* when you really thought about it. So don't think about it, I told myself.

The phone rang. It was Winslow. I didn't put him on-screen. I didn't want to see the white face and the black suit. "Mr. Thorpe," he said, "I just want you to know that if you want to tell me anything, anything at all, I will see to it that it'll be safe for you. With respect to prosecution."

"You're with the FDA, not the FBI, Winslow. You seem to get them mixed up."

"Let's just say that this investigation is a little special. If you can tell me about the Corporeal Side Effects report on the Club Eden phenomena—"

"I really don't know what you're talking about," I said sincerely.

"If you want to play that game—fine. But we'll see who wins."

"FDA, Winslow, FDA. The other one is the Federal Bureau of—"

He hung up.

I shrugged. But then I thought: *Either he's a loon, or we're in trouble and we don't know it.*

Don't think about it. It's Gannick's problem.

I went home.

I sat in my confoam chair, nestling into its artificial hug, with the windows opaqued and the lights dimmed, playing my hiding game, pretending it was nighttime and dark out; anyway, it was dark *in.* I sat there sipping Johnnie Walker and listened to the TV talk about vacationing in Heaven, and I thought: *I don't like this life. I don't like this world. So why don't I go?*

The Special Report anchormen talked about "the Club Eden phenomenon". Described the depression and ennui Club Eden returnees slipped into when the afterglow wore off. Noted that there was no actual physical addiction, but there was an indication of compulsiveness. "After you get over the depression," a returnee told the cameras, "you get back into the groove of regular life. Everything seems kind of dingy and dirty and tired and stiff, for a while—but pretty soon you start to enjoy life again, and, you know, you stop yearning for Heaven all the time. But as soon as you've got the money again, man, you *sign up!*"

Certain psychiatrists, whom I knew to be in the pay of Club Eden, made great, soft-edged, rolling claims for the therapeutic benefits of a Club Eden vacation. A few Southern senators muttered darkly about the religious implications. Club Eden had stopped calling the projection plane "Heaven," but that's what everyone thought it was. So the Moral Majority stamped their feet and pouted.

Senator Wexler called for an investigation into the risks, stating it was only a matter of time before the transport rigs went haywire and projected someone into a mountain, or the ocean—or maybe into Hell. And if that didn't happen, there was a danger someone might develop "bootleg" transport rigs. Club Eden had resisted franchising. It held onto the monopoly with all the legal strength that the $400 million they'd made could give them. That was a lot of strength.

After the Special Report, I had my third scotch, and listened to the regular newscaster dolefully announce that, yes, the government had admitted that the country was sliding into a severe recession. Yes, there was a rather unexpected oil shortage, a general energy crunch, epidemic problems with power plant generators around the country; indeed, around the world. And the Shacktowns were growing.

I rewound the cassette, so I could listen to Buckner again, and take notes.

Club Eden was hot. Club Eden was The Buzz. There was suspicion, outrage, and investigations. But Club Eden kept on through it all, and Gannick and I did our work.

Don't take Paradise for granted . . . until you've tried Club Eden. And: *So you think this* (a slick Kodachrome photo of glorious South Pacific beach: deep blue sky, crystal waters, emblematically perfect palm trees) *is Paradise? You haven't tried Club Eden.* And: *Club Eden: Who needs drugs?*

I had my free pass, locked up at home. Gannick encouraged me to go. Putchek encouraged me. Putchek went himself sometimes. There was a limit to how often you could go, and how long you could stay, something to do with electromagnetic stress on the body, but Putchek went as often as the safety regimen would allow.

Gannick didn't go. He said poker at the club with a pretty girl bringing the dry martinis was heaven enough for him.

"But I want you to go," he said. "OK, Barry?"

So I sat in my apartment on a Saturday evening, a year after Buffy had vanished and came back, thinking about using my pass. Not worrying about Winslow—he'd come only once more, and it had been more of the same. I'd almost forgotten about him.

The Shacktowners couldn't afford a ticket to Heaven. But I had one. So why didn't I use it? I went to the safe I kept the pass in, and opened it. I looked at the pass. I couldn't quite—

That's when the doorbell rang, and somehow I knew it would be Winslow.

Guiltily, I locked the pass away and opened the door for him—and stared. He looked different now. The veneer was gone. So was the badge and the alumitech briefcase. He wore a cheap printout paper suit and dark glasses; and the left lens on the dark glasses was cracked. He smelled like beer, and he listed to the right.

I was seeing a different Winslow here and I liked him better. "Gotta talk to you," Winslow said.

"Come on in and have a drink," I said. "As if you needed one."

He reached into a pocket and took a gun from it. It was small, a .25, but it would put a hole right through me, at this range. "No. You come out. Were going for a drive."

We were walking along a pitted gravel road, under a lowering gray sky. The clouds at the horizon were reddening in sunset and beginning to shed rain; in the red tint it looked as if the clouds were bleeding. We walked between the shanties of Shacktown, through smells that would have stopped me like a brick wall if the gun hadn't been in Winslow's coat pocket. Winslow was talking, talking, talking, with a sort of excessive care that only underlined his drunkenness. "Mr. Danville—my supervisor—and I received a sort of anonymous tip, a transcription of a conversation between two lawyers, one for a certain Janet Rivera and the other working for Club Eden. Club Eden was offering Janet Rivera a fat settlement, a million newbux, and she took the money and ran. It seems that with a very minor adjustment of the transport rig—or a power surge at the wrong time—the vacationer will arrive in something very like Hell. Perhaps it's like this . . ."

He gestured vaguely at the packed-in, mud-encrusted, sewage-reeking shanties; the drawn faces peering from beneath plastic sheets nailed over crooked doorways. He went on, "Perhaps it's worse. Ms. Rivera was sent to such a Hell. Apparently, Ms. Rivera barely kept her sanity. Watch out, that dog wants a piece of your thigh. He's wild . . ." It was a bony yellow mongrel, its eyes cloudy, its muzzle ribbed with a snarl. Winslow took the gun from his pocket and said, "This'll feed some'a these kids." The gun cracked, making me jump, as he shot the dog in the head. Its legs buckled, and it fell twitching. An old woman, muttering to herself, scurried out and dragged the dead dog by the tail into her hut.

"The transcript got us interested," Winslow went on as we continued down the road. (I glanced over a shoulder and saw a small crowd following us at a careful distance; a convention of scarecrows.) "And we saw our chance to pull down the commissioners. They were corrupt, and we'd had enough. We probed, and probed, and came up with something we didn't expect. A correspondence between the increase in Club Eden vacationers and the statistical deterioration of the living conditions of people around them. Putchek knew about it: it was called 'launchpad charring' because they likened the trips to Heaven to the launchings of rocket ships—and the launchpads are charred by rocket-ship engines, Thorpe. Club Eden's launchpad is our world; its charring is the side effects on the world: the worsening recession, the widening gap between rich and poor. And as it went on, the exchange became more . . . literal. Look Thorpe . . ." He gestured at something.

We had come to a pit in the earth. It was about four hundred yards across, and deeper than I could see, coated with fine gray-black dust. The shanties were built right up to its rim; those nearest it were half fallen, partly sunk in soft, ashen ground.

Thick, oily drops of rain pattered down, freckling the gravel and drumming tin rooftops, drumrolling faster and faster as the downpour increased. Under its impact, three of the shacks around the rim of the crater collapsed at once, buckling like the shot dog, crumbling like sand castles under a wave; I heard human voices crying out from the shambles, a dissonant choir, wailing; glimpsed faces in the muddy ash, faces stamped with resignation. Swallowed up a moment later. "There are lots more like these, Thorpe. All over the world. They sprang up after Club Eden got really big. Thousands of people have gone into these pits. They're all caught up in some kind of . . . of inertia. Despair. So they don't fight it. You can feel the pit pulling at you . . ." He was right: I felt the pit tugging at me, a sort of vacuum sucking at my sense of self-worth, my need to survive. Pulling me apart, making me want to take a step forward, to pitch myself in.

"There's a Federal coverup of all this—" Winslow was saying.

"Shut up," I said. I wrenched my gaze from the pit. The urge to throw myself in had almost overwhelmed me. I couldn't stand it there anymore. "Shoot me or not," I said. "I'm leaving." I turned and started walking back the way we'd come. I waited for the gunshot. After a moment he was walking beside me, hunched against the rain. Once, he had to fire into the air to disperse the crowd. But in twenty minutes we were in his car.

"Perhaps what happened to me and Danville is part of the pattern of effects that hits anyone who doesn't visit Heaven," Winslow said. "Perhaps it'll hit *you*, eventually." We sat in his car, listening to the rain hammer the roof. He took off his sunglasses and focused his pink eyes on nothing at all. "We were fired. They said we'd gone beyond the confines of our job, which we had. That we'd made things up. We hadn't." He tugged idly at a sleeve of his paper suit; the acid rain had worked on it, and the sleeve came away in his fingers. "I've run out of money. My clothes are rotting on my back. But what matters—what should have mattered—" he looked at me "—are those people out there."

I didn't say anything. I was choking on what I had seen.

He said, "Why didn't you take the trip?"

"Just a feeling. That it was going too far into pretending that everything was all right. That it was going too far to wallow in our private Heaven when there are so many people in Hell. It was always wrong, but this way I couldn't look away, somehow. It was just a step too far. Guilt, I guess, is what it boils down to."

"You had the right instincts, Thorpe. I knew it when I interviewed you—I could tell the whole thing bothered you. I did my homework on you. Read those pieces you wrote a few years back. I know you're not happy about what you do for Gannick; persuading people to squander millions on the pointless consumption of crap. It *bothers* you. But you were addicted to the money."

"Mostly I was just scared. Of not having an income big enough to save up a safety margin. I was scared of ending up like those people . . . So I had to do it."

"No, you didn't. You don't. You saw what it led to . . . So, Thorpe— what are you going to do about it?"

"I don't have any proof of bribery. Or anything else. And let me tell you something: the public doesn't want this thing to go sour. They don't want it questioned, or fought. They want Heaven, and damn the consequences, and they're paying into a lot of senatorial campaigns to see to it their chances for Heaven aren't disturbed. I can't do a goddamn thing."

"You're wrong, Thorpe. What you can do is, precisely, a God Damned Thing, '

I knew what he wanted me to do. No reason I should do it. I could get away; I could escape this. I could begin going to Heaven myself. I could . . .

I couldn't. I saw the faces whose expressions had gone to dust. I felt the suction of the entropy pit. Having seen that, I was transformed by knowledge. I had lost my moral innocence. And knowing: I couldn't turn my back on it. "What do you want me to do?"

"It starts with a trip to Heaven."

It's going to be hard, Winslow had said. *Maybe the hardest thing you've ever done.* It was. It was like someone who loves puppies being forced to throttle one; it was like seeing your mother for the first time in ten years, and then—though you love her—having to spit in her eye at the moment of reunion.

It was like being in Heaven and spurning it. The vista was sweet, soft, warm, like living in an Impressionist's landscape—and, like great Impressionism, never dull. I was nude but unashamed; for the first time I felt nudity without awkwardness. I was drifting weightless over the treetops, basking in just the right amount of sunshine, feeling the caress of the music they gave off, and reveling in the surge of joy that was arrival: the sight of Friends (Friends I had never known before) awaiting me in the garden, turning with a luminous gladness in their faces—

I wrenched myself away and began to Seek.

The act brought the Prefects of Heaven; they emanated from the trees like a thought from a synapse, and spiraled gracefully round me: soft lights, living questions. They drew closer to assuage the misplaced Desire in me—but, with a crackle of lightning that was an expression of Will, I thrust them back. Refused to let them soothe me into Heaven.

What, then? they asked.

Without speaking, I asked them: How is it we're permitted here at all? For surely this place was something to be earned.

You are permitted here because you have come here. The Great Organizer has made this place; the Great Organizer is the living Principle, who creates all orderliness and harmony. You are here, in Absolute Harmony, so the Organizer must intend it.

I told them what had happened on our world, to the poor. How things had worsened. I asked them why it had happened.

There are Laws regarding the conservation of matter and energy. If you fill a cup from a bottle, the bottle will be that much emptier. Your world is the bottle. Your privileged are emptying it out: the others must suffer. There are machines of metaphysical truth that underlie physical things. You have tampered with the machines. Your wealthy surround themselves with stolen Grace, with the subatomic essence of orderliness, stolen from the exploited. This stolen Grace prevents them from paying the price: so others must.

This place, then, is no supernatural paradise?

It is a function of Law: all laws incorporating what you call Physics, all laws of what you call Science, and laws your people haven't learned. This place is a great device; just as in your world a church is a physical construct to represent the idea of holiness, here we used a physical construct to materialize holiness.

Heaven is created by a machine?

Yes. A machine birthed by the great Machine that is the universe.

Then tell me how I can make adjustments, to right the imbalance in the machine, to arrest the deterioration on our end of things.

The obvious, they said.

"For me, it began with a can opener. I saw a hand holding an old-fashioned can opener, the kind you have to stab into the can. But the hand was stabbing it into my belly, opening it like a lid, sawing toward my groin; through the pain I looked harder at the, hand and saw it was my own. I could not say that I had no control over it. I controlled the hand, but I was making it cut me open. I was no masochist; I did not enjoy it. I screamed for it to stop, and I meant it. After a while the wound went away, but of course, by then I was making another. Not wanting to, but doing it voluntarily. The paradox sneered at me. At the same time I was watching the great screen where my humiliations and stupidities replayed, and knew my mother watched on another screen as I bought the favors of a small boy in Spanish Harlem . . . My sensations of humiliation and suffering, in all their permutations, were not diminished in the least by time or familiarity. None of it brought me relief or a sense of expiation . . . Later I found gasoline and tools and glass with dog shit on it, and I used all these things to—

—From an interview with Frank Putchek,
in the security ward of Bellevue Hospital's
Mental Health facility.

REALLY, REALLY, WEIRD STORIES

It was imprinted in my mind when I came back from Heaven. The Prefects had imprinted the adjustments: the literal, electronic adjustments, the equations for the new guidance chips to go into the transport rig. We went from one Club Eden transport station to another, across the country, Winslow and I, wearing the Club Eden technicians' jumpsuits I'd stolen, pretending to be doing routine service checks. Making the adjustments.

We set it up so our readjustments applied exclusively to the new ten-minute vacations, which were available only to the wealthiest vacationers. The industrial barons, their spoiled children; the corporate vampires; the corrupt politicians.

And of course, there was Putchek. We saw to that. Because Winslow had spoken to Putchek, who had admitted he'd known early on about the side effects of granting First Class Tourist passage to Heaven. Putchek had known, and had not cared. Putchek was the first to go; the first of many.

By degrees, it began to work: the suffering of the exploited and the abandoned began to be reversed, and some of the garbage pits became gardens. The ashpits cleared up like the healing of geological chancres. The Shacktowners found strength: they organized, and built, and made demands. There was no Utopia there, and never will be. But there was dignity, and soon there was food and shelter.

We restored the balance. The adjustments worked. It worked because Club Eden had gotten sloppy about security. Which meant we were able to send a surprisingly large number of people to Hell.

But then again, maybe that shouldn't have surprised us.

Really,
Really,
Really,

WEIRD
STORIES

ASH

A police car pulled up to the entrance of the Casa Valencia. The door to the apartment building, on the edge of San Francisco's Mission district, was almost camouflaged by the businesses around it, wedged between the stand-out orange and blue colors of the Any Kind Check Cashing Center and the San Salvador Restaurant. Ash made a note on his pad, and sipped his cappuccino as a bus hulked around the corner, blocking his view through the window of the espresso shop. The cops had shown up a good thirteen minutes after he'd called in the anonymous tip on a robbery at the Casa Valencia. Which worked out good. But when it was time to pop the armored car at the Check Cashing Center next door, they might show up more briskly. Especially if a cashier hit a silent alarm.

The bus pulled away. Only a few cars passed, impatiently clogging the corner of 6th and Valencia, then dispersing; pedestrians, with clothes flapping, hurried along in tight groups, as if they were being tumbled by the moist February wind. Blown instead by eagerness to get off the streets before this twilight became dark.

Just around the corner from the first car, double-parking with its lights flashing, the second police car arrived. By now, though, the bruise-eyed hotel manager from New Delhi or Calcutta or wherever was telling the first cop that *he* hadn't called anyone; it was a false alarm, probably called in by some junkie he'd evicted, just to harass him. The cop nodded in watery sympathy. The second cop called through the window of his SFPD cruiser. Then they both split, off to Dunkin' Donuts. Ash relaxed, checking his watch. Any minute now the armored car would be showing up for the evening money drop-off. There was a run of check cashing after five o'clock.

Ash sipped the dregs of his cappuccino. He thought about the .45 in the shoebox under his bed. He needed target practice. On the slim chance he had to use the gun. The thought made his heart thud, his mouth go dry, his groin tighten. He wasn't sure if the reaction was fear or anticipation.

This, now, this was being alive. Planning a robbery, executing a robbery. Pushing back at the world. Making a dent in it, this time. For thirty-nine years his responses to the world's bullying and indifference had been measured and careful and more or less passive. He'd played the game, pretending that he didn't know the dealer was stacking the cards. He'd worked faithfully, first for Grenoble Insurance, then for Serenity Insurance, a total of seventeen years. And it had made no difference at all. When the recession came, Ash's middle-management job was jettisoned like so much trash.

It shouldn't have surprised him. First at Grenoble, then at Serenity, Ash had watched helplessly as policyholders had been summarily cut off by the insurance companies at the time of their greatest need. Every year, thousands of people with cancer, with AIDS, with accident paraplegia, were cut off from the benefits they'd spent years paying for, shoved through the numerous loopholes that insurance industry lobbyists worked into the laws. That should have told him: if they'd do it to some ten-year-old kid with leukemia—and, God, they did it every day—they'd do it to Ash. Come the recession, bang, Ash was out on his ear with the minimum in retirement benefits.

And the minimum wasn't enough.

Fumbling through the "casing process," Ash made a few more perfunctory notes as he waited for the armored car. His hobbyhorse reading was books about crime and the books had told him that professional criminals cased the place by taking copious notes about the surroundings. Next to Any Kind Check Cashing was Lee Zong, Hairstyling for Men and Women. Next to that, Starshine Video, owned by a Pakistani. On the Valencia side was the Casa Valencia entrance—the hotel rooms were layered above the Salvadoran restaurant, a dry cleaners, a leftist bookstore. Across the street, opposite the espresso place, was Casa Lucas Productos, a Hispanic supermarket, selling fruit and cactus pears and red bananas and plantains and beans by the fifty-pound bag. It was a hardy leftover from the days when this was an entirely Hispanic neighborhood. Now it was as much Korean and Arab and Hindu.

Two doors down from the check-cashing scam, in front of a liquor store, a black guy in a dirty, hooded sweatshirt stationed himself in front of passing pedestrians, blocking them like a linebacker to make it harder to avoid his outstretched hand.

That could be me, soon, Ash thought. I'm doing the right thing. One good hit to pay for a business franchise of some kind, something that'd do well in a recession. Maybe a movie theater. People needed to escape. Or maybe his own check-cashing business—with better security.

Ash glanced to the left, down the street, toward the entrance to the BART station: San Francisco's subway, this entrance only one short block from the check-cashing center. At five-eighteen, give or take a minute, a north-bound subway would hit the platform, pause for a moment, then zip off down the tunnel. Ash would be on it, with the money; escaping more efficiently than he could ever hope to, driving a car in city traffic. And more anonymously.

The only problem would be getting to the subway station handily. He was five-six, and pudgy, his legs a bit short, his wind even shorter. He was going to have to sprint that block and hope no one played hero. If he knew San Francisco, though, no one would.

He looked back at the check-cashing center just in time to see the Armored Transport of California truck pull up. He checked his watch: as with last week, just about five-twelve. There was a picture insignia of a knight's helmet on the side of the truck. The rest of the truck painted half black and half white, which was supposed to suggest police colors, scare thieves. Ash wouldn't be intimidated by a paint job.

He'd heard that on Monday afternoons they brought about fifteen grand into that check-cashing center. Enough for a downpayment on a franchise, somewhere, once he'd laundered the money in Reno.

Now, he watched as the old, white-haired black guard, in his black and white uniform, wheezed out the back of the armored car, carrying the canvas sacks of cash. Not looking to the right or left, no one covering him. His gun strapped into its holster.

The old nitwit was as ridiculously overconfident as he was overweight, Ash thought. He'd never had any trouble. First time for everything, Uncle Remus.

Ash watched intently as the guard waddled into the check-cashing center. He checked his watch, timing him, though he wasn't sure why he should, since he was planning to rob him on the way in, not on the way out. But he had the impression from the books you were supposed to time everything. The reasons would come clear later.

A bony, stooped Chicano street eccentric—aging, toothless, with a squiggle of black mustache and sloppily dyed black hair—paraded up the sidewalk to stand directly in front of Ash's window. Crazy old fruit, Ash thought. A familiar figure on the street here. He was wearing a Santa Claus hat tricked out with junk jewelry, a tattered gold lamè jacket, thick mascara and eyeliner, and a rose erupting a penis crudely painted on his weathered cheek. The inevitable trash-brimmed shopping bag in one hand, in the other a cane made into a mystical staff of office with the gold-painted plastic roses duct-taped to the top end.

As usual the crazy old fuck was babbling free-form imprecations, his spittle making whiteheads on the window glass. "Damnfuckya!" came muffled through the glass. "Damnfuckya for ya abandoned city, ya abandoned city and now their gods are taking away, taking like a bend-over boy yes, damnfuckya! Yoruba Orisha! The Orisha, *cabrón*! Holy shit on a wheel! *Hijo de puta*! Ya doot, ya pay, they watch, they pray, they take like a bend-over boy ya! El-Elegba Ishu at your crossroads shithead *pendejo*! LSD not the godblood now praise the days! Damnfuckya be sorry! Orisha them Yoruba *cabrónes*!"

Yoruba Orisha. Sounded familiar.

"Godfuckya Orisha sniff 'round, *vamanos*! *Chinga tu madre*!"

Maybe the old fruit was a Santeria loony. Santeria was the Hispanic equivalent of Yoruba, and now he was foaming at the mouth about the growth in Yoruba's power. Or maybe he'd done too much acid in the sixties.

The Lebanese guys who ran the espresso place, trying to fake it as a chic croissant espresso parlor, went out onto the sidewalk to chase the old shrieker away. But Ash was through here, anyway. It was time to go to the indoor range, to practice with the gun.

On the BART train over to the East Bay, on his way to the target range, Ash let his mind wander, and his eyes followed his mind. They wandered foggily over the otherwise empty interior of the humming, shivering train car, till they focused on a page of a morning paper someone had left on a plastic seat. It was a back-section page of the *Examiner*, and it was the word *Yoruba* in a headline that focused his eyes. Lurching with the motion of the train, Ash crossed the aisle and sat down next to the paper, read the article without picking it up.

Yoruba, it said, was the growing religion of inner city blacks—an amalgam of African and Western mysticism. Ancestor worship with African roots. Supposed to be scads of urban blacks into it now. Orisha the name of the spirits. Ishu El-Elegba was some god or other.

So the Chicano street freak had been squeaking about Yoruba because it was getting stronger. His latest attack of paranoia. Next week he'd be warning people about some plot by the Vatican.

Ash shrugged, and the train pulled into his station.

∞ ∞ ∞

Ash had only fired the automatic once before—and before that hadn't fired a gun since his boyhood, when he'd gone hunting with his father. He'd never hit anything, in those days. He wasn't sure he could hit anything now.

But he'd been researching gun handling. So after an hour or so—his hand beginning to ache with the recoil of the gun, his head aching from the grip of the ear protectors—he found he could fire a reasonably tight pattern into the black, man-shaped paper target at the end of the gallery. It was a thrill being here, really. The other men along the firing gallery so hawk-eyed and serious as they loaded and fired intently at their targets. The ventilators sucking up the gunsmoke. The flash of the muzzles.

He pressed the button that ran his paper target back to him on the wire that stretched the length of the range, excitement mounting as he saw he'd clustered three of the five shots into the middle two circles.

It wasn't Wild Bill Hickok, but it was good enough. It would stop a man, surely, wouldn't it, if he laid a pattern like that into his chest?

But would it be necessary? It shouldn't be. He didn't want to have to shoot the old waddler. They wouldn't look for him so hard, after the robbery, if he didn't use the gun. Chances were, he wouldn't have to shoot. The old guard would be terrified, paralyzed. Putty. Still . . .

He smiled as with the tips of his fingers he traced the fresh bullet holes in the target.

Ash was glad the week was over; relieved the waiting was nearly done. He'd begun to have second thoughts. The attrition on his nerves had been almost unbearable.

But now it was Monday again. Seven minutes after five. He sat in the espresso shop, sipping, achingly and sensuously aware of the weight of the pistol in the pocket of his trenchcoat.

The street crazy with the gold roses on his cane was stumping along a little ways up, across the street, as if coming to meet Ash. And then the armored car pulled around the corner.

Legs rubbery, Ash made himself get up. He picked up the empty, frameless backpack, carried it in his left hand. Went out the door, into the bash of cold wind. The traffic light was with him. He took that as a sign, and crossed with growing alacrity, one hand closing around the grip of the gun in his coat pocket. The ski mask was folded up onto his forehead like a watch cap. As he reached the corner where the fat black security guard was just getting out of the back of the armored car, he pulled the ski mask down over his face. And he jerked the gun out.

"Give me the bag or you're dead right *now!*" Ash barked, Just as he'd rehearsed it, leveling the gun at the old man's unmissable belly.

For a split second, as the old man hesitated, Ash's eyes focused on something anomalous in the guard's uniform; an African charm dangling down the front of his shirt, where a tie should be. A spirit-mask face that seemed to grimace at Ash. Then the rasping plop of the bag dropping to the sidewalk snagged his attention away, and Ash waved the gun; yelling, "Back away and drop your gun! Take it out with thumb and forefinger only!" All according to rehearsal.

The gun clanked on the sidewalk. The old man backed stumblingly away. Ash scooped up the bag, shoved it into the backpack. *Take the old guy's gun too.* But, people were yelling, across the street, for someone to call the cops, and he just wanted *away.* He sprinted into the street, into a tunnel of panic, hearing shouts and car horns blaring at him, the squeal of tires, but never looking around. His eyes fixed on the downhill block that was his path to the BART station.

Somehow he was across the street without being run over, was five paces past the wooden, poster-swathed newspaper kiosk on the opposite corner, when the Chicano street crazy with the gold roses on his cane popped into his path from a doorway, shrieking, the whites showing all the way around his eyes, foam spiraling from his mouth, his whole body pirouetting, spinning like a cop car's red light. Ash bellowed something at him and waved the gun, but momentum carried him directly into the crazy fuck and they went down, one skidding atop the other, the stinking, clownishly made-up face howling two inches from his, the loon's cocked knee knocking the wind out of Ash.

He forced himself to take air and rolled aside, wrenched free, gun in one hand and backpack in the other, his heart screaming in time with the throb of approaching sirens. People yelling around him. He got to his feet, the effort making him feel like Atlas lifting the world. Then he heard a deep, black voice. "Drop 'em both or down you go motherfucker!" And, wheezing, the fat old black guard was there, gun retrieved and shining in his hand, breath steaming from his nostrils, dripping sweat, eyes wild. The crazy was up, then, flailing indiscriminately, this time in the fat guard's face. The old guy's gun once more went spinning away from him.

Now's your chance, Ash. Go.

But his shaking hands had leveled his own gun.

Thinking: The guy's going to pick up his piece and shoot me in the back unless I gun him down.

No he won't, he won't chance hitting passersby, just run—

But the crazy threw himself aside and the black guard was a clear-cut target and something in Ash erupted out through his hands. The gun banged four times and the old man went down. Screams in the background. The black guard clutching his torn-up belly. One hand went to the carved African grimace hanging around his neck. His lips moved.

Ash ran. He ran into another tunnel of perception; and down the hill.

Ash was on the BART platform, and the train was pulling in. He didn't remember coming here. Where was the gun? Where was the money? The mask? Why was his mouth full of paper?

He took stock. The gun was back in his coat pocket, like a scorpion retreated into its hole. His ski mask was where it was supposed to be, too, with the canvas bag in the backpack. There was no paper in his mouth. It just felt that way, it was so dry.

The train pulled in and, for a moment, it seemed to Ash that it was *feeding* on the people in the platform. Trains and buses all over the city pulling up, feeding, moving on, stopping to feed again . . .

Strange thought. Just get on the train. He had maybe one minute before the city police would coordinate with the BART police and they'd all come clattering down here looking to shoot him.

He stepped onto the train just as the doors closed.

It took an unusually long time to get to the next station. That was his imagination; the adrenaline affecting him, he supposed. He didn't look at anyone else on the train. No one looked at him. They were all damned quiet.

He got off at the next stop. That was his plan—get out before the transit cops staked out the station. But he half expected them to be there when he got out of the train.

He felt a weight spiral away from him: no cops on the platform, or at the top of the escalator.

Next thing, go to ground and *stay*. They'd expect him to go much farther, maybe the airport.

God, it was dark out. The night had come so quickly, in just the few minutes he'd spent on the train. Well, it came fast in the winter.

He didn't recognize the neighborhood. Maybe he was around Hunter's Point somewhere. It looked mostly black and Hispanic here. He'd be conspicuous. No matter, he was committed.

You killed a man.

Don't think about it now. Think about shelter.

REALLY, REALLY, REALLY, WEIRD STORIES

He moved off down the street, scanning the signs for a cheap hotel. Had to get off the streets fast. With luck, no one would get around to telling the cops he'd ducked into the Mission Street BART station. Street people at 16th and Mission didn't confide in the cops.

It was all open-air discount stores and flyblown bar-b-cue stands and bars. The corners were clumped up, as they always were, with corner drinkers and loafers and hustlers and people on errands stopped to trade gossip with their cousins. Black guys and Hispanic guys, turning to look at Ash as he passed, never pausing in their murmur. All wearing dark glasses; it must be some kind of fad in this neighborhood to wear shades at night. It didn't make much sense. The blacks and Hispanics stood about in mixed groups, which was kind of strange. They communicated at times, especially in the drug trade, but they were usually more segregated. The streetlights seemed a cat-eye yellow here, but somehow gave out no illumination—everything above the street level was pitch black. Below it was a dim and increasingly misty. A leprous mist that smudged the neon of the bars, the adult bookstores, the beer signs in the liquor stores. He stared at a beer sign as he passed. "Drink the Piss of Hope," it said. He must have read that wrong. But farther down he read it again in another window: "Piss of Hope: The Beer That Sweetly Lies."

Piss of Hope?

Another sign advertised Heartblood Wine Coolers. *Heartblood*, now. It was so easy to get out of touch with things. But . . .

There was something wrong with the sunglasses people were wearing. Looking close at a black guy and a Hispanic guy standing together, he saw that their glasses weren't sunglasses, exactly. They were the miniatures of house windows, thickly painted over. Dull gray paint, dull red paint.

Stress. It's stress, and the weird light here and what you've been through.

He could feel them watching him. All of them. He passed a group of children playing a game. The children had no eyes; they had plucked them out, were casting the eyes, tumbling them along the sidewalk like jacks.

You're really freaked out, Ash thought. It's the shooting. It's natural. It'll pass.

The cars in the street were lit from underneath, with oily yellow light. There were no headlights. Their windows were painted out. (That is *not* a pickup truck filled with dirty, stark-naked children vomiting blood.) The crowds to either side of the sidewalk thickened. It was like a parade day; like people waiting for a procession. (The old wino sleeping in the doorway is not made out of dog shit.) In the window of a bar, he saw a hissing, flickering neon sign shaped like a face. A grimacing face of lurid strokes of neon, amalgamated from goat and hyena and man, a mask he'd seen before. He felt the sign's impossible warmth as he pushed through the muttering crowds.

The place smelled like rotten meat and sour beer. Now and then, on the walls above the shop doors, rusty public address speakers, between bursts of static and feedback, gave out filtered announcements that seemed threaded together into one long harangue as he proceeded from block to block.

"Today we have large pieces available . . . the fever calls from below to offer new bargains, discount prices . . . prices slashed . . . slashed . . . We're slashing . . . prices are . . . from below, we offer . . ."

A police car careened by. Ash froze till he saw it was apparently driving at random, weaving drunkenly through the street and then plowing into the crowd on the opposite side of the street, sending bodies flying. No one on Ash's side of the street more than glanced over with their painted-out eyes. The cop car only stopped crushing pedestrians when it plowed into a telephone pole and its front windows shattered, revealing cracked mannequins inside twitching and sparking.

Shooting the old guard has fucked up your head, Ash thought. Just stare at the street, look down, look away, Ash.

He pushed on. A hotel a hotel a hotel. Go in somewhere, ask, get directions, get away from this street. (That is not a whore straddling a smashed man, squatting over the broken bone-end of a man's arm to fuck it in the back of that van.) Go into this bar advertising *Lifeblood Beer* and *Finehurt Vodka*. Christ, where did they get these brands? He'd never . . .

Inside the bar. It was a smoky room; the smoke smelled like burnt meat and tasted of iron filings on his tongue. One of those sports bars, photos on the walls of football players smashing open the other players' helmets with sledgehammers; on the TV screen at the end of the bar a blurry hockey game. (The hockey players are *not* beating a naked woman bloody with their sticks, blood spattering their inhuman masks, no they're not.) Men and women of all colors at the bar were dead things (no they're not, it's just . . .), and they were smoking something, not drinking. They had crack pipes in their hands and they were using tiny ornate silver spoons to scoop something from the furred buckets on the bar to put in their pipes and burn; when they inhaled, their emaci-ated faces puffed out: aged, sunken, wrinkled, blue-veined, disease-pocked faces that filled out, briefly healed, became healthy for a few moments, wrinkles blurring away with each hit, eyes clearing, hair darkening as each man and woman applied lighter to the pipe and sucked gray smoke. (Don't look under the bar.) Then the smokers instantly atrophied again, becoming dead, or near-dead, mummies who smoked pipes, shriveled until the next hit. The bartender was a black man with gold teeth and white-painted eyelids, wearing a sort of gold and black gown. He stood polishing a whimpering skull behind the bar, and said, "Brotherman you looking for de hotel, it's on de corner, de Crossroads Hotel—you take a hit too? One money, give me one money and I give you de fine—"

"No, no thanks," Ash said, with rubbery lips.

His eyes adjusting so he could see under the bar, in front of the stools— there were people under the bar locked into metal braces, writhing in restraints: their heads were clamped up through holes in the bars and the furry buckets in front of each smoker were the tops of their heads, the crowns of their skulls cut away, brains exposed, gray and pink; the clamped heads were facing the bartender who fed them something that wriggled, from time to time. The smokers used their petite, glimmering spoons to scoop bits of quivering brain tissue from the living skulls and dollop the gelatinous stuff into the bowls of their pipes—*basing the brains* of the women and men clamped under the bars, taking a hit and filling out with strength and health for a moment. Was the man under the bar a copy of the one smoking him? Ash ran before he knew for sure.

Just get to the hotel and it'll pass, it'll pass.

Out the door and past the shops, a butcher's (those are not skinned children hanging on the hooks) and over the sidewalk which he saw now was imprinted with fossils, fossils of faces that looked like people pushing their faces against glass they pressed out of shape and distorted like putty; impressions in concrete of crushed faces underfoot. The PA speakers rattling, echoing.

"*. . . prices slashed and bent over sawhorses, every price and every avenue, discounts and bargains, latest in designer footwear . . .*"

Past a doorway of a boarding house—was this the place? But the door bulged outward, wood going to rubber, then the lock buckling and the door flying open to erupt people, vomiting them onto the sidewalk in a Keystone Kops heap, but moving only as their limbs flopped with inertia: they were dead, their eyes stamped with hunger and madness, each one clutching a shopping bag of trash, one of them the Chicano street crazy who'd tried to warn him: gold roses clamped in his teeth, dead now; some of them crushed into shopping carts; two of them, yes, all curled up and crushed, trash compacted, into a shopping cart so their flesh was bursting out through the metal gaps. Flies that spoke with the voices of radio DJs cycled over them, yammering in little buzzing parodic voices: "This is Wild Bob at KMEL and hey did we tell ya about our super countdown contest, we're buzzing with it, buzzzzzzzing wizzzz-zzzz—"

A bus at the corner. Maybe get in it and ride the hell out of the neighborhood. But the bus's sides were striated like a centipede and when it stopped at the bus stop its doorway was wet, it fed on the willing people waiting at the bus stop, and from its underside crushed and sticky-ochre bodies were expelled to spatter the street.

"*. . . one money sale, the window smoke waits. One money and inside an hour we'll find the paste that lives and chews, prices slashed, three money and well throw in a—*"

He paused on the corner. There: the Crossroads Hotel. A piss-in-the-sink hotel, the sort filled with junkies and pensioned winos. Crammed in between other buildings like the Casa Valencia had been. He was afraid to go in.

Across the street: whores, with crotch-high skirts and bulging, wattled cleavages and missing limbs that waved to him with the squeezed out, curly ends of the stumps. (It's not true that they have no feet, that their ankles are melded into the sidewalk.)

"*One money will buy you two women whose tongues can reach deeply into a garbage disposal, we also have, for two money—*"

The whores beckoned; the crowd thickened. He went into the hotel.

A steep, narrow climb up groaning stairs to the half door where the manager waited. The hotel manager was a Hindu, and behind him were three small children with their faces covered in black cloth (the children do not have three disfigured arms apiece), gabbling in Hindustani. The Hindu manager smiling broadly. Gold teeth. Identical face to the bartender but long straight hair, Hindu accent as he said: "Hello hello, you want a room, we have one vacancy, I am sorry we have no linen now, no, there are no visitors unless you pay five money extra, no visitors, no—"

"I understand, I don't care about that stuff," Ash babbled. Still carrying the backpack, he noted, taking stock of himself again. *You're okay. Hallucinating but okay. Just get into the room and work out the stress, maybe send for a bottle.*

Then he passed over all the money in his wallet and signed a paper whose print ran like ink in rainwater, and the manager led him down the hall to the room. No number on the door. Something crudely penknifed into the old wooden door-panel: a face like an African mask, hyena and goat and man. But momentum carried him into the room—the manager didn't even use a key, just opened it—and closed the door behind him. Ash turned and saw that it was a bare room with a single bed and a window and a dangling naked bulb and a sink in one corner, no bathroom. Smelling of urine and mold. The light was on.

There were six people in the room.

"Shit!" Ash turned to the door, wondering where his panic had been till now. "Hey!" He opened the door and the manager came back to it, grinning at him in the hallway. "Hey, there's already people in here—"

"Yes hello yes they live with you, you know, they are the wife and daughter and grandchildren of the man you killed you know—"

"What?"

"The man you killed, you know, yes—"

"*What?*"

"Yes they are in you now at the crossroads and here are more, oh yes—" He gestured, happy as a church usher at a revival, ushering in seven more people, who crowded past Ash to throng the room, shifting aimlessly from foot to foot, gaping sightlessly, *whining* to themselves, bumping into one another at random. Blocking Ash, without seeming to try, every time he made for the door. Pushing him gently but relentlessly back toward the window. The manager was no longer speaking in English, nor was he speaking Hindi; his face was no longer a man's, but something resembling that of a hyena and a goat and a man, and he was speaking in an African tongue—Yoruba?—With a sound that was as strange to Ash as the cry of an animal on the veldt, but he knew, anyway, with a kind of *a priori* knowledge, what the man was saying. Saying . . .

That these people were those disenfranchised by the old man's death: the old armored-car guard's death meant that his wife will not be able to provide the money to help her son-in-law start that business and he goes instead into crime and then to life in prison, and his children, fatherless, slide into drugs, and lose their hope and then their lives and as a direct result they beat and abuse their own children and those children have children which *they* beat and abuse (because they, themselves, were beaten and abused) and they all grow up into psychopaths and aimless, sleepwalking automatons . . . Who shoved, now, into this room, made it more and more crushingly crowded, murmuring and whining as they elbowed Ash back to the window. There were thirty in the little room, and then forty, and then forty-five and fifty, the crowd humid with body heat and sullen and dully urgent as it crowded Ash against the window frame. He looked over his shoulder, peered through the window glass. Maybe there was escape, out there.

REALLY, REALLY, REALLY, WEIRD STORIES

But outside the window it was a straight drop four floors to a trash heap. It was an air shaft, an enclosed space between buildings to provide air and light for the hotel windows. Air shafts filled up with trash, in places like this; bottles and paper sacks and wrappers and wet boxes and shapeless sneakers and bent syringes and mold-carpeted garbage and brittle condoms and crimped cans. The trash was thicker, deeper, than in any airshaft he'd ever seen. It was a cauldron of trash, subtly seething, moving in places, wet sections of cardboard shifting, cans scuttling; bottles rattling and strips of tar paper humping up, worming; the wet, stinking motley of the air shaft weaving itself into a glutinous tapestry.

No, he couldn't go out there. But there was no space to breathe now, inside, and no way to the door; they were piling in still, all the victims of his shooting. The ones killed or maimed by the ones abandoned by the ones lost by the one he had killed. How many people now in a room made for one, people crawling atop people, piling up so that the light was in danger of being crushed out against the ceiling?

One killing can't lead to so much misery, he thought.

Oh, but the gunshot's echoes go on and on, the happy, mocking Ishu said. *On and on, white devil cocksucker man.*

What is this place? Ash asked, in his head. Is it Hell?

Oh no, this is the city. Just the city. Where you have always lived. Now you can see it, merely, white demon cocksucker man. Now stay here with us, with your new family, where he called you with his dying breath . . .

Ash couldn't bear it. The claustrophobia was of infinite weight. He turned, again to the window, and looked once more into the air shaft; the trash decomposing and almost cubistically recomposed into a great garbage disposal chum, that chewed and digested itself and everything that fell into it.

The press of people pushed him against the window so that the glass creaked.

And then thirty more, from generations hence, came through the door, and pushed their way in. The window glass protested. The new-comers pushed, vaguely and sullenly, toward the window. The glass cracked—and shrieked once.

Only the glass shrieked. Ash, though, was silent, as he was heaved through the shattering glass and out the window, down into the air shaft, and into the innermost reality of the city.

TRIGGERING

It was one of those protectiplated Manhattan brownstones, rewired in the 'teens, every square inch evenly coated with a thin, flexible preserving plastic. The old building was a jarring sight, snugged between the glassy high-rises. It was the distant past all neatly wrapped up and embalmed. It seemed appropriate, considering the job I'd been sent there to do.

I went up the slippery hall stairs, one hand on the plastic-coated wooden railing, wondering what unprotected wood felt like. They'd even preserved the quaint twentieth-century graffiti spray-painted in bright crimson on the faded walls: NUKE SADDAM and CRIPS RULE.

I pressed 2-D's doorbell. An old-fashioned glass peephole. The place apparently had no inspection cameras. The door opened—on real hinges—and I was looking down at a four-year-old boy. Behind him was the chair he'd been standing on. He pushed it aside.

He glanced at my clingsuit, and at the department's suit-and-tie stenciled sharply on the front (the white hankie and the tie clip were beginning to fade), and chuckled grimly. He noticed my dark eyes, my short black hair, my duskiness, and his recognition of me as an Americanized East Indian showed in his face: a flicker of suspicion. It was a very adult expression.

I stared. They hadn't told me what the Tangle was. I had a feeling it began here. With the boy. The boy had curly brown hair, big blue eyes, a pug nose, and pursed lips. He wore a formal spiral-leg suit. It was an adult's suit, in miniature. In his mouth was clamped a black cigarette holder containing a Sherman's Real Tobacco burnt nearly to the butt. Smoke geysered at intervals from his nostrils.

A midget? But he wasn't. He was a four-year-old boy.

"You're staring at me," he said abruptly, his voice high-pitched but carefully articulated, accented almost aristocratically. "Is there some specific reason for this intrusive scrutiny, or are you simply a man who practices his penetrating glance on any unsuspecting citizen he encounters?"

"I'm Ramja," I said, nodding politely "I'm from the Department of Transmigratology. And your name?" I covered my astonishment well.

He frowned at his cigarette, which had gone out. "Care for a smoke?"

"I don't smoke, thanks."

"Self-righteous, the way you say that. But you Federal men are always self-righteous bastards. There was another here, fellow named Hextupper or something. You're the followup. Very orderly. You can go and dance with Dante for all I care, friend. But if you must know—" he gestured me inside and moved to close the door behind me "—my name's Conrad Frampton. How-do-you-do, salutations, and etcetera."

"You're overcompensating about being a little boy," I said, returning his hostility.

He shrugged. "Could be. If you were a forty-year-old man trapped in a four-year-old body, you'd feel like overcompensating, too. You'd feel like leaping out the window now and then. Believe me." He led me to a couch, and I sat beside him.

"When did you die?" I asked, watching him. He made me nervous.

"I died in 2002," he said, not even blinking. "Care for a drink?"

"No, thanks. You go ahead."

"Damned right I will." There was a low yellow table beside the couch. He punched for a cocktail on the table's programmer.

I looked around. The room wasn't antique; it seemed like a broken promise after the outside of the building. It was a standard decorbubble, done in various shades of pastel yellow, the curved walls blending cornerlessly into the concave ceiling; the floor was more or less flat but of the same spongy synthetic. The walls, floor, ceiling, and furniture were all of a piece, shaped by the inhabitants. The room spoke to me about those inhabitants.

"Who else lives here?" I asked. The department had told me nothing about the people involved in the Tangle, except the address. It's better that way.

Conrad took a silvery cigarette case from a table, his infant fingers struggling for smooth movements; he lit a thin Sherman sulkily with a thumbnail lighter. "A couple of degenerates live here," he said, blowing smoke rings, "who call themselves my parents. *Fawther* is a musician. George Marvell, snooty concert guitarist. Plays one of those hideous flesh-guitars. They're both flesh machine fetishists. Mother works at the genvats, helping make more genetic manipulation horrors. She's not so bad, really, though it nauseates me when she looks at me with her big brown eyes welling, hoping I'll turn into her widdoo Ahmed again. Her name's Senya. They named me Ahmed, but I make them call me by my real name."

"I take it you don't approve of flesh machines." I sensed there was a flesh machine near at hand. A big one.

He made a something-smells-bad face. "Soulless things. Ugly. I don't know which is worse, the flesh guitar or that living *pit* they call a bed-room. They are soulless, aren't they? You're from the Department of Transmigratology. So you're allegedly an expert on souls. What's your stand on flesh machines, old boy?"

"Depends on what you mean by soul. For us, a 'soul' is a plasma field composed of tightly interwoven subatomic particles, capable of record-ing its host's sensory input. And capable of traveling from body to body, evolving psychically so that species survival is more likely. It's not reli-gion. It's a function of the first law of thermodynamics, but we use cer-tain mystical techniques to work with it. Training for seeing life patterns, that sort of thing. Karma-buildup release. But if we use words like *karma* and *soul* in our reports to the National Academy of Sciences, we'll lose our funding. It took us decades of regressing people, and trac-ing facts, to get them to admit it was a bona fide science."

"I don't know about science. But in my current circumstances . . ." He made a bitter face. "I'm forced to believe in reincarnation." He looked at me. "Why the hell are you here? Level with me."

"We had a report of a rather nasty Tangle here. The lines of spiritual evolution tangled. Sometimes a gross emotional trauma from one life sur-faces in the next. The people involved in the trauma are reborn in close circumstances in the next life, and the next, until the things cleared up."

I considered telling him more. I might have said I came because a Tangle needs a Triggering. And they sent me, Ramja, specifically, because I'm part of the Tangle. Not sure how yet. But I'm one of the few department staff-ers who can't remember his last life. Part of it's repressed irretrievably. The computer model connected me with this Tingle.

But I didn't say that. Instead: "As for flesh machines, I don't know how much so-called soul they have. Or even how much awareness. The de-partment believes that they're part of the evolution of the lower orders. Animal minds, animal souls." I shook my head. "I'm not sure, Conrad, what do you remember of your death?"

He shakily relit his cigarette. "I . . . I drowned. Scuba . . . uh, scuba-diving. Sickening circumstances. Trapped underwater. My air ran out.

Big pain in my chest. Gigantic buzzing in my ears. And a white rush. Next thing I remember is hearing this sad guitar song. Only it was a flesh guitar; so it sounded like they do—like a guitar crossed with a human voice. I looked around, and there was Senya looming over me, her arms outstretched, and I was staggering toward her. It must have looked like toddling. And then the guitar *screamed*. That's what brought me to myself. I remembered who I was. . . My *real* parents are Laura and Marvin Frampton. Were. They died together in a nursing-home fire, I'm told."

He crossed his small legs and propped an elbow on one knee, his cigarette holder poised continentally between thumb and forefinger. "George would like to have me adopted. He doesn't like me, and neither does his room. But then the room is rude to George, too. It shakes when he strokes it. Unpleasantly. I'll show you the damn thing."

We got up. I followed him to a doorway on the right and into the bedroom.

The room was in pain.

The cave-like walls were all rosy membranes, touched with blue, pulsing. Across the room and near the living floor was a blue-black bruise, swollen and pustulant, a half-meter across. Conrad carefully didn't look at it.

"You're just full of hostility, Conrad." I said softly "You've been kicking the wall there. Or hitting it with something."

He turned to me with a very adult look of outrage. "If I have, it's in self-defense. I sleep in the next room, but I can feel this thing *radiating* at me even in there. It won't let me sleep! It wants something from me. I'm half-crazy living in this kid's body anyway, and this thing makes it worse. I can feel it nagging at me."

"And you kicked it to make it stop. In the same spot. Repeatedly."

"What do you know about it?" Conrad muttered, turning away.

I felt uncomfortable in the room, too. It wasn't hostility that I felt from the walls. It was the shock of recognition.

The moist ceiling was not far over my head, curvingly soft, and damp. It wasn't much like a womb. It was more like a boneless head turned inside out.

The wall at the narrower end, to my left, contained the outlines of a huge unfinished face. The nose was there, but flattened, broad as my chest. The eyes were forever closed, milky oblongs locked behind translucent lids.

The room was a genvat creation, a recombinant-DNA organism expanded to fill an ordinary bedroom. The old bedroom's windows were behind the eyes; the light from the windows shining through them as if through lampshades, defining the outsize capillaries in the lids. The face's lips were on the floor, puckered toward the ceiling. The lips were the room's bed, disproportionately wide. They were soft looking, about the size of a single-bed; they would open out for two. There would be no opening beneath them, no teeth.

"It was grown from Senya's cells, you know," Conrad said. He deliberately ground out his still-smoldering cigarette on the room's floor. The fleshy walls quivered.

I controlled the impulse to box Conrad's ears as he continued. "There's a tank of nutrifluid outside the window. Personally, I think the creature is disgusting. I can hear it breathe. I can smell it. You should see the lips move when Senya stretches out on them. Ugh!"

The room's odor was briny, smelling faintly of Woman. It breathed through its nose with a gentle sigh.

Returning to the main room, Conrad said, "Sure you won't have a drink?"

"This time I will have one, thanks." The womb-room had shaken me. I stood on a secret brink. My heart was beating quickly and irregularly.

Waves of fear swept through me. I focused on them, brought them to a peak, shuddered, and let the fear vaporize in the light of internal self-awareness.

I sipped my plastic cup of martini, for the moment relaxing. Sitting beside Conrad, I said, "You said something about George's guitar being sick."

Conrad smirked. "George is hoping his guitar will be better today. But it won't sing for him. I know it won't. It'll start screaming again as soon as he plays it. It sounds vicious—the most awful screams you can imagine. He may have to go back to playing electric guitar."

"It's screaming of its own volition? Maybe it's allergic to him."

"Possibly. It doesn't scream when Senya plays it."

I felt my trance level deepening. The outlines of the furniture seemed to hallucinogenically expand, softly strobing. I glimpsed ghostly human figures on flickering paths; the apartment's inhabitants had left their life patterns on the room's electric field. In those subtly glowing lines I could see the Triggering foreshadowed.

"Conrad," I said carefully, trying not to show any excitement, "tell me about your life just before transition. Give me details of the death itself." I waited, breathless.

Conrad was pleased. He lit another cigarette and watched the smoke curl up as he spoke. "I was a copy editor for a book publisher. I was a good one, but I was becoming bored with the work. I'd accumulated a lot of vacation time; so I accepted Billy Lilac's invitation to go on a cruise with him and his friends. I felt sort of funny about it, because I was having an affair with his wife. But she insisted that it would be good because we would remain casual for the duration of the trip—four days—and that would cool Billy's suspicions about us. Billy was rolling in the Right Stuff. He owned a chain of fast-food restaurants."

"His yacht had what he called a mousetrap aquarium built into it. The boat had a deep draft, and by pressing a button, he opened a chamber in the hull. Water would be sucked into it, along with little fish and sometimes squid or even a small shark. Then the gates at the bottom would close, temporarily trapping the creatures in there, and we would watch them through a glass pane in the deck of the hold.

"There were five of us on the cruise. Lana Lilac, Billy's teenaged wife, thirty years younger than Billy; his secretary, Lucille Winchester; Lucille's son Lancer—"

"Who? Who did you say? The last two?" My interruption was too eager.

Conrad looked at me strangely. "Lucille and Lancer Winchester," he said impatiently. "*Anyway,* Billy asked a bunch of us to go down and scare some octopi into the aquarium. We were over a certain Jamaican reef where they were quite common. So we went down in scuba gear. There were me and Lana and—"

"And Lucille. You three went down," I interrupted. My head contained a whirlpool. *Calm. Perceive objectively. Perceive in the perspective of time. Evolutionary patterns.*

The mummified hurt. Tonight I would resolve the hurt.

"You three went down," I repeated, "and when you approached the gate where the hull opened, good old Billy pressed the button that opens the gate and makes the current that pulls things in, and all three of you were sucked into the mousetrap aquarium. He closed the gate behind you, and then he stood in the hold, over your heads, watching. And you ran out of air."

For a few minutes I couldn't talk. I felt as if I were choking, though it hadn't been me who'd drowned on that occasion. I'd drowned later, choking to death on my own vomit; drug overdose. Years later.

Conrad's irritation visibly became astonishment.

But I was only peripherally aware of him. I was seeing myself, as fifteen-year old Lancer Winchester, hands cuffed behind me, lying facedown on the glass floor, watching as my mother drowned. My gasping and my tears misted the glass, but somehow the blur emphasized their

frantic movements as they tried to pry the gate. Their frenzied hand signals. Their fingers clawing at the glass.

While Billy Lilac stood with his hands in his pocket beside me, like a
man mildly amused by a zoo, chuckling occasionally and sweetly chatting
to me, politely explaining that he'd killed Conrad because Conrad had
been having an affair with Lana. And he'd killed my mother because she
helped them keep the secret and had permitted Lana and Conrad to use
her apartment.

I'd expected him to kill me. But he simply uncuffed me and put me
ashore. He knew that my history of emotional disturbance destroyed my
credibility. No one would believe me when there were three others testify-
ing differently. He'd bribed his two crewpeople handsomely. They
claimed a mechanical failure had caused the gate to open prematurely, and
Billy had been on deck and hadn't seen it. They'd been with him the whole
time. Craig and Judy Lormer, husband and wife, were his crew. Only, after
a while, Judy began to have nightmares about the people drowning in the
hold. Judy had threatened to go to the police. I knew this, because Billy
came to me in the asylum and told me in the visitors' room.

He enjoyed talking about it. Billy was the quintessential son of a bitch.
"I drowned Judy in the aquarium in my house, Lancer," he'd said, his
voice mild and pleasant. Like a taxidermist talking shop.

"You want to explain yourself, friend, hmm?" Conrad said, in the
present.

I was thinking about my own death. I'd been in and out of institutions
for the four years after my mother drowned. Treated for paranoid
schizophrenia and drug abuse—the drug abuse, heroin, was real—'til I
wondered whether I *had* hallucinated Billy's quiet enjoyment as he stood
on the glass, watching the bubbles, forced from exhausted lungs, shatter
on the pane between his feet.

I died of an overdose in 2007.

"No coincidences, Conrad," I said suddenly "I'm here because I knew
you in your last life. I was Lancer Winchester. I watched you die. You and
Lana Lilac and Mother. Strangling under glass." I paused to clear my
throat. I tranced to calmness. "Really, Conrad," I said distantly, gazing
down the corridors of time, "you ought to slow down on the drinking."

Ignoring my advice, he gulped another cocktail, swearing softly.

I turned my eyes toward the doors, first the front door and then the
door to the bedroom. The orifice in the womb-room had contracted a
little, twitching, so that its blue-pink flesh showed at the open door's
corners.

REALLY, REALLY, REALLY, WEIRD STORIES

I felt its excitement subliminally, and I shared its half-slumbering yearning. Conrad felt it, too, and glanced at it, irritated.

But only the womb-room and I were aware that George and Senya Marvell were climbing the plastic-coated steps to the apartment. Now I felt them stopping on the landing to rest, and to quarrel. I felt the Trigger near. I hadn't quite located it.

"Conrad," I began, "Senya is—"

The door opened. Senya came in, toting something behind her. She and the man I took to be George were carrying a large transparent plasglass case between them. Within the case's thick liquids, something wallowed like a pink sea animal. A flesh guitar. An expensive one, too.

But I could hardly take my eyes from Senya. She was lovely. I had a disquietingly powerful sense of *déjà vu*, taking in her strong, willowy shape; a campy Old Glory flag pattern worked into the thick spill of flaxen hair flipped onto her right shoulder. Something in the gauntness of her face excited me. There was both curiosity and empathy in her expression, out of place with her black, clinging Addams Family Revival gown and her transparent spike heels.

"Who the hell is *he?*" George puffed, looking me over as they carried the flesh guitar's case into the bedroom.

"He'd be the man from the Department of Transmigratology, George," she replied offhandedly "I had them send someone over about, umm, about Conrad."

The *déjà vu* resurged when I listened to her voice. The tone of it wasn't familiar. The familiarity was in the way she used it.

George and Senya returned from the bedroom. In contrast to Senya, George was stocky and pallid, his hair permaset into a solid yellow block over his head. His smoky-blue eyes swept over me, then flicked angrily at Conrad. "The kid's drunk again." His voice, when he spoke to me, was a distillation of condescension: "So you think you can clear the garbage from the kid's head here?"

"If there is any garbage to be cleared in this room," Conrad interrupted, "it's coming out of your mouth, George."

As George bent to punch for a drink, his motions set off reverberations containing within them, coded, all the actions of his lifetime. And implications of earlier lifetimes.

"Actually, I'm not here to clear anything from Conrad in particular," I said, crossing my legs and leaning back against the couch. Watching Senya, I went on, "In this lifetime my name's Ramja; in the last it was Lancer." Her eyes met mine. She was puzzled. I hadn't hit the Trigger yet. I smiled at her, felt a flush of pleasure run through me when she smiled back.

"No, George, I'm here," I continued, trying to keep eagerness from my voice, "to deal with a rather complex transmigrational entanglement. It results from a past-life trauma shared by everyone here. A memory that brought us back together. For Triggering. And the funny thing is, George, I don't really have to do much of anything. My being here completes the karmic equation. I'm not sure how it's going to trigger." I sipped my drink and asked, "How did your guitar perform today, George?"

George just shook his head at me. He was close to throwing me out.

Senya answered for him. "It screamed. As usual! Every time George touched it." She looked at George as if she could understand perfectly why *anyone* would scream if George touched them.

"I rather suspected that," I said. "And I suspect, too, that there's a growing alienation between you and George lately, Senya. Since the day the guitar started screaming–and Conrad appeared in your son."

"What the bad-credit do *you* know about it?" George blurted. He was tense with fear. He, too, could feel the Triggering coming.

"The man's right, George." Conrad put in, grinding his cigarette out on the table, his little-boy fingers trembling. "The guitar's screaming and my, ah, my *coming out* came close together. And then the tension between you and Senya got nasty. I saw it. But it's not like it's *my* fault. The damn guitar may not have more than the brains of a squirrel, but it knows a creep when it senses one. George was playing it, and this scream came out of it. It finally got fed up with the creep."

George said suddenly, "If you think there's some link between *him*—" he jabbed a thumb at Conrad without looking at him "—and what's wrong with my guitar, then maybe you can—I dunno, uh—clear it away so the guitar works again?"

"Maybe," I said, smiling. "Let's go into the bedroom. And—clear it away."

A moment later we were standing around the plasglass case, beside the bed-sized, up-thrust lips at one end of the womb-room. Senya opened the case and lifted the guitar free as the floor's lips quivered and the room's walls twitched. The guitar dried almost immediately. It was the approximate shape of an acoustic guitar, but composed of human flesh, covered in pink-white skin, showing blue veins. The neck of the guitar was actually fashioned after a human arm, with the elbow fused so that it was always outstretched. The tendon-like strings were stretched from the truncated fingers, which served as string pegs. But the guitar's small brain kept the strings always in tune. It's lines were soft, feminine, its lower end suggesting a woman's hips. Where the sound hole would be on an acoustic guitar was a woman's mouth, permanently wide open, it's lips thin and pearly-pink; toothless, but with a small tongue and throat. There were no eyes, no other physical suggestions of humanity.

Senya held it in her arms, leaning its lower end on her lifted knee, her right foot propped on the brim of the open guitar case. She played an E chord, her fingers lightly brushing the strings. The strings vibrated, and the guitar's mouth sang the note. The tone was hauntingly human, melancholy, sympathetic. An odd look came over Senya's face. She glanced up at me, and then at Conrad, who reeled, drunk, to one side. And back at me.

"Well?" George said.

"You play the guitar, George." I said. "Go on. I think all the integers of the equation are here, in place. You play it."

"No, thanks." he said, looking at the pink, infant-like guitar in his wife's arms.

I could feel the lines of karmic influence tightening the room. Unconsciously we'd moved into the symmetrical formation around the glass case: myself, Conrad, Senya, George, and the guitar, which Senya held over the case, her arms trembling with its weight. We were the five points of a pentacle, encircled by the waiting, brooding presence of the womb-room.

"Go on, George," said Conrad, slurring his words. "Don't be a simpering coward. Play the guitar." Like a defiant midget, he sneered up at George.

George snorted and took the guitar from Senya. Its strings contracted with a faint whine when he touched it. He strummed a chord and relaxed as the notes came out normally. He strummed again, shrugged, and glanced nervously at the living blue-pink ceiling and the bruise low on the ceiling walls.

The guitar's scream shattered the glass of the window hidden behind the flesh wall and made me clap my hands over my ears. The walls rippled and from somewhere gave a long sigh. Blood ran from the lower edge of the closed eyelids, like crimson tears. An ugly, ripping sound made me look up; the ceiling had ruptured. Blood rained on us in fine droplets. Conrad began to laugh hysterically, his voice piping maniacally. His eyes rolled back, into his head.

George flung the guitar down furiously. I had to look away as the flesh guitar struck the edge of its case. It howled again as something vital within it snapped. It rolled onto the floor, facedown, moaning. The room moaned with it. Panic enlarging his eyes, George looked at each of us. He looked as if we'd suddenly become strange to him. He was seeing us differently now, all his self-assurance gone.

I said, loudly, staring hard at George, "Yours was the sort of crime that required a major effort at karmic justice, Billy."

"You call him Billy . . ." Conrad said, staring at George.

"Billy Lilac," I said, smiling at Senya. "By now you should be remembering. And wondering, maybe, why a man should be punished for things he did in another life. Was Billy the same man as George, really? He is the same man, at the root. Remember what he did? That sort of crime, Billy . . . ah! The womb-room remembers, on some level. The guitar remembers. Their brains are small, but their memories are long. You drowned three people, and, perhaps worse, you chuckled while you watched. You destroyed my life. Me? I was Lancer Winchester." I waited for the full impact of my words to hit the others.

The red mist sifted down on us. The floor's lips snapped open and shut soundlessly. Senya and Conrad listened raptly, their eyes strange. "You killed my mother, Billy. But she's here with us. Everyone you killed is here. It's going to be a big shock to the genvat industry when I tell them we've got evidence that human spirit-plasma fields can incarnate into flesh machines. It will shake up my department, too. My mother? She incarnated into the room that surrounds us, Billy. And Lana is here in Senya. The guitar woke up in your arms one day and remembered what you had done. So it screamed. The guitar is Judy Lormer. Remember Judy? The crewwoman you drowned when she threatened to talk?"

I didn't mention the fact that young Lancer had been genuinely in love with Lana Lilac.

George, a.k.a. Billy Lilac, wasn't listening. He was backing into a corner, making funny little subhuman sounds and swiping at his eyes. Overwhelmed by the sudden remembrance I'd triggered. Realization: who he was and what he'd done and how it had always been a shaping influence on his life.

The room's walls were closing in around us. The room itself was undergoing contractions, squeezing us. We felt waves of air pressuring us, slapping us toward the door. We staggered.

Howling, his voice almost lost in the room's keening and the dischording of the dying guitar, Conrad struggled on all fours after us. He looked like a frightened child.

Senya and I stumbled out into the main room, both of us fighting panic, shuddering with identity disorientation.

REALLY, REALLY, REALLY, WEIRD STORIES

Choking, I turned and looked through the shrinking entranceway. The aperture was irising shut. I glimpsed George standing over the guitar case. The bleeding flesh guitar yowled at his feet. George swayed toward us as the room got smaller around him, his arms outstretched plaintively, face white, his expression alternating terror and confusion, mouth open in a scream lost in the room's own clamor. Behind him, the fused lower edges of the lids over the room's eyes tore free; the lids snapped abruptly open. The eyes glared, pupils brimmed with blood. The room contracted again, and George tripped. He fell against the open plasglass guitar case, facedown over churning liquids. The aperture closed.

"Ahmed!" Senya shouted, recovering herself. "Ahmed's trapped!"

She was calling Conrad by the name she'd given him. The doorway was blocked by a convex wall of tense, damp human tissue; it was puckered into a sort of closed cervix at the middle. But slowly the "cervix" dilated. The top of a head poked through. Conrad's head. His eyes were closed, his face blank.

Gradually the room pressed him out. He was unconscious but breathing. Senya held him in her arms. His clothing was badly torn and slickwet with the room's blood. When he opened his eyes a minute later, he said nothing, but gazed up at her, all trace of Conrad gone. Conrad had withdrawn to whatever closet of the human brain it is that erstwhile personalities are kept in.

The womb-room had shrunk to a bruised, agonized ball of flesh less than two meters across, clamped rigidly around the plasglass case. It died, mangled by the corners of the big glass case, and inwardly burst from its own convulsions.

George, Billy Lilac, died within it. He'd been forced by the shrinking enclosure into the glass case, into its glutinous, transparent fluids. He died under glass. He died by drowning.

WHEN ENTER CAME

There was no contact. He was hard, or hard enough anyway, and he was inside her. He had his arms around her, their tongues worked expertly together. She groaned on cue, and thrust her hips to meet his. But there was no contact. The whole thing was a lifeless minuet performed by skilled dancers. It was sex for Buzz Garret and his wife Elena Garret.

David Letterman was in the room. The TV was still on, in the background, but the sound was off. The only light in their bedroom was videolight, shape-shifting in pixel colors and shadow. Garret ejaculated, and thought of a line from a Lou Reed song: *Something flickered and was gone . . .*

Afterward, Elena went to the bathroom. He heard the faint plastic rattling that meant she was getting a prescription bottle. Taking a Xanax.

He thought: How did we get this way? Is it Elena? It's me as much as her. She's a bit more openly nasty sometimes, is all. She can't blame me for the career thing. She was in graduate school when we met; I was in a rock band, then. One that never made any money. She had the career momentum. I never asked her to give up her Physics R&D . . .

But somehow Garret became a booking agent, Elena became a housewife, set quantum physics aside for the glib comfort of astrology and mysticism; stays up late reading about the occult, never says a word to Garret about what she really believes . . .

She came back to bed. "Elena?" he asked.

"Hm?"

"What do you really believe? I mean, about what we're here for, what the universe is—all the stuff you read about."

"What the hell kind of time is this to ask me, Buzz? It's almost one-thirty in the morning, Jenny's going to come prancing in here waking us up promptly at seven—"

"Okay forget it."

"I mean, I'm too tired to get into—"

"Okay, okay."

No contact.

Three weeks and no further sex later.

"Come off it, Buzz, you love booking bands. It's the best job in the world except maybe astronaut, and that's quoting you." Elena said. He could tell she didn't like the direction of the conversation; she stared into the middle distance and used her weary, patronizing tone. "You're kind of young for a midlife crisis. Thirty-one. I mean, Christ."

It was all just her way of saying, Don't talk about it, it makes me nervous. Warning him that if he insisted on talking about it, there'd be a fight. They had a house to pay off, this was no time for a change in careers.

They were sitting in the back yard, in lawn chairs by the lawn table, on which the bones of T-bone steaks soaked grease through paper plates. The brick barbecue gave up a faint ghost of gray smoke. Elena and Garret: lounging in the soft California sunlight that went like an accessory with any Bay Area suburb, with this moderately pricey development in Walnut Creek. Elena was smoking a cigarette through one of those attachable filter-holders that strains the smoke to help you cut back. She chain-smoked to compensate.

He was tempted to point that out. But it would precipitate more snippiness. Pointless wrangling. He would be using it against her because he was angry . . .

Around and around in his head. Thinking, no contact, no real contact. We could take X, maybe, like Barry recommended, the drug MDMA, supposed to get you closer to your spouse. But Garret was scared of drugs, after putting in a year in NA to get off cocaine. And he didn't know if he *wanted* to get closer to Elena. She wasn't particularly interested in him, not really. She didn't even know why he was nicknamed Buzz. She'd never asked, and probably thought it was like Buzz Aldrin. But it was short for Buzzard. Because Garret had been in one of the first West Coast punk bands.

He looked around at his big yard, his barbecue, his two-story pastel-blue split level house, and thought, How did I get from shrieking obscenities under a mohawk, to this?

He loved the house, in his way. It was like one big baby crib for him and his kids. Being punk, by contrast, was like being a flagpole sitter. It had a limited appeal. It was not a career move. But it'd had one thing. It had contact, of sorts.

He could never go back to it, of course. But maybe there was some other kind of deep contact to be had . . .

Louis and Birdy were over by the rose bushes playing He-Man and She-Ra. They had the prop swords, bought at Toys-R-Us. Louis was being She-Ra, which irritated Elena, made her worry about the boy's sexual identity. "Oh He-Man," four year old Louis was saying in a fluting voice, "you're so strong, only you can stop Skeletor!"

Garret's seven year old daughter, in her best low voice, said, "Don't worry, She-Ra! I'll help you!"

Louis stopped playing, like an actor on a stage startled by the manager turning up the house lights. Looking around. Distracted.

There was a rumble you couldn't hear. Elena frowned.

Garret felt a kind of indefinable dread, coming out of the very bottom of his gut in slow, diffuse waves of anxiety. Resonating with the unheard rumble in the air. A subsonic shiver.

Garret said, "You feel . . . anything? Kind of like something's out of whack or . . . ?"

Elena hugged herself, and pursed her lips, and said, "No." Lying through her teeth. Looking at her workroom window.

The rumble, again. Felt but not heard. Rising again and then gone. Garret saw Louis shiver, and look around. Then Louis shrugged, and raised his She-Ra sword. "HeMan—Skeletor's coming!"

And Garret thought, for no reason in particular. *Contact.* It sounded in his mind twice, in the voice of some mental phone operator. *Contact.*

"Skeletor is here!" Louis said. "But so is She-Ra and He-Man!"

If you write poetry when you're a teenager, you probably write bad poetry. Especially if you were young in the late 70s, early 80s, with all the dour, gothic rock people around, and you were sensitive, a bit alienated, fairly smart. In that case, you wrote poetry that matched your clothes. Poetry dressed all in black, poetry with little silver skull earrings and kohl around its eyes and maybe a tattoo that said BORN TO DIE.

But bad poetry isn't meaningless. The day before Enter came, Garret was going through a box of press clippings in his office, looking for a nasty review of one of his own early bands—he was going to show it to one of the bands he was booking. On top of a thin book of clippings, Garret found one of the high school notebooks he'd filled with bad poetry. Found himself reading some stuff he wrote one night after his parents came home drunk—they always came home drunk, and usually left home drunk. Drunk and snarling at one another.

He was the child of alcoholics. The poetry, in consequence, could have been cited in a psychological casebook, with lines like:

Loneliness comes in concentric circles
Like the circles in Dante's Hell
And the innermost circle is the hardest to see.

Pretty heavy-handed stuff, he thought. Garish. But now, fifteen years later, it rang true, somehow. He was married, had two kids, once had a lot of girlfriends; still had a lot of friends. And he wasn't as lonely as it was when he was a young misfit teenager, no. But he was still a circle away from knowing anyone.

She came to Garret when he was trying not to masturbate. He was working late in his office, upstairs in their house. He had his feet up on the transparent plastic desk, next to the PC he never used, a cup of espresso in one hand from the espresso machine on the file cabinet, a machine that he did use a great deal. He was making phone calls that simply seemed to breed more calls. He was trying to get the TinTones on the same bill with Wind Window, despite the irritating sound of the dual wordplay names, and at the same time fighting the randiness that had plagued him all week. He was tempted to slip into the upstairs bathroom run through one of his repertoire of sexual fantasies, discharge some of the sexual tension. Then get back to work. But he knew it was a way to avoid sex with Elena. Sex they were overdue for. Something she was getting bitter and sarcastic about. So he was trying to hold the randiness in for her . . .

It happened when he was absentmindedly changing a light bulb. He was talking to Chalky, the Brit who was the manager of the TinTones, telling him, "I just talked to Bill Graham Presents, and if you can make a concession on the band's paycheck—Hey, Chalky, man, this gig is an important showcase for the Bay Area because the programmers will all be there, especially the guys from KROQ and KNET—" The walls hummed with a distant, almost unfelt rumble. And then, *phht*, the overhead light burnt out, leaving Garret in a darkness broken up by streetlight glow coming blue-white through the blue curtains. It was like suddenly being put into photonegative. But he kept talking to Chalky on the speakerphone as he got a bulb out of a desk drawer, stood on a chair, tilted the fixture aside, unscrewed the dead bulb. Telling Chalky, "You do this one for me, pal, I'll do one for you—"

And then a thick, shining, violet fluid dripped out of the empty light socket.

Pop. The sound of the dead light bulb breaking on the floor. Slipped from his fingers as he stared.

The glowing fluid dripped in slow motion.

As Chalky rattled on about something, "The trouble is, luv, I've got more people to please than just my dear, dear mate Buzz Garret. There's the promoter, the record companies . . ."

A filmy ribbon of purple and violet plasma was issuing from the socket, swirling and dripping, fluid but gaseous too; like smoke, but it wasn't smoke. It crackled softly and flexed itself like an idea. Unevenly lighting the room in twisty neon

Garret said, numbly, "Chalky, call you back." Hit the hang-up button. Stared at the socket.

Some kind of electromagnetic peculiarity? Some kind of swamp gas sort of thing? A hallucination? Was he that stressed out?

The ribbon thickened and turned in the air, and took shape as it torqued, like a figure emerging on a slow lathe. The shape . . .

He thought of certain paintings by Georgia O'Keefe. And others by Judy Chicago. He thought of women.

The shape was mercurial and full of promise. It reached octopally to-ward him—

He fell off the chair, onto his ass. One hand went into a patch of broken light bulb glass, cutting the heel of his thumb. His butt hurt from the fall. He hardly noticed any of this. He couldn't take his eyes off the shine, the shape growing, getting big. Big as Mindy Gretch. Mindy, the ebullient expanse of nude Mindy Gretch, his first sexual partner. She was a two hundred pound nineteen year old glitter rocker, into Bowie and Alice and the Dolls. Davie Garret, at sixteen, was mesmerized by the Niagran fullness of her breasts. Mindy put on a chilling tough-rocker-chick act, and though the young David Garret identified with her outsider status, he was kind of unnerved when she asked him to come over to sneak some of her parents' vodka. Maybe she'd get drunk and kick him around or something. But that night in her parents' basement she was tender and tentative . . . Where was she now?

She was here, now. Standing there, nude, in his office. One of her eyes was smaller than the other; one of her breasts the size of an apple, the other enormous. She was listing to the side because one of her legs was six inches too short. Then the shape adjusted for parity, like a parade

balloon inflating, and she was symmetrical. Her eyes and legs and bo-
soms equalized. The Venus of Willendorf with Mindy's face.

She was not quite there in the flesh. Her pink skin had a violet
underglow, and there was a faint purple light in the very middle of her,
shining like the filament in the new bulb he held in his right hand. The
bulb, with no power source, for no damn good reason at all, was lit up in
his hand. Glowing.

"Mindy?"

She'd died, and this was her ghost. It was the only thing he could
think of.

He ought to be scared. Instead he was disoriented and—

And drunk. It came over him like a wave of drunkenness, as if he'd
had grain alcohol intravenously. A rubberiness, a pliancy, rippling
through him. The room rippling with it too; a rumbling wave of The
Unseen that passed through everything around them. It emanated from
that purple glow at the center of her.

The drunkenness that was more than drunkenness kept him from
screaming when she closed in around him.

Pop. The other light bulb hitting the floor, as Mindy clamped home
around him like the jaws of a gentle bear-trap. A great soft pink and violet trap.

He was surrounded by Mindys. Six of them, all interconnected somehow, seamlessly joined at the hips and rolls of fat at her middle; six
Mindys facing inward, a circular accordion of Mindys, pressing against
him, naked and reeking deliriously of flesh and female lubrication, six
pairs of enormous Mindy breasts . . .

His hard-on hurt him.

The drunkenness left him inhumanly loose, but didn't leave him flac-
cid or numb or tired the way booze did. This was being drunk on Mindy.

She peeled his clothes from him. He had enough rationality left to
wonder what Elena would think if she came in, Would she even be able
to see it? If Elena saw it would she scream?

Should I be screaming? he wondered, as he squirmed close to this
Mindy apparition, felt her embrace on every part of him, all 'round.
Closing in on him so he could barely breathe. Succulently warm.

Embraced by her at 360 degrees of the compass, the six interlocked
Mindys around him, blended together at their hips and arms and legs;
six faces, six pairs of breasts, six vaginas: six two hundred pound women
symmetrically arrayed like fleshy petals, like the inner parts of a Claes
Oldenberg flower, and for a moment he had a hideous, frightening vi-

sion of himself sucked into a venus flytrap made of this all-encompassing woman, sucked down into some sickening tube and slowly devoured . . .

But then she reached down, under her hugely pliable belly, and two of her hands guided his cock into one of her vaginas. Smoking with sensation as he entered her. Drunk with euphoria, a wallowing in woman . . .

Contact. *Hello.*

His erect cock was a phoneline to her, and the phoneline was open.

All lines are open, she said. *Call our 800 number . . .*

"What?" he asked. In a gasp; pumping into her. Into the purple shine at the mysterious heart of her.

Contact, she said, *You wanted contact.*

"Who . . . oh Christ . . ." Feeling like he could go on doing this forever. Standing here, making love to her. To all six of her. Hands exploring other orifices as his direct line to her jacked into the vagina directly in front of him. . . . Six tongues, all from one woman, lapping at him.

"Who? Are . . ."

Identity. You're asking about my identity. She didn't say it, and she didn't exactly think it at him. She formed concepts and he became aware of them, but it was as if they were occurring to him with a kind of cognitive synchronicity he shared with her . . .

She answered his question, though he didn't know it for a while. She shifted. *Closer,* she said.

Picture a woman stretched like an image on silly putty, for one second; picture a strangely iridescent taffy in a transparent taffy-pulling machine, for about two seconds. Then the taffy loses its palpability, becomes a translucent matrix of light, for another incandescent second; then the light takes a shape in the air like an iris, a six petaled iris, each petal vaguely reminiscent of a woman, some undefined woman. The woman becoming less human but more palpable, more physical, as she flows over you . . .

This time it was an effort not to scream. But he was afraid that if he screamed, he'd disrupt the rapport, break some fragile balance between them, and he wanted desperately for what was happening to go on. The contact was an unspeakable relief.

So he didn't scream when she enfolded him like a cocoon.

His eyes were open, when the cocoon closed completely over him, and what he saw was something like the patterns in peacock feathers, but made out of the faces of women, women he'd known and women he'd never known, overlapping, sliding one into another. Faces lined in knowledge and. perception; a depth of feeling he'd only glimpsed before. He thought of making love to them–his erection was as rigid as a radio tower, and it was transmitting–and the women's lips blossomed, sucking, nibbling, kissing; an organ that was both a mouth and a vagina drew his erection into it. His hands skied the curves of waists, the fullness of hips and thighs, the roundness of arms; every epidermal inch of him coming into contact with her: with them. With the tautness of skin over collarbone, the exquisite silk stretched under a jawbone, a sweetly slithering chain of damp labia drawn past his shoulder, down his torso; a padded room of buttocks and breasts embracing him; a glittering panoply of eyes looking piercingly into his. A bouquet of mouths sweeping past his genitals. Everything was wet but nothing was uncomfortably sticky; was redolent of flesh, sweat and lubricant, and all those scents and effluents melted together into a symmetrical harmony in keeping with the kaleidoscoping visuals of her. She was an endlessly reproduced variant on pattern, like the ornate embellishments of the Sun King's palace decor, but none of it was simple decoration; it was *expression*. And none of it was fragmentary; it was all of a piece, symphonically articulated by a guiding mind.

She was around him like a great vagina, his body the penetrating organ, but the organ that enclosed him was charged with radiant intelligence, and was at the same time the electric piquancy of all sexuality. He moved peristaltically within her, his entire body pumping through her. When he thrust out his tongue, a tongue arose to meet it. When he squirmed away from one vagina and thrust his cock in another direction, another opened to receive him. Breasts filled the hollows of his body. He swam between them. He could breathe, he could move freely, and yet she was everywhere.

He writhed to escape and at the same time yearned to stay within her. And light and flesh began to intermix.

Light and flesh were one, was all around him (somewhere, the office phone was ringing, ludicrously ringing again and again, answered by the answering machine, Chalky yammering after the beep, wanting to try some stupid scam on him), sliding against him, interpenetrating his own skin on the waves of some exotic electromagnetic field, stimulating each of his nerve ends so that he was sweetly feeling everything, not with sensory overload but with sensory renewal. His erogenous zones beaming like klieg lights.

The boundaries began to dissolve. He was no longer able to sense clearly where his own flesh ended and hers began. A shattering panic whistled through him–and then was absorbed into a long slow undulation of reassurance from her.

You will not be destroyed in me.

He believed her. He let go. Felt himself turn head over heels. Saw himself from the outside . . .

And she shifted again. She was a specific someone, now. She was Jane Wasserstein. When was it? 1975? He was eighteen, she was seventeen, had jumped a grade. Jane, the girl he'd dated for five months before she'd broken down and . . .

And put out. What kind of expression was that, "put out?" It was both barbarically sexist and touchingly resonant of an adolescent boy's wistfulness. Put out: put it to the outside. Give, in a way that makes insiders of outsiders.

Here she was. Jane. Slender, curly blond, sylphlike Jane. A half-Jewish girl with asthma, who blinked rather often, as if her quick mind was taking in more frames per second than everyone else. Eyes like a blue-violet premonition of the underglow in this creature's skin. "Just don't say 'Me David you Jane,'" she'd said, on their first date, a breathless half second before he would have said it. Second date she'd said, "You going to ask me to go to the drive-in or are we going to work up to that?" She was always a step ahead of him. He felt like he was playing chess with her. He'd make a pass and she'd snort, "Oh *listen* to him!"

The undefined woman had shifted, now, in 1989, in the office of Buzz Garret and Black Glass Productions. Mindy had become the shifting cocoon which had become Jane, Jane all 'round him, Siamese sextuplets formed in a circle, but somehow all variations of one, and not a confined joining of many.

He knew this creature wasn't Mindy or Jane. But drove himself into the nearest Jane, and made contact. Hello again.

Jane's voice, coming on as if triggered by a mnemonic answering machine. Something she'd said to him, when they were both seniors in high school. *David you're a professional misfit, and you'll probably make big money at it like Alice Cooper or Frank Zappa. But you're not kidding me with this Rimbaud of rock act, all you really want is for everybody to love you, which is all every Joe Normal wants, too . . .*

No, he told her, that's not all. I want them to love me as I am. No matter how I am. I want that much acceptance.

Now, in '89, his tongue brushing Jane's small, hard breasts, her nipples becoming stiff as little .22 bullets, the electric contact of his tongue on her was like a switch triggering more astrally recorded memories.

Buzzard Garret, punk romantic. Jane's words, riding on a sneer, as she broke up with him in their freshman year at UCB. Two weeks before he dropped out to focus on rock. *You always had a feel, David, for what women wanted to hear. They invariably thought it was endearing, too, that you were a punk romantic who could leave silver-spray-painted roses on a doorstep, quote morbidly romantic stuff from Verlaine in a letter, talk about psychic union in lovemaking, and still go out on stage and tell the world you hated it. That made you a tragic figure of romance, right? So why'd you do it, Buzz? Just to get laid? That was never enough. You insisted they had to fall in love with you. When I gave up the nookie, it wasn't enough. You had to make me say I loved you. You fucking pig.*

She'd gone right to the heart of him. He saw himself, through this Contact, as she had seen him: He needed them to be in love with him. He needed them to believe he was in love with them. But he couldn't be, not really. He could say all the right things and make the right moves. Could give them a good semblance of sexual passion. Surprise them with romantic gestures, call them funny pet names. Could even marry them. But he could never really, honestly love them. This way, he had them under his thumb. This way he controlled them, and this way he was safe from abandonment.

And all the time he thought these things, he kept plunging into Jane. Who was not Jane anymore. She was Sandy. Pleasantly plump, busty, spray of freckles across her cleavage. The same exact pattern of freckles reproduced on six linked manifestations of Sandy all around him.

Because if you don't want to have a baby, Sandy'd said, *you're not serious about living life. You're full of yourself and you'll never live that way.*

She'd wanted kids, and he hadn't, and they'd broken up over it. After that he'd dated sometimes three women a week for three years, and then he'd met Elena while he was booking a college where she was working in the student affairs office, he was blown away by the crystalline vastness of her intellect, the subtlety and intensity, alternating, when she made love. Her odd combination of spiritual emphasis and hard science. *The Tao of Physics* ruling their lives. She'd got pregnant and informed him she didn't believe in abortions.

So okay, babies and marriage. Their conjugal lovemaking was good up to a point till she realized he was holding back, holding back more than ever now that he felt trapped by marriage. Withdrawing more and more as the resentment in him quietly grew. Elena sensing it and withdrawing to protect herself.

Communication between them became businesslike or brittle with sarcasm and acrimony. They were caught up in the vicious circles of quietly angry marriage, endless reflections in a hall of mirrors—mirrors that were funhouse warped . . .

And suddenly, now, standing up in his office, he found himself making love to his wife.

Six of her, at first. Then, the six Elenas collapsed into one woman. Like a string of paper dolls folding up into one.

He was making love to an Elena with a violet underglow to her translucent skin, and a purple orb shining at the center of her.

He wanted to run. But then he looked into her face, and saw none of the sophisticated hostility that Elena normally kept there like a falcon in a cage. He saw only the basic Elena, perceptive, vulnerable, curious, private and more emotionally complex than he'd ever guessed.

The impulse to run faded. He sank into her, more deeply yet. His fingers tracing the hollow of her back, her buttocks, finding them entirely new; and finding that his hands were dipping into her skin, shallowly sliding through her skin as if it were a fur of electrically charged flesh.

And then he struck gold.

He drove deeper into her vagina, and the electrode of his organ made contact with the electrical receiver of hers, some inner node of sheer receptivity. Contact.

Hello.

"You're not Elena," he said, ludicrously trying to identify her even as he feverishly pumped into her.

This time she spoke aloud. "Yes and no. Call me Enter. I need your help. I'm trapped in this otherness, trying to get to my husbandside. I'm trapped—" All the time both of them copulating deliriously, joyously, as she gasped into his ear: "Need your help getting through to the free level."

"What are you?"

"A consciousness; a body of different principles but similar essence. A woman. A connection to women, from your viewpoint."

"Where do you come from?"

"An otherness. Not this world; not this plane; not this universe. But with roots in it."

"How can I help?"

"Don't come."

"What?"

"You're about to have an orgasm. The electrical discharge that accompanies the reproductive discharge will come too soon. Don't come, David. Don't orgasm. Wait. Timing is crucial."

He saw it like a tidal wave on the horizon of his mind's eye. An orgasm rolling toward him with the inexorability of a force of nature.

He withdrew from her, just in time. The build of orgasm slowed, faded, stayed aching just on the brink of his groin . . .

He acted on intuition, or perhaps following some instruction she gave him through the secret connections they'd explored. He stepped *through* her, as if she were a door. Walked through Elena; through Enter, who became amorphous and plasmic. Feeling a shock that was almost a burn sear through him as he went. Coming out on the other side knowing that if he looked back, she wouldn't be there. But she was still here, unseeably, waiting for him to complete the favor.

He was standing nude in his office. Clothes heaped on the floor. Skin slippery with sweat and lubricant.

He walked to the door of his office, his erection wagging, transmitting, still, like a radio antenna. Opened the door, the doorknob crackling with sparks under his touch. Walked down the hall to Elena's studio. The room she kept for her hobbies. The door opened for him, before he got there. No one near to open it.

He stepped through. Saw Elena lying back on the rug, naked, her clothes heaped untidily about her. She was panting, glistening with sweat. Her legs apart.

Between Garret and his wife was a low metal table. On it was an intricate design of copper and silvery metal, some sort of occult ideogram made of metals, wired to the electrical socket overhead. Shimmering with violet glow.

With some strange combination of quantum physics and ancient female witchcraft, his wife had invoked Enter, drawn her from another world, channeled her through this one. And drawn someone else too. He could feel his presence. The husbandside. The male one. The one Enter was trying to rejoin. He'd been here, making love to his wife, even as Enter had been making love to Garret.

Like Enter, he was gone now, from the visible world; but he was here.

The wave of intuition that had brought Garret to this room filled in the blanks for him: Elena had been desperate for contact. Found herself unable to break through to him directly. Blocked. Neither of them could bear the humiliation of a marriage counselor. So Elena had tried something exotic and indirect, a quirky synthesis of physics and ancient magic, never expecting it to work. Some personal ritual, performed for psychological reasons, which had translated into objective reality.

Don't question it, Garret thought.

He went to Elena, lay down beside her. The true Elena. He lay beside her and then with her, entering her very soon after the embrace began. Feeling the first orgasm buck through him. Breaking down the barrier between worlds. Enter passing through her to him; Enter's male counterpart passing through Garret to her. Enter and Husbandside meeting and joining and passing on, freed now, into their own world. Having left Elena and Garret transformed behind them.

Garret had a glimpse of something, just before Enter and Husbandside passed on. That Enter and her lover were one creature, with two aspects; two sides of one coin, meeting here where dimensions intersected. And they had connections, interfacings with other consciousnesses—with Garret's, and Elena's. With all others.

Garret made love to his wife several times that night.

And each time—

Contact.

Skeeter Junkie

It struck him, then, and powerfully. How consummate, how exquisite: A mosquito.

Look at the thing. No fraction of it wasted or distracted; more streamlined than any fighter jet, more elegant, for Hector Ansia's taste, than any sports car; in that moment, sexier—and skinnier—than any fashion model. A mosquito.

Hector was happily watching the mosquito penetrate the skin of his right arm.

He was in his El Paso studio apartment, wearing only his threadbare Fruit of the Loom briefs because the autumn night was hot and sticky. The place was empty except for a few books and busted coffee table and sofa, the only things he hadn't been able to sell. But as soon as he'd slammed the heroin, the rat-hole apartment had transformed into a palace bedroom, his dirty sofa into new silk cushions, the heavy, polluted air became the zephyrs of Eden, laced with incense. It wasn't that he hallucinated things that weren't there; but what was there had recast into a heroin-polished dimension of excellence. As he'd taken his shot, he'd looked out the windows at the refineries that studded the periphery of El Paso, through the lens of heroin transformed into Disney castles, their burn-off flames the torches of some charming medieval festival.

He'd just risen out of his nod, like a balloon released under heavy water, ascending from a zone of sweet weight to a place of sweet buoyancy, and he'd only now opened his eyes, and the first thing he saw was the length of his arm over the side of the old velvet sofa. The veins were distended because of the pressure on the underside of his arm, and halfway between his elbow and his hand was the mosquito, pushing its organic needle through the greasy raiment of his epidermis . . .

It was so fine.

He hoped the mosquito could feel the sun of benevolence that pulsed in him. The china white was good, especially because he'd had a long and cruel sickness before finding it, and he'd been maybe halfway to clean again, so his tolerance was down, and that made it so much better to hit the smack in, to fold it into himself.

Stoned, he could feel his Mama's hands on him. He was three years old, and she was washing his back as he sat in a warm bath, and sometimes she would kiss the top of his head. He could feel it now. That's what heroin gave him back.

She hadn't touched him after his fourth birthday, when her new boyfriend had come in fucked up on reds and wine, and the boyfriend had kicked Mama in the head and called her a whore, and the kick broke something in her brain, and after that she just looked at him blank when he cried . . . Just looked at him . . .

Heroin took him back, before his fourth birthday. Sometimes all the way back.

Look at that skeeter, now. Made Hector want to fuck, looking at it.

The mosquito was fucking his arm, wasn't it? Sure it was. Working that thing in. A proboscis, what it was called.

He could feel a thudding from somewhere. After a long moment he was sure the thudding wasn't his pulse; it was the radio downstairs. Lulu, listening to the radio.

Lulu had red-blond hair, cut like in the style of English girls from the old Beatles movies, its points near her cheeks curled to aim at her full lips. She had wide hips and round arms and hazel eyes. He'd talked to her in the hall and she'd been kind of pityingly friendly, enough to pass the time for maybe a minute, but she wouldn't go out with him, or even come in for coffee. Because she knew he was a junkie. Everyone on Selby Avenue knew a junkie when they saw one. He could tell her about his Liberal Arts B.A., but it wouldn't matter: he'd still be just a junkie to her. No use trying to explain, a degree didn't get you a life anymore, you might as well draw your SSI and sell your food stamps; you might as well be a junkie.

Lulu probably figured if she got involved with Hector, he'd steal her money, and maybe give her AIDS. She was wrong about the AIDS—he never ever shared needles—but she was right he'd steal her money, of course. The only reason he hadn't broken into her place was because he knew she'd never leave any cash there, or anything valuable, not living downstairs from a junkie. He'd never get even a ten dollar bag out of that crappy little radio he'd seen through the open door. Nothing much in there. Posters of Chagall, a framed photo of Sting, succulents over-flowing clay pots shaped like burros and turtles.

She was succulent; he wanted her almost as much as her paycheck.

He watched the mosquito.

If he lifted his arm up, would the mosquito stop drinking? He hoped not. He could feel a faint ghost of a pinch, a sensation he saw in his mind's eye as a rose bud opening, and opening, and opening, more than any rose ever had petals.

Careful. He swung his feet on the floor, without moving his arm. The mosquito didn't stir. Then he lifted the arm up, very, very slowly, inch by inch, so as not to disturb the mosquito. It kept right on drinking.

With excruciating languor, Hector stood up straight, keeping the arm motionless except for the slow, slow act of standing. Then—walking very carefully, because the dope made the floor feel like a trampoline—he went to the bookshelf. Easing his right hand onto the edge of a shelf to keep the arm steady, he ran his left over the dusty tops of the old ency-clopedia set. He was glad no one had bought it, now.

The lettering on the book-backs oozed one word onto the next. He was pretty loaded. It was good stuff. He forced his eyes to focus, and then pulled the M book out.

Moving just as slowly, his right arm ramrod stiff, so as not to disturb his beloved—the communion pinch, his precious guest—he returned to the sofa. He sat down, his right arm propped on the arm of the sofa, his left hand riffling pages.

Mosquito . . .

(There was another shot ready on the coffee table. Not yet, *pendajo*. Make it last).

. . . the female mosquito punctures the skin with equipment contained in a proboscis, comprised of six elongated stylets. One stylet is an in-verted trough—the rest are slender mandibles, maxillae, and a stylet for the injection of mosquito saliva. These latter close the trough to make a rough tube. After insertion, the tube arches so that the tip can probe for blood about half a millimeter beneath the epidermal surface . . . Two of the stylets are serrated and saw through the tissue for the others. If a pool of blood forms in a pocket of laceration the mosquito ceases move-ment and sucks the blood with two pumps located in her head . . .

Mosquito saliva injected while probing prevents blood clotting and creates the itching and swelling accompanying a bite . . .

Hector soaked up a pool of words; here, a puddle there, and the color pictures—how wonderfully they put together encyclopedias!—and then he let the volume slide off his lap onto the floor, and found the other syringe with his left hand, and, hardly having to look, with the ambidexterity of a needle freak, shot himself up in a vein he was saving in his right thigh. All the time not disturbing the mosquito.

He knew it was too big a load. But he'd had that long, long Jones, like mirrors reflecting into one another. It should be all right. He stretched out on the sofa again as the hit melted through him, and focused on the mosquito.

Hector's eyelids slid almost shut. But that worked like adjusting binoculars. Making the mosquito come in closer, sharper. It was like he was seeing it under a microscope now. Like he was standing—no, floating—floating in front of the mosquito and he was smaller than it was, like a man standing by an oil derrick, watching it pump oil up from the deep places, the zone of sweet weight . . . thirty-weight, ha . . . An *Anopheles gambiae,* this variety. From this magnified perspective the mosquito's parts were rougher than they appeared from the human level—there were bristles on her head, slicked back like stubby oiled hair, and he could see that the sheath-like covering of the proboscis had fallen in a loop away from the stylets . . . her tapered golden body, resting on the long, translucent, frail-looking legs, cantilevered forward to drink, as if in obeisance . . . her rear lifted, a forty degree angle from the skin, its see-through abdomen glowing red with blood like a little Christmas light . . .

. . . *it is the female which bites, her abdomen distends enormously, allowing her to take in as much as four times her weight in blood . . .*

He had an intimate relationship with this mosquito. It was *entering* him. He could feel her tiny, honed mind, like one of those minute paintings obsessed hobbyists put on the head of a pin. He sensed her regard. The mosquito was dimly aware of his own mind hovering over her. He could close in on the tiny gleam of her insect mind—less than the "mind" of an electric watch—and replace it with his own. What a rare and elegant nod that would be: getting into her head so he could feel what it was like to drink his own blood through the slender proboscis . . .

He could do it. He could superimpose himself and fold his own consciousness up into the micro-cellular spaces. Any mind, large or small, could be concentrated in microscopic space; microspace was as infinite, downwardly, as interstellar space, wasn't it? God experienced every being's consciousness. God's mind could fit into a mosquito. Like all that music on a symphony going through the needle of a record player, or through the tiny laser of a CD. The stylet in the mosquito's proboscis was like the record player's stylus . . .

He could circle, and close in, and participate, and become. He could . . .

. . . see the rising fleshtone of his own arm stretching out in front of him, a soft ridge of topography. He could see the glazing eyes of the man he was drinking from. Himself; perhaps formerly. It was a wonderfully malevolent miracle: he was inside the mosquito. He was the mosquito. Its senses altered and enhanced by his own more-evolved prescience.

His blood was a syrup. The mosquito didn't taste it, as such; but Hector could taste it—through his psychic extension of the mosquito's senses, he supposed—and there were many confluent tastes in it, mineral and meat and electrically charged waters and honeyed glucose and acids and hemoglobin. And very faintly, heroin. His eggs would be well sustained—

Her eggs. Keep your identity sorted out. Better yet, set your own firmly atop hers. Take control.

Stop drinking.

More.

No. Insist, Hector. Who's in charge, here? Stop drinking and fly. Just imagine! To take flight—

Almost before the retraction of her proboscis was completed, he was in the air, making the wings work without having to think about it. When he tried too hard to control the flight, he foundered; so he simply flew.

His flight path was a herky-jerky spiral, each geometric section of it a portion of an equation.

His senses expanded to adjust to the scope of his new possibilities of movement: the great cavern, the massive organism at the bottom of it: himself, Hector's human body, left behind.

Hector sensed a temperature change, a nudge of air: a current from the crack in the window. He pushed himself up the stream, increasing his wing energy, and thought: *I'll crash on the edges of the glass, it's a small crack . . .*

But he let the insect's navigational instincts hold sway, and he was through, and out into the night.

He could go anywhere, anywhere at all . . .

He went downstairs.

Her window was open.

From a distance, the landscape of Lulu was glorious, lying there on the couch in her bikini underpants, and nothing else. Her exposed breasts were great slack mounds of cream and cherry. She'd fallen asleep with the radio on; there were three empty cans of beer on the little end table by her head. One of her legs was drawn up, tilted to lean its knee against the wall, the other out straight, the limbs apart enough to trace her open labia against the blue silk panties.

Hector circled near the ceiling. The radio was a distorted boom of taffied words and industrial-sized beat, far off to port. He thought that, just faintly, he could actually feel radio and TV waves washing over him, passing through the air.

He wanted Lulu. She *looked* asleep. But suppose she felt him, suppose she heard the whine of his coming, and slapped, perhaps just in reflex, and crushed him—

Would he die when the mosquito died?

Maybe that would be all right.

Hector descended to her, following the broken geometries of insect flight-path down, an aerialist's unseen staircase, asymmetrical and yet perfect.

Closer—he could feel her heat. God, she was like a lake of fire! How could the skeeters bear it?

He entered her atmosphere. That's how it seemed: she was almost planetary in her glowing vastness, hot-house and fulsome. He descended through hormone-rich layers of her atmosphere, to deeper and more personal heats, until he'd settled on the skin of her left leg near the knee.

Jesus! It was revolting. It was ordinary human skin.

But up this close; hugely magnified by his mosquito's perspective . . .

It was a cratered landscape, orange and gold and in places white; here and there flakes of blue, where dead skin cells were shedding away. In the wens of pores and around the bases of the occasional stiff stalks of hair were puddly masses of pasty stuff he guessed were colonies of bacteria. The skin itself was textured like pillows of meat all sewn together. The smells off it were overwhelming: rot and uric acid and the various compounds in sweat and a chemical smell of something she'd bathed with—and an exudation of something she'd been eating . . .

Hector was an experienced hand with drugs; he shifted his viewpoint from revulsion to obsession, to delight in the yeasty completeness of this immersion in the biological essence of her. And there was another smell that came to him then, affecting him the way the sight of a woman's cleavage had, in his boyhood. Blood.

Unthinking, he had already allowed the mosquito to unsheathe her stylets and drive them into a damp pillow of skin cells. He pushed, rooted, moving the slightly arched piercer in a motion that outlined a cone, breaking tiny capillaries just inside the epidermis, making a pocket for the blood to pool in. And injecting the anti-coagulant saliva.

Her blood was much like his, but he could taste the femaleness of it, the hormonal signature and . . . alcohol.

She swatted him.

He felt the wind of the giant hand, before it struck. She struck at him in her sleep, and the hand wasn't rigid enough to hit him, the palm was slightly cupped. But the hand covered Hector like a lid for a moment.

The air pressure flattened the mosquito, and Hector feared for his spindly legs, but then light flashed over him again and the lid lifted, and he withdrew and flew, wings whining, up a short distance into the air . . .

She was mostly quiescent now. Looking from here like the rolling, shrub-furred hills you saw in parts of California: one hill blending smoothly into the next, until you got close and saw ant colonies and rattlers and tarantulas between the clumps.

She hadn't awakened. And from up here her thighs looked so sweet and tender . . .

He dipped down, and alighted on Lulu's left inside thigh, not far from the pale blue circus tent billow of her panties. The material was only a little stained; he could see the tracery of her labia like the shadows of sleeping dragons under a silk canopy. The thigh skin was a little smoother, paler. He could see the woods of pubic hair down the slope a little.

Enough. Eggs, outside.

No. He was in control. He was going to get closer . . .

When at last he reached the frontier of Lulu's panties, and stood between two outlying spring-shaped stalks of red-brown pubic hair, gazing under a wrinkle in the elastic at the monumental vertical furrow of her vaginal lips, he was paralyzed by fear. This was a great temple to some subaquatic monster, and would surely punish any intrusion.

With the fear came a sudden perception of his own relative tininess, now, and an unbottling of his resentments. She was forbidden, she was gargantuan in both size and arrogance.

But he had learned that he was the master of his reality. He had found a hatch in his brain, and a set of new controls that fit naturally to his grip, and as he chose.

A sudden darkness, then; a wind—

He sprang up, narrowly escaping the swat. Hearing a sound like a jet breaking the sound barrier—the wind of her hand and the slap on her thigh. Then a murky roaring, a boulder-fall of misshapen words. The goddess coming awake; the goddess speaking.

Something like, *"Fucking skeeter . . . little shit . . . get the fuck out . . ."*
Oh, yes?

The fury swelled in him, and as it grew—Lulu shrank. Or seemed to, as rage pushed his boundaries out like a parade balloon, but unthinkable fast. She shrank to woman size, once more desirable.

She screamed, of course.

He glimpsed them both in her vanity mirror . . .

A man-sized mosquito, poised with slender but strong front legs; Lulu screaming, as he leaned back onto his hind legs and spread her legs with the middle limbs and drove his piercer through the fabric of her panties and into the forbidden temple of the goddess, into the tube of what was now only the tender little outer membrane of her reproductive organs. He thrust the thirty-inch proboscis stylets deep into the vagina. He pulled out a little; he thrust in . . . feeling her writhe in a disgusted ecstasy . . .

He might go the next step. Thrust through her cervix, into the womb, and beyond to an artery; suck her so hard she turned inside out and atomized and sucked whole into him, making him three times bigger.

But he held off. He pumped his proboscis like a dick and—

In her delighted revulsion, she struck at the mosquito's compound eyes.

The pain was realer and more personal than he'd expected. He jerked back, withdrawing, floundering off the edge of the bed, feeling a leg shatter against the floor and a wing crack, one of his eyes half blind . . .

The pain and the disorientation unmanned him. Emasculated him, intimidated him. As always when that happened, he shrank.

The boundaries of the room expanded and the bed grew, around him, into a dirty white plain; Lulu grew, again becoming a small world to herself . . . Her hand sliced down at him—

He threw himself frantically into the air, his damaged wings ascending stochastically; the wings' keening sound not quite right now, his trajectory uncertain.

The ceiling loomed; the window crack beckoned.

In seconds he had swum upstream against the night air, and managed to aim himself between the edges of the crack in the glass; the lips of the break like a crystalline take on her vagina. Then he was out into the night, and regaining some greater control over his wings . . .

That's not how it was, he realized: *she*, the mosquito had control. That's how they'd gotten through the crack and out into the night.

Let the mosquito mind take the head, then, for now, while he rested his psyche and pondered. That great yellow egg, green around the edges with refinery toxins, must be the moon; this jumble of what seemed sky-scraper-sized structures must be the pipes and chimneys and discarded tar buckets of the apartment building's roof.

Something washed over him, rebounding, making him shudder in the air. Only after it departed did it register in his hearing: a single high note, from somewhere above.

There, it came again, more defined and pulsingly closer, as if growing in an alien certainty about its purpose.

The mosquito redoubled its wing beats in reaction, and there was an urgency that was too neurologically primitive to be actual fear. *Enemy. Go.*

Hector circled down between the old brick apartment buildings, toward the streetlight . . .

Another, slightly higher, even more purposeful note hit Hector, reso-nating him, and then a shadow draped him, and wing beats thudded tympanically on the air. He saw the bat for one snapshot-clear moment, superimposed against the dirty indigo sky. Hector knew he should de-tach from the mosquito, but the outspread wings of the bat, its pointed ears and wet snout, caught him with its heraldic perfection—it was as perfect, poised against the sky, as the mosquito had seemed, poised on his arm. It trapped him with fascination.

Sending out a final sonar note to pinpoint the mosquito, the bat struck its head forward—

But Hector was diving now, under it, swirling in the air, letting himself fall for a ways just to get the most distance.

He glimpsed the hangar-like opening of a window and flew for it. He sensed a body inside and newly flowing female blood. An even bigger woman.

He had to rest first. He found a spot on a wall near the ceiling. Some-time later there was the sound of a radio alarm coming on to wake the sleeper below him, the radio in mid-monologue . . .

And this is the KRED crack-of-dawn-news, all the news that's fit to trans-mit. Look out for your hamburgers, folks, that's the story that comes to KRED radio from Lubbock where a woman was shot by a burger. It seems that some twisted soul has been putting .22 caliber bullets into ground meat sold at Lubbock supermarkets. The bullet exploded while the burger was cooking last night and the woman suffered a minor facial wound from a bullet fragment . . . Chrysler has announced two new plant closures and plans to lay off some 35,000 people . . . Give us about, oh, an hour and we'll give you the first KRED morning traffic report . . .

REALLY, REALLY, REALLY, WEIRD STORIES

∞ ∞ ∞

When Lulu woke, she had cramps. But it was the aftertaste of the dream that bothered her. There was a taintedness lingering on her skin, as if the nightmare of the giant mosquito had left a sort of mephitic insect phero-mone on her. She took two showers, and ate her breakfast, and listened to the radio, and, by comforting degrees, forgot about the dream. When she went downstairs the building manager was letting the ambulance attendants in. They were in no hurry. It was the guy upstairs, the manager said. He was dead.

No one was surprised. He was a junkie. Everybody knew that.

Next day Lulu was scratching the skeeter bites, whenever she thought no one was looking.

WHAT JOY! WHAT FULFILLMENT!

Henry was a bit disappointed by his suicide.

It wasn't, he told himself, that he'd really wanted the spectacular sort of suicide he'd once imagined for himself, just eleven years before, when he'd been a seventeen-year-old role-playing gamer in Covina, California. He'd pictured strapping dynamite to himself, then walking into Congress and blowing them all up along with himself. No particular political grudges involved; he'd simply wanted a suicide that would earn him a place in history.

And neither had he wanted the melodramatic sort of suicide that his friend Lydia had genuinely pulled off: hanging herself, with a sign on her chest, outside her parents' bedroom door one night so that the next morning they'd opened the door to find their fifteen-year-old daughter dangling crookedly, hours dead, bearing a sign that read:

THIS *IS* WHAT YOU WANTED, ISN'T IT?

No. Too over-the-top, even had he still entertained those kinds of childish motivations for suicide. His suicide wasn't really a suicide at all: it was the first step through the Gate, first step in a journey to a reunion. It was *cosmically* motivated, in the true sense. It was a purification, Marshall had said, a transcendance.

Anyway, he thought, now, as he waited for his journey to really begin, simple though the suicide was, it had been done *right*. He'd carried it off perfectly. He stood—if stood was the word—gazing appreciatively at his body lying there, in its orange robe, with the candles about it, the ritual incense still smoking. His face hadn't contorted; there was no spray of vomit from the mouth. His pudgy late-twenties body had never looked better. And it had been as Marshal had said it would be, quite painless. Take the pills, eat the toxified Jell-O, drink the wine. Wait for the sleeping pills to do their work, and so they had; he didn't even remember losing consciousness. Then the poison had stirred itself into his bloodstream, completing the recipe, and *voilá*; there was not even a sense of wrenching in the parting. His spirit had slipped out of his body as easily as he'd shrugged out of his bathrobe before the ritual cleansing in the Motel 6's shower.

It wasn't perfect, though, not really: he'd had to go solo, having left the Passengers before Marshal declared them ready. And he'd never had the courage to remove his testicles, as some of the others had. He'd been there when it had been done to Jerry. The drugs, the garden clippers. The blood, the little splash into the bucket. He'd gotten dizzy and almost thrown up. And the sight had led to his leaving them; running home to Mother. Who, of course, was pained to see him back at home. "Pain when you first came out, a pain in the ass when you walk back in, too," she'd said, sipping her dry Manhattan. Thinking herself funny, too. That was the amazing thing. But she'd been humiliated when someone at the Women's Creativity Circle had said she'd seen him interviewed on TV as a 'cult survivor'.

He wished she could be here now; wished she could be here with him spiritually, and see, just see, really see for herself—

The far wall of the motel room was gone. When had it vanished? It was just dark there, a sucking darkness, a smiling, hungry darkness—

Then he was spinning through it, flying through space, through—yes, it was The Tunnel! And through The Tunnel to . . .

A kaleidoscope of his past, all osterized together: getting kicked out of Boy Scouts for masturbating; Mr. Smith taking him into the showers after PE and playing with his thing; birthday with his Dad, good feelings because his Dad had really loved him; his Dad's death; the funeral; school and school and school and smoking hash after school with Buddy who was the first one who asked him if he believed in UFOs; seeing *Close Encounters* and believing he saw himself going into that spaceship with Richard Dreyfus; getting laid and feeling sick afterwards and the girl laughing; Mother telling him he was "a mistake who keeps on making them;" *Dungeons and Dragons,* and he saw the characters in all the role-playing games there before him, as real people, real beings; games and games and games; miserably realizing he was failing in college; the flying saucer he'd seen, a shining oblong that his brother had insisted was just a blimp catching sunset light, but Henry had known . . . It was *them.* And they were looking for him . . .

Buddy telling him about Marshal. Marshal, the old man with the sexless, eternally smiling eyes, welcoming him to the Passengers, to Heaven's Gate . . .

But now, as he hurtled through the curtains of eternity where were the stars? Had Marshal said anything about this kaleidoscope of memories? Henry didn't think so. It was hard to think. It was all . . .

Where were the stars?

Where were the stars that Marshal had promised? Where was the comet that accompanied the great Mothership of the Space Angels, those beings of light who appeared to human beings more like oversized newts, but who—

There! The stars! As if his expectation, his seeking had summoned them, there were the stars, the nebulae, the majestic planets, marbled with color, whirling by; and there—yes, there! There was the comet! And beside it . . . That Saturn-shaped vehicle of shining silver, its power-ring encrusted with energy gems . . . The Mothership!

A starship, yes—but with a whole other spiritual dimension to it, just as Marshal had described it. A starship with its own aura, propelled through space by the divine energy of the space angels within it.

He was falling toward it now. Funny how in space you seemed to be flying along without an up or down but when you approached a thing you fell toward it . . . And so it was now, the Mothership seeming "be-low" him, getting bigger and bigger . . .

Would it admit him? Or would it turn him away, because he'd run away from what his brother had sneeringly called a cult, because he'd refused to keep the faith?

"Marshal!" he shouted, but the shouting was soundless here in the vacuum of space. And he didn't have a mouth, really, to shout with—did he? But he kept trying. *"Marshallll!"*

Then he saw Marshal like a ghostly giant against the stars; Marshal in a shimmering robe, a translucent projection of Marshal emanating from the giant Mothership . . . Welcoming him with open arms!

And lo! Heaven's Gate opened for him! A great hatchway had rolled back on the curved surface of the giant starship below him, and a shaft of golden light shone up on him from within, and it caught him in it, drew him closer, like a tractor beam in *Star Wars*, and he passed the glittering outer hull of the starship and was drawn through a corridor of silver-flecked glass, diamond walls flickering with the inner fires of the ship's divinely energized stardrive.

Then he passed through—just as Marshal had described it!—the Rain-bow of Purification, which removed the last stains of sin and doubt from him, making him feel ecstatically buoyant, the lightest element in the universe!

And then, two great golden doors swung back for him . . . and a celestial music filled the air, a music you could feel like a spray of cool mist and a warm sea breeze, a music that carried you like a butterfly on an updraft . . . A music with a beat!

It sort of reminded him of a John Tesh song he'd heard once, a kind of New Age dance song

Maybe John Tesh *had* been an alien! But of course—there he was, Tesh in person, dancing with the others! Hundreds of others! Human and alien, dancing together on and above a crystalline dance floor that shimmered with rainbow light to the music's beat . . .

And there was Buddy! And Linda, and Drew and Luce and Wendy and Hassan and . . . there was Marshal, up on that dais, standing beside a grey alien who wore a crown of tiny stars caught in an little web of antigravity forces. The Queen of the Galaxy herself!

Then he was down among them, with all his old friends whirling around him, and the joy was incandescent in him, and the relief was enormous. It had all been true! And he danced beneath a weightless floating chandelier of light, within high walls of mother-of-pearl, floating over the glassy, shining floor: the ballroom of the gods.

And so they danced in the travelling disco of the stars, to the rave music of the spheres, human beings in shimmering robes dancing with the little grey aliens who moved like spiraling smoke to the music, loving greys laughing like elves, and his human friends, too, dancing around him smiling, Jerry and Buddy and all the girls . . . He spoke to Buddy . . .

"Isn't this great? It was all true!"

Buddy's happy expression never changed, he just danced and waved his arms over his head.

"Buddy? Hey Buddy! Isn't this great?"

He shouted it now, leaning nearer. Not sure how physical these people would be, though occasionally he could feel someone jostle him. Buddy turned him a happy look, like the expression on the face of a bot, some character in a computer game. A computer animated face, almost. But . . . Then he saw another Buddy's face—beneath Buddy's face. Another face behind the outer one. It looked anguished. For a moment it pushed through the membrane of the outer, smiling face and it screamed and he heard the scream in his mind:

Henry we can't get out of them! . . . They're doing something to us, they're . . . Henry try to get out before—

But then the music changed; it was as if someone had taken the coherent stream of music in sonic hands and twisted it, like a wet towel, and ripped it, and another music was revealed within the first like Buddy's anguished face within the happy one.

That's when Henry noticed the aliens were growing; the little happy greys stretching out like Gumby, fleshing out, swelling like balloons, becoming taller than the humans—and then each one embraced one of the humans . . . One of them had embraced Buddy and now Buddy's outer face simply fizzled out and was gone, and his inner face, the true face, screamed soundlessly as the thing drew him into itself the way an amoeba sucks in a smaller organism, and Buddy was inside the thing, pushing on its now-transparent skin from within its hollow innards, like a man inside a balloon pushing to get out and not able to break the rubbery sac; and the grey began to shrink, its face changing, its body shrink-wrapping over Buddy's—and others doing the same to Luce, to Jerry, to all the others . . . and yes the queen was doing it to Marshal! And the music had become a triumphant cacophony, and the mother-of-pearl walls had cracked, began to issue yellow pustulence, to leak red like festering wounds, and the floor had become a glutinous, bubbling acid with bits and pieces of human bodies floating in it, and giant sections of carrot and chunks of half digested meat, and the chandelier had become a tube that spat down two more luckless late-coming suicides; and it was all a giant stomach, and the aliens inside it were spirits who used this great external stomach to break them down so they could consume them, and he saw them now as they really were: sadistic mockeries of human faces, grossly diabolic, with pendulous tongues and eyesockets that extruded maggots, each maggot with one tiny eye on it that the demon used to see, and Luce—Henry'd had such a crush on her!—screamed and clawed and tried to get out of the interior of one of the transformed greys and it howled with laughter.

And now one of the creatures was looming over Henry, grinning down at him and he tried to run but the soupy floor sucked at him and he sank down—

But with a huge effort of the spirit he tore himself free and rocketed straight upward, flying, carried by pure will, jetting on the fuel of ectoplasm toward the spewing tube in the ceiling—

He heard Marshal wailing after him, screaming at him to come back, to have faith, it must be a test, it must be!

But then he was in the ceiling tube, ascending up it like a bird flying up a well, spiraling, his lower parts burning, exhaustion pulling on him like gravity, but up he went—and burst out through a vertical wound in the hide of the thing . . .

And now that he was free of the mothership he saw that it was a great and hideous and eternally hungry creature itself, a bloated, wounded thing of gray scales and ooze, and he knew its name: ASMODEUS . . . Asmodeus floating not amongst stars but in a gray nothingness, the betweenness of limbo, and he knew that he and the others had seen . . .

Had seen . . .

Had seen, at first, only the afterlife that they'd expected to see. They'd seen the afterlife Marshal had coached them to see, until the truer afterlife had broken through the decaying consensual vision; and the hungry creatures who waited, there, for the mindless, for the unconscious, for those who followed their fears and petty impulses, for those who followed stronger minds from birth to death: these hungry ones had made use of their group fantasy, held them in it until the trap had finally closed and the moment had come for their wholesale and salacious consumption.

Henry ascended still, trying to put as much distance as possible between himself and the hideous creature he had once thought a beautiful "mothership" . . .

Then a whipping pseudopod issued from the crown of tortured tendrils on the giant head of Asmodeus, and it gripped Henry about the middle and drew him close to its vast, stinking mouth and he tried to remember a prayer, to prepare himself for the death within a death . . .

But instead it spoke.

"I perceive a provocative little independence here . . . Beginning with your first escape from the trap, and showing itself again with your second attempt . . . Just enough initiative to make you useful . . . The other lure insisted on believing his own lies—but you, you will not make that mistake . . . Now if you would be other than digested, make your bargain, small one . . ."

Henry had been dead and reincarnated for twenty-eight earthly years before the Great Revelation came to him. He now had another body, another name to go with it: he was now Ervin Holmes, known to some as the Penultimate Prophet, teacher to the twenty-first century's own Lost Generation, and until this moment—

Sitting in the dressing room of the little auditorium, waiting to go on, to speak to a few hundred followers.

It was at this moment that he saw his real mission. Looking into the dressing room mirror, he saw Asmodeus himself, floating in the silvery glass as in the gray betweenness of limbo.

"Now, small one . . . bring me food, or become food yourself . . ."

And so he went on stage, and smiled, and a hush descended over the crowd, and he said, "I have good news for you. You don't have to stay in this dark, brutal world anymore. The Space Angels have spoken to me—and they are ready to receive you . . . the transition will be a bit frightening to contemplate. But once you get there . . . oh, once you get there—"

"Oh my friends—"

"What joy, what fulfillment!"

And his followers cried out in glad assent.

199619971998*

She was a small soft thing walking in the shadow of great hard things, under the sullen gray sky of a November morning. She was in North Central California, and she was quite alone. She was Little Connie Depthcharge, taking a walk into the year 1996. That's how she thought of it. Every second, she reasoned, took her further into the year. And the year was unfolding around her, bleak and relentless, pervading this edifice of decay. The year 1996 was a place, Connie thought. This time is a place. Not all times are places, not so you'd notice, but this one was.

Connie was nine years old. Until this year she had perceived the world as a sort of efflorescence blossoming symmetrically out from her; she had imagined herself at the center of it. Now she saw that the world had no center, or none visible. Perhaps there was some great sucking whirlpool of events somewhere, like the black hole in that old Disney movie she'd panned in the videocassette section of her column for *Weekly Reader* (the column was called "The Cinematic Bitch." Now that the children's newspaper had gone yellow tabloid, with blaring headlines like "My Mom Has Sex with the Vacuum Cleaner and I'm, Like, So Embarrassed," it had room for Little Connie's penetrating if spiteful analyses.)

Connie was thinking about these things as she walked along the weed-thatchy railroad tracks. She was walking through the old industrial park. It was closed today. Much of it had been closed continuously since the Dream Plagues. The smokestacks were streaked with rust, marbled with cracks; the acid rains had pitted the gray and black walls of the monolithic buildings squatting on both sides of her. She liked to walk here because the place had a dreary, *cinémavérité* quality that she found reassuring. It had no *affect*. It could be trusted, she thought, to remain itself. She was weary of the unpredictable, since the Dream Plagues; since the

* Don't you remember when all this happened?

War of the Weirdos; since the jarring sight of the people spinning by overhead, high on antigravity drugs . . . Here, at least, there were no surprises.

A lizard surprised her by scuttling from a hole. It seemed too cold for lizards to be about. The lizard was a leathery sizzle, here and gone. Then another, darting from another hole. And another. And then the warm-blooded things, rats and mice, oozing from holes in the ridges of cinders to either side of the rusty tracks, shimmying from the cracks in the dusty foundations of the old factories, small living things moving like a fear hormone through this industrial vein, scrambling randomly about, ignoring her, and she read the signs for what they were. She could feel it herself, then: felt it in the soles of her feet. In *that* spot, the place in her foot that Mother said contained a gland of some kind. (Poor crazy Mama; poor dead Mama; she'd insisted on a coffin shaped and painted like a *Deep Space Nine* lunchbox. It was, like, so embarrassing. But it was *her* funeral.)

Staggering to remain upright, Little Connie felt the vibrations ripple up from some epicenter below the railroad tracks; saw the dust rise in matched ripples to either side as it traveled outward; saw the symmetry become confusion as the vibrations collided with quake vibrations coming from the opposite direction. She thought of blenders and taffy machines and Mama's candy-striped vibrator.

She was too fascinated, just then, to be afraid. This was her first earthquake, and she thought of it as a storm in the earth, weather underfoot, and, swaying, she sought to find its groove, the way her mother had taught her. "Every storm has a groove," Mama had said.

But then the buildings began to move. They weren't falling, they weren't caving in. They were moving toward one another. The newer ones were moving faster, she noticed. They were moving with an impossible ease, sailing the ground like ships across water, either making the earthquake or made to move by the earthquake, thunderous but absurdly graceful. Like improbably swift icebergs, coming together . . . and she was going to be caught between them.

But still the terror refused to come. She wondered at its absence. Perhaps she was numb; perhaps resigned to death. She was alone in the world. Why not?

Closer. The buildings sailed across the open ground, plowing up the gravel, coming corner first like a prow making a wake in the dirt, raising fantails of dust, shrieking with the grind of metal and concrete like a ghost in chains. Closer, looming over her; she could smell friction, see sparks rising like spray from the prow of these industrial ships . . .

Maybe this was all hallucination, she told herself. But the Dream Plagues were over, and she knew what *that* felt like. Hallucinations had a distinctive quality. No, this was no dream, she knew, as a chunk of rock, smashed by one onrushing building against another, flew apart and a fragment hit her cheek. It stung nastily, and blood ran along her jawline. No, this was real. Objectively real.

The buildings loomed over her . . . and then the corners of the buildings had pushed past her on either side, grinding the railroad steel into tangled ribbons that whipped through the air . . . She dodged a cobra of torn steel and, staggering in the shockwaves cracking the ground, she stepped into the interstice between the two onrushing prows, where outthrust bulkheads, passing one another, made a sort of alleyway a few feet wide . . .

The buildings stopped moving; cacophony gave way to eerie silence. She waited, breathless, as the dust settled. The buildings on either side had moved together, leaving only a few gaps here and there, like the gaps between wrongly fitted jigsaw-puzzle pieces. She was safe in one of these, for the moment.

The buildings had moved very deliberately, she thought. Not like things nudged by some geologic randomness. Who is moving them? Why?

She knew it wasn't over. She could feel it.

That's when the smokestacks tilted over and began to snake toward one another. She watched as, overhead, a set of smokestacks from two separate buildings met mouth to mouth and, somehow, locked together.

The tortured metal squealed. The windows of the buildings shattered. Connie ducked flying shards of oily glass as sections of machinery thrust themselves through windows and moved click-click, snick-snick, creak-creak, together, locking into unity like the smokestacks: sections of pipe and wire and gauges and robotic arms and struts and more wire and tubing and gears and cogs and the rollers from conveyor belts and metal hooks and stamping units and stainless-steel presses and a thousand intricate variations of metal and plastic and rubber innards she couldn't identify; self-animated, they began to rewire and reconstruct themselves, grinding and caterwauling and moaning and sparking in the process, making a mazelike roof of odd machine parts a few feet over Connie's head . . .

"Right this way, Little Connie! Big sale on small favors!" It was a man's voice, melodious and warm and perhaps a touch unctuous. But a voice to inspire confidence. She crawled toward the sound, under the writhing nest of living metal. Half expecting to be caught up by the wires and pipes, forced into the woof of their rigid weave, crushed and incorporated in living death.

REALLY, REALLY, REALLY, WEIRD STORIES

No. She emerged from beneath the ceiling of the living unliving, and found herself on her knees before a doorway at the end of the alley. It was a cobwebby old back door of one of the factories, and standing in the open door was a sign shaped like a man. One of those cardboard cutout life-size photos you see promoting things in a supermarket. But then it moved and she saw it wasn't a sign, it was quite three-dimensional and human. Some quality of absolute emblematic expression—as if this man were *only* semiotics—had made him seem artificial at first. Looking at his face, the fixed expression of faintly self-deprecating glee, the drugged eyes and idiotic grin, the unwavering diagonal of the ordinary brown pipe clenched in teeth so white and even they looked all of a piece . . . the perfect quizzical brows and immaculate swept-back short black hair . . .

Looking up into that face she once more had the sense of emblem, of semiotic absolutes . . .

And then he spoke. His mouth moved; the pipe bobbed-some noxious herb in it tracing a wavery line of blue smoke in the air—his head tilted . . . but the expression remained the same. "Connie," he said, "we have to move quickly. The Prototime is upon us. Am I right? You coming? Or do you prefer to die horribly, by remaining here?"

She blinked. He hadn't asked the question sarcastically, or facetiously. It was as if he sincerely thought she might actually *want* to die horribly. As if it were a viable option, like, would you prefer to take the train or a jet? "Lead the way," she said.

They went through the door and behind her the buildings closed up the gaps, sidling and edging till they fit perfectly together. The right jig-saw-puzzle pieces after all.

The factory was reconstructing itself around them. It was merging with another factory; thesis, antithesis, synthesis, and the synthesis was heavy-metal pandemonium. The feverish self-redesigning was clearly guided, conscious—but what consciousness was the guiding force was a palpable mystery Connie could taste in her mouth and smell in her nostrils, along with the stink of random lightning bolts and the ancient scent-of uneasy petroleum and tortured metal and ozone.

She walked in the lee of the briskly striding stranger, a tall man in a timeless suit, her eyes stung by the smoke from his pipe. They plunged through a mechanical Armageddon, as machines threw themselves through the air at one another—but instead of crashing the machine sec-tions merged perfectly; machines that could not possibly have been de-signed to interface somehow *tilted and gyrated* to interface. She thought again of puzzle parts. All this time the puzzle parts have lain about us on the table and we didn't know they fit together. To make . . . what?

Sparks flew, smoke belched, wires whipped, pipes clanged, things flashed past, moved in a blur in search of unity, a dance of death all around them, and somehow, miraculously, they walked through the gauntlet untouched. The man never seemed to look around, never seemed to watch where he was going at all. He just blundered through and somehow, so far, was unhurt. Once, a year before, looking through the window of a factory, she'd seen a mouse run along a conveyor belt. The conveyor belt carried bits of soft metal to stamping presses that stamped the metal into Dabney the Poodle doorbell ringers, a faddish novelty item. The mouse ran under the stampers—and past them, narrowly avoiding getting crushed five times before it leapt free. Just the luck of the very stupid, she'd thought.

Was that what was happening now?

Not for everyone. She glimpsed people—maybe workmen, maybe caretakers—caught in the machinery, skewered and crushed like cockroaches caught in a garbage disposal . . . she couldn't bear to look, to think about it. She tried to think of something to talk to the man about, to get her mind off what she'd seen.

"How'd you know my name?" she asked, shouting it over the uneven racket of the place.

"It was written on your pstench!" he shouted. "I whiffread it! Your mom had it coded into your DNA so I could find you!"

A lunatic, she thought. But he had saved her life. "What's *your* name?"

He stopped and turned to her. An enormous razor-edged pendulum of metal swept by in the spot he would have been in had he kept going. It would have pulped him, she thought, if I hadn't asked him his name just then. He thrust out a hand to her, like an encyclopedia salesman who'd come to the door once. (Mom had broken the guy's fingers.) She shook his hand. Feverishly warm. Possibilities squirmed under the skin. "The name is Dobbs! J.R. "Bob" Dobbs!" You could hear the quotation marks around *"Bob."* He turned and swept onward, plunging recklessly through the storm of flying metal. She followed, trying not to look around, tasting the fear now.

Up ahead, a conveyor belt was taking cryptically shaped segments of crystal up an incline, toward the ceiling, and through a hole in the roof.

They stepped off the conveyor belt, onto the roof. Beside them, the fist-sized irregular chunks of crystal fell off the belt and rolled with effortless serendipity to fit perfectly into irregular holes pocking the roof. To the left the expanse of tarpaper was unbroken. "Bob" strode off to the edge of the roof; Connie followed. When she got there she saw with a flush of embarrassment that he'd unzipped his pants and was peeing off the edge of the building. With his free hand he gestured sweepingly at the great world. "Behold, the Prototime!"

She gazed out over the city. The buildings on the Strip, beyond the edge of the industrial park, were moving and changing too. They were all franchises and chains of some sort: 7-Eleven, Soy-Boy, PetroPup, In-n-Out, PigeonPie, Pioneer Chicken, Colonel Sanders, McDonald's, Carl's Jr., Horse Habit, ArtiFish 'n' Chips, and the discount department store chains, K-mart and Target and Bozo's Re-Cycled Goods and the other places like Kragoff's Soviet Auto Parts . . .

They were all moving together, like a film of an explosion run backwards, leaping together, or stumping on their signs like they were crutches and falling together in some cryptic organization that, once achieved, seemed natural and normal . . . because they all fit. K-mart fit with Pioneer Chicken and PetroPup fit with Carl's Jr., they locked together like machine parts, signs snicking into place in door slots, oddly angled roof peaks fitting neatly into drive-in windows, all the jumble of architectural ineptitude she'd always wondered about suddenly made sense when they were locked together, and an *über*building came about, the gestalt fruit of this fevered mating . . . an enormous quasi-crystalline structure that reached out multicolored limbs of fiberglass and plastic and impossibly flexible roofing tiles to interface neatly with the reconstructed shapes of the industrial park, all of it becoming One Thing, some minatory self-contained environment . . .

The clangor and roar of it resonated the surface of the planet like a cymbal.

Afraid, feeling so tiny in the sight of this mighty reconstruction (and seeing that "Bob" had put his majestic privates back in his pants and zipped them up), Little Connie took "Bob's" hand and moved close beside him. " "Bob" . . . is it happening everywhere?"

"No. But it *will* happen everywhere, unless we stop it, Little Connie. This is the Prototime, the precursor to X-Day, Connie, the Con's prep for July 5th, 1998. They're setting a trap for us, so we will be lost to those charismatic strangers from Planet X when they arrive on Earth . . . a trap set by the Conspiracy and triggered by the Malign Sendings of the Yacatisma! What you're seeing is the Conspiracy preparing the way for the Yacatisma (not to be confused with Yacatizma) who seek to prevent me from interceding with the Xists. The Conspiracy hid this one from us,

Connie . . . they hid it from us using the power of the Smog Monster, who blanketed the Earth with toxic complacency. The poisons spread through the air slowly, subtly, and we accepted them. The 'intelligent' among humanity found a thousand intelligent ways to rationalize them—so no one fought them . . . and they affected our minds. Made even those of us who See into the Higher Wire a little blind, just enough so they created a psychic smoke screen, enabling the Conspiracy to plant their submolecular nanotechnological machinery in the paint and insulation and plastics and lubricants of these structures hence, this went unpredicted, Little Connie. Fuck! The Smog Monster fooled us all . . . for the Smog Monster is a sending of . . . *GBROAGFRAN!!!, the Rebel God* from *Deep Space!*" With the uttering of this arcane name, his voice took on an amplified reverb quality that should have been possible only with recording-studio equipment. "I was driving to Kragoff's Soviet Auto Parts to see if they had something that would work as a water pump for a '57 Studebaker, when I felt the submolecular Conspirals of self-organizing quantum-mechavibrational systems in the Material Reality Underpinnings—and knew we'd been snookered. *The Smog Monster is creating an enormous mechanized concentration camp for the processing and subjugation of SubGeniuses and non-Normals of all kinds!* We should have guessed, seeing the franchises and chain stores scab up around the periphery of the cities, like ringworm, like an encamped army around us, tightening the noose, subjecting us to bombardments of mind-numbing consumer-conditioning symbols. I should have guessed they were simply preparing the ground for this . . ." He paused to stuff a wad of multicolored herb into his pipe—somehow the pipe never quite went out as he did this . . . Puffing, talking out of the side of his mouth, chattering rapid-fire but offhandedly the whole time: "Lucky for you I came to investigate. *Lucky for you* is a blessing, dear child, that makes the mealymouthed prayers of the 'Holy Father' in the Vatican smell like a dog fart, my Little Connie . . ."

"All of this"—Connie looked out at the gigantic artifact building itself around them—"is going to trap us? It's some kind of prison?"

"Exactly. A Conspiracy concentration camp . . . a camp without guards for it has *a life of its own* . . . it is its own guards . . ."

"You talk just like my Mom," Connie observed. "Did you know my Mom? Betty Furnace? She used to talk about the Yacatisma and used to say 'not to be confused with Yacatizma' just the same way you did . . ."

"Bob" turned to her and laid a hand on her head, ruffling her hair gently. "Yes," he said tenderly, allowing ashes from his pipe to drop into her eyes, "Yes, I knew your mother. Betty was—"

REALLY, REALLY, REALLY, WEIRD STORIES

He was interrupted by an explosion.

There was a narrow section of ground—narrowing more as the concentration camp construct creaked and shuddered nearer—four stories beneath their roof edge. It had erupted, a fissure opening in it to gout violet and sulfur-yellow smoke that geysered upward, a furious spew that towered over them like a Djinn . . . and a sort of Djinn it was . . .

Little Connie and "Bob" staggered backwards ("Bob" had a quality about him of having *planned* to stagger or stumble though he couldn't possibly have planned it . . .), Connie clinging to "Bob," choking in the stink of the thing, the rotten-eggs-mixed-with-semitruck-smoke gas-chamber stench of it, as its rolling mass shaped into . . .

"It is the one called AH'OOGAH!" "Bob" shouted. "The Smog Monster!"

"YOU MUST NOT INTERFERE WITH THE GESTATION!" came a voice from within the foul whirlwind. It was a voice belched from exhaust pipes and smokestacks . . . a voice without a muffler. "TRY YOUR FAMOUS LUCK OUT ON DEATH ITSELF!"

And AH'OOGAH swung toward them like a tornado wielded as a hammer—

—as "Bob" grabbed Connie's hand and stumbled with her off the edge of the roof.

She was falling. The Earth rushed up at her . . .

And then the Earth was *above* her. The ground was a sort of ceiling

She was falling *up* to "Bob" was beside her, still holding her hand, his head thrown back, the pipe clenched in his teeth gushing a locomotive cloud of blue (and green-sparkled) smoke that surrounded them, made her choke with its cloying incense . . . but somehow as she inhaled it, a certain ethereal clarity created a magnification lens for her perceptions, and she saw that "Bob," through the medium of this envelope of smoke, was clearing a path of some sort for them. All this she perceived in the half-second it took them to fall upward to the ground . . .

And then they struck the ground, which was, despite appearing un-yielding as concrete, a mist, an atomic illusion like all matter, mostly space, and the space came together around them so they passed harmlessly through, and emerged—

—in the midst of a city. Downward into an upside-down city. The city was hung from above like one of those trick rooms where the chairs are glued to the ceiling. The buildings were upside down. They fell past them, down toward the sky. And then her stomach flip-flopped, followed by her perceptions, as suddenly sky and ground changed places and they were ascending, levitating upward from the ground.

They ceased ascending, alighting on the roof of a bus laying over on a corner, where it blocked traffic and the crosswalk. The driver, unaware of them, smoked an angel dust joint and massaged his crotch.

Feeling detached and objective and weirdly bodiless—and yet *not at all dreamlike*—Connie looked around, and knew that the city had been vivisected for her.

The skin of its consensus reality had been peeled away; she saw now the pulsing inner organs of it, the skein of its hidden organic relationships, and she recognized it all.

"Where's the Smog Monster?" Connie asked.

"Hundreds of miles from here," "Bob" said. "We took a shortcut through the Luck Plane. By the time the Rebel Gods find us it'll be too late. With luck."

"Luck cuts both ways, "Bob"," Little Connie said.

"Little Connie, you were always too old for your age," "Bob" replied, through his ceaseless grin. "I was absent when you grew up and yet I was there. Where two and three gather in my name, there am I also: Can you not feel my hands in your pockets? . . . Notice anything about this place?"

Connie was staring at a crowd of people milling on the sidewalks of the great city, people on their way somewhere, oblivious of the Ipsissimus of Sales and his charge atop the bus, and she saw now that a series of coruscating lines were connecting some of the people in the crowd; they were like translucent puppet strings of energy, defining relationships the people in the crowd were entirely unaware of. They belonged to herds within the herd; to cultural phyla whose attributes governed what they supposed to be their freewheeling impulses. And looking closer at those people she saw past their superficial semblances, saw them as they could not see one another: as they really were. There were tall men who were dwarfs and short men who were ten-foot giants from Hell; there were beautiful women who were revealed as twisted harridans, and hunchbacked, shrunken old women who were actually the stately winners of beauty contests; there were bankers who were actually giant worms with lamprey mouths, and there were smiling, friendly cops who were really werewolves in Nazi-SS uniforms; there was a priest who was a mincing drag queen and there was a mincing drag queen who was a genius of dizzying mathematical perceptions. She saw four men in tailored suits coming out of a Hilton, approaching, their forty-foot eight-wheeled limousine. They were surrounded by bodyguards who wore black suits and sunglasses; looking beyond their veneers she saw that the men in the suits were hideous slug-bodied things of palpitating tendrils and oozing suckers, hungry aliens with the mouths of giant horseflies; their bodyguards were robots, she saw, things of sheer intent and nothing more. She shivered, and was grateful that "Bob's" psychic cloaking screen protected her from being seen.

Then "Bob" took her hand, and blew a plume of smoke above them, which somehow drew them with it into the air. Like a sex-changed and depraved Mary Poppins, Dobbs drew Little Connie higher and higher into the sky, till they reached the thirteenth-story level. There they drifted along, paralleling the impatient procession of traffic, gazing down at a whole new web of interrelationships. Connie saw, from this greater height, the oscillating blueprint of the Luck Plane superimposed on the street. She saw which cars were likely to collide (but weren't necessarily destined to) and which were likely to make it home unscathed; she saw which individuals would fall in with drug addicts and be sucked into the conditioning quicksand, and which would instead likely fall to a fundamentalist preacher or the deadly programming of network television; she saw which ones would accidentally become wealthy, and which would . . .

Wait. There was something more: She saw the skein of interrelationships as it stretched out to the event horizon . . . she saw something hideous and something glorious taking shape out there . . . she saw . . .

Saucers.

She blinked, and looked back at the present. Amongst the crowd she saw a few who were like self-propelling steel balls in a pinball game, making havoc of the rules, introducing a Brownian motion where the others strove for regimentary order. There was something about them that reminded her of her mother—could they be the ones Mother had described? The other race hidden amongst the humans . . . the privileged and divinely aberrant . . . the SubGenius?

"I see you perceive your tribe," "Bob" told her. "The tribe of the Untribal. Do you also see the webs of probability?"

"I do."

"Then keep your eyes on them and learn, Little Connie . . . because we're dive-bombing the Luck Plane!"

And with that "Bob" dove down, straight down, rocketing headfirst toward the bus they'd alighted on earlier. The bus had moved on, was entering the stream of traffic. And now they entered the bus through the roof—

passing through it as if it were the skin of a soap bubble. "Bob" came to a screeching stop in the air over the driver, floating beside a sign that said, "PINKVILLE VOCATIONAL SCHOOL IS A STEP UP TO MORE WORK!"

"Bob" reached out and tapped the back of the man's head with his pipe . . . tapped it precisely. In a particular spot.

The man shuddered, and giggled, and jerked the wheel to the left into the flow of oncoming traffic.

"Uh oh!" "Bob" said, grinning. "I made a mistake. Accident. Wrong car. We're going to cr—"

Crash, as the bus rammed the forty-foot limo they'd seen earlier, buckling it so it was shaped like a boomerang. The limo spun and struck a semitruck, which swerved and drove through the wall of a power station and crashed into a set of enormous transformers, causing a short circuit which caused a mighty power surge (Connie could see all this taking shape on the Luck Plane like a video animation) which roared through the wires to an airport a hundred miles away garbling the transmissions of the air traffic controllers causing the wrong signals to be sent to a Learjet crammed with undersecretaries of the Trilateral Commission who went into a screaming panic when the plane, its computer controls confused, veered wildly and went out of control, going into a tailspin, nosing down . . . crashing thunderously into the industrial park where Connie had met "Bob." The cargo of nanotechnological submolecular reprogramming proteins the undersecretaries had been carrying to Washington exploded along with the hundreds of gallons of fuel in the plane's tanks, spreading in a diffuse cloud over the living concentration camp construct, the nanoprogramming molecules colliding with submolecular guidance systems for the minatory mechanism, reprogramming it—quite by lucky accident—into a complete reversal of the process, so that the living concentration camp began to deconstruct itself . . . and in so doing released another cloud of deprogramming nanotech molecules that drifted over the land, reversing the process wherever they encountered it . . .

"Whew!" "Bob" said. "That was lucky." He turned to Little Connie. "Young Miss, how would you like to visit your brothers and sisters in Malaysia?"

"Brothers and sisters? But I'm an only child!"

"Not at all. You're my daughter. You have hundreds of brothers and sisters, products of the Supreme Seed, thriving in Dobbstown, learning, awaiting X-Day . . . would you like to meet them?"

"You're my . . . Dad?"

REALLY, REALLY, REALLY, WEIRD STORIES

"Yes!"

"Shit! What a disappointment . . . Mom told me you were a rock star." The eternal grin almost wavered. Then he ruffled her hair tenderly. "You'll like your brothers and sisters," "Bob" said. "They're just as disrespectful as you are. Care for some 'Frop?"

And so, borne on a purposeful plume of green-sparkled blue, they rose from the twisted wreckage of the traffic accident, oblivious to the screams of the approaching sirens, and hurried on into the year 1996, on their way to a date with destiny, seeing the years 1997 and 1998 unfold ahead of them, like a place in the distance, where, clearly and far away, the Saucers were landing . . .

PREACH

The following was recorded as the tragic events of February 10th, 1999, unfolded at the New Gate Chapel, near Redding, California, during the sermon of a visiting minister, The Reverend Johnny Ess. General narrative observations are interpolated by a recording engineer with literary pretensions, one Marzo Deafstein:

The Reverend Ess was a lean, fiftyish man, with a rumpled suit, snakeskin cowboy boots, a day's growth of beard, a little tremble in his hands, a little rounding of his shoulders and something singularly alive in his hips, something that kept pulsing its way to other parts of him . . . He had seen better times, having lost his one-time multimillion dollar ministry, a whole TV channel . . . But he could still preach, right through an accent thick as rancid butter . . . He started out saying, "I'm here to talk about sin . . ."

I'm here to talk about sin, and the payment for sin. And I know sin, I know it intimately. My name is The Reverend Johnny Ess, E for Every, S for Sin, and S for sssssssssertainly. Sure, that's kind of funny, you can laugh, I'm just a damn hick. No, no need for that wince of embarrassment, folks, Lord knows it's true, I'm an Arkansas Po'bucker; my Daddy kept a rusting Dodge up on cinder blocks in front yard, and some nights we had to steal chickens to eat. My situation wasn't so bad, though. We all got it bad our own special way; the Lord tests us all, makes us all suffer with great particularity, each to his best and deepest capacity. Tests us and tests us. There ain't no cheatin' on that test.

Now, when I look out at y'all, and I say sin, some of you are almost lickin' your lips. Now I ask you, is that the appropriate response? Why sure, with some of y'all, it's the way it was with me: there's no relief without sin and there's no real party as is bereft of relief. And relief, it comes from bigtime fun, fun with weightlifter muscles on it, fun that concentrates first in this part of the body and then that part. Well now: Let me tell you something, our sweet Lord's eternal life is NO FUN—and it's not supposed to be. No fun, my babe, no fun.

Are you thinkin' this redneck Biblethumper don't know turkeydroppings about sin . . . ?

[At this point the Reverend became increasingly agitated. We took this as a tent-revivalist working himself up to a passion of charisma and outpouring. But there was something jumpy, twitchy about it. Watching the Reverend Ess I was reminded of something: When I was a kid my parents used to take me to a gas station and at this station was a menagerie—they used to allow this in the '50s—and there was some moth-eaten monkeys and one truly miserable leopard. This big cat had been in a cage about as big as a Volkswagen Bug for twenty some years and it showed a certain twitchiness, a certain exotic fusion of advanced decay and bottled, boiling energy . . . you knew it would kill people if it ever got out . . . I used to whisper to it, "I'd do it to them for ya if I could . . ."]

Let me tell you, my friends, oh yes, good Lord forgive me yes I have sinned. I have been up to my neck in SENSE-YOU-ALITY, in the charging and the discharging of the senses; I have sunk myself in that particular La Brea Tarpit of Life—and it is only thanks to our sweet precious Lord that I have escaped that ravenous suction, that tarpit suction that seemed to fasten itself on my lower parts and suck and SUCK until it drew the LIFE OUT OF ME. Yes, I know sin.

I won't tell you what my sins were—oh yes, I could talk about my time as a counselor at a girl's camp . . . hell, fourteen, fifteen year old girls, soft as little kittens, out there on the aching side of that mountain where the smell of the pines seemed to call me out every night to prowl the cabins like a cougar . . . But no. It's best that sin remains hidden. Neither will I befoul your ears with the long nights in bars and brothels, yes and of rutting with marijuana dreaming whores in puddles of vomit—I cannot bring myself to mention it. Those numberless faceless WHORES—my name is LEGION cried the Whore of Babylon!

[The Reverend is ignoring the microphone on the podium, is strutting back and forth, his voice really booming—then going soft all of a sudden

. . . but we could hear every word, though there was five hundred of us in that fairly sizeable church . . . every whispered word . . .]

. . . I never think of those whores now; those whores of argent hair and ebony pubes, of eyes that wander the space between you like midges. And YES I KNOW THE DEVIL'S SNOW! YES YES I KNOW THE DEVIL'S SNOW! that crystal LILITH, that medicinal tasting temptresss COCAINE, yes LORRRRRRD, I know cocaine—preferably cocaine cut with a little smack—and I have flown through CLOUDS OF COCAINE and yes, yes, yes I know sin and . . .

I cannot tell you about it. That night on the tar-roof of Bluesteak Billy's New Orleans condo, that crazed mightily-pierced teenyboppstress and I, the both of us gone wild on angel dust—the irony of that name angel dust, can you imagine! And mad with peeceepee driving my degraded but engorged manhood again and again into that hysterically laughing punk rock bitch whore—1979 it was—as the rain lashed us and the lightnin' unzipped the sky!!

I will not tell you of it. But you can take my word for it. I know sin.

And I know the DEVIL PERSONALLY. And you feminist ladies, you postmodern pomo homo feminist ladies, you think there's a PATRIAR-CHY here on Earth—you don't know phallocentricism till you get to HELL because Satan is a gonna make you dance around a steaming phal-lus in the green and gold flames of RETRIBUTION.

Satan, ladies, is no sensitive Berkeley male.

But get up to Heaven—and you find that Jesus and Mother Mary are receiving equal pay and don't you, don't you, don't you fool yourself into thinking there's no money in Heaven—was there ever anyplace worth being for long without money? You see money and faith—wellsir, one is a unit of the other. Money is a unit of faith and if you give the Ministry of the Reverend Johnny Ess one dollar then you have one dollar's worth of faith; and when you give him five dollars you have five dollars worth of faith; and when you give him five hundred dollars that's FIVE HUN-DRED MOTHERFUCKIN' DOLLARS WORTH OF FAITH redeemable at the gate of Heaven.

As in Luke verse forty-four, "And turning to the woman he—Jesus—said unto Simon, "Seest thou this woman? I entered into thine house, thou gavest me no water for my feet but she hath wetted my feet with her tears, and wiped them with her hair. Thou gavest me no kiss but she hath not ceased to KISS MY FEET."

Folks that's nothing less than the right attitude.

And if you think a Faith Payment is a questionable investment ladies and gentlemen you forget that I have the God-given power to SEE INTO YOUR SOULS and—right here I can see your heart before me like a devil's dinner on a plate and I can tell you—you sir!—that the heart I see within your breast, the soul quivering on that plate—it . . .

It MAKES ME SICK!

Imagine seeing a quivering cube of Jell-O and instead of fruit salad there are maggots, the maggots of sin, quivering in that cube of Jell-O and LORD HELP ME TURN AWAY!

And you young lady . . . Yes you . . .

I'm a lookin' into your heart young miss and YES HE HAS GIVEN ME THAT POWER PRAISE GOD FOR IT, the power to see the naked . . . the naked truth.

And in your heart, young lady I see—LORD NO, I MUST LOOK AWAY, for that grinning, quivering bearded clam of a demon's face is a laughin' and laughin' hysterically at me like a punk rock bitch with her legs spread on a tar roof LORD NO, take it away!

And in this man's heart I see a quivering bucket of tarantulas and in this one I see an eel pie with livin' eels and in this one I see a spitoon overflowing with spit, phlegm, cigar butts and marijuana roaches!! Excuse me . . . while I retch.

[A moment of shaken silence . . . He stares at the floor boards and then looks up, begins again in a quieter voice . . . soft but audible even to the creatures between the walls . . . and then thundering through the room like a sonic boom . . .]

And yet . . . And yet I'm hear to tell you . . . that there is help. There is hope. There is a Heavenly housekeeper who cleans the heart and you do not have to pay taxes for her Social Security, because she is God's grace and she's here right now for you to take and take and take again!

She is here, she is here with me, I can transmit her to you, and I'm askin' for witness, I'm askin' you to get up off your sinful rear ends and witness the power, the nonsatirical power, the AC/DC electricity of God's CLEANSING CURRENT and NO NO NO don't you fear the trade in lives for life loves force and force loves life for this wedding in heaven was made up in Hell with the victim as bride to life life itself, yes I'm OD'd on life, the ETERNAL LIFE OF THE GOOD LORD JESUS CHRIST ALMIGHTY!

I can feel him, I can FEEL HIM, I can feel his power in this room with us right now and it's lightin' up my spirit like a Christmas tree GOOD

GOD THANK YOU for pulling me out of that sucking pit of eternal desire and I'm begging you right now lord to help me pull and pull again . . . pull these sinners right here up from that same stinking black tarpit that is the ROOF OF HELL, Lord let your power rise up in me RIGHT NOW, Lord let me pull their souls from the pit and lord let me TOUCH THEM DEEP WITHIN THEIR MOST PRIVATE RECESSES–CAN YOU FEEL IT my friends there's hope here tonight–TOUCH ME AND FEEL IT, TOUCH ME AND FEEL IT, FEEL IT, FEEL IT, praise Jesus FUCKING CHRIST and . . .

[As some disgusted twentysomething who'd come for a lark decides to leave . . .]

Now waitaminnut now where the Hell you goin' you young sourpussed Generation X piece of ephemeral human trash! You come up here and TOUCH ME and you GET A CHANCE AT ETERNAL SER-VICE or BY GOD you will pay the price RIGHT NOW and wait a GODDAMN MINUTE, you two! You are offended, I reckon, is that it?!

[The Reverend hesitates . . . seems to make up his mind about some-thing . . .]

Well FUCK YA! Because you're going straight to HELL with the rest of us!

[A final hesitation and then he speaks with meth-amped rapidity . . .]

I spoke of money and faith and payment–tonight money won't be enough folks, tonight we pay in lives! We pay in LIVES and in BLOOD AND WE PAY for our SINS because I cannot, I cannot, I CANNOT GO ON and neither can you, the least I can do is take some of you fucking hypocrites with me straight to HELL–

[And it was then the Reverend pulled the M-16 with the custom doubleclip from inside the back of the podium and opened up on the audience, screaming at them as he fired, killing some two dozen people before the Sheriff burst in, firing as he came, and the Reverend shouted something about sucking the Angel Gabriel's bluesteel member and stuck the gun in his mouth and blew his brains all over the cross behind the podium . . .]

Preach: Part Two:
The Apocalypse of
The Reverend John Shirley

Truly, I say unto you, I have seen it: in a dream of sticky sheets have I seen it; in a golden haze of sacred frop have I seen it; in the daily newspaper have I seen it: THIS I HAVE SEEN, and here foretell:

First I saw the many-headed Beast, whom some call THE CONSPIRACY, and in one aspect is called ALSO: Military Industrial Complex; this I see under a dome, in a welter of yellow cloud, dipping its heads into many troughs round about, and lo, swimming in terror in those troughs were women and children, blackened and shriveled with cancer they were; even were they brain damaged with toxins, and in great suffering. And in other troughs were boiling the war-mutilated, and the bombed; and the heads of the M.I.C. Beast wore toupees and dandruffed glasses, and some wore dark glasses, and designer shirts, and some had capped teeth, and Rolex watches pierced their nostrils, even those nostrils marked with much drinking of good Scotch; and on their heads were golf caps and yet were they without arms, and truly without dicks except that their heads were dicks, but had only the bodies of serpents, and tongues that were whips of many lashes, each lash with a different name: Pension, was one called; Group Health Insurance was another; Salary a third; "Shut up or we'll blow your fucking brains out" was another marked, and truly.

And one of these heads was called, in those days, General Electric; and its eyes were of television sets, of NBC daytime and night-time programming, and here were lies to the number five million.

And one of these heads was called General Motors, and Ford by some, and by others Chrysler; and I saw this head of chrome-plate and metalflake raising itself so to vomit laid-off workers even as it laughed, and from the rectum that was also its mouth excreted faulty tanks, which nevertheless knew murder; also it excreted faulty cars, and a great smog that choked the world, and brought the world into a slow roasting like unto a barbecue chicken, which in those days was called Global Warming.

And another was called Chemical Industry; who laughs even unto the bank as children die in Bhopal; and whose pesticides and herbicides sicken the land, and produce great famines, whereupon the people starve.

And another of these heads was five-sided, to the shape of a pentagon, and was called ROACH BRAINED SHAMBLER; its head reached beyond the trough to suck the strength from the land, like a leech on a mouse, which in the end was almost bigger than the mouse, and a repugnant sight withal. And its tongue was also a rectum, and poisons it excreted, which were in those days called *military toxic waste* and *nuclear waste* and *hidden radioactive contamination*, and these it concealed in a great spew of paperwork, the nests of featherless birds who are its brainless offspring, who are called Bureaucrats; and in its throat was a garbage disposal, wherein for all Eternity Lieutenant Calley throws a switch to grind up the innocents, and in its skull are the machine men, who will order other machine men buried alive in trenches, and burned alive, and a great foul laughter will rise up within the Beast at this, and other atrocities which it greets with great joy.

And then another head there was, called *CIA/Russian Intelligence*, and called also *Israeli Intelligence*, and *P2 Nazi conspiracy network in the world of secret intelligence*, also called by some *Bumbling Idiots with too much power and not a clue, truly*, and these shall in their trough spawn Death Squads and torture, and in their jaws I see a President, killed these many years ago, forever ground between molars, as each tooth had its name: Justice Department, and FBI, and CIA Black Ops and truly it was also CRACK COCAINE CONTRAFUNDING, and also was it called Mafia Connection, and Secret Nazi Power.

And sprouting beside this head, and in obscene congress with it, was one called Cocaine Cartel, in whose trough a million children suffered; and one called Heroin, and others of their like, and they were like unto CIA, and yet had they agendas unto themselves, and much murder and bloody masturbation.

And I saw these heads also on the Beast: Who is called Vatican; who is called Muslim Fundamentalist Lunatics; who is called Media (the Blinding One, the Liar who makes Satan look like Mother Teresa); who is Multinational Oil Conglomerates; and who is called Health Care Industry; who is called Congress, the slut *Politicia*, the Whore and Harlot; and International Arms Trade; and Mindless Communism known to men as the Servants of Mao, and Pol Pot, who wallow in butchery; and the body of the beast did also have a name, and was known as he who is the Stupefaction of the Common Man, and under its belly will the children of the Common Man sleep, and sleep will hold them in bondage.

And U2 shall play a benefit, whereupon the Beast will dance with embarrassing ineptitude on its clawed feet; and also Guns N Roses are seen to play, and even unto the one called Sting, and others who shall be known as hypocritical ass kissers.

And the Sacred Motorhead shall not be asked to play; nor the Saint Iggy Pop; neither Henry Rollins nor The Band That Dare Not Speak Its Name; nor Captain Beefheart, nor the Frank and the Zappa.

But there shall be two parties; and one shall be within the dome, and one outside; and the one outside the dome will perish first, and yet will not just party, but will party the hell out of it, and these latter will party in the burning mud outside the dome, and under the sky, which with ultraviolets shall scorch them even unto stir-frying, and yet their death will be joyous, and will come with exquisite contortions in the throes of their divine toxicity, even as their astral forms are released, and they thereupon enter the waiting saucers of the Xists, and know that the Beast trapped within the dome will perish without rescue: The Beast with one foot upon the golf course and the other upon the Resort which is called Palm Beach, and its tail upon Beverly Hills and thence across the pesticide-slain sea to Tokyo, even to Peking and Moscow, and its groin resting on Manhattan, and its Lowermost Rectum (for it has of these a multitude) pierced by the World Trade Center, doubly and with hemorrhoids to the number ten thousand, and in this party shall dullness and blandness flourish, and this mediocrity become a toxic liquid in itself, which will thicken and choke those who sport with the Beast beneath the dome, while the dome itself—this I have seen, verily—prevents the entry of the saucers with its own hell-wrought insularity, who might have rescued some few in their mercy, but by the Dome of Class and Privilege were prevented, and so those beneath the dome perished, even like Robert Alton Harris in the gas chamber, or like unto obscenely squirming termite queens in poisoned walls.

These things I have seen, before the fact, and outside of Time; and let the Sacred Scribe record them, and let Pink Men take warning: For the end times approach, and they're just the beginning, dumbshit.

MODERN TRANSMUTATIONS
OF THE ALCHEMIST

She struck him in the face with the deliberation of a musician who makes each note as precisely on pitch as he can: exactly thus, precisely now. The musician in her hand had little confidence in himself; he would sit on the balcony of his Mediterranean villa (a gift from his father, a soloist with the Symphony de Paris) and watch the slow billow of clouds or the light fading on swallows that curveted like little stunt planes, and tell himself that he should be inspired to music by them. He would say, "Now, you see beauty, hear music in what you see, as Papa used to say," and then he would compose drastically uninspired jazz. Afterwards, he would feel the need to reward himself; so, like a rat finishing a maze with a drink of sweetened water, he would fix himself a martini and relax with one of those long-legged escorts from Marseilles, preferably a brunette. The rat who pokes its nose over his shoulder, sharing his drink, was huddled in its cage in a nondescript corner of the pet shop behind a revolving rack of collars and leashes. It wrapped the stench of its cage around itself like the cloak of a rodent king as it rolled in the excrement-soaked sawdust on the tin floor. The cage was bare except for the mason jar lid of water in one corner, and a handful of sawdust and droppings heaped before the wire-mesh gate. The cage's sole occupant had never seen another rat. It had been separated from its parents and family before its eyes had opened, a measure the shop owner thought necessary to prevent the cannibalization of the rat by its mother who had eaten her other offspring alive. The only indication given the rat of the existence of other sentient beings was the occasional face at its cage door, and the chirrupings of other rats; and though it did not know what made the sounds it responded to them with its own meager peeps, while its dirty white snout wriggled and its scaly pink tail rasped. It did not associate the daily arrival of yellow mash through the door with the care of a living creature. It presumed it to be a phenomenon as natural as the fluctuations in temperature that made it fluff up its coarse fur when someone opened the door of the shop in cold weather. After a while it did not answer the rat-calls from the contiguous cages, so their hollow squeaks vibrated alone in the thin tin walls like the jaw of the man who was slapped with the deliberation of a musician. The man flinched and closed his eyes, putting his hand to his face almost as if to clasp the fingers of the red handmark left by the blow. He stifled a welling curse that he knew would only make her angrier. Instead, he decided to lower his eyes as if he were martyred. She crossed her arms over her chest and bit her lips to keep from crying. She did not want him to know that she was still vulnerable. She had gray-blue eyes which reflected nothing and therefore drew all other eyes to them. She had high cheekbones and cheek-hollows made up gaunt in the fashion of German models that year. Her eyes were incised with eyeliner; when she ducked her head the copper of her hair boiled round her face like ocean foam around a dolphin. The dolphin luxuriated in the uterine embrace of the Mediterranean. The dolphin had been a long time in Arctic waters but had returned to her birthplace to have her children. She lay in the shallows, her pale belly on the paler sand, her blue dorsal fin just six inches above the bluer water. She had hoped to lie there awhile to rest, but with a start she felt the first pangs of labor (and a searing image of her lover: he leaps out of the green face of a cresting wave, his scaleless silver blue hide striking a cymbal clash with the sun. The image broke from her memory as the surface of the Mediterranean parted for her torpedo blunt snout). Her spaceship body went rigid, her back arched, straightened and an almost motionless mercuric brushstroke darted from her belly. She raised her blowhole above the water-line and, dilating it, she sucked cool air into her lungs, using them to press the second offspring free as her body shook with a series of tympanic throbs. She trembled, relieved, and took two more quick breaths, blew them sweetly out, like the musician blowing tunes through his flute. With two quick breaths the jazz musician gave birth to the second run of his latest improvisation. He was sweating, trying to wring each note for its moisture. He paused, and saw that Frellen, the American guitar player, had the audience's complete attention: grandstanding as usual, gyrating about the stage. Frellen invariably stole his thunder, then had the nerve to weep on his shoulder about yet another fight with his wife. "I hope she slaps him again tonight," he said to himself. His bitterness distracted him just long enough to make him miss his cue. As he frantically sought to catch up he caught a disheartening glimpse of the band's manager scowling at him from the wings. The look on Michel's fat face—the son-of-a-whore could make you feel like a rodent with that look—gave the flutist a sensation in his stomach like a rat chasing its own tail in panic. The rat squealed its terror and scuttled to one corner of its cage, turning to lash at the monstrous five-headed pink thing, the hand that clutched at it. The rat hadn't believed the universe could be breached; that the vague fluttering in the non-existence beyond the bars could be concretely real. With a gut sensation like the nervous trill of a flute, the rat fainted long enough for a massive pink claw, awful in furlessness, to scoop it up and fly beyond the confines of the universe. The rat was plunged into a kaleidoscope of gawking faces and gleaming metal. It saw, briefly, the universe from the outside, until its frail perceptions began to dissolve. But the hand lowered the rat into a brown cardboard box. The rat responded gratefully to the enclosing walls, closed its red eyes, and shivered. From one Universe to another, this one barer than the first. A lid clamped over the box and the rat sank into a rhythmically pendulous darkness just like the motion of a red haired woman's hips in her black dress as she walked impatiently back and forth in the apartment. Waiting for her husband to return home, her mind seethed; but one thought recurred clearly: retribution. Frellen left her alone for two months four times this year to tour with his band as its lead guitar. He had refused to take her along, claiming that it would interfere with his dedication to the band. But at last, after much argument, he had promised to go away no more. He had allowed her to make plans for parties, to make arrangements for trips to Paris, just the two of them. And then he'd told her offhandedly, as if it were only an inconvenience, that he would be leaving again "for a short tour," and all plans must be canceled. "I'll show him just what he is, to treat me as if my needs are nothing, like I'm a dog to be kenneled." She stamped her foot, her silver slippers jumping like baby dolphins. The dolphin's offspring slid around the flute-player's legs as he stood in the surf in his stiff tuxedo, stiff with drunkenness, holding a bottle of sherry and a long platinum flute that flickered in the sunset like the flashing fin of a fish. He did not see the dolphins yet, as they zipped like electric toy trains around his knees. Nor did he notice the protective bulk of their mother basking a few yards away. He swayed, murmuring to himself (that bastard Frellen threatening to force him out of the band). And suddenly the flute seemed a threat, and its touch repugnant to him. Hating himself, he threw the flute into the sea. He watched it disappear into the blue waters like a fading smile. He turned to stagger up onto the deserted beach, suddenly wanting a bed to hide in. He had taken several unsteady steps when something sharp, a broken shell, cut his bare foot. He yelped and jerked his foot up, lost his balance, fell into the arms of the surf. The water closed over his head, burned his eyes with salt, chafed his lungs and made his formal suit a burden. A swift undercurrent siphoned him backwards and he slid down the slope of sand. His head swam from drink and he drank the sea, sobered but despairing as the twilight was sucked into darkness and he was sucked downward. But he felt something thump him from beneath, as the dolphin pushed him to the surface, and then onto the sand above the lapping tongues of surf. He coughed, spat saltwater and laughed: He was alive! He had given himself up to death. But the sea had thought him too fine a musician to waste; had sent its servants to rescue him. He laughed. But the laughter froze on his face as he remembered: something *real* had pushed him from the water. He turned and looked into the sea, seeking out his rescuer. The waves neoned red in the sunset, rocking like an old man's sleepy head. Then the old man opened his silver-blue eyes. His eyes were dolphins, mother and two dart children. They followed one another in the shallow surf, describing a lazy figure-eight with their wakes. He put his hands in his pockets, laughed to find a small crab, and then peeled off his soaked black suit. He was warmed by the evening breeze. Stripped down to his shorts, he threw the soggy clothes away like his anger at Frellen and Michel, his work with the band. He looked at the dolphin and tried to think of some way to ask her why she had saved him. As he watched her he saw something bright flashing from her snout. The dolphin came nearer and he saw that she held his flute in her mouth. Placing his steps very carefully, he walked into the surf and took the flute. The dolphin seemed unafraid and watched him with curiosity as he dried the flute with the bow tie he had thrown on the beach, before he'd gone into the water. He tried the flute; blew a little water out of it. He began to play. He sat cross-legged by the surf for many hours, swaying and playing to the strobing of the dolphin's tails, and the percussion of the surf. The fluteplayer's eyes closed, and Frellen's hand closed on the knob of his apartment door. He hesitated there, dreading to open the door. She would never understand. Frellen sighed and opened the door. His wife was there with just the expression that he'd anticipated on her long face. As he put down his guitar case she said, "Welcome home. I've got good news for you. I've had your child." Her voice was the scratch of claws on tin. He gaped at her in real amazement and she was pleased. "In fact, he looks just like you," she went on. "Here, your son." She picked up a cardboard box and reached inside, plucked out something that wriggled, and threw it at him. She ran from the apartment, out the door that led to the beach. The faint trilling of a distant flute came through the open door. Frellen looked down at the dead rat at his feet. It convulsed from its swift death of fright.

Really,
Really,
Really,
Really,

WEIRD
STORIES

JUST LIKE SUZIE

Perrick is in his underwear, standing in the middle of the room, trying silently to talk himself out of slamming crank. He's a paunchy guy, early forties who looks ten years older than he has to, and knows it. He's in a weekly rates hotel room in San Francisco. It's not boosh-wah but it's not a piss-in-the-sink room, as it has a small bathroom. Perrick lives here, for the moment. He's used to these rooms, because he's lived half of his double life in them, but he's not used to *sleeping* in them; not used to the shouts in the hall at night, the heavy tread of cops, the shrieking fights of the two junkie gays downstairs. But this Bedlam is genteel, one of his neighbors assures him, compared to other weeklies on the street.

The room contains, besides Perrick, a double bed, a dresser on which is lined up aftershave, cologne, a box of tissues, a man's comb, a cheap chrome-faced radio. There's a lamp table by the bed, with a squat lamp on it, a wastepaper basket below it. A window onto the street. A raincoat hanging on a hook.

Perrick is alternately pacing and going over to a table on which there is a syringe, already filled and capped up, and a spoon. He nervously pokes at the syringe, holds it up to the light, puts it down, whines a little to himself. Of two minds about using it. He picks it up again, puts it down and goes to the bathroom door. He calls through the door, "Suzie! Damn, come on, girl!"

Suzie's hoarse voice from the bathroom: "Just take a fuckin' chill-pill, man, you gotta get your stuff in you so you be a little fuckin' understandin' about me getting' mine!"

"Heroin," Perrick mutters to himself. "Sick bitch. She's gonna give me AIDS or something." He yells at the door again. "Come on baby let's do it!"

Suzie emerges from the bathroom—she's skinny, with bad skin, thin bleached blond hair, a white girl who's affected a lot of the local homegirl mannerisms, mixes them all up with her white Valleytrash SouthernCal roots. "Your princess is here, dude!" She walks a little unsteadily on her heels, and she's nodding a touch. "You got my money?"

"I paid you when you came in!"

"That was like a down payment thing." She sinks onto the edge of the bed and fumbles a cigarette out from her purse, which is still on her shoulder strap . . . Her movements become slow and deliberate as she lights it.

Perrick yells, "The fuck it was! I can't believe you pullin' this shit after rippin' me off last time—my fuckin' credit cards—I can't believe I'd go for you again but . . ."

"OK fuck this, I'm goin', I don't need no accusations, you totally illin', you dissin' me, fuck you." She starts to get up, sways, falls into sitting back on the bed. "Shit."

"OK OK fuck it. Here." He slaps more money down beside her, it's gone almost before it hits the mattress, into her purse . . . then she droops a little, nodding . . . comes out of it, shaking herself.

"Wow. Shit's good. Let's do the Thing. Before I nod out or something. You want it like before?"

Perrick nods, unzips his pants, then hesitates, takes his wallet out of his back pocket and puts it where he can keep an eye on it, in the middle of the dresser. Then goes to the raincoat, puts it on over his underwear. Buttons it up. He goes to her, taking up the syringe. Perrick makes as if he doesn't notice her. He's looking at the ceiling and humming absently but breathing rather rapidly.

Suzie, in a practiced little girl's voice: "Oh! I wonder what would happen if I looked inside this big grown-up man's coat when he's not watching me! *My goodness!* I wonder what's in here?"

She unbuttons the bottom button of his coat and puts her head under it. Feels around. "Oh what's this nummy yummy! Mmmmm! I wonder what the big man will do . . . !"

Perrick gasps as she begins giving him head, her own head bobbing. Perrick snatches up the syringe, drags back his coat sleeve and fixes, registers immediately. His back arches and his jaw quivers as he rushes. Never as good as the first rush he had the first time he did it and every time he does it he feels a little more strain on his heart and he half hopes that this time the ticker goes blooey but still he's riding what rush there is, enough to make him go: "Oh jeezus oh yes little girl you bad dirty little girl oh yes take it take it oh yes you ripped me off you dirty little girl my credit cards but I forgive you because you are the little girl who loves me loves to oh yes—" Faster and faster as the drug takes hold. "Good crystal good meth little girl you ripped me off and my wife found out and had to tell her the whole story and she kicked me out and here I am can't believe I'm back with you, you caused it, you got me kicked out bad little girl bad little girl . . ."

His movements are convulsive as he grabs the back of her head . . . his repressed anger emerging in the violence of his hip thrusts and hands taloned on the back of her neck. Faster and meaner. She's gagging. Choking. He's oblivious. He's gasping, " . . . Shouldn't do it shouldn't do it but you made me bad little girl you made me buy the stuff made me buy you made me I didn't want to I don't know what to do how'd I get into it I don't know Andrea left me . . . your fault your—" He punctuates the words now with vicious thrusts into her. "*—fault!* Your *fault!* Your *fault!*"

She's still gagging, choking, but now only resisting feebly. The heroin was the synthetic stuff, hard to gauge its strength, more than she bargained for.

Perrick's singing idiotically. "Heroin and speed, you and me, heroin and speed, you and me, you down and me up, never quite enough, heroin and speed make her bleed make her sorry she stole from me—"

She's choking more and more. He holds himself deep in her, forcing a sustained deep throat—her struggles are now like mock motions of a sleeper acting out a dream.

Perrick's babbling "Bad girl little ripoff artist broke my heart take my dick show you're sorry . . . SHIIIIIT!" As he orgasms and she . . . stops moving. He slumps over her. Hugs her to his groin. "Fuck. I'm sorry I got too . . ." He straightens up, panting. "Hope I didn't hurt you . . ."

He tries to pull away from her. Frowns. Sees he's stuck or she's not letting go. She's otherwise totally limp.

Perrick muttering: "Said I was sorry. Come on. Let go. You're hurting me. Shit you got my nuts in your mouth too . . . how'd that—?" Yelling now: "Hey! Suzie? You're hurting me, seriously! What is this, I'm supposed to give you more money or—" He stops, grimacing with clamping pain at his groin. Bending to look under the coat. She's beyond unconscious. He can see the profound emptiness of her. A slackness beyond slack. Already tinged blue. And at the corners of her jaws the muscles are bunched with a signature of finality. She's clamped onto his dick and his balls, both in her mouth, her teeth clamped like a sadist's cock-ring over the root of his maleness. "Jesus fucking Christ! Suzie! Don't be dead, come on, that's a fuckin' bitchy thing to do to me! Don't be—" He checks her pulse at her throat. "I don't fucking . . . She is. She's dead. Shit shit *shit!*"

He tries to ease her off . . . when that doesn't work, makes an effort, tells himself Stay Calm, as he attempts to yank free. "Awwwwwwwwwhhhhh shiiiiiit! Fuuuuuuck!"

It hurts.

He takes a deep breath. Forces a measure of relaxation into his limbs. Then tries again to wrench her loose.

Searing pain.

He yowls. Then he stands there, panting, feeling the weight of her hanging from his genitals. He's holding her up by his genitals. He moves to try to get her head more in the light, then attempts to work his thumbs between her teeth, try to pry her off. Pushes—

Crunching pain. Some sorta death-reflex. She's crunching down harder on him every time he tries to pry her loose. Like punishment for the attempt . . .

"Owww fuck goddamnit!"

A banging at the door.

He recognized Buck's geeky voice coming from outside the hotel door "Yo! You got Suzie in there! Say hey you got my lady in there, dudeski?!"

Perrick mutters breathlessly to himself, "Oh shit it's her fuckin' pimp!" Then yelling at Buck, "No, no man she—she split!"

"Hey bullshit! Come on, man! Get over here, open this door!"

Whining, Perrick grabs the corpse under the armpits and drags it along with an awkwardness that seems a weirdly apt choreographic parody of his path through life. When he gets to the vicinity of the door he's got her turned the wrong way, she'd be visible if he opened the door, and there's not enough room for a 'U-turn' so he has to bend over—grimacing horribly—and grab her skirt and sort of lift her at the hips, so her back is humped, and he does a little capering hump-swivel hump-swivel hump-swivel move, 'til he gets her turned round. He whines some more as Buck pounds the door. Now Perrick's standing sideways with respect to the door, the body behind it. He adjusts the raincoat. Unlocks the door and opens it some—trying his best for fake composure—and opens the door only enough so that he's peering around the side of it.

There's Buck. He's emaciated, his blond hair in a white boy's approximation of dreadlocks. Under his arm is an expensive skateboard with a lot of cartoony stickers on it; he's wearing Levi jacket sans sleeves, stupid looking surfer shorts, tattoos.

Perrick attempts: "Hey. Buck. I paid her, man. She's out hittin' the pipe an' hittin' the needle, slammin' your money."

"Heeeeey dudeski, the bitch does that again she's gonna be a bad memory an' she knows that. And I hope she hears me." He shouts past Perrick. "You hear me, bitch?!'

Perrick is holding her up with one hand to take the weight off his dick and the strain is hacking away at his veneer. Can't take much more.

Was she going to bite through? She can't–she's dead. Right? Right?

Buck's saying, "I bet she's in the bathroom doin' up some shit and laughin'. I always know when she's laughin' at me no matter where she is. I can feel it. Right now. I'm like, psychic. Her mouth's open and she's laughing right now–"

Perrick ventures, "I don't think so." He's walking a line, between whimpering and hysterical laughter. He feels like he has the weight of the planet hanging from his dick. The pregnant mass of the fucking bitch Mother Earth.

Buck ignores him, he's shouting, "–And I'm gonna KICK HER ASS FOR IT!" And he kicks the door, smashing it into the corpse and Perrick so that the pain dances through Perrick And expresses itself with a long ululating howl and he tries to edge aside but the door is kicked again and wham, bangs into the corpse again and Perrick howls again, tries desperately to get out of the way until. At last Buck pushes in and past him, turns and sees the body with its head under his coat.

"Oh this is cute, right when I'm talkin' to you she's givin' you head, dude!" He starts yanking at the body to get her out where he can slap her around. "Tryin'a pretend you're not here, I bitch-slap you, let go of that shit and get your ass over here!"

Perrick is making a hot-coals kind of dance, his face a rictus of pain, trying to prevent his dick from being pulled off–starts following Buck's pull around the room in a Chinese parade dragon effect with the body, making funny little marching shuffles with his feet like a kid playing choochoo.

Perrick yelling, "No no don't you don't–no wait!"

Suddenly Buck stops and stares. Looks at the body. Lets it fall limp. Steps over to the panting Perrick and peeks into the coat. Takes a startled step back.

"Jeezus! You fuckin' murdered my old lady with that puny little dick of yours!"

Perrick's sobbing, "I didn't mean it, Buck she just–she was all nodded out and I guess I got carried away on some crystal and I guess I was kinda mad at her anyway so I was kinda chokin' her and I didn't see what was happenin'–and she just croaked, man! And she clamped down on there some kinda deathgrip reflex thing and I'm fuckin' stuck, man!"

REALLY, REALLY, REALLY, REALLY, WEIRD STORIES

"The balls too?"

"Yeah yeah yeah. Yeah. I really got carried away, you know?"

"This . . ." Buck shakes his head as if in high moral judgement. "This . . . this is gonna cost you extra."

Perrick suddenly feels a cold melty feeling in his dick. He thinks, at first, she's bitten right through. But then he checks it out. He sees . . . "Oh shit. Oh no. I'm losin' feelin' in it It's *not hurting.* "

"Well, you oughta be glad, dudeski!"

"You don't fucking understand! If I can't feel it—that *means it's dying!* MY DICK'S DYING!"

Buck crosses his arms, considers the strange union of the corpse and the dick with a philosopher's judiciousness. "Yo, calm down, there's a way . . . we make a deal, we get you out . . . This is so totally gnarly."

Buck starts moving around, looking at the thing from different angles, sniggering behind his hand.

Perrick yells, "It ain't fuckin' funny, Buck."

"Sure it is. You know what else? This is just like Suzie. It really is. And you know what *else*? It was in all the signs today, man." He takes out a glass crack pipe, blackened with use, thumbs in a rock and fires it up, poofs in a thoughtful way. Buck's head seems to expand slightly like a toy balloon. He exhales and chatters, "Astrology, it was her planets, man, they're all fucked up with her lunar signs. And it was in the smog colors. You ever read smog colors. Like tea leaves? And the way people was walkin' in the Mix, I always know, I'm kinda psychic like that, I see the patterns in the Mix, you know? Somedays there's wack shit in the air that just gets a life of its own."

Perrick's on the gelatinous rim of the Grand Abyss called Hysteria. "Stop hittin' on that fuckin' pipe and get her the fuck *off me!!*"

Buck blows white smoke and says, "Hey don't be comin' at me like that, dudeski, 's bullshit."

"I got a few thousand dollars in the bank, I can get you two hundred fifty bucks right away, get you two thousand tomorrow, you get her off me. It's all I could get out of the joint account I had with my wife when I left her but you can have it all man. Just . . . Just . . . shit . . ."

Buck's interested now. "Two grand?" He looks speculatively again at the corpse: "Maybe I get a screwdriver and pry her jaws or something?"

"No no you do stuff like that she clamps down harder. Some kinda reflex thing or something. And I don't want anybody to get crazy with a knife because *my fucking DICK is in there, you know what I'm saying?* It's still all swollen up, I don't want just anybody cutting around in there—I got to have a surgeon."

"But you go to the emergency room, the cops will come around. I tell you what. I know a doctor. He does bullet work and shit. He'll do it and he won't roll over on you. He's good. But we can't get you to him with that thing hangin' down there and he don't make housecalls no matter what—he don't never go out. He's a speedfreak worsen you. Totally tweakin'. But he cuts good. He smells bad but he cuts good . . ."

"So . . . what are you saying?"

"Gotta cut off her head . . ."

Perrick stares at him. "What?"

"I'm waiting for another idea, dudeski. Cut off her head first—or, anyway, cut off her body I guess—do it quick, we can get you out of here with it . . ." He takes a big buckknife from his pocket and opens it, flourishes it . . .

Perrick hesitates. Hands jittering as he pokes at the head, trying to see how his genitals are doing. "I don't know . . . it's all purple. Oh God. I . . . I'm gonna get gangrene. And I gotta piss. I can't . . ."

Buck suggests, perfectly seriously: "Heeeeey, wait'll we get the head separated from the shoulders, you can piss out her neck." He hits the pipe again.

Perrick retches at this, a retching from deep inside him . . . he screws his eyes shut . . . then he takes a deep breath and manages: "Just . . . Just do it, just do it. Cut off her . . . her body. Her head. You know."

Buck laughs, "Me?! NO way, Jose! Fuckin A no-way!" He folds up the knife and drops it in Perrick's coat pocket. 'That's your jobby, kimosabe! I just paid eight bucks for a good organic vegetarian lunch and I ain't gonna lose it!"

Perrick protests, "Hey look, seriously, I can't—"

"You wanna lose your dick? You did her man, it's your fuckin' responsibility. I come back later. Oh first—" He takes her ankles. As if to a chauffeur: "To the bathroom, James."

Clumsily, each step risking Perrick's ability to reproduce, they carry her between them to the bathroom. Buck chuckles. "I swear to God this is just like her . . . I was gonna kill her myself tell you the truth but I'd never do it that way, wouldn't trust the bitch . . ."

In the bathroom Perrick is standing in the tub. Takes out the knife, then removes his coat and tosses it on the floor next to Buck. Trying not to think about it, he opens the knife and begins to saw at her neck.

"Yo yo yo yo whoooooa!" Buck blurts. "Wait a motherfuckin' minute I wanta get outta here before you . . ." He backs out of the bathroom, grimacing, heads for the hall door, pauses to take a hit from his pipe, goes out the door stage whispering just loud enough for Perrick to hear in the bathroom, "I'll be back, man, I got to cop some rock but I'll be back, take you to that doctor, a thousand bucks and that's between you, me and the rollers if you don't come through . . ."

Perrick still sawing. Sawing and sobbing. He expects her to react by biting down harder but—though blood spurts and then levels off, simply wells out of her, she doesn't react and that's horrible. How can morticians do it? Just . . . sawing at someone. They should scream or something, dead or not. Maybe she *was* clamping harder? There was no feeling down there now. How could he tell? "Oh God oh no. I'm gonna throw up on her. This is . . . I can't feel a thing now I think I . . . I think she's biting through Oh God . . ."

The blood making hollow spatters and dripdrops into the tub. Wet crackly noises as he goes through the spine. Letting his eyes glaze, his hands seem to know the work. CRICK-CRICK-CRACKLE.

SPLURT.

Thump.

The body thumping down onto the tub. He drops the knife onto it. Turns quickly because he can't keep it down anymore: the vomit. Painful vomiting. Then he turns on the shower. Vomit and blood going down the drain.

He steps out, dries himself off—and dries off the head too. It has mostly finished its draining. It's bluish yellow now. The eyes sunken into the head more. Cheeks sunken. His dick, where it shows at the root, above her teeth, is angry red and blue. He wonders if he should wash her hair. Give her a shampoo. What the fuck. Maybe *brush her teeth too* while he's at it.

Crazy thoughts. Control yourself. Walk your ass through it, Perrick.

He steps through the bedroom door with the head dangling from his groin. It bounces ludicrously as he walks. A bloody towel wrapped around the neck stump. The head's eyes are open now and looking up at him. Once more he's wearing the raincoat and underwear. Raincoat isn't blood soaked but his stomach is spattered and the underwear is scarlet brown and his legs are streaked. He looks somewhat relieved and yet in shock. Staggers over to his rig, his syringe, draws some crank from the spoon. Looks down at the head. Starts to giggle. Suppresses it.

Says to himself, "Wish I had some horse. Like to take some. Share some with you. Don't worry, I don't have to pee no more, I can't feel nothin down there . . . Hey . . . close your eyes, Suzie . . ." He reaches

down and tries to close them . . . doesn't work . . . nervous GIGGLE . . .
"OK, I understand, sure: we got to have *some* communication." A
peacock's tail of garbage in his head. He thinks: I'm losing it. He looks
at the needle. A friend. "Speed ain't right for this. Need champagne for—
I don't know if this is a marriage or a divorce . . ."

He says the Magic Words: "Fuck it." He injects the speed. Rushes.
Giggles. Sobs. Giggles. Sobs. Babbles.

"Suzie . . . Suziebitch talk to me, tell me: is this . . . this is your way to—"
He's interrupted by a delicate knock on the door.

He hears a fluting female voice, sort of silly flirtatious "Andy! Oh
Annnn-dyyyy!"

Perrick at first thinks this is Suzie's voice. Stares down at the head. It's
pulsing from the drug rush. Emanating.

"Suzie—How'd you say that with your mouth full?" Laughing and crying both as he says it.

The voice again and this time Perrick realizes it's coming from the
hall door. "Annn-dyyyy! The Pakistani lady at the front deh-esk said
you were ho-ommme!" A more normal voice: "Come on, open up,
hon, let's talk!"

It sinks in who this is. His wife. Andrea. He mutters, "Jesus Fuck. My
fucking wife I don't even—but oh yeah sure—sure uh-huh makes sense . . ."

He starts to giggle and tosses the syringe into a wastebasket, buttons
up his coat over the head. Throws a bedspread haphazardly over the
small amount of blood on the floor that dripped through the towel.
Funny head-hump bobbling under the coat as he goes to the door, opens
the door for his fairly straight wife who looks around with distaste. She's
Jewish, well dressed.

She says, "This place even *smells* horrible, doll. Listen—" She closes
the door and comes toward him. "You look awful. So—you've been using? You ready to come home? I thought about it and thought about it
and I don't think you would've gone to that whore if you weren't on the
drugs. I mean, you weren't in your right mind, and we're gonna take you
to one of those twenty-eight day programs and start over—if you're willing I mean you really have to be willing. And no more women, Paid for
or otherwise . . ." She stares at his legs. "Why are you wearing a raincoat
and no pants? It's not even raining. You got shorts on under there?"

"No I . . . Got a head. Ahead of . . . myself." Trying to keep down the
crazy half giggle. "Put on the coat before the pants. Come on, sit down."

Andrea looks around skeptically. "Where? I don't know if I want to sit
on any of this . . . I mean, do you launder any of this bedding?"

"The bed's OK. Just . . . *head* over here." Laughter creaking down in his throat as he gestures to the bed. She moves to it and sits gingerly.

"You threw the bedspread on the floor? Very nice.'"

Perrick giggles moronically. *"Head* to." He walks awkwardly toward her.

"You're walking funny, YOU got a back ache?"

Perrick's close to tears now, getting it out spastically. "Got to keep your HEAD down in this world!" Fairly *barking* the word "head." He snorts, "If you don't keep your HEAD down, you've HEAD it, pal!"

She gapes at him. He begins to laugh hysterically. She looks at the lump bobbing under his coat. "Whatever have you got . . .?"

Perrick is sobbing openly now, breaking down."HEADN'T THOUGHT ABOUT IT!"

And then the towel dislodges and falls to his feet in a wet bloody lump.

Andrea gives a rabbity little shriek and jumps to her feet. "You've been doing something again. Something . . ."

Perrick approaches her, feeling madly earnest. Seeing a crepuscular ray of hope. "Andrea—talk to her. You're a woman. Talk to her for me. Convince her to let go."

It might work. It might.

Andrea just backs away, the bitch, whenever you really need them they pull shit like this . . .

She squeaks: "What?"

Perrick pleads, "Talk to her! Woman to woman! What do they call it? Yeah: *Tête à tête!* Talk to her—!"

Blood is dripping down his leg . . . he starts to open his coat . . .

Andrea bursts out: "You don't have to open that!" She's angling for the door. "You really don't have to. I don't—I mean, everybody should have their personal space, the marriage counselor said that and uh—"

But he opens the coat and flings it off. Andrea's eyes are pingpong balls in her head as she sees Suzie. She takes a long noisy breath that sounds as if she's choking on something . . . touches her throat with her hand . . .

Perrick approaches her, weeping, smiling, idiotically appealing: "Talk to her about it, Andrea, just get down there and jaw with her! Woman to woman! If you want to talk to her face to face I could—" He squats and bends over so the head sort of half dangles between his legs . . . he's quite serious and sincere as he goes on: "—and you could, you know, go around behind me and put your face under me there—if you don't mind, I mean, you always said I had a cute tush—you could just—"

Andrea's backed into the door. She turns and claws at it. Yanks it open with a sound of animal fear and sprints out into the hall. Perrick stares after her, a little disappointed but already forgetting about it. He turns away from the door and begins to caress the head, to move his hips against it, not like fucking but more like . . . dancing. Then Buck appears at the door, staring down the hall at the retreating Andrea.

"Yo dudeski your old lady's really geeking out behind—"

He breaks off, seeing Perrick dancing. As Perrick dances over to the dresser, turns on the radio. It's playing "Cheek to Cheek." Buck looks ill and disgusted.

Perrick is tenderly dancing with the head, singing along, badly but sincerely. ". . . when we're out together dancing cheek to cheek!"

Buck murmurs, "Oh wow. Dudeski."

The music swells in Perrick's head. Buck looks at him calculatingly now. Then goes to him, drapes the coat over his shoulders, leads him—still dancing—to the door. "You know what? Your old lady's going to call the cops . . . let's get out of here . . . Get to that ATM . . . I bet that cunt has your bank account frozen but we got another wheeze maybe . . ."

To Perrick, the part of him that used to plan his life and drive his body about, all this is seen detached, like from behind a trick mirror. He's just watching as he body dances out the door with Buck. He watches without feeling as it goes along with him down the stairs and down the street.

A vacant lot. A half-dozen neighborhood homies and dudeskis hanging around a lazy blue flame in a rusting oil barrel. One of this group, a black guy calls himself Hotwinner, is arguing with Buck. Saying "I say it's a load of fuckin' bullshit."

Buck shrugs. "Put your money down and check it out. I'm lying, I pay off three to one."

Hotwinner says, "I get to look close."

Buck nods. "Rockin'."

"You got it. Just don't pull any gafflin' bullshit—" And he forks over five bucks.

Buck says, "Anybody else?"

Two others pony up. "Yeah here, it's a waste of good wine money but fuck it—you goin' to pay off or we keep you ass fo' my dog to have his dinner—"

Buck yells at the rickety van parked at the curb. "Hey yo, Perrick! Let's do it!"

No response. Buck makes a sound of irritation, hustles to the back of the van, drags Perrick out. Perrick's wearing his long coat over the bulge. Perrick is giggling. Mumbling to himself—". . . telling me all the secrets so hard to understand what she's saying sometimes but she knows it all knows it all . . . she's a Head of her time hee hee . . ."

Buck brings him to the firelight, pulls back Perrick's coat, exposing Suzie's purulent head still clamped on his dick and balls, one eye hanging down from the skull, dangling next to his testicles, jigsaws of the scalp rotted off, pig bristles of hair remaining, maggots dripping now and then, squirming . . . halfway to a skull . . .

"That's a pig head or somethin', that ain't no bitch!" a dudeski protests, but Buck draws him closer, makes him bend and really look. He backs away making phlegmy sounds in his throat as Buck says to the others, "OK, dudeskis, take a good look, you paid for it." A few other people drift over to check it out. Buck covers the head. "Anybody else want a look? Five bucks!"

Buck taking more money, murmuring to vacant eyed Peffick, "This is way cool, the bitch still workin' for me, tha's, like, loyalty to the max, you knooooo? I mean, it's just like Suzie to hang in there, dude . . . Lemme count the money dude . . ."

COLD FEET

Didn't like the looks of the wheatfield beside the apple orchard. The wheatstalks looked stiff and uncompromising, and she suspected that they were actually sharp rods of yellow-painted steel which would impale her if she tried to lie down. But he had said to wait at the corner of the wheatfield. And her doctor had told her to start seeing men, escape her introversion. At least, this meeting with Clancy wouldn't be as boring as the usual drive-in dates. She tossed her red corduroy coat onto the wheat and lay down on it, wincing at the feel of crushing wheatstalks brittle underneath. She looked around nervously for insects, shading her eyes against the glare of the Indian summer sun. Clancy was approaching through the apple orchard, taking bites from a bruised yellow apple. *Clancy couldn't be his real name*, she thought.

He stood over her, tossed aside the apple, his silhouette blotting the sun into a halo. He just stood there, watching, trying to seem confident. "I knew you'd come," he said in a measured monotone.

"Pretty sure of yourself?"

"I didn't come here just for myself, you know." He sat down close to her.

"Well," she said, in a conscious effort at unnerving him, "Let's dispense with all the game playing and get down to brass tacks. You didn't ask me to meet you in a secluded place for a discussion about psychology. The grass is high, and no one is around."

"You're kinda . . ." He cleared his throat. "Well, that's fine with me."

She removed, with ritualistic aplomb, her purple wool skirt and light pink blouse, leaving only pink see-through briefs. She laid her clothes in a neat pile and waited for him to remove his blue workshirt and dungarees. She closed her eyes and daydreamed:

A neatly furnished room, with couches, easy-chairs, coffee tables, doilies, and pre-Raphaelite prints. In one corner a very average-looking man of middle age in a dark business suit stood perfectly still. He was completely unmoving, unblinking, unbreathing. Another man–a chubby and cherubic butler in coat and tails–entered, humming to himself. He dusted all the furniture with a large feather duster. He then approached the immobile man as though he were a suit of ornamental armor and began to dust the right arm. There was no response from the frozen man. But strips of white were produced in the wake of the butler's brushing. The white was the shirt under the coat of the man being dusted. In a few minutes the coat and trousers had completely vanished, having been brushed away by the feather duster like paint darkening a wall. The butler continued matter-of-factly, breaching none of his outward calm as the shirt and underwear of the stationary man fell into dust at the lightest feather touch, heaping gray particles between his polished black shoes. The butler raised the cocktail duster to the stationary man's head and dusted away his hair and epidermis. Brushing in equanimous spirals, front to back, peeling him candy-stripe away, the butler left an oozing red surface on every inch of the frozen man (who still hadn't moved or changed expression). Whistling "It's a Long Way To Tipperary," the butler removed the second layer of flesh under the outer skin, leaving a filmy blue transparent membrane with the tendons and muscles clearly outlined underneath it. The butler dusted inexorably through tissues of crimson dampness down to fat and flesh. He exposed underlayers of veins and cartilage without inflicting damage on them when brushing the layer directly above. He chafed down to the muscles and glands, melting down to primary organs and veins which hung loosely from the skeleton like baubles on a Christmas tree. Though the heart was not beating, nor the lungs filling, the organs seemed soft and fresh as if preserved in the amber of an instant's hiatus between beats of metabolism. The butler, still whistling and stepping carefully around the multicolored heaps of dust on the floor, said to himself, "Tsk, I should have put down some newspapers."

He brushed away layer after layer until only the skeleton remained. He took out a rag and applied furniture polish, shining the bones for some minutes.

The sunlight seemed to want to pierce her eyelids, insistently telling a story like light from a movie theater's projection booth. She opened her eyes and saw that Clancy still wore his pants. A peculiar expression danced on his thin nervous face.

She reached casual fingers to unzip his jeans. He arrested her fingers with his sweaty palm.

"What's wrong?" She asked irritably, "Getting cold feet?"

"No. I should tell you though, Clancy's not my real name. My real name is Avram. And I'm not here for dreams."

She reached back to brace herself against the ground; and gasped. She had stabbed her hand on a wheat stalk. Stiff and metallic, yellow paint was flecking from its wiry shaft.

The Peculiar Happiness
of Professor Cort

It was three minutes before the IAMton explosion, and Professor Brian Cort was finding it difficult to concentrate.

Cort was a tall, stooped, balding man with worry lines around his foggy gray eyes. He wore the traditional white lab smock and underneath it the traditional rumpled suit.

Cort's wife was bothering him that day; his wife bothered him the way other people were bothered by rheumatism or migraines. Cort was in his lab at Pennyworth College; his wife was at home, probably totting up a new list of grievances. But Cort felt as if an imp-sized ghost of Betty were sitting on his shoulder, fussing into his ear. Sneering.

Betty's harangue that morning had been so piquant, so barbed, he could hear it still, and it was maddeningly distracting as he strove—In the overlit, chrome and white-tile lab—to concentrate on adjusting the particle gun.

At a minute and a half before the explosion he didn't know was coming, Cort was wondering why he stayed with his wife. Why cultivate misery? Maybe he deserved it.

He accessed the particle-gun gradiation program, absently tapped out the first few designations; sighing, recalling what his wife had said to him that morning.

"What I don't understand, *Professor—*" she'd said, calling him Professor in the most biting and skeptical of her repertoire of nasty tones, "is why I remain with a man who ignores my emotional needs. Maybe it's part of my transactional script. My therapist says—"

Gritting his teeth as he remembered what her therapist said, Cort distractedly tapped out the wrong series of digits, programming the particle gun to an excess of both tangency and acceleration.

In consequence: the explosion.

It was a strange explosion, because it did no real damage. Nothing broken, or burned. Cort simply heard a sort of high-pitched *screeeeeeee,* felt a spiteful heat and a malicious chill go through him. Saw only light.

A profound light, and a peacock one. More colors than were perceivable engorged the outpouring of light, that brilliant explosion.

For a full minute after the explosion, Cort was blind. He saw only a sort of light-infused Jackson Pollock painting wherever he looked. And then the lines and contours of the room leached back into the painting, looking gray and black in contrast to the filter of unbridled color, finally asserting themselves, and the dazzle faded. He looked down at himself— he was unhurt, unchanged.

But the room had been materially altered. At first, Cort thought he was seeing some sort of after-image, some distortion of damaged nerve-ends. But no, he realized: this was the way things looked now, objectively. Everything was crusted in iridescent crystal. Like a zircon-crusted nail file.

The iridescence was everywhere. On the lab tables, the instrument panels; on computer consoles and spectrographic analyzers and the other arcana of a particle physicist. And on windows, ceilings, floors. He was inside a gem-walled box. It was like some variant of an Egyptian treasure tomb—jeweled renderings of what the dead physicist will need in the next world.

His mind reeling, Cort tried to grasp what had happened—and, as if his mental effort were the stimulus, the room changed again.

Now, every surface crawled with pictures. Kaleidoscoping imagery that slid, overlapped, folded symmetrically into itself, appearing within the glimmering crust. He saw charts, photos of fog chamber events, equations, diagrams . . . and recognized it all as material from his own research on IAMtons. He thought: Hallucinations. But he'd taken LSD, once, years before, and he knew what hallucinations were like. Not like this.

Remembering his dismaying experience with lysergic acid made him think of Susan Pritchett, the dizzy, bleached blonde who had given him the stuff . . . a simple-minded girl, but one who'd have made him happier than Betty . . .

He saw Susan Pritchett walking toward him, out of the wall. He smiled—but then Betty's image materialized, and warped to encompass Susan, devouring her; Betty became an attacking antibody.

Cort closed his eyes and thought: Sister Mary Jane. He opened his eyes and saw, within the wall like a penguin locked in amber, the nun who'd courageously tried to teach him to play piano, thirty years before.

"Oh, I see," Cort said to himself. He turned away and walked toward the open door leading out of the lab, trying to keep his eyes focused on that door, not wanting to see his unexpurgated free-association projected on the walls, the ceiling, the floor . . .

He stepped through the door, blinking, into the April sunshine, and looked out at the park-like grounds of Pennyworth College. "Oh, no," he said.

Oh, yes: it was here too. The crystalline crust; the cinematic collaging. And now, as he watched, it became more than projected mental imagery. Now, things began to reshape *physically*.

It was early Sunday morning. The campus was almost deserted. And yet it was thronged. To his right, for example, was the burning bush. "That expression of mawkish, gaping surprise on your face, Cort," the burning bush said, as Cort stepped onto the blacktop walkway that led across the lawns to the street, "is unbecoming for a man your age." The burning bush was waist-high, with dark green foliage; a nondescript bush except for its fluttery sheath of bright red flame. It burned but was not consumed. The burning bush went on, in its Cecil B. DeMille voice, "And your confusion is really inappropriate, Cort. You've irradiated the area with IAMtons, after all. I quote from your IAMtons *Defined for the Layman:* 'IAMtons are a hypothetical subatomic or superatomic particle. Essentially, the essence of awareness . . . the particles work in collaboration with the inherent electrochemical actions of the brain to produce a psychically holographic entity, the Self; real awareness is impossible without them; they are our link to the Universe's reservoir of collective awareness; IAMtons, further, act as reflective mirrors for the informational input of the perceptual organs—'"

The bush paused to clear a throat it didn't have. "In my case, the intense, localized concentration of IAMtons released by the explosion evidently induced in me—and in other plants and substances hereabouts—a psycho-reactive state, the particles of raw awareness reacting with a kind of psychological echo to the electromagnetic influence of your brain, drawing on the paradigms of your subconscious to—"

Cort had ceased to listen: he was staring at the large abstract sculpture that stood a few paces from the burning bush. The sculpture had always struck Cort as an idealization of vagueness rendered in marble, suggesting at times a cloud solidified in the act of changing shape; at other times, when the light was different, it might have been a rendering of a multiple amputee break-dancing. Today, irradiated and interpenetrated with IAMtons, the sculpture's knobs and whorls and flowing contours reacted to Cort's mind by writhing into new configurations. Its abstract topography divided and subdivided, becoming more intricate, re-sculpting into shapes that emanated a sinister familiarity.

He stepped onto the grass and crossed to the sculpture. He found himself staring at it from two feet away, looking into it is if it were a TV screen. And on TV, as it were, was his least favorite show: *Cort, the Boy.*

Within the sculpture was a vivid, three-dimensional moving image of the precocious Brian Cort at seven years old, sitting in his room, turning the pages of a book written for twelve-year-olds, and looking bored. Looking bored and pale and neurasthenic. And lonely.

"Cort!" A voice from the real world. Cort turned away from the image in the sculpture, to see Bucky Mackenzie standing on the tarmac, blinking at the burning bush and the image-rippling sculpture. "So you see it too?" Cort said. He was still afflicted with a nagging doubt that, despite the clarity of his perceptions, all of this was hallucination.

"I do indeed," Bucky said breathily. "Lord!"

"Lord? Not this time," the burning bush said.

"I'm dreaming," Bucky said. Bucky was the head of the physics department; just over forty, he was slender but, unlike Cort, his slenderness was compact, neatly proportional. His close-cut black hair was teased down into short, spiky bangs, a style intended to be youngishly hip without being risky. He was scrupulously tanned, immaculately manicured, and faddishly fit. Bucky was a climber, a glad-hander, a man who guarded his own flank first and could be counted on to set things up so there was someone else to blame if a project went awry.

Looking from Cort to the shifting shapes in the sculpture and back again, Bucky murmured absently, "I was just coming over to see if you had the results that . . . that you'd hoped for and, ah . . . it would appear that *something* has, ah . . ."

Noting that the sculpture was now replaying with embarrassing exactitude a certain very familiar sexual fantasy, Cort stepped between the sculpture and Bucky and said, "I'm conducting an experiment and our presence will prejudice the, uh . . ." His voice trailed off as he stared at the water sprinklers. Bucky was staring at them too.

The sprinklers on the other side of the walk had automatically started up, and were spraying the crystal-crusted grass of the lawn . . . but the water was no longer itself.

Bucky was standing nearer than Cort to the sprinkler's outpour, and the up-fanning water, evidently affected by the ambient field given off by the IAMton concentration, was arcing higher, warping itself to conform to some emanation of Bucky's unconscious. As if shaped on a lathe the water spun into a translucent replica of what Cort thought at first was a ten-foot-high bowling trophy and then perceived to be a giant version of the *Pursbinder Award for Excellence in the Encouragement of Scientific Progress*. It was the figure of Broderick Pursbinder holding a globe out in front of him, the globe configured with DNA molecules and atom-symbols and EEG lines, a clumsy representation of the World Of Science.

Bucky, of course, had been angling for the Pursbinder, having "shepherded," to use his own modest expression, a number of studies which later came to be regarded as "seminal." None of which he'd done the work on, nor had he come up with the initial ideas. But he'd swung the grants for them. His success rate in swinging grants was Bucky's equivalent of a record-breaking home run average.

Bucky took a mesmerized step toward the rippling, aqueous, ten-foot-high Pursbinder award—it looked rather like an unstable ice sculpture—with an expression on his face that made Cort think of John the Baptist experiencing a vision of Paradise.

So it's not just me, Cort thought. Other people see them too. And I see what Bucky sees.

He turned back to the marble abstract, was relieved to see the image had shifted. He was relieved, that is, until he was what it had shifted to . . .

That day in the principal's office. Himself, his mother, the principal at his grade school; the crust of iridescence gave depth, startling semblance of real life to the figures so that, after a moment, Cort forgot he was watching a simulation. He was engrossed in remembering. He was there, once more, in that stuffy office on a wet October morning . . .

When you're eight years old, wet is *wet*; scary is *scary*. Outside the school it was wet; raindrops made leaden patterns down the window behind Mr. Jameson, so it looked like a herd of snails had stampeded down the glass. Inside the room it was scary, because Brian Cort was in trouble.

Brian and his mother sat to the right of the door; across from them Mr. Jameson sat behind his desk, his big, thick, hairy-knuckled hands clasped on the desk's flawless glass. Brian was sitting on an orange plastic chair. He was gripping the plastic seat to either side of his Wrangler jeans, rubbing his thumbs on the almost slimy plastic, and he was staring at Mr. Jameson's forehead. If you stared at the duck-shaped mole on Mr. Jameson's forehead, you could give the impression you were looking attentively at him, without really having to look him in the face. Jameson's wide, froggish face was slightly cockeyed; one of his eyes was glass. He maintained a look of patronizing amusement, like the lily pad for the frog of his face, as he said, "Mrs. Cort—Brian here has been my delight and my disappointment both. He's two grades ahead of his peers, and he's still right on top of his classes, but sometimes—it's kinda funny—it's like the bottom will drop right out of his motivation, and he'll do *just nothing* for two weeks at a time—"

"Brian," his mother said sharply, "what have you got to say to that?" His mother was tall and birdlike, her neck too long, her lips pressed into an almost invisible line in her mouth; those wing-frame glasses making her small, bitter green eyes weirdly malevolent. She wore a crisp gray dress-suit; kept her olive purse clenched in her lap. She leaned forward toward Brian over the purse, her knuckles white on its brass jaws as she looked at him. He imagined her turning into a bird . . .

Professor Cort, staring into the sculpture's animations, saw a reenactment of the cartoon-like sardonicism of the young Brian Cort's imagination. His mother was transforming, the purse melding to her neck to become part of a buzzard's wattles, her shoulders narrowing, arms growing feathers, becoming *wings,* chin sinking into her face, her small sharp nose lengthening, getting sharper, harder, becoming a beak, her gray suit becoming dirty gray plumage . . . the mother-bird darting her beak to crack the boy's head, to redden her beak with his brains . . .

Fighting nausea, Cort looked away from the sculpture. He shook himself, trying to shiver the image loose. He watched Bucky to take his mind off it.

Bucky was dancing with a crowd of young, semi-transparent co-eds. Young coeds are always semi-transparent in a way, but these were girls made of flowing water contained, now, in sheaths of crystal iridescence. They were life-sized, and nude, and their various parts were detailed in frothy bubbles; water ran out of the back of their heads and down their backs like long, flowing silvery-blue hair . . . They were caricatures of nubility, impossibly buxom . . . They were dancing with Bucky around the giant Pursbinder award; Bucky was stripping off his shirt as he pranced, dancing to a sort of libidinous perversion of Mozart that seemed to emit from the giant award.

Bucky looked entranced, Cort noted. More than entranced, he looked positively drugged. Cort suspected that Bucky's immersion in the IAMtons—now and then he made a grab for a water baby and splashed right through her—was sticking IAMtons into his bioelectric field, whereupon they went, quite literally, right to his head.

It may yet happen to me, Cort thought. I'd best get well away from her . . .

But he turned back to the memory sculpture, as if invisibly tugged, and found himself gazing into it once more . . .

The young Brian Cort, sitting in the principal's office, was trying to answer his mother's acid-dripping question. *What do you have to say to that, Brian?*

"Um, Mom, see, uh . . . those times I couldn't work I just got tired, felt like was going to fall asleep all the time or something. I mean you make me stay up to study so—"

But Jameson was rattling on, "I mean, dammit Mrs. Cort—if you'll excuse my lingo—this boy has so darn much potential—"

"Oh dear, I know, Mr. Jameson—it's sad to see him waste it—"

"I mean he's basically a good boy but . . . well, in order to fulfill all that potential, Mrs. Cort, he's got to push himself a little harder, and a little more often, and that's just the unpleasant fact of the matter. What have you got to say, Brian, eh?"

"Uh, well, the problem is—"

"I think he understands, Mrs. Cort, don't you?"

"I certainly hope so." She gave Brian a look that was too reserved to be a glare, but somehow it cut more deeply than one. "I'll let you in on a little secret, Mr. Jameson. When his father died, the last thing he said to me was, "Make sure Brian works hard to be everything he *can* be—for his own sake. That's all I ask . . .'"

Even Jameson looked a little embarrassed hearing this. It was too obviously a fabrication.

Brian was certain his father had never said anything of the sort. But it didn't matter. His mother made him feel as if Dad had said it.

Professor Cort took a step backward from the sculpture, blinking, breathing hard. He felt strange. Like his skull had gone soft as the skin over Jell-O. Like the blood in his brain had gone ice cold.

Something drew his attention to the grass at his feet. The grass was encrusted with IAMton iridescence, and it reacted to his cognizance, began to rearrange itself into words eight inches high: CORT, PSYCHIC PARADIGM SEQUENCE ENGAGED: LOOK AGAIN.

He snorted in disbelief and irritation. Now the grass was talking to him. The grass was telling him what to do.

But he looked at the sculpture again. Something kept pulling him back to it . . . Some part of his mind nagged, "For Heaven's sake, Cort, get to a hospital, have yourself checked out for radiation burns, arrange to get the lab's IAMton irradiated material analyzed–it could be invaluable! It could advance your career! Act responsibly! *Look away from the sculpture!*"

But he couldn't look away. Seeing himself as a boy . . . the sight gripped him. It was as if it closed some mental circuit, and he was rooted to the spot by a kind of psychological electricity. And as he gazed at the sculpture–no, gazed into it–the configurations shifted again. He saw and remembered.

Brian was tired. But he felt good. It was his birthday, he was fifteen years old today, and he'd aced the trig and Introduction to Philosophy tests he'd stayed up all night studying for. Probably hadn't been necessary to stay up and study, but Mom had been adamant.

Winter had sealed Cincinnati under three feet of snow. The late afternoon sunlight sparkled the snow's crust. Brian's black rubber boots squeaked through the muddy rut as he turned up the drive of the small, rickety wooden house, thinking, *Today's my birthday and I aced the tests.*

Fifteen years old today, and already a senior in high school. He was up for half a dozen scholarships. Mr. Greensburg, the boy's counselor, had suggested Brian take a year off before going to college. Maybe get a job, buy a used car, "enjoy being a teenager."

God it sounded good. Mom wouldn't like it. But today was his birthday, today he'd done well. She wouldn't be able to say no.

The warmth of the kitchen tingled his nose and ears as he came in the back door. The room smelled like mentholated tobacco. Mom was sitting in the small breakfast nook, smoking, talking on the red wallphone.

She put her hand over the mouthpiece and shot him one of Those Looks. "Brian you're tracking slush all over my floor. Take your boots off on the back porch. For such a smart boy you can be so thoughtless. Sometimes I think you're an idiot savant."

He looked at her, then at his boots. *Shrug it off, Brian.*

But as he took his boots off on the back porch, he heard over and over: *Sometimes I think you're an idiot savant.* No humor in her voice. *Sometimes I think you're an idiot . . .* When he came back into the kitchen, though, there was a gift-wrapped box on the wooden table. His mother was still on the phone. He sat at the table, waiting to tell her how well the tests had gone.

"Okay, I'll see that he's there, Horace. Six o'clock sharp! No, he's not as punctual as he should be—but I'll make sure he gets there!"

She hung up. "That was Horace Cress at Cincinnati U, he says there'll be no problem with your getting into school there next fall, and he thinks the plan for you to go to Stanford for your Masters is the ticket." She clapped her hands together once, in a way that announced finality. And smiled, the smile that always seemed to say, *I'm pleased but dubious. Let's just hope you don't blow it.*

He looked at the gift.

"Go *ahead*, Brian, *open* it!" Rolling her eyes.

He did, slowly, thinking about the new shoes he'd hinted about; the shoes he had were too small and they were falling apart, embarrassing him at school . . . and the package came apart and—three pamphlets, and a framed certificate. The framed certificate was his father's Master degree.

"I thought you'd like to have that. Give you a little incentive."

The pamphlets were things like, *Your Career in Research Chemistry!*

"There's good money to be made in that field, working for those big deodorant corporations, Brian. Judy Clapper's brother-in-law Tony works at Glass Bell Toiletries. He helped invent Pore-Plug, you know. And Glass Bell's not even one of the big companies, and he makes—"

"Jeez, Mom, I don't wanta spend my life making deodorant!"

"Pore-Plug has been very good to Tony. If you—"

Desperately changing the subject, Brian put in, "Mom—don't you want to know how I did on my term tests?"

"I know how you did. I called your teachers. You got A's on both. But I want you to know I'm very disappointed in you."

He stared at her, numbed.

She went on, "I spoke to Mrs. Gilmore and she says you take no interest in extra-curricular activities. Brian, you should get involved, those things look good on your record when you're looking for a job after college. You could join some school clubs—"

"Mom, I don't have *time,* I'm taking extra classes—"

"What else have you got to do with your spare—"

"I don't *have* any spare time! And I don't know what else I'd do if I had some—but I want to find out, Mom, jeez, I need some time to . . . Mom, Mr. Greenburg suggested I take a year off from school after I graduate and, uh, get a job and use the money to buy a car and maybe, I don't know, go out or—"

"I can't believe you'd do that," Her dangerously-flat voice. "I can't believe it. All our plans—*phhbt!* You'd do that to your mother—to your *father?*"

"Mom, it wouldn't hurt my GPA—"

"I really can't believe it." Shaking her head with exaggerated incredulity. "I just . . . can't . . . believe it."

He knew, then, that it wasn't going to happen. She just wouldn't let it. He'd go to summer school of some kind after high school, to "give him an edge," and then to college, straight through into college. At fifteen years old. He saw a vista of drudgery opening up before him . . .

She stared at him. "My God—you're crying! At fifteen!"

Stop it, he told himself. Stop crying.

She went pitilessly on. "I mean, it's not enough that you don't have the gumption to get involved in extra-curriculars, you have to be a cry-baby too. Your father would be just plain disgusted."

Cort, the adult, had to look away from the scene.

The lawns had humped up and reshaped themselves for Bucky, Cort saw. They'd disgorged rock and soil and agate that'd melded together into a sort of instant alloy of simulated metal, and formed itself into the life-sized shape of a Lincoln Continental. The earthen luxury car carried Bucky around and around the giant Pursbinder trophy, and around the quivering translucent girls, with a kind of ritualistic redundancy; miniature mansions grew up from the ground, formed of the local silicon, into fantastic shapes somewhere between miniature golf castles and Bucky's fantasy of the perfect home . . .

A couple of students had discovered the IAMton concentration, one of them screaming in horror as the earth erupted his phobia—which he'd just been trying to come to terms with in the biology lab: white rats made of roots and silicon, rats the size of dogs, capering on their hind legs in a Disneyesque square dance . . .

The girl student with him was backing away from an enormous baby, a house-sized baby of yellow clay. The elephantine infant playfully slapped a gardener's wheelbarrow so it arced up, over the roof of the lab and struck a chimney with a lovely clang, showering sparks and bricks; the baby giggled earthshakingly.

Cort closed his eyes, took a series of deep breaths, and once more heard the nagging disembodied voice, "Cort! Get to work on this thing! The explosion could be a breakthrough! Why are you wasting your time playing mind-games with your memory? Get back to work!"

But after a moment he found himself looking at the living sculpture once more.

Saw himself within it: as a young man at his mother's funeral.

Saw the expression on his face and knew what he'd been thinking: *I can do what I want, now.*

Then came the wince of guilt. *How can you be glad she's dead? Your father would be . . . disgusted.* Telling himself. *There's no reason I should feel guilty. I'm not glad she's dead. But since she is, since the cancer came along . . . well it's not as if I gave her cancer.*

Reply: *But she implied it was my fault, that all her worrying about me made her prone to it.*

Around and around, guilt and resentment like snakes devouring one another and endlessly regenerating and devouring again.

Cort looked away from the sculpture, thinking: *But I went on to do what I wanted.*

He didn't take the chemlab position at Glass Bell Toiletries or the one at Dow. He was interested in particle physics, and he pursued that interest, in defiance of his mother's dying wish. Ending up at the one place that would give him a free hand in research: Pennyworth College.

Where he met Betty.

Within the softly contoured stumpy torso of marble, the living hieroglyphs were again coming alive, taking on three dimensional shape, filling his eyes, whispering to him . . .

Dr. Winslow Garland's party. Celebrating the grant for the new super-miniaturized particle accelerator. Garland's shabby little backyard, that summer evening. Bach playing softly from the wheezing stereo; groups of professors, assistants, deans, a few students most of them clumped near the big clamshell-shaped bowl of cloying wine punch on the checkercloth-covered cardtable; chatting, drinking the awful punch. Betty was helping Mrs. Garland lay out fresh canapés. But now and then she glanced up at Cort, who was standing alone at the rose-twined back fence.

He'd seen Betty watching him, calculating and predatory. Somehow she'd decided on him. He could feel it, though she hadn't said much to him at the party, hadn't wound her coils of precious, dryly flirtatious small talk around him this time.

Go on, he told himself. Talk to her. You're lonely. She's interested. You're a research prof at a minor college and you can't expect starlets or even sex-hungry coeds to come nuzzling up to you. You can't hope for anyone more attractive than Betty.

Replying to: But I tried it, I dated her twice and she annoys me. She prattles, she pretends to an interest in physics she doesn't have, she doesn't like the opera, she doesn't like the theater only because "why pay to go sit in an uncomfortable seat and watch those things when you can see them free on public television?" She's tight with her money which means she'll be tight with mine. She's selfish about a thousand little things which means she'll be selfish about all the big things. She wants to get married, I can feel it, and I don't want to spend my life with someone who annoys me.

She was coming over to talk to him.

Cort thinking: This is my chance to put an end to it, I'll simply snub her. She'll leave me alone. It doesn't matter what she says about me, these people don't like me much anyway.

But that voice again, telling him: It does matter. Her uncle is Joshua Pennyworth. You'd be advancing your career if you married her. Do something right for once . . .

Looking at the miniature re-enactment in the sculpture, Cort shuddered, seeing something jarringly out of place in it.

Impossibly, his mother was there, at Professor Garland's party. Years after she'd died.

Mother was standing beside the image of Cort at the party. No, she was standing *in* him. Half in, half out of him, almost like a Siamese twin. Her image was semi-transparent; his was solid. She wasn't there, really— but the IAMtons were showing him the psychological reality, this time.

And when he walked, he walked strangely—"the Cort shuffle," he'd overheard one of the students calling it. He saw now that he walked oddly because his mother was merged into his leg. Was tugging it her way. And she was bent over him, her face gone birdlike as she dug her beak into his ear and whispered, "Don't be an idiot. Betty's perfect for you . . ."

He knew the voice now. The voice that had said, *Do something right for once.* His mother's voice.

She looked out of the sculpture at him. His mother in miniature, cobbled grotesquely onto the miniature, earlier Cort. Mother, gazing out at him with contempt.

Cort turned away from the sculpture. Stomach churning, he lurched across the grass to walk, looked around, trying to re-orient himself.

Bucky had collapsed with exhaustion, was lying asleep on the grass; his IAMton constructions had degenerated into fuzzy-edged abstracts, geometrical cut-outs that took on anthropomorphic shape from time to time, then fell back into component geometry; they shimmered in and out of free-associative definition, reflecting his dreams.

A group of children had run out onto the IAMton zone and were giddily helping the Coyote chase the Roadrunner, the figures three-dimensional and child-sized and giving every appearance of being alive; the children laughed every time the Roadrunner went *beep-beep!*. Bugs Bunny looked on, jeering, while GI Joe, squatting besides Bugs, cleaned his rifle, looking around tensely for some real action.

Cort thought: *I'd better get out of here before I get caught up in something I can't get out of . . .*

He moved off down the path between a row of small trees—and stopped, staring. The trees were writhing, re-shaping with nightmarish familiarity. A squat holly tree was bulging here, contracting there, rustling with the movement as it rearranged and recolored itself, becoming a pointillistic reproduction of his wife Betty. A Betty twenty-eight feet tall.

Berries in the holly bush rearranged to become Betty's sulky lips; leaves and shadows conspired to form her beak-like nose—so like Mother's—and her sunken, accusatory eyes. The holly bush bent over him and said, "You didn't love me, but you married me anyway and now I have to suffer because of your hypocrisy, and oh yes, I *know* you don't love me, I can *feel* you not caring—"

He felt the requisite stab of guilt—and then heard another furious rustling, turned to see a willow tree, green-furred with buds, whipping its long, drooping branches about, shaping itself into a likeness of his mother.

His mother was traced in the sky with a willow-twig filigree, droning through her nose, as always: ". . .if your father was alive he'd be disgusted . . ." and, "I'm very disappointed in you . . ." and on, and on.

Betty yammering on one side, Mommy Dearest droning on the other, and the grass rustling, shifting, the blades bending and bunching to form two-foot high letters in green: *IAM* CORT AND *IAM* DISAPPOINTING . . . *IAM* NOT LIKE MY FATHER . . . *IAM* A BAD HUSBAND . . . *IAM* A FAILURE, *IAM* A LOSER . . . As the sidewalk before him humped up, buckling, IAMton-impregnated concrete that should have cracked, instead going rubbery, elastically bulging, reddening, pulsing . . . a great red boil waist-high, swelling on the sidewalk before him; splitting open, glutinously erupting a slime-coated, inchoate human figure emerging from it as if from a soft egg: Cort himself, but a Cort deformed, a dwarfish parody, its face a rigid mask of self-pity; its hunched back striped with welts.

Cort saw it for what it was: his own guilt-deformed self-image. And beyond it he saw the ground rippling as the roots of the willow tree nosed like enormous earthworms across the grass, under the walk, through the ground to the holly tree, to "Betty," to entwine the trunk of the Betty-shaped tree. And he saw the roots of the holly tree elongating, stretching to entwine the base of the willow; and he saw that the wife-tree and the mother-tree were bent over the twisted image of himself, incanting at it, and he saw that it reacted to their accusations, their condemnations, by deforming further, becoming more repulsively toad-like . . .

Seeing all this enacted, he knew: He'd married Betty because he knew she'd treat him as his mother had. Because the nagging, deriding part of his mind that his mother had planted in him had pushed him into it. The mother that he carried around with him had recognized Betty for what she was . . .

It was horribly, laughably absurd. And exposed as absurd it lost all its power to mold him. He walked past himself, past his guilt-ridden self, and left it behind.

Light as a soap bubble, he could laugh at the wasted years. And a great, shuddery wave of sheer relief swept him almost running out of the campus, past the area of IAMton impregnation—which was already beginning to disperse with entropy. He'd think about the scientific implications of all this later. First, he had to get his life in order. Beginning with finding a new place to live—a place where he'd live alone, really alone, for the first time.

And as he passed a church on that Sunday afternoon, the people arriving for services stared at him—and wondered why he looked so goddamned happy.

Tahiti in Terms of Squares

Now: I'm going to tell you something—

Go right ahead. Parent paid for it, not me, so talk away.

—and you'd better be paying strict attention. First I'll tell it to you, then you'll begin to see it, manifesting before you. Because that's the way things work here.

Okay. I'm listening.

Listening isn't good enough. If you want to *see* you must give me your complete attention. Concentration.

All right! I'm paying attention.

Good. This concerns Tahiti. I offer a cinematic exegesis in arbitrarily selected stages of that continuum.

Which continuum?

That one . . . over *there*.

Oh, okay. I'm with you—

Before I begin, read off the pertinent points of the introductory pamphlet. I want to be utterly assured you know exactly what we're up to, coming here. Why the Between is useful to us.

The Between? I don't need to read the pamphlet. Anyhow, I threw it away. Ummm . . . what we're doing here is-

Threw it away? Threw away the *pamphlet?* After the agency spends involuted Karmas to have those pamphlets 'grammed! I hardly think that's a—

Doesn't matter, I memorized it. More or less. It said this field trip will enable me to "attain objectivity in the antiduality perspective achieved through the externalization of parity". . . which is one of those attitudes Parent thinks it's so necessary to adopt. Privately I don't understand why Parent is so anti-Subjectivist. Anyhow, it said I've been brought to this vast, clammy, pearly-white place with the two definitionless curving walls so . . . could I have a drink off your bulb? I didn't bring one.

Go on, go on; why were you brought here?

Oh. So I'll learn something by graphic example. A lesson concerning the mechanics utilized in the insemination of zones of reality. So the pamphlet claimed. Something like that. Personally, I think Parent assumes the whole thing will engender in me a reactionary Objectivist philosophy or some such nonsense . . . I'm *dry* after all that ranting, can I have a drink off your bulb? Ah, thanks—

"Some such nonsense"! Puerile half-weaned! It is far from nonsense. This exercise will help to assure you never get lost while plane-sifting. In the Between we can objectively observe the means with which zones of reality radiate from archetypal cusps, after which everything else in that sphere of wavelength-specific influence is patterned. Got it?

Yeah, sure. Got it.

Hey—don't drink it all. You could have exchanged for your own bulb. Now. Let me . . . here it is . . . this is *Prime A for Tahiti Continuum.* Look—right over *there.* Come a few steps this way. Now look where I'm pointing. See him? *There.*

He glanced at the watch strapped on his left wrist. The face of the watch said noiselessly: "It's time." The watch had no hands or dial, nothing but two pale rubbery lips set into the face and he read the lips as would a deaf person, though he wasn't deaf. He might as well have been deaf because he was alone in the abode of silence and as far as he knew there was no one outside of silence's abode at all, and even if there were, surely no one would be capable of breaking in through silence's unspeakable defenses. And he didn't comprehend speaking except in terms of squares . . . you'd have thought the room that contained him was about fifty feet square with three yards between floor and ceiling. No furniture. He didn't need furniture, and although he possessed a human body he didn't sleep or rest or ingest or digest or excrete (except in the nonmaterial terms of the squares). The palpitating tissues, the anticipatory wetness of his human flesh was ready and waiting to sweat/eat/spit/digest/excrete/excite but none of those reactions were indigenous to the time frame in which the body was ever-presently coded. It had been deliberately coded into the flicker between two heartbeats, between two breaths. But he moved about and he had the false impression that it was under his own power . . . that's all you need to know about *him,* as he stands as an individual, except if you want to know what he looked like.

Yes, I rather would.

Oh. You would? Troublesome of you. But all right. He had an average man's body, for the middle twentieth century era, Tahiti continuum; he was English, Caucasian, six foot and one hundred sixty pounds, sparse and extra-soft brown hair, watery-blue eyes. But he would have looked strange to the biological refractions patterned after him because his face and head were that of an infant of three weeks, homo sapiens baby, soft and inchoate, vague like a baby though the volume of the head was proportionate to his body

No eyebrows?

None. When his watch told him it was time which it periodically did—

I can see him! Over against that curving wall, by all those checker-things in—

Obviously, idiot. Why else would I be explicating him? Verbal description is the token for this vending machine. As you can see, he is and was . . . I'll restrict my narrative to past tense because past tense *here* sparks the present tense *there*, which is the apropos mechanics of that locale—

Or maybe you're just nostalgic and sentimental.

Shut up and listen. Now: He was alerted by the watch to the necessity of palming the squares. You can see the squares on the walls, there.

Squares in a variety of colors, yeah. Pastel shades.

Yes. Each square a foot in diameter and six inches from the others, evenly patterning the walls. None on ceiling and floor—

I can see that for myself.

Shut up, it's necessary for me to say it. Where were we? Oh: He went to the walls and pressed his palm against the light brown square. When the palm of his soft, uncalloused hand—his right hand—pressed onto the surface, it is adhered gently, with a sticky commingling—

Hey! You're narrating that in the present tense! You said "*is* adhered gently . . ."

Ah, thank you. Very kind of you to bring that to my attention. Very kind. Naturally I'd have noticed it myself in time.

Naturally. But . . . why can't you narrate this scenario in present tense? It's dangerous.

Dangerous! Oh *really*—

Laugh if you like. It is dangerous.

What happens if you narrate this scenario in present tense?

I suppose I can demonstrate if I do it in a very cautiously controlled manner. *Observe:*

He smiles, enjoying the onrush of physicalized data, abandoning himself to it like a death-dwarf-junkie to a rush, he sighs and presses his arm further in, to the wrist, to the forearm, elbow, until the arm is immersed in the stuff, vanished into the wall, and his shoulder begins to sink also, his head grows rubbery and pliant as it is sucked into the square—

Hey! You'd better cut that out. He's disappearing, his head is *going.*

The longer I do it the more difficult it is to reverse. Now, as you can see, the image is frozen, he is half in the square, its precipitous consumption of him halted because I've stopped narrating altogether. But if I were to continue, the inertia of the present tense narration, which tends to proliferate its own future because its inception in *now* causes a hollow in the *to be* which must be filled since time follows the path of least resistance, like everything else.

Well—can you get him out of there?

I can now; the inertia didn't build up to the degree that I lost control. *Listen:* Realizing he'd gone too far, he drew his arm out of the dun square, slowly, letting the data-dew drain cleanly away and back to its source, as his head and limb returned to their normal aspects . . . He stood back, stretched, sighed, and began again, this time more conservative in his rate of induction. When the palm of his soft, uncalloused right hand pressed onto the surface, it was adhered gently with sticky commingling. Now he experiences the tea gustatorially, smells its boiled aroma, is aware of its initial texture on his lips.

Hey, aren't you narrating in—

Don't interrupt again, you're distracting me. I have to concentrate. Keep your eyes on him; how else do you expect to learn? *Heed:*

The drink is silvery, it is earthcolored, it is velvet, it is mischievously steamy. He does not linger amongst these superficial sensations. He goes on. His hand slowly sinks into the brown square, the edges of tea-data brinking his flesh seeping up, around his knuckles and over the back of his hand, creeping over his wrist. If he chooses, he can press his entire arm up to the shoulder into the brown square which would then expand to accommodate the remainder of his body, the other squares shrinking to compensate. But he sinks only up to his shoulder . . . *Comprende?*

Solid. Yeah.

So this provides him with an orderly immersion into the whole matrix between the origins, the empirical and the conclusions of various strains of *Thea Sinensis.* Tea. He is aware of the tea in every cell and pore now, and his back is rigid, his eyes rolled upward, as he relishes the trance. He is aware (in rippling fibrillations coursing his fingers and arm, traveling down into his spine by unbroken but oscillating channel) of the etiology of the earliest forms of the plant identifiable as a strain of *Thea Sinensis,* its taste relative to the latest flavor in the manifold tea hybrids, its genetic makeup, how it came to cross-pollinate into yet another form of tea, and another, how that tea was discovered and savored in turn by a clan of naked savages, how those savages were affected by the tea, the trading of that tea to other tribes and the articles for which it was traded, the effect of the tea on the other tribe, the cultural reverberations of the tea, the various comparative hybrid phases and related species developed deliberately or accidentally by these tribes and by the civilizations engineered by their progeny and the status of tea therein, all books written about tea including recipes and treatises on the various complementary additives, the names and life histories of all tea manufacturers, plantation owners, connoisseurs; the cultural effect of tea on every society into which it is introduced, the colors, scents and textures of the leaf and flower and their configurations in botanists' schematics, the microscopically discerned panoply of a crosssection of tea-plant cells, the plants viewed through the filter of the fourth and the fifth dimensions, the rituals and traditions stemming from the various historic derivations of tea, the names and life stories of the first person who ever used tea and the last who ever will—

All this and more?

Exactly. But the information, somatically calibrated data, does not linger in the brain cells of our babyface; it lights the lamps and then snuffs the flame an instant after it is lit. When at last babyface extracts his arm from the square he recollects none of what he's just experienced and measured. His arm is clean when it is removed. The brown substance (physical realization of data) does not cling to his skin, and its information eschews internment in memory. And the surface of the square closes up as if it had never been disturbed . . .

Hey, you've changed from past—

Don't interrupt! Watch him! Now having finished tea it is time for a walk down the beach. He goes to—

Hey, listen, should you have changed from—

Shut up! He goes to the next square in line, to the left, which is pastel shades of sunset red and tropical sky blue and beach-sand white and bamboo yellow and palm-trunk brown, all gently blended strata. He places his palm against this polychromatic square and sinks only up to the wrist. He is no longer aware of his arm as entering the square, now he is all rapport with the sensory-eidetic organ-music of data; surrounding and permeating this beach in Tahiti about is confluence. He raptures in the atomic structure of "1910 A.D.," relative to this confluence. He raptures in the atomic structure of sands and wavelength dissection of photons in refraction with sea spray and contrasted with the various poems written about the tropics (read in alphabetical order) and theses concerning Tahiti written up till January 1, 1910.

Ah, as with tea but more so?

Just so.

I see. But still you've changed your—

Quiet! Now he glances at the watch on his left wrist—he does this with that part of his reflexes specially reserved for that action—and registers: "Time for lunch." So he begins to withdraw his arm, shedding cognizance as he does, preparing to depart to the beach square so that he can progress to the lunch square that is the absolute fact of a sandwich, a ham and cheese sandwich on stale imported rye and all the background and layers of sensation infinitely minute and macrocosmically unfolding from that node of perception. He draws his arm out—

Hey! I'm trying to *tell* you, you've gotten into present tense!

What? I . . . Oh *damn*, I've gone and done it now. That'll result in a stress pattern and rupture the membrane unless I can keep up, overtake the verbal realizations, catch up, slow it down to past tense. Get control again. Like trying to harness maddened horses, at this point. Why the Monitor didn't you tell me this before I—

I'm sorry. I tried.

Never mind. I've got to concentrate or it's going to fly out of its groove and strike off on its own. Ah, his arm is emerging—was emerging?—from the square and suffers a spasm, his fingers get caught on the edge of the square, the inner edge on the interior of the pastel shades. He tugs, a little furrow of frustration invading his otherwise dispassionate face, and the wall quivers under the pull. He cannot disengage his fingers from the inner edge of the wall-frame and, angrily, he gives it a furious yank. This time there is a crackling sound—

I feel all cold inside. I don't like this feeling in my guts. A chill. Unpleasant, brittle. Something getting loose inside me. I—

Quiet! I'm losing ground, damn it! Ah, a crackling sound and a portion of the seemingly unbreakable wall comes loose in his fingers, chipped off, (Oh damn it all!) and the liquid inferential being in the square comes pouring out of the gap and splatters babyface about the feet. He staggers, he turns to run but is overwhelmed and vanishes from view as the section of the square that was green-yellow licks out and expands like a fire in a match factory and the room begins to fill up with bamboo shoots shooting and leaves unfolding. Quickly after comes the brown and the blue and the white formulating into magically upspringing palm trees and billows of sky-gas and the room is suddenly filled to capacity with shifting arabesques of sand and water and foliage, exceeding the bursting point as babyface is compressed and annihilated, processed

into seminal droplets which fertilize the soil of the frenetically proliferat-
ing island paradise growing like a self-inflating rubber raft and *oh damn*
I can't catch up, I've lost the reins—

What's happening? I can't see! It's all a boiling of liquified leaves and
sandstorm and there went a swordfish! The wall is crackling, the walls of
white . . .

Hey! It's coming out *here.*

It's making a break for it, spilling into the Between, it's going to have
to compensate itself now, engender a plane in which to root the tropical
belt—oh damn—hold your breath, I'll attempt an—

"Harold! Look at those two on the beach up there. In the shade of those
palms."

He shrugged. "Just a couple of beachcombers, dear, I doubt they'll be
any trouble. They look a trifle dazed, don't they?"

"*Dazed* is hardly the word. Harold they're *naked!*"

"Ah . . . yes indeed. So they are . . . Well bother! Come about, dear,
we'll do well to turn back. We'll complain to the desk clerk at the Captain Bligh. He said the riff raff had been cleared off the beach. Hedo-
nists of some sort, by the look of them. And white, too! Oh, *do* stop
crying, Emily."

"I can't help it. They look *mad.* We've got to hurry. And I shall expect
you to complain to the consulate."

"Of course. But I'm sure they . . . quite harmless. The light was sort of
. . . ah . . . diffused about them. And I could swear that neither one had
a nose . . ."

Shading her eyes against the sun's tropical glare she gazed timorously
over her shoulder.

She shrieked.

"They're coming *after* us."

(Running footsteps, heavy breathing, curses from the British gentleman as he stumbles. His wife valiantly pauses to help him rise.)

Excuse me, said one of the odd, pallid men as he caught up with
them, *I wonder can you direct us back to the Between? We've no idea
how to get back from here. Frankly, we're quite lost. Terribly sorry
about all this. The world. Spilled something. Sorry. Dreadful inconvenience, I know.*

He said it in a language that anyone anywhere in the universe would
instantly have understood.

EQUILIBRIUM

He doesn't know me, but I know him. He has never seen me, but I know that he has been impotent for six months, can't shave without listening to the news and TV at the same time, and mixes bourbon with his coffee during his afternoon coffee break. And is proud of himself for holding off on the bourbon in the afternoon.

His wife doesn't know me, has never seen me, but I know that she regards her husband as "something to put up with, like having your period"; I know that she loves her children blindly, but just as blindly drags them through every wrong turn in their lives. I know the names and addresses of each one of her relatives, and what she does with her brother Charlie's photograph when she locks herself in the bathroom. She knows nothing of my family (I'm not admitting that I have one) but I know the birthdays and hobbies and companions of her children. The family of Marvin Ezra Hobbes. Co-starring: Lana Louise Hobbes as his wife, and introducing Bobby Hobbes and Robin Hobbes as their two sons. Play the theme music.

I know Robin Hobbes and he knows me. Robin and I were stationed together in Honduras. We were supposed to be there for "exercises" but we were there to help train the anti-rebel troops. It was a couple of years ago. The CIA wouldn't like it if I talk about the details much.

I'm not the sort of person you'd write home about. But Robin told me a good many things, and even entrusted a letter to me. I was supposed to personally deliver it to his family (no, I never did have a family . . . really . . . I really didn't . . .) just in case anything "happened" to him. Robin always said that he wouldn't complain as long as "things turn out even." If a rebel shoots Robin's pecker away, Robin doesn't complain as long as a rebel gets *his* pecker blown away. Doesn't even have to be the same rebel. But the war wasn't egalitarian. It remained for me to establish equilibrium for Robin.

Robin didn't want to enlist. It was his parents' idea.

It had been raining for three days when he told me about it. The rain was like another place, a whole different part of the world, trying to assert itself over the one we were in. We had to make a third place inside the first one and the interfering one, had to get strips of tin and tire rubber and put them over our tent, because the tent fabric didn't keep out the rain after a couple of days. It steamed in there. My fingers were swollen from the humidity, and I had to take off the little platinum ring with the equal (=) sign on it. Robin hadn't said anything for a whole day, but then he just started talking, his voice coming out of the drone of the rain, almost the same tone, almost generated by it. "'They're gonna start up the draft for real and earnest,' my dad said. 'You're just the right age. They'll get you sure. Thing to do is, join now. Then you can write your own ticket. Make a deal with the recruiter.' My dad wanted me out of the house. He wanted to buy a new car, and he couldn't afford it because he was supporting us all, and I was just another expense. That was what renewed my dad, gave him a sense that life had a goal and was worth living: a new car, every few years. Trade in the old one. Get a whole new debt. My mom was afraid I'd be drafted too. I had an uncle was in the Marines, liked to act like he was a Big Man with the real in-the-know scuttlebutt; he wrote us and said the Defense Department was preparing for war, planning to invade Honduras, going to do some exercises down that way first . . . So we thought the war was coming for real. Thought we had inside information. My mom wanted me to join to save my life, she said. So I could choose to go to someplace harmless, like Europe. But the truth is, she always was wet for soldiers. My uncle Charlie use to hang around in his dress uniform a lot. Looking like a stud. She was the only woman I ever knew who liked war movies. She didn't pay attention during the action parts; it wasn't that she was bloodthirsty. She liked to see them displaying their stripes and their braid and their spit and polish and marching in step, their guns sticking up . . . So she sort of went all glazed when Dad suggested I join the Army and she didn't defend me when he started putting the guilt pressure on me about not getting a job and two weeks later I was recruited and the bastards lied about my assignment and here I fucking am, right here. It's raining. It's raining, man."

"Yeah," I said. "It'd be nice if it wasn't raining. But then we'd get too much sun or something. Has to balance out."

"I'm sick of you talking about balancing stuff out. I want it to stop raining."

So it did. The next day. That's when the rebels started shelling the camp. Like the shells had been waiting on top of the clouds and when they pulled the clouds away, the trap door opened, and the mortar rounds fell through . . .

Immediately after something "happened" to Robin, I burned the letter he'd given me. Then I was transferred to the Fourth Army Clerical Unit. I know, deeply and intuitively, that the transfer was no accident. It placed me in an ideal position to initiate the balancing of Equilibrium and was therefore the work of the Composers. Because with the Fourth Clerical I was in charge of dispensing information to the families of the wounded or killed. I came across Robin Hobbes's report, and promptly destroyed it. His parents never knew, till I played out my little joke. I like jokes. Jokes are always true, even when they're dirty lies.

I juggled the papers so that Robin Hobbes, twenty years old, would be sent to a certain sanitarium, where a friend of mine was a Meditech who worked admissions two days a week. The rest of the time he's what they call a Handler. A Psych Tech. My friend at the sanitarium likes the truth. He likes to see it, to smell it, particularly when it makes him gag. He took the job at the sanitarium with the eighteen-year-old autistics who bang their heads bloody if you don't tie them down and with the older men who have to be diapered and changed and rocked like babies and with the children whose faces are strapped into fencing masks to prevent them from eating the wallpaper and to keep them from pulling off their lips and noses—he took the job because he *likes* it there. He took it because he likes jokes.

And he took good care of Robin Hobbes for me until it was time. I am compelled to record an aside here, a well-done and sincere thanks to my anonymous friend for his enormous patience in spoon-feeding Robin Hobbes twice daily, changing his bedpan every night, and bathing him once a week for the entire six months interment. He had to do it personally, because Robin was there illegally, and had to be hidden in the old wing they don't use anymore.

Meanwhile, I observed the Hobbes family.

They have one of those new bodyform cars. It's a fad thing. Marvin Hobbes got his new car. The sleek, fleshtone fiberglass body of the car is cast so that its sides are imprinted with the shape of a nude woman lying prone, her arms flung out in front of her in the diving motion of the Cannon beach towel girl. The doors are in her ribs, the trunk opens from her ass. She's ridiculously improportional, of course. The whole thing is wildly kitsch. It was an embarrassment to Mrs. Hobbes. And Hobbes is badly in debt behind it, because he totaled his first bodyform car. Rammed a Buick Marilyn Monroe into a John Wayne pickup. John and Marilyn's arms, tangled when their front bumpers slammed, were lovingly intertwined.

Hobbes took the loss, and bought a Miss America. He is indifferent to Mrs. Hobbes's embarrassment. To the particularly judgmental way she uses the term *tacky*.

Mr. Hobbes plays little jokes of his own. Private jokes. But I knew. Mr. Hobbes had no idea I was watching when he concealed his wife's Lady Norelco. He knew that she'd want it that night, because they were invited to a party, and she always shaved her legs before a party. Mrs. Hobbes sang a little tuneless song as she quested systematically for the shaver, bending over to look in the house's drawers and cabinets, and *behind* the drawers and cabinets, peering into all the secret nooks and burrow-places we forget a house has; her search was so thorough I came to regard it as the product of mania. I felt a sort of warmth, then: I can appreciate . . . thoroughness.

Once a week, he did it to her. He'd temporarily pocket her magnifying mirror, her makeup case. Then he'd pretend to find it. "Where any idiot can see it."

Bobby Hobbes, Robin's younger brother, was unaware that his father knew about his hidden cache of Streamline racing-striped condoms. The elder Hobbes thought he was very clever, in knowing about them. But he didn't know about me.

Marvin Hobbes would pocket his son's rubbers and make *snuck-snuck* sounds of muffled laughter in his sinuses as the red-eared teenager feverishly searched and rechecked his closet and drawers.

Hobbes would innocently saunter in and ask, "Hey—you better get going if you're gonna make that date, right? What'cha looking for anyway? Can I help?"

"Oh . . . uh, no thanks, Dad. Just some . . . socks. Missing."

As the months passed, and Hobbes's depression over his impotence worsened, his fits of practical joking became more frequent, until he no longer took pleasure in them, but performed his practical jokes as he would some habitual household chore. Take out the trash, cut the lawn, hide Lana's razor, feed the dog.

I watched as Hobbes, driven by some undefined desperation, attempted to relate to his relatives. He'd sit them at points symmetrical (relative to him) around the posh living room; his wife thirty degrees to

his left, his youngest son thirty degrees to his right. Then, he would relate a personal childhood experience as a sort of parable, describing his
hopes and dreams for his little family.

"When I was a boy we would carve out tunnels in the briar bushes.
The wild blackberry bushes were very dense, around our farm. It'd take
hours to clip three feet into them with the gardener's shears. But after
weeks of patient work, we snipped a network of crude tunnels through
the half-acre filled with brambles. In this way, we learned how to cope
with the world as a whole. We would crawl through the green tunnels in
perfect comfort, but knowing that if we stood up, the thorns would cut
us to ribbons."

He paused and sucked several times loudly on the pipe. It had gone out
ten minutes before. He stared at the fireplace where there was no fire.

Finally he asked his wife, "Do you understand?" Almost whining it.

She shook her head ruefully Annoyed, his jaws bruxating, Hobbes
slipped to the floor, muttering he'd lost his tobacco pouch, searching
for it under the coffee table, under the sofa. His son didn't smile, not
once. His son had hidden the tobacco pouch. Hobbes went scurrying
about on the rug looking for the tobacco pouch in a great dither of
confusion, like a poodle searching for his rawhide bone. Growling low.
Growling to himself.

Speculation as to how I came to know these intimate details of the
Hobbes family life will prove as futile as Marvin's attempt to relate to
his relatives.

I have my ways. I learned my techniques from other Composers.

Presumably, Composers belong to a tacit network of free agents the
world over, whose sworn duty it is to establish states of interpersonal
Equilibrium. No Composer has ever knowingly met another; it is impossible for them to meet, even by accident, since they carry the same
charge and therefore repel from each other. I'm not sure just how the
invisible Composers taught me their technique for the restoration of
states of Equilibrium. To be precise, I am sure as to how it was done—I
simply can't articulate it.

I have no concrete evidence that the Composers exist. Composers
perform the same service for society that vacuum tubes used to perform
for radios and amplifiers. And the fact of a vacuum tube's existence is
proof that someone must have the knowledge, somewhere, needed to
construct a vacuum tube. Necessity is its own evidence.

Now picture this: Picture me with a high forehead crowned by white
hair and a square black graduation cap with its tassel dangling. Picture

me with a drooping white mustache and wise blue eyes. In fact, I look a lot like Albert Einstein, in this picture. I am wearing a black graduation gown, and clutched in my right hand is a long wooden pointer.

I don't have a high forehead. I don't have any hair at all. No mustache. Not even eyebrows. I don't have blue eyes. (Probably, neither did Einstein.) I don't look like Einstein in the slightest. I don't own a graduation gown, and I never completed a college course.

But picture me that way I am pointing at a home movie screen with my official pointer. On the screen is a projection of a young man who has shaved himself bald and who wears a tattered Army uniform with a Clerical Corps patch on the right shoulder, half peeled off. The young man has his back to the home movie camera. He is playing a TV-tennis game. This was one of the first video games. Each player is given a knob which controls a vertical white dash designating the 'tennis racket', one to each half of the television screen. On a field of blank gray the two white dashes bandy between them a white blip, the 'tennis ball'.

With a flick of the dial, snapping the dash/racket up or down, one knocks the blip past the other electronic paddle and scores a point. Jabbing here and there at the movie screen I indicate that the game is designed for two people. I nod my head sagely. But this mysterious young man manipulates left and right dials with both hands at once. (If you look closely at his hands, you'll note that the index finger of his left hand is missing. The index finger of his right hand is missing, too.) Being left-handed, when he first began to play himself, the left hand tended to win. But he establishes perfect equilibrium in the interactive poles of his parity. The game is designed to continue incessantly until fifteen points are scored by either side. He nurtured his skill until he could play against himself for long hours, beeping a white blip with euphoric monotony back and forth between wrist-flicks, never scoring a point for either hand.

He never wins, he never loses, he establishes perfect equilibrium.

The movie ends, the professor winks, the young man has at no time turned to face the camera.

My practical joke was programmed to compose an Equilibrium for Robin Hobbes and his family. Is it Karma? Are the Composers the agents of Karma? No. There is no such thing as Karma: that is why the Composers are necessary. To redress the negligence of God. We try. But in establishing the Equilibrium—something far more refined than vengeance—we invariably create another imbalance, for justice cannot be precisely quantified. And the new imbalance gives rise to a contradictory inversity, and so the Perfect and Mindless Dance of Equilibrium proceeds. For there to be a premise there must somewhere exist its contradiction.

Hence I present my clue to the Hobbes encrypted in a reversal of the actual situation.

In the nomenclature of the Composers, a snake symbolizes an octopus. The octopus has eight legs, the snake is legless. The octopus is the greeting, the snake is the reply; the centipede is the greeting, the worm is the reply.

And so I selected the following document, an authentic missive illicitly obtained from a certain obsessive cult, and mailed it to the Hobbes, as my clue offered in all fairness; the inverted foreshadowing:

My dear, dear Tonto,

You recall, I assume, that Perfect and Holy Union I myself ordained, in my dominion as High Priest—the marriage of R. and D., Man and Wife in the unseeing eyes of the Order, they were obligated to seek a means of devotion and worship, in accordance with their own specialties and proclivities. I advised them to jointly undertake the art of Sensual Communion with the Animus, and this they did, and still they were unsatisfied. Having excelled in the somatic explorations that are the foundation of the Order, they were granted leave to follow the lean of their own inclinations. Thus liberated, they settled on the fifth Degree in Jolting, the mastery of self-modification. They sought out a surgeon who, for an inestimable price, fused their bodies into one. They became Siamese twins; the woman joined to his right side. They were joined at the waist through an unbreakable bridge of flesh. This grafting made sexual coupling, outside of fondling, nearly impossible. The obstacle, as we say in the Order, is the object. But R. was not content. Shorn of normal marital relations, R.'s latent homosexuality surfaced. He took male lovers and his wife was forced to lay beside the copulating men, forced to observe everything, and advised to keep her silence except in the matter of insisting on latex condoms. At first this stage left her brimming with revulsion; but she became aware that through the bridge of flesh which linked them she was receiving, faintly at first and then more strongly, her husband's impressions. In this way she was vicariously fulfilled and in the fullness of time no longer objected when he took to a homosexual bed. R's lovers accepted her presence, as if she were the incarnate spirit of the frustrated feminine persona which was the mainspring of their inner clockworks. But when their new complacency was established, the obstacle diminished. It became necessary to initiate new somatic obstacles. Inevitably, another woman was added to the Siamese coupling, to make it a tripling, a woman on R.'s left. Over a period of several months more were added, after the proper blood tests. Today, they are joined to six other people in a ring of exquisite Siamese multiplicity. The juncturing travels in a circle so the first is joined to the eighth, linked with someone else on both sides. All face inward. There are four men and four women, a literal wedding ring. (Is this a romantic story, Tonto?) Arrayed as they are in an unbreakable ring, they necessarily go to great lengths to overcome practical and psychological handicaps. For example, they had to practice for two days to learn how to collectively board D.'s Learjet. Four, usually the women, ride in the arms of the other four; they sidle into the plane, calling signals for the steps. This enforced teamwork lends a new perspective to the most mundane daily affairs. Going to the toilet becomes a yogic exercise requiring the utmost concentration. For but one man to pee, each of the joined must provide a precisely measured degree of pressure . . . They have been surgically arranged so that each man can copulate with the woman opposite him or, in turns, the man diagonal. Homosexual relations are limited to one coupling at a time since members of the same sex are diagonal to one another. Heterosexually, the cell has sex simultaneously The surgeons have continuated the nerve ends through the links so that the erogenous sensations of one are shared by all. I was privileged to observe one of these highly practiced acrobatic orgies. I admit to a secret yen to participate, to stand nude in the center of the circle and experience flesh-tone piston-action from every point of the compass. But this is below my Degree; only the High Priest's divine mount, the Perfect and Unscrubbed *Silver*, may know him carnally . . . Copulating as an octuplet whole, they resemble a pink sea anemone capturing a wriggling minnow. Or perhaps interlocked fingers of arm wrestlers. Or a letter written all in one paragraph, a single unit . . . But suppose a fight breaks out between the grafted Worshippers? Suppose one of them should die or take sick? If one contracts an illness, all ultimately come down with it. And if one should die, they would have to carry the corpse wherever they went until it rotted away—the operation is irreversible. But that is all part of the Divine Process.

Yours very, very affectionately,
The Lone Ranger

Mrs. Hobbes found the letter in the mailbox, and opened it. She read it with visible alarm, and brought it to her husband, who was in the backyard, preparing to barbecue the ribs of a pig. He was wearing an apron printed with the words, DON'T FORGET TO KISS THE CHEF. The word FORGET was almost obliterated by a rusty splash of sauce.

Hobbes, read the letter, frowning. "I'll be goshdarned," he said. "They get crazier with this junk mail all the time. Goddamned pornographic." He lit the letter on fire and used it to start the charcoal.

Seeing this, I smiled with relief, and softly said: "Click!" A letter for a letter, equilibrium for the destruction of the letter Robin Hobbes had given me in Honduras. If Mr. and Mrs. Hobbes had discerned the implication of the inverted clue I would have been forced to release Robin from the sanitarium, to the custody of the Army.

When the day came for my joke, I had my friend bring Robin over to my hotel room, which was conveniently two blocks from the Hobbes' residence.

It should be a harmless gesture to describe my friend, as long as I don't disclose his name. Not a Composer in face but one in spirit, my Meditech friend is pudgy and square shouldered. His legs look like they're too thin for his body. His hair is clipped close to his small skull and there is a large white scar dividing his scalp, running from the crown of his head to the bridge of his nose. The scar is a gift from one of his patients, given in an unguarded moment. My friend wears thick wire-rim glasses with an elastic band connecting them in the rear.

Over Robin's noisy protests I prepared him for the joke. To shut him up I considered cutting out his tongue. But that would require compensating with some act restoring equilibrium which I had not time to properly devise. So I settled for adhesive tape, over his mouth. And of course the other thing, stuck through a hole in the tape.

Mr. Hobbes was at home, his Miss America bodyform car filled the driveway. The front of the car was crumpled from a minor accident of the night before, and her arms were corrugated, bent unnaturally inward, one argent hand shoved whole into her open and battered mouth.

Suppressing sniggers—I admit this freely, we were like two twelve-year olds—my friend and I brought Robin to the porch and rang the doorbell. We dashed to the nearest concealment, a holly bush undulating in the faint summer breeze.

It was shortly after sunset, eight-thirty p.m. and Mr. Hobbes had just returned from a long Tuesday at the office. He was silent and grumpy, commiserating with his abused Miss America. Two minutes after our ring, Marvin Hobbes opened the front door, newspaper in hand. My friend had to bite his lip to keep from laughing out loud. But for *me,* the humor had quite gone out of the moment. It was a solemn moment, one with a dignified and profound resonance.

Mrs. Hobbes peered over Marvin's shoulder, electric shaver in her right hand; Bobby, behind her, stared over the top of her wig, something hidden in his left hand. Simultaneously, the entire family screamed, their instantaneous timing perhaps confirming that they were true relatives after all.

They found Rob as we had left him on the doorstep, swaddled in baby blankets, diapered in a couple of Huggies disposable diapers, a pacifier stuck through the tape over his mouth, covered to the neck in gingham cloth (though one of his darling stumps peeked through). And equipped with a plastic baby bottle. The shreds of his arms and legs had been amputated shortly after the mortar attack on Puerto Barrios. Pinned to his chest was a note (I lettered it myself in the crude handwriting I thought would reflect the mood of a desperate mother.) The note said:

PLEASE TAKE CARE OF MY BABY

WHAT CINDY SAW

The people from the clinic were very nice. Of course, they lived on the shell, and people who lived on the shell often behaved nicely, and with uniformity of purpose, like the little magnetically-moved toy players on an electric football game. They seemed very sincere, and they had a number of quirky details making them ever so much more realistic. The way Doctor Gainsborough was always plucking things from the corner of his eye, for example. And the way Nurse Rebeck was forever rubbing her crusty red nose and complaining of allergies.

Doctor Gainsborough admitted, with every appearance of sincerity, that, yes, life was mysterious and ultimately Cindy might well be right about the way things were under what she called "the shell." Doctor Gainsborough couldn't be sure that she was wrong—but, Cindy, they said, we have our doubts, serious doubts, and we would like you to consider our doubts, and our reasoning, and give our viewpoint a chance. Doctor Gainsborough had known Cindy would respond to his pretense of politely considering her ideas. Cindy was, after all, fair-minded.

And she simply refused to respond at all when people told her she was crazy and seeing things.

Yes, Cindy, Doctor Gainsborough said, you could be right. But still, we have severe doubts, so it's best that we keep up the treatments. All right?

All right, Doctor Gainsborough.

So they'd given her the Stelazine and taught her how to make jewelry. And she stopped talking about the shell, after a while. She became the clinic's pet. It was Doctor Gainsborough himself who took her home, after "just three months this time, and no shock treatments." He let her off in front of her parents' house, and she reached in through the car window to shake his hand. She even smiled. He smiled back and crinkled his blue eyes, and she straightened, took her hand back, and stepped onto the curb. He was pulled away down the street; pulled away by the car he drove. She was left with the house. She knew she was turning toward the house. She knew she was walking toward it. She knew she was climbing the steps. But all the time she felt the pull. The pull from the shell was so subtle that you could think: *I know I'm turning and walking and climbing,* when all the time you weren't. You were being pulled through all those motions, so it wasn't you doing it at all.

But best you think it's you.

She had practiced it, that steering amongst the obstacle course of the mind's free associations. She did it now, and she manage to suppress her sense of the pull.

She felt fine. She felt fine because she felt nothing. Nothing much. Just . . . just normal. The house looked like a house, the trees looked like trees. Picture-book house, picture-book trees. The house seemed unusually quiet, though. No one home? And where was Doobie? The dog wasn't tied up out front this time. She'd always been afraid of the Doberman. She was relieved he was gone. Probably gone off with the family.

She opened the door—funny, their not being home and leaving the door unlocked. It wasn't like Dad. Dad was paranoid. He even admitted it. "I smoke Paranoid Pot," he said. He and Mom smoked pot and listened to old Jimi Hendrix records and, when they thought Cindy was asleep, screwed listlessly on the sofa.

"Hello? Dad? Mom?" Cindy called, now. No answer.

Good. She felt like being at home alone. Playing a CD, watching TV, nothing to cope with. No random factors, or scarcely any. And none that weren't harmless. Watching TV was like looking into a kaleidoscope: it was constantly shifting, going through its motions with its own style of intricacy, but there was never anything really unexpected. Or almost never. Once Cindy had turned it on and watched a Japanese monster movie. And the Japanese monster movie had been too much like a caricature of the shell. Like they were mocking her by showing what they knew. What they knew she knew.

Now, she told herself. Think about *now*. She turned from the entryhall to the archway opening into the living room.

In the living room was something that looked very much like a sofa. If it had been in the rec-room of the clinic she'd have been quite sure it was a sofa. Here, though, it sat corpulent and dusty blue-gray in the twilight of the living room, scrolled arm-rests a little too tightly wound; it sprawled ominously in the very center of the room. There was something unnatural in its texture. It had a graininess she'd never noticed before. Like one of those ugly, irregular scraps of jellyfish at the seashore, a membranous thing whose stickiness has given it a coating of sand.

Even more disorienting was the sofa-thing's ostensibly familiar shape. It was shaped like a sofa. But there was something bloated about it, something tumescent. It was just a shade bulkier than it should have been. As if it were swollen from eating.

So that's their secret, she thought. It's the sofa. Normally I don't notice anything unusual about it—because normally I don't catch it just after it has eaten.

She wondered who it had eaten. One of her sisters? The house was silent. Maybe it had eaten the whole family. But then Mother had said that they wouldn't be home when she got there: she remembered now. One of the nurses had told Doctor Gainsborough. Sometimes the Stelazine made Cindy forget things.

They had gone out to dinner. They wanted to go out to dinner, probably, one last time before Cindy came home. It was embarrassing to go out to dinner with Cindy. Cindy had a way of denouncing things. "You're always denouncing things, Cindy," Dad said. "You ought to mellow out. You're a pain in the ass when you do that shit." Cindy would denounce the waitress, and then maybe the tables, the tablecloths, the folds in the tablecloth. "It's the symmetry in the checker-pattern on the table that reveals the deception," she would say earnestly, like a TV commentator talking about terrorism. "This constant imposition of symmetrical pattern is an attempt to delude us into a sense of a harmony with our environment that isn't there at all."

"I know you're precocious, Cindy," her dad would say, brushing crumbs of French bread from his beard or maybe tugging on one of his earrings, "but you're still a pain in the ass."

"It could be," Cindy said aloud to the sofa, "that you've eaten one of my sisters. I don't really mind that. But I must hastily and firmly assure you that you are not going to eat me."

Still, she wanted to find out more about the sofa-thing. Cautiously.

She went to the kitchen, fetched a can opener and a flashlight, and returned to the living room.

She played the light on the thing that sat on the polished wooden parquet floor.

The sofa-thing's legs, she saw now, were clearly fused to the floor: they seemed to be growing out of it. Cindy nodded to herself. What she was seeing was a kind of blossom. It must have roots far underground.

The sofa-thing quivered self-consciously in the beam of her flashlight.

With the flashlight in her left hand—she could have turned on the over-head light, but she knew she'd need the flashlight for the caverns be-neath the shell—she approached the sprawling, blue-gray thing, careful not to get too close. In her right hand was the can opener.

All the while, she seemed to hear a backseat driver saying: *This isn't part of the program. You should go upstairs and watch TV and move from moment to moment thinking safely, steering around the obstacles, turning the wheel away from the dangerous clumps of association, pretending you don't know what you know.*

But it was too late. Her Stelazine was nearly worn off and the couch had startled her into a wrong turn, and now she was on a side road in a foreign suburb and she didn't know the route back to the familiar high-way. And there were no policemen she might ask, no mental cops like Doctor Gainsborough.

So Cindy crept toward the sofa-thing. She decided that the sofa couldn't hurt her unless she sat on it. If you sat on it, it would curl up, enfold you. Venus's-flytrap.

She knelt by its legs. Sensing her intent, it bucked a little, dust rising from its cushions. It contracted, the cushions humping. It made an awful sound.

She began to work on its legs, where they joined the floor. For thirty-eight minutes she worked busily with the can opener.

The sofa-thing made a series of prolonged, piteous sounds. Her arm ached, but the can opener was surprisingly sharp. Soon she had the cav-ity under the sofa partly exposed; you could see it under the flap-edge of the shell. Cindy took a deep breath, and prised the flap so it opened wider. It was dark in there. Musky smell; musky and faintly metallic, like lubricant for a motor. And a faint under-scent of rot.

By degrees, working hard, she rolled back the skin of the floor around the sofa. Nature was ingenious; the skin had looked like a hardwood parquet floor till now. It had been hard and solid and appropriately grained. Marvelous camouflage. The skin *was* hard—but not as hard as it looked. You could peel it back like the bark of a tree, if you were patient and didn't mind aching fingers. Cindy didn't mind.

The sofa-thing's keening rose to a crescendo, so loud and shrill Cindy had to move back and clap her hands over her ears.

And then, the sofa folded in on itself. Its sirening folded too, muffled like a scream trying to escape from a hand clamped over a small child's mouth.

REALLY, REALLY, REALLY, REALLY, WEIRD STORIES

The sofa was like a sea anemone closing up; it deflated, shrank, vanished, sucked down into a dark wound in the center of the living-room floor. The house was quiet once more.

Cindy shined the flashlight into the wound. It was damp, oozing, red flecked with yellow. The house's blood didn't gush, it bled in droplets, like perspiration. The thick, vitreous underflesh shuddered and drew back when she prodded it with her can opener.

She tucked the can opener into her boot, and knelt by the wound for a better look. She shined the flashlight into the deepness, into the secret, into the under-shell . . .

The house supposedly had no basement. Nevertheless, beneath the living room floor was a chamber. It was about the same size as the living room. Its walls were gently concave and slickly wet—but not organic. The wetness was a kind of machine lubrication. In the center of the chamber was a column, the understem of the creature that had masqueraded as her house. The column, she reflected, was actually more of a stalk; a thick stalk made of cables. And they wound about one another like the strands in a powerline. The sofa must have been sucked into its natural hiding place, compressed within the stalk.

She wondered why the house hadn't struck till today. Why hadn't it got them all while they were sleeping? But probably the undershell people, the programmers, hadn't bred it to be a ravenous, unselective carnivore. It was there for the elimination of *select* people—she realized this must be the explanation for the disappearance of their houseguests. Mom had brought four such people home in the last two years, bedded each one on the sofa, and each of them hadn't been there for breakfast. Awfully curious, awfully coincidental, Cindy had thought, every houseguest deciding to leave before breakfast. Now Cindy knew that they hadn't left the house at all. They'd become part of it. Probably that was what had happened to Doobie—Mom usually wouldn't let him sleep in the house, and never allowed him on the sofa. But her sister Belinda sometimes let Doobie in after Mom had gone to bed; the dog must have snuck onto the sofa for a nap, the sofa's genetically programmed eating hour had come around, and it had done to Doobie what a sea anemone does to a minnow. Enfolded, paralyzed, and digested him.

Cindy didn't mind. She'd always hated Doobie.

She lay face down, peering into the gap in the house's skin. The underfloor was about fourteen feet beneath her. She considered dropping to the sub-world, to explore. Cindy shook her head. Best go for help. Show them what she'd found.

A funny feeling in her stomach warned her to look up.

REALLY, REALLY, REALLY, REALLY, WEIRD STORIES

∞ ∞ ∞

The living-room archway was gone. It had sealed off. The windows were gone. A sort of scar tissue had grown over them. She had alarmed the creature, cutting into it. So it had trapped her.

Cindy made a small, high *uh!* sound in her throat. She stood, and went to the nearest wall, pressed her hands flat against it. It should have felt like hard plaster, but it depressed under her fingers, taking her handprint like wet clay. Softening. The house would ooze in on her, collapsing on itself like a hill in a mudslide, and it would pulp her and squeeze the juices from her and drink.

She turned to the gash she'd made in the floor. Its edges were curling up like paper becoming ash. But it was closing, too. She got a good grip on the flashlight, knelt, and wriggled through the opening, dropping to the floor below. The impact stung the balls of her feet.

Cindy straightened, breathing hard, and looked around.

Tunnels opened from the chamber on both sides, stretching as far as she could see. She stepped into the right-hand tunnel. The ceiling was just two feet overhead; it was curved and smooth. She walked slowly, feeling her way with one hand, shining her flashlight beam at the floor. The darkness was rich with implications, and Cindy felt her nerve falter. She had a vice-squeezing sensation at her temples, and a kind of greasy electricity in her tongue. She tried to picture the flashlight's beam as a raygun's laser, straight and brightly furious, burning the darkness away— but the light was weak, and set only a small patch of the darkness afire. Gradually, though, her eyes adjusted, and the darkness seemed less dense, less oppressively pregnant, the flashlight beam no longer important. At intervals the oblong of light picked out what looked like transparent fishing lines passing from floor to ceiling. The plastic wires came in irregularly spaced sheaves of eight or nine. Sometimes there was hardly room to squeeze between them. Then, she'd sidle through, twisting this way and that. When she brushed a wire, it would resonate like a guitar string, but with an overtone to its hum that was like the call of a desert insect. She sensed, somehow, that the wires had to do with events in the upper world. *They certainly weren't installed by the utility company,* she said to herself.

She came to a place where the wall was transparent, a clear patch big as her two hands put together. It was a little cloudy, but Cindy could see through it into another chamber; two men sat in there at a metal table. They were playing cards, the little white rectangles in their hands marked with mazes and mandalas instead of the usual kings and queens and jacks and spades. Each man was hunched over his hand, deep in concentration. One sat with his back to her. He was the smaller man; he had gray hair. The other was a round-faced man: stocky, a little overweight, his brown beard streaked with white. The bigger man wore a rumpled jacket and trousers of a contemporary cut; the other wore a threadbare suit many decades outdated. The room looked like a jail cell. There were two bunks, a toilet, trays of half-eaten food, empty beer cans lying under the table. "It's your bid, Mister Fort," said the bearded man, with humorous formality "Right you are, Mister Dick," said the other man lightly. He slapped a card face-up on the table and said, "M.C. Escher against Aztec Maze." The other man sighed. "Ah, you've locked again. You win. It's not fair: you had decades to practice, playing against Bierce. Dammit I wish they'd let us smoke . . ."

Cindy banged on the glass, and shouted, but she couldn't make them hear her. Or perhaps they pretended not to. She shrugged, and went on.

Another ten strides further something glimmered on the left, reflecting her flashlight's beam. It was a long, vertical, rectangular mirror, set flush into the wall. The mirror distorted Cindy's reflection, making her seem ludicrously elongated. She reached out to touch it, and accidentally brushed one of the wires; the transparent wire thrummed and her image in the mirror shimmered, vibrating in and out of visibility in a frequency sympathetic to the wires quivering. She struck the wire again, harder, to see what it would do to the image in the mirror. Her reflection fluttered and vanished, and in its place was a flickering image of the upper world. A mundane street scene, children walking home from school, cars honking impatiently behind a slow-moving VW Rabbit driven by an elderly lady . . .

On a hunch, a hunch that became an impulse, Cindy struck the tunnel wires repeatedly, as hard as she could.

The mirror—really a kind of TV monitor—showed the traffic careening out of control, the VW Rabbit backing up at great speed, ploughing into the others, the children losing control of their limbs and flapping haphazardly at one another.

Cindy tittered.

She took the can opener from her boot and slashed at the wires, watching the "mirror" all the while. The strings parted with a protesting *whang*.

And in the upper world: children exploded, cars began to wrap around one another, suddenly becoming soft and pliable, tying themselves round telephone poles . . . a great invisible current swept the street, washing the buildings away . . .

Cindy smiled and went her way down the tunnel, randomly snipping wires.

REALLY, REALLY, REALLY, REALLY, WEIRD STORIES

∞ ∞ ∞

Every few hundred yards she came to an intersection of tunnels; three opening to the right, three to the left, her own continuing on ahead. Sometimes Cindy changed direction at these subworld crossroads, following her intuition, vaguely aware that she had a specific destination.

At length the tunnel opened out into a circular room in the center of which was another thick, red-yellow stalk; a corded, man-thick stalk, grown up to merge with the ceiling. But here, the walls swarmed with what looked like oversized aphids. Mechanical aphids, each big as her hand, and the color of a blue-metal razor blade. They clung to the walls in groups of twenty or thirty, only a hand's width between each group; the aphids crawled methodically on small metal legs thin and numerous as the bristles of a hairbrush; on the right-hand wall they swarmed between banks of TV monitors. She switched off her flashlight; there was enough light from the TV screens. Standing at the monitors, spaced more or less evenly, were a score of dusty blue fellows, vaguely human wearing jumpsuits of newspaper. Looking closer, Cindy could see that the newspaper print was in some kind of inscrutable cipher, quite unreadable. And the news photos showed only half-recognizable silhouettes.

For the first time, real uneasiness shivered up in her, and bits and pieces of fear, like irregular hailstones, rattled down through the chill focal-heart of her sensations.

Fear because the men at the monitors were entirely without mouths, without noses, without ears. Each had only large, blinking, watery-gray eyes. And fear because: with Cindy's arrival in the room, the aphids, if that's what they were, began to move feverishly—but somehow purpose-fully—in mandala patterns over the walls, rustling through a thick coating of shag-rug cilia: the cilia, she saw now, covered the walls everywhere. It was the color of a throat with a bad cold.

The mouthless men used three-fingered hands to manipulate knobs on the frames of the TV monitors. Now and then one of them reached up and brushed an aphid; something in the touch galvanized the creature so that it scurried furiously up the wall, parting the cilia and altering the symmetrical patterns made by the collective motion of the other aphids.

The TV pictures were black-and-white. The floor was alabaster, patterned with inset silver wires; the wires were arcanely configured, and occasionally sparked at the touch of the metal shod feet of the almost-people.

Cindy had decided to call them almost-people.

Her eyes adjusted to the dim light, and she saw that in the small of each almost-person's back was an umbilicus. The long, attenuated black umbilicus drooped, then rose to attach to the base of the thick red-yellow stalk in the center of the chamber, much as a May Day reveller's ribbon attaches to a maypole. Cindy supposed that the umbilici made mouths and noses unnecessary for the almost-people.

Cindy was afraid, but that always put her on the offensive. *Take control*, she told herself.

So just to see what would happen, she went about the room and—with her can opener—methodically clipped the umbilici severing the almost-people from the stalk.

The almost-people stopped what they were doing; they turned and looked at her.

Cindy wondered how they felt. Were they alarmed or surprised or outraged or hurt? She couldn't tell.

One by one they fell, clutching their spindly throats. They writhed and twitched, making the wire-patterns on the floor spit blue sparks, and Cindy supposed that they were choking to death.

She felt a little sorry this time. She even said so. "Oh, I'm sorry."

After a few minutes, they stopped moving. Their big eyes shut. Breathing shakily, Cindy stepped over the corpses and went to one of the TV screens. She was careful not to step on the silver wires in the floor; she was sure she'd be electrocuted if she did.

The TV screens monitored life on the upper world. Reticulating charcoal-and-chalk video images of houses and motels and traffic and dogs. Junkyards. Traffic lights changing. Farms. Seaside resorts. Canadian hikers. Rock singers. A teenage boy with stringy blond hair and a thin chest shakily trying to fill a syringe from a rusty spoon. Jazz players. Masturbating children. Masturbating men and women. Masturbating monkeys. She gazed for a while at a TV showing two people copulating in a hotel room. They were both middle-aged and rather doughy. The man's hair was thinning, and his paunch waggled with his hip motions; the woman's hair was as defined and permanent in shape as a hat. A bell-shaped hat.

Impulsively, Cindy reached out and twiddled the monitor's unmarked black-plastic knobs. The picture shimmered, changed: the woman's head warped, bent out of shape, reified—it had become the head of a chimpanzee. The man screamed and disengaged and backed away. The woman clawed at herself.

Cindy made a moue with her lips, and tilted her head.

She reached up and prodded a number of the metallic aphids with her can opener. They scurried, frightened at the unfamiliar touch, and set the others to scurrying more frantically, till the thousands of aphids clinging to the rounded ceiling were reshaping in the cilia in swarming hysteria, their symmetry of pattern obliterated.

Cindy looked at the TV monitors. Now they showed only crowd scenes. People at football games, looking confused and distressed, as if they'd all gone blind and deaf; they staggered into one another, arms flailing, or tripped, went tumbling down the grandstands, upsetting other people—but, as Cindy watched, the people began to move cohesively down toward the playing field. They streamed onto the field, crowding it, and began to arrange themselves according to the dictates of a spontaneously reconceived psychic schema: people wearing white or yellow shirts moved together, people with dark shirts congregated, till the bird's eye view of the stadium showed the crowd spelling out words with their re-ordered color scheme. They spelled out:

ZEITGEIST

and then

LOVE TIMES DEATH EQUALS ACTION

and then

LACEWORK REBELLION

Cindy turned away. She approached the stalk in the center of the room. With the can opener stuck in her teeth, she began to climb. The going was slippery, but she was determined, and soon reached the ceiling. Arms and legs aching, she clung there and, with one hand, began to carve an opening.

The skin parted more easily from the underside. Ten minutes of painful toil and the gap was wide enough to climb through. Cindy dropped the can opener and wormed her way upward, through the wound in the ceiling.

She broke through a second layer, gnawing with her teeth, coming up through the skin of another seeming-floor.

She found herself under what looked like an ordinary four-legged wooden table. Around her were four empty wooden chairs, and a white floor-length tablecloth.

She dragged herself out of the wet, shuddering slit, and onto the floor. Gasping, she pressed aside the tablecloth, which had so far concealed her from those outside, and crawled into the upper world, once more atop the shell.

She was in a restaurant. Mom and Dad and Belinda and Barbara sat at the next table.

They stared at her, open-mouthed. "What the hell have you got all over you, Cindy?" her father asked. The girls looked a little sick.

Cindy was coated with the wetness, the stickiness, the halfblood death essence of underplace things.

Still breathing hard, her head pounding, Cindy reached down and lifted the tablecloth aside, revealing the ragged, oozing wound shed crawled out of. This time, her family saw it too.

Her father got up from the table rather convulsively, so that he nearly upset it, and his wine glass splashed his wife's dress. He turned away and, fumbling for his pot-pouch, staggered toward the exit. Her sisters had covered their eyes. They sobbed. Her mother was staring at her. Mom's face was changing; the eyes growing bigger, the lips vanishing, her skin going dusty-blue. So, then. Her mother was the one they'd planted in the family. "They're not under every house," Cindy tried to explain to her sisters. "They aren't always there to find. You might dig under our house and not find it—you have to know *how* to look. Not *where* to look. They keep us blinded with false symmetries."

Her sisters followed their father outdoors.

Cindy turned away. "Fuck them all, then," she said. She felt her mother's subworld eyes on her back as she fell to her knees and crawled back under the table. She slid feet-first into the wound, and dropped into the room below. She searched through the monitors, and found a screen showing her dad and her sisters getting into the car. She turned the knobs, and laughed, seeing the car rising into the sky like a helium balloon with the string cut turning end over end, Belinda spilling out of it and falling, her father screaming as the car deliquesced, becoming a huge drop of mercury that hung in the air and then burst into a thousand glittering droplets, falling to spatter the parking lot with argent toxicity.

THE ALMOST EMPTY ROOMS

As images seen in a dream, thus should one see all things.
—Vajracchedika Sutra

PART I OF PRIMARY SYNTAX

AIR RAID ALERT

It was on television at 8:36 A.M. when no one expects catastrophes.

AIR RAID ALERT: LISTINGS OF LOCAL FALLOUT SHELTERS/ALPHABETIC ORDER (Alphabetical shelter listings for the county. Screen flickers, distant siren. Blank screen.)

My wife made a blank scream: Nothing came out of her opened mouth. She ran to get the children. Charles and Andrea had just left for school.

It was a pleasant morning, other than for the alert, and the sky was clear and crisp. I felt no apprehension, seeing the TV announcement. I had expected it; it was right on time.

I'd just risen, and was wheeling between kitchen and study in my electric wheelchair, looking out first one window, then another, mildly curious to see all the neighbors were running in and out of their houses.

The children had laughed, watching the ludicrous scene through the window. The neighbors flung themselves into cars or scurried about on their front lawns like tawdry rags caught in a dust-devil, huffing in circles about the mounds of furniture, clothing, and appliances, quibbling over what to take. I gazed over their heads: it was crisp and chilly, the cloudless sky was hollowed out turquoise.

FALLOUT SHELTER LIMIT OPTIMUM: EQUIVALENCY OF 500 POUNDS PER REGISTERED FAMILY OF TWO PERSONS IN POSSESSIONS OR RELATIVES said the stark letters on the TV screen. The message played over and over. The men at the TV station had left it on automatic replay and gone home to their respective families. No one remained at the TV station, but the machines there still told us to run.

AIR RAID ALERT/CIVIL DEFENSE COMMAND 56648.

REALLY, REALLY, REALLY, REALLY, WEIRD STORIES

I went outside to see what was keeping my wife and children (but I knew). I had no intention of taking them to a fallout shelter (though I'd known). It would do no good, not a bit. As I rolled onto my ramp by the front steps I heard a roar, clutched at my wheel-rims. The ground shuddered.

I looked up: My six-year-old girl and my eight-year-old boy were in the air, far overhead. My wife was nowhere to be seen. A great gust of wind had picked the kids up like plastic kites. They became crosses stark against the sky. X-factors on a blackboard, my children. They hovered up there: in abeyance. I waited with my arms outstretched, instinctively waiting, to catch them as they fell. But they never fell.

A great light from the east.

I shaded my eyes. Light, piercing and sudden as a labor pain. But it was not blinding. It was penetrating; the atomic flash was a revealing light, and my eyes did not melt nor my face scorch. I remembered what day this was—I had shut the eroding calendar out of my mind till that moment. I had stopped up expectancy with self-hypnotism. This day was February 10, 2048.

I had expected all of this.

The nuclear vortex reared up black-bellied with scar-white plumage. White-hot lathing wind cut our flesh from us in spiral strips, but—and here's the amazing grace, the happy surprise—gracefully, smoothly, painlessly. I was almost disappointed. It didn't hurt, not even for a moment. It was as loving as the fingers of a mother undressing a child for the bath. Our skins didn't fly off in crazy bits and ragged pieces, but in coherent spirals, a slack minaret above us, whirling us like toys (yarn unwinding from a spindle), faster, faster until my skeleton fused into a single long bone, molded by centrifugal force. It was all quite painless. And consciousness never ceased nor faltered, but fluttered in my fused remains like a caged songbird. We were not blown away and up like the neighborhood children (those thirteen and under). My neighbors and I were rooted each at our special point, afloat above the lawns whose grasses were now ash. We resonated from the explosions which detonated harmoniously, complementing one another pleasantly, their force snatching the ground neatly upward like a pickpocket artistically plucking a wallet.

There was no pain or discomfort, even when our bodies were only vague memories. There was to be no pain at all in this surgery. It was performed by professionals.

PART I OF SECONDARY SYNTAX

Hypothesis: Events are animals. Events are living creatures, whose complete anatomy and fleshly dimensions are invisible to us, because we are functioning cells ignorantly but efficiently comprising their body make-up.

Corollary: If an event could be predicted and confirmed according to the characteristic metabolic cycle and inductive-excretive requirements of the event-organisms body, then it might be possible to alter the course of anticipated incidents through working with the event-creature's nervous system to shift its actions in midcourse. Confuse it, perhaps.

I was going to try to interfere with a certain sad but small-scale disaster I had predicted would take place on the afternoon of August 11, 2047.

This was to be a test.

If I could stop this small-scale mishap concerning a young man named Simon Chelsez, then I might use this model for the manipulation of events, to divert World War III.

For I knew: World War III would arrive on the morning of February 10, 2048.

If the experiment with Simon Chelsez was successful, I would trace my way through the interacting clusters of event-organisms busily constructing the foundations for the structure they called Fun and we knew as the End of Humanity, and there, at the nexus of the crises, intercept the gestation of the Third World War.

The origin of this complex and circumlocutionaty ludicrous series of endeavors was disillusioningly simple:

I didn't want to die.

PART II OF SECONDARY SYNTAX

In form Astral, with sensations Subtle, I conducted myself along the damp web-work of the incident-neural system to the apartment of a young man and his mother who lived across from the elementary school. I traced my way from a teacher's repressed memory of a child's death (ghostly reenactment) to the young man's recollection of the accident: a teacher had seen a child killed on the street corner on which Simon Chelsez and his mother lived; Simon had seen the truck hit the little girl, watching from his bedroom window, and it had not moved him. The little girl had been nearly divided in half by the truck's right front tire. The child's blood left a Rorschach inkblot on the white concrete, the blot's red configuration reminding him of a knight killing a dragon.

The teacher was an acquaintance of mine, I had her vibratory identity code *down*. She was connected eternally with Simon, though she'd never met him face to face, by their mutual cross-referenced recollections of the accident; together they were functioning memory-cells in the mnemonic bank of the event-animal in which they lived. I worked my way, psychically, from one person to the other: from one brain cell to the next.

And I was invisibly sharing a room with Simon Chelsez.

Simon was gazing at a holographic programmer, trying to decide which program to play. He was completely unaware of me, since I was with him in astral form only I secluded myself amongst programmer circuits. Observing him through the reticulating eye of the event-organism, I perceived his surface thoughts clearly as plays and flares of polychromatic lights defining the crown of the sinuous tube of incident-compositions marking his wake of passage.

All of his holographic movies starred the same hero: Captain Horatio Alphonso. The holos were projected onto the center space of the large, almost empty room through lenses set flush into the ceiling. The white room was fifty by fifty feet, empty except for a single bed in its exact center. Nineteen-year-old Simon Chelsez, the present owner of the holoprogrammer, was a short, stocky, and muscular Chicano. Like Captain Alphonso, Simon knew all the Alphonso holos by heart. He punched up the program-selector, leaving the setting on *Pride and Punishment*. The overhead laser-projector hummed, fell silent, as the image of the heroic Alphonso appeared in the middle of the room, at the foot of the bed. If you'd walked into the room without knowing that Simon owned an expensive holo set you'd have thought that Captain Alphonso was actually *there*. He was three-dimensional in that you could walk around him, look up at him from beneath, always without interfering with the focus or proportionate volume of his body. If you approached Captain Alphonso from behind, you saw a holo reproduction of his back; when you walked around to his front you'd see that his sides were perfectly formed into his chest without a seam.

Simon fidgeted impatiently as Alphonso waited, stoically immobile in his dashing black toga with the silver Liberator's arrow on the right shoulder, arms outspread as if holding up the ghostly words which floated under his forthright jaw:

PRIDE AND PUNISHMENT
A REALER-THAN-LIFE PRODUCTION
STARRING ESTEBAN MANTABLU AS
CAPTAIN ALPHONSO

REALLY, REALLY, REALLY, REALLY, WEIRD STORIES

PETULA ANKENY AS LIDIA
PAUL CHELSEZ AS VORGAS
COPYRIGHT ©2039 3-D LTD.

Simon possessed a complete collection of the Alphonso series. He had inherited it because his late father, Paul Chelsez, had played the role of Vorgas, the Villainous Arch-Foe of Alphonso, in each of the thirty-nine episodes.

Simon and Alphonso were remarkably alike in physique.

And as the statuesque hero vanished, Lidia appeared, reclining on a silken air-turbulence bed in an apartment hung with streamers like smoggy cobwebs. Lidia was peacefully asleep. Alphonso entered from the balcony and stood beside her, gazing deep into the vacant eyes of his slumbering beloved. In keeping with the glamor fad of that period she slept with her eyes opened, their membranes bathed in artificial protective fluids sprayed from tiny hoses attached to her head. Her eyes gleamed in the bars of rainbow light from the overhead DreamTone. She had set the Dreamtone for *Fanning Reds*, guaranteed to color her dreams with scenes of passion. Her passionate dreams were about to be made concrete reality with the coming of Captain Horatio Alphonso, personification of all that is gallant and debonair. Bars of vermilion luminescence played over her delicate features, making her blankly-staring blue eyes red as small forges.

Simon, who had waited beyond the border of the holoscenario, waded suddenly through the projected image, without disturbing it, and slipped into Alphonso.

He merged with Alphonso's every action, striding the archetype's strides, a fraction of a second behind in the holo's choreography, slightly blurring its outline. His limbs and head were one with Alphonso's, his features moving in the same stereotyped holo's smug expressions.

Simon had memorized the holo so completely his voyeur enactment developed into a self-hypnotized reflex. He knew all the words, mouthed them with perfect inflection and precision timing. He could act it all out without a single mistake. For the hundredth time.

He even made love when Alplonso did. Which Alphonso did frequently. While involved in the holoscenario Simon believed that he was Captain Alphonso, Guerilla Hero of the Silver Liberators. The visual illusion was complete enough that he could fill in the rest of his senses with his imagination. So he had orgasms when Alphonso did. Which Alphonso did frequently.

Really, Really, Really, Really, Weird Stories

It hadn't been difficult for Simon to memorize the tapes for the Alphonso series. It was all very primordial and basic, each Alphonso holo lasting no more than twenty minutes. Alphonso would make love to Lidia, or begin to, Vorgas would come in to interrupt with his kidnapping attempt on Lidia, and Alphonso would defeat Vorgas and spend the remainder of the holo making love to Lidia.

Simon/Alphonso stepped onto the sunken bed, still standing, straddling Lidia like the Colossus of Rhodes. Then he knelt gracefully beside her and she woke: stretching luxuriantly, removing the DreamTone with a delicate sweep of her jewel-bangled hand, squeezing her eyes shut and then opening them with a euphoric giggle.

Purring, Lidia reached for Alphonso/Simon.

Simon could feel Lidia's slim body in his arms. Almost. Enough. There was a real bed onto which the holo bed was projected, supporting Simon over his loving mirage. But he was forced to slip slightly out of synch with Alphonso in order to keep himself from falling through the incorporeal form of the naked Lidia as he mounted her. The outline wavered, stained.

Alphonso threw his toga and briefs aside and bestowed his affections on Lidia . . . After a few minutes of her spider embrace Vorgas crept into the scene, as he always did at those indelicate moments. Vorgas also looked very much like Simon, though thinner, much older because he was played by the man who had leased this apartment and bought the holo-projector shortly before his death. He was wrapped in a white shroud that contrasted sharply with his long black train of hair and dark, sunken features. He slithered toward the bed on all fours and unfurled a lanky, corded arm at the end of which was a paralysis-gun, dart-shaped and silvery. He pointed the gun at Alphonso who shielded Lidia with his naked but magnificent body . . .

. . . at this point in the holoscenario Alphonso was supposed to whip out his handy paralysis-ray reflector concealed in the utility belt lying within reach . . .

I concentrated on the narrow band of electric charges traveling Simon's optic nerve. I changed what he saw. I concentrated on the narrow band of electric charges traveling his audio nerve. I changed what be heard.

Instead of the usual reiteration of Vorgas's defeat, Alphonso screamed and flung himself away from Simon, toppling, paralyzed. Simon stood up, uncertain, split from his vicarious self-image, and watched in growing horror as Vorgas leapt onto Alphonso's bare breast and plunged a needle-dagger deep into his throat. Alphonso spurted blood, squealing like a pig at slaughter.

Simon covered his eyes and whimpered.

He staggered to the wall panel and flicked the holo off. The holoscenario faded like the blotchy after-image of a bright light. The room ached with near-emptiness.

Simon's face was calm, almost empty. There should have been surprise or fury.

I was becoming worried. The eventual organism's neural predilection was cloudy. I levered, see-sawed, bounced from and was pumped into . . .

He opened a door, went down a hall to his mother's bedroom, approaching her soundlessly. She was lying under a sunlamp and listening to the radio on earplugs. He flicked the radio into silence.

"Simon?" his mother said, her eyes wide open, sprayed by protective fluid as Lidia's had been. "Simon, dear, why don't you come back later? Mother was just about to go to sleep. But while you're here shut off the sunlamp and turn on my DreamTone, will you?"

Simon reached up and deliberately made the sunlamp brighter. "Lights!" he intoned histrionically, "Cameras!"

"Hey, turn that off, son, will you? She switched off the eye filters and peered at him. Her hair, in sharp hooks around her puddly, watered-down face, had the exaggerated gloss of synthetic implanting, plastic sky-blue.

Simon's face was ingenuous, eyes-wide. "You've been playing the holo again, haven't you?" Mother accused. "I'd prefer you didn't, Simon. Really. You know why. Doctor Hannaly warned you. It's best to forget Paul." Her bland, middle-aged features creased meridians of blue-gray. Self-consciously, she tried to relax her face; strong facial expressions were said to promote wrinkles.

"Lidia . . ." Simon murmured, throwing his arms around his plump mother, who resembled Lidia only in the lack of facial expression. He kissed the breasts dumping from her terrycloth robe.

His mother was profoundly shocked. She allowed her forehead to wrinkle. "Stop it!" She slapped him.

He stood up and his look of naiveté became cunning. "So you are Vorgas, with a new ploy! You could hardly think to disguise yourself as Lidia for long, Vorgas!" He bellowed, with a melodramatic flourish of his hand.

His mother bit her lower lip and leapt clear of the bed, flinging herself at the door.

REALLY, REALLY, REALLY, REALLY, WEIRD STORIES

Simon caught her under the throat with his right arm and with his left hand tugged the cord of the sunlamp from its socket and wrapped it around her neck. His face tightened into a snarl exactly when his hands tightened the cord. His mother gurgled briefly, thrashed, then became limp, a cumbersome weight. He let her fall onto the bed. Then he stood up to wait for the credits for the next episode.

Blood from his mother's parted lips flowed enthusiastically and spattered the pillow with a red Rorschach inkblot. To Simon the inkblot resembled a small girl run over by a truck.

I couldn't bear to watch any longer. Failure. And now cathartic tides of the event-organism's cleansing organs swept me away. I allowed myself to be sucked into the undercurrent that led back to my body which waited in cataleptic torpor on my office couch . . .

A manganese blue light poured thickly through the window slats and blurred the spare furnishings in my office into the viridian gray of things seen underwater.

I sat up, feeling numb around the edges, and my eyes cleared some. I adjusted slowly to my physical husk. I concentrated, raising my blood pressure, accelerating breathing, quelling dizziness. At first, moving my arms was an indirect process, like manipulating the handle of a steam shovel to pick up a bauble in a penny arcade game. For a vertiginous instant I was fitting myself into my body like Simon into Alphonso's. But I locked in, thinking of myself as arms, legs, torso, head, and tolerating the erection which plagued my resurrections.

PART III OF SECONDARY SYNTAX

I agonized for a while. I had nightmares about the murder of Simon's mother. I didn't eat for a few days. I agonized and decided.

I would try once more.

I had projected another mishap, concerning a young woman, a virtuoso musician, Phylla Bertran. I'd listened to her solo performances and memorized the recordings of her own compositions. I had her vibratory identity code *down.*

So I traced my way through the neural channels of the event-animal, arriving in: A large and vacuous room, empty except for the four taut, thick strings of metallic black stretching from the center of the concave ceiling to the coastered fixture firmly magnetized to the black plastic floor. The walls were contoured to throw back a greatly amplified resonance of any string, when struck. The entire room was the hollow body of a huge acoustic bass viola, large enough to contain its musician inside itself.

Phylla was red-haired, with preoccupied blue eyes and thin, impatient lips. She wore a skintight leotard and tights and walked with footsteps clipped and minced, to the upright strings. The door hushed shut automatically behind her.

. . . Except for me, she was alone. And I was only there in spirit, observing via the optical membrane of the event-organism. Waiting my chance to test the corollary to my hypothesis one last time . . .

She pressed the chrome stud on her bracelet releasing the wheels for the string-pickup carriage mounted into the ceiling. Directing it with a remote-control device in her silver bracelet, she could coerce the strings from one part of the room to another. The room narrowed at the farther end, and when Phylla brought the strings there, they were tuned by that constricted space to a higher pitch. When the perpendicular strings traveled to the larger end of the room their tone became more bass.

Fingers strumming like running children, she played the encompassing instrument and lightly danced to and fro, one arm looping the mobile strings as if they were her dancing partner. She played expertly, each note as deep and pronounced as a church bell but with the thunderous rapidity of artillery fire. For a while she dashed through her bass viola solo in the Bartok piece she performed with the New York Philharmonic. But she couldn't complete the composition without a bow and anyway she was happy in improvisation, embellishing with her own compositions. Her bobbing breasts and short tosses of her hair marked rhythm in intimate wavelength as she pirouetted and furled through the belly of the huge bass.

. . . for me the music was filtered through the membrane of the event-organism, emerging as a ghost of its actual tone. But its echoes, reverberations of a lonely woman, made the body temporarily abandoned by my mind, waiting, dreaming in my office, shudder. I waited and watched for the high-water mark of those intimate wave-lengths . . .

Phylla was an enthralled artist, internationally applauded. But a part of her was numbed by supernumerary desires placing the pinnacle of the music, her personal essence just beyond her reach. Never quite satisfied, though critics vainly insisted that her interpretations were letter-perfect, she wanted the whole cup, every drop. To this end she had the bass-room customized into a musical instrument designed to envelop her in her own self-expression. For a month she'd practiced here, ever closer, always closer, not quite: not just yet.

Now she was scarlet, sweating; yet her fingers nimbly flakked the strings. Each finger dipped into the scale like a surgeon seeking a special nerve within an incision.

After thirty-two minutes Phylla was nearly sated. But not quite.

. . . and I knew that if I let her go on uninterrupted she would exceed the limitations of the room and it would not be enough. And what I hoped to forestall would inevitably come about. The time approached for the second test. If I could toss a mental probe into her impressions now, altering, amplifying, enlarging her capacity for receptivity to her own compositions. Satisfaction, perhaps . . .

She moaned. *I reached out . . .* She made the cry of an exhausted deer chased beyond its limit.

She sat down heavily on the floor. The fading reverberations of the strings hummed mournfully, like a departing jet.

The four strings in their metal fixture rolled silently, with finality, to the center of the room.

Phylla was left sighing.

. . . I sensed the mercury bursting from the cap of the thermometer . . .

Phylla stood up unsteadily, and taking her steps carefully, left the room.

. . . The test was positive. It might be possible to avert . . .

Phylla returned with a stepladder which she placed by the four strings.

. . . World War III . . .

She climbed to the stepladder and tied a silver-white cord to the metal fixture on the ceiling. She fixed the other end of the cord in a loop around her neck. She pressed the bracelet's remote control for *Automatic Response.*

The strings' fixture rolled toward the narrow end of the room, yanking Phylla off the stepladder. She sagged from the slim cord, making not a spasm, towed wherever the strings bounced, here and there in the echoing chamber. As she swung, a pendulum, her dead face bloated and mottled with purple, she bumped into the strings, which gave out a discordant thrumming.

She was dragged about the room, gyrating in her noose, body striking the strings, played a melody as void of predictable structure as death.

. . . I had been unable to change the predicted event-organisms' metabolic reaction: Suicide, as I had projected . . . OK, nobody's perfect. It wasn't my doing. Only. Only the corollary of my hypothesis had been negated twice . . .

PART II OF PRIMARY SYNTAX

So you see, I wasn't at all unprepared when the TV said AIR RAID ALERT.

I had done what I had done the night before; I had seen the consequences; I had redefined the word *failure*; I had drugged myself and hypnotized myself to forget, so that my family could have the last six hours of the illusion of self-determination. I had done what I had done.

I had seen the consequences. I knew myself as a note in a symphony which had no human hand in its composition.

And the TV said AIR RAID ALERT.

I'd laid off trying to convince anyone that Armageddon was going to happen. The FBI just laughed. It wouldn't do them any good to know, anyway. I suppose I had some illusions about the world going out in the dignified splendor of fatalistic comprehension.

Still, for a while, I sought out fissures or weak spots in the skin of the event-organism enclosing me, through which I might pass to stand apart and regard it impartially. A nonsense proposition. That would be as if my own lungs ripped their way from my rib cage to stand outside and survey me.

I gave up trying to escape. I got drunk for a week. I stared, soddenly, at the calendar. I experimented with heroin. I discarded that and went to Jesus, for a weekend. When faith-healing failed to revive my legs I gave up on that, too. I removed all the calendars from my house. When my wife asked why, I told her to shut up.

As a trifling hobby, I studied the social habits of the event-organisms. Sometimes they come together in the equivalent of committee meetings. Those take place as devastating earthquakes or wars or gold rushes. Sometimes they have fights amongst themselves. Those take the form (from our narrow viewpoint) of interchanges like the Olympics or the United Nations General Assembly or midnight on New Year's eve in Times Square.

Once every 500 millennia or so, events have festivals.

World's Fairs. They get together to have fun and enjoy themselves, and from our viewpoint this takes the persona of World War III. Their latest World's Fair was scheduled, in terms of our time system, for February 10, 2048.

Fancy that, I said, when the firestorm's prologue of hurricane winds swept our children half a mile into the sky. My boy, Charles, had babbled on about what glory he would find as a jet pilot. I wanted him to be a Doctor of Metaphysicis.

A throat of spasming energy. The nuclear fire took our city apart neatly, with sterile, rubber-gloved fingers. Like a child carefully removing plastic toy bricks from his play-castle now that the game was done. All of the leaves of the trees were stacked as neatly as dollar bills in the Treasury. Everything in its place. Japanese floral arrangement with the entire landscape. The explosions were metallic notes and the nation was a xylophone, cities ringing euphoniously where steel missiles impacted.

Fireworks heralding the commencement of the festivities.

PART IV OF SECONDARY SYNTAX

All right then, perhaps my attempts to intercept the deaths of Phylla and Simon had caused them. But it couldn't be my fault. There are no accidents.

Something nagged at me. It was three days till February tenth. I was trying to decide what to do.

Whether or not.

Something rattled around in the back of my mind like some object rolling loose in the trunk of a car, and as I drive along, listening to the unidentified things bumping as I turn corners, I try to decipher it from the muffled sounds it makes. Slowly I got the picture and began to wonder if I was a dupe.

Because there is simply *no such thing* as an accident. And it's a damn shame.

I sat in the study, stoking the fire on the permaplast hearth, hotter and hotter though it was already hot in there from the central heating. I sat in a plush chair and sweated and went without dinner but the answer didn't sweat itself out of me.

Finally I got in bed next to my wife. I lay in bed looking at my wheelchair. My wife, Elaine, tried to hug me. I shrugged her off.

"What's wrong?"

I decided to be honest with her for once. Maybe the legendary wifely intuition would make an appearance. For once. "It's the event-organism thing—"

She made a small sound of weariness.

"Oh, cut it out, will you?" She put her head under the pillow. "I'm sick of hearing that crap," came her muffled voice. Not muffled enough. "You made an ass of yourself when those FBI agents came to our house. You were always big-mouthed with rhetoric. Like the first time I met you in that ludicrous transfinite geometry class. I was impressed then. But what about your children? Are you going to explain your theories to them? Can you philosophically explain why you ignore them?"

"I don't ignore them. I bought them those plastic kites yesterday, didn't I?"

"Big deal. Do you know what your son does, lately? He collects tapes of *Bernie Backsterr the American Dreamer* and he memorizes every goddamn thing about that moron Backsterr and imitates him. He takes *notes* about what Bernie Backsterr's room looks like on the holo set and rearranges his own damn room to look exactly the same way. He dresses like that moron, wears his hair the same way—"

I couldn't repress a shudder. It connected too closely with Simon. I began to wonder if Charles contained hidden antipathy for his mother. Andrea, though only six, already wanted to be a musician. Elaine wanted her to play viola . . .

Elaine's makeup was smeared on the mauve pillow. She always put on her makeup just before she went to bed. Eye shadow, lipstick, glitter. She'd wash it off directly on getting up the next morning. It was an idiosyncrasy like her aversion for Chinese people. She wouldn't go near Chinese restaurants; she wouldn't allow a Chinese in the house, or watch them on TV. It was a peculiar prejudice for an educated woman, a professor of English. I used to think that she put the makeup on for me. But I suppose she wore it for whoever it was who made her moan so passionately in her sleep. When talking in her sleep she mumbled monosyllables which sounded distinctly Chinese.

I turned my back on her and tried to sleep.

I had to choke down an omelet for breakfast. I herded the greasy remnants of breakfast listlessly about the plate with my fork.

My daughter, Andrea, sat or rather teetered madly, across from me. Charles had gone to school. Andrea was six, healthy, blonde, and blossoming. She was one of those children who explode outward, looking at as many things simultaneously as practical. She fashioned her unfinished breakfast into tiny castles with her knife. If she didn't like something she always found some kind of use for it. Nothing was wasted, with her. And a child like this, I thought, should not be wasted on radiation poisoning.

I looked at the giddy stammer-play of her lips as she sang a TV-jingle; I ran through my calculations again: eighty-nine percent probability that my involvement in the metabolic gestation cycle would cause the war.

That left eleven percent.

I'm not sure if the man I influenced was the Secretary of Defense. I knew, through the jack-o-lantern buttered light, veined and notched with the footprints of meteorites that this was the man who was about to make a decision about a certain debacle with the Chinese. He was the man at the cusp, the one whose interpretation of the problem made all the difference. He was the living turning point. He made a phone call from his desk in his cozy, simulated red-velvet office to someone who might have been the President. The caller was a tight-faced little man with a gray mustache and an out-of-place black toupee. In his right hand he gripped the leather handle of a briefcase, unobtrusive except for the handcuffs chaining it to his wrist. They rattled out a code I couldn't understand. I was able to interpret very few of his thoughts: his output was sparse. I could tell he was thinking about his ulcer and about calling his mother. He hung up the phone and placed the briefcase on an empty desktop.

He unlocked the handcuffs with a murmur of satisfaction.

He opened the briefcase. Inside was a sheaf of papers. figures on the build-up of nuclear arms bases in certain strategic regions owned by the Chinese. I scanned, selected what I wanted to change.

I saw something out of the corner of my event-animal's eyes: Phylla and Simon's mother. They were there, with me, though I could see the files on the opposite wall through their denseless forms. They wavered but remained, expressionless, but trying to say something.

I looked back at the little man who couldn't see me, his eyes running down the column of figures . . .

. . . *I changed what he saw* . . .

PART III OF PRIMARY SYNTAX

The entire world was caught up in the nuclear devolution.

The bombs only fell on select cities, but those were mere torches illuminating the field for the event-animals' construction crew. Fallout shelters were utterly without value. Fingers of nuclear fission plucked shelters neatly from the ground and unpacked them, laying everything out primly on the picnic table. Each individual person was suspended—not levitated, it was more like hanging from an invisible hook—a foot above the naked, flattened earth, where we were spaced out evenly from one another.

Half of us, my half, were stripped of our flesh, quite painlessly. And symmetrically arranged. Like a mother unwrapping her Christmas present while conscientiously saving the wrapping for next year, our clothes, skin, muscles, tissues, cartilage, and vestigial organs such as amazement were all lifted cleanly away and stacked one by one to the side. Empty skins like discarded wetsuits were folded on one pile; organs placed neatly in transparent receptacles.

We couldn't see exactly who was responsible. On the other hand, everything we saw was responsible.

Our bodies were gone, our minds (stripped of initiative) remained microfilmed onto long white rods of pure ossified perception, rods which trembled with every wayward stimulus, like tuning forks for sight and smell as well as sound.

The other people were still paralyzed, always would be—locked into their bodies, dead but seeing, corpses with feeling. But no one was killed in World War III.

All of us: frozen above the ground like leaping ballet dancers crucified in mid-jump. No shadows blotted the frozen, ash-coated earth.

Light from everywhere.

No sun. No houses. No horizon. No argument.

We could not see farther than—ahhhh, it seemed five miles, but then, through the eye of the event it might have been five thousand. Gray haze tastefully presented the grounded verge of the vast transparent hemisphere that was World War III's interpretation of the sky. Inside our hemisphere, pleasing arrangements of cones and cubes and pyramids were constructed of the stripped houses and parks, of rough, prosaic wooden texture or rust-flaked metal offsetting mathematical spareness of geometry.

All the city's children floated, bobbing about one another in an aloof pavane in the sky above us. A cloud of babies.

Those who still possessed flesh began to revolve around the calcium rods like myself. I vacillated faintly, like an antenna aerial. An ultrasonic hum sings: Fun Fun Fun Fun Fun Fun Fun.

We rods formed an axis like a circular picket fence circled by the fleshed; like maypoles surrounded by dancing virgins. A carrousel of weightless, stark humanity comprising the nuclear merry-go-round, we the nucleus, they wooden-horses electrons.

There was no sound for that detached time-space. And no wind. Everywhere was the colorless light. The light that never warms.

FINAL SEGMENT OF PRIMARY SYNTAX, IN PRESENT TENSE

This place is full with motion, but nearly empty. I don't know how long we'll revolve like this, or if measures in duration apply, or what the event-animals intend for us after that. I envision myself chasing an ice cream truck. I am a small child. I am lured by the jangling bells of the ice cream truck. I've run six blocks to catch up with the cruising Moby Dick white Good Humor truck, but it outruns me and my lungs ache and my knees shake. I clasp a quarter so hard in my fist it hurts my palm. I can almost taste the ice cream and its color mixes and its texture melts into the sun-bleached color of my hair and the tropic steam of perspiration behind my ears. I hear the jangling and I chase on after the truck: within me, in memory. But externally the inner circle of rods and resonating bone whirls faster and faster and counterclockwise faster within the larger circle of paralyzed folk who stare straight ahead, with their arms at their sides and their children floating above them. There are no shadows, now, for the light is everywhere.

I cannot follow the organic twine of events into the future, now. I'm perceptually fixed in time, pinning the function of this organ of the event onto the present moment with my calcium nail. Time, the continuity of motion, revolves happily around me, riding the carrousel.

I get the impression that Time is an entity. He is a high officiary attending this, the World's Fair of Events. Time is judging World War III, attaching blue ribbons to the best exhibits. I am gratified: Detroit is a winner!

On one side I see, flashing by, an immense rectangular glassy construction resembling an oversized aquarium. In this container, dutifully recycling, recurring again and again, are the events which led up to World War III. I can see myself over there. I can see my interference with the lives of Phylla and Simon. Whizzing past, I catch a glimpse of Simon's murdering and Phylla's suicide. I can see myself floating wraithlike over each of them. I watch as I make the fatal decision to attempt to avert World War III. I see the cerebral scan-projections of Phylla and Simon's mother distracting me, deliberately muddling my judgment. I see myself adjusting the wrong set of figures, inadvertently influencing the little man in the cozy office to conclude that it is best to attack China before they attack us.

I glimpse missiles ejaculating from the USA which wave a friendly hello to missiles of retribution on their way from China. I try to perceive why Phylla and Simon's mother made me do it all, and I catch a glimpse of myself, one of my submerged personalities, laboring while I sleep, conjuring through my magically endowed wheelchair-talisman the visions of Simon's Mom and Phylla, placed to confuse me at that crucial instant: I deliberately distracted myself. And I chuckle (without a mouth) as I see (without eyes) that the steps I took to prevent the projected deaths of

Simon's Old Lady and Phylla Dedicated Artist, and the final effort to prevent the Third World War were as a whole predetermined reflex-reactions to the signals of the event-animals of which I am a cell; the same kind of inexorable spasms which led to the destruction of the civilization we now call Lemuria and the uncountable societies the event-animals allowed humanity to think it had personally built prior to that. If a man is killed in a car accident (Fun Fun Fun), why, that seems the sheerest chance; but that man (as a child I loved to play with marbles) had, perhaps even genetically, every intention of getting himself mutilated. I went willfully into the car accident that made me a cripple. The captain of the Hindenburg steered into that tower deliberately; Dewey wanted defeat at the hands of Truman (I enjoyed games of chance, especially as a means of escape; never chess, always dice) and Simon Chelsez's mother spent her entire life preparing to be strangled by her son.

Unconsciously, I had every intention of igniting World War III.

But why not? And why the hell not? Now that I mull it over, it's turning out to be a jolly affair, lots of fun. I can see the beginning of this delightful festival of events, and I cannot (Fun! Fun!) imagine what errant kill-joy impulse possessed me to try to put it off. It's a dandy, lovely show. They display it in that huge aquarium over there—*there*—for Time or one of the other visiting dignitaries should they chance to stroll by.

Hey! All kidding aside, I feel shamelessly giddy! It's all happening here and now: and I'm recording it.

I suspect I've hit on my assignment, my role as part of this gay, carnival affair: I'm a recording device.

And also a broadly smiling Master of Ceremonies.

Streamers of radiation fall golden from the sky like festival confetti and tickertape. I'm plumage on a parade float. I'm performing, a clown in the center of three rings.

From here, there is (Fun Fun Fun) nothing wrong with World War III. Nothing sad about Armageddon.

Everything, symmetrically right now, performs in the present tense. Like a burglar alarm ringing. The present is extremely tense, straining every fiber of the bubble sky's sumptuous fabric almost to the point of ripping it.

Fine and good. The tension is half the fun.

Ten Things to be Grateful For

In this fickle world . . .
In this coy and cloying world . . .
In this the best—can it be true?—of all possible worlds . . .
One must butter one's bread on the sunny side of the street. One must keep a stiff lower grip. One must . . .
One must remember: there are things to be thankful for. We have so much to be grateful, to be thankful for.
Here are ten things to be thankful for.

I.

Be thankful that you are not strolling through a park on a pretty spring day, minding your own mind, and thinking about whether or not to call the corporate head-hunter back, when you find that you have to pee, you have to pee badly and there's nowhere to go within a quarter mile, and it's a big park, a bushy park, and you've taken that liberty in the park's bushes before, and you sort of enjoy the occasional outdoors pee, so you step off the path and pee off an embankment, through some ferns, watching them bob with the impact of the stream, and you finish and turn and see two men standing there blocking your way and they tell you that you've just peed on their home, their mattresses, because there's a homeless encampment under the embankment, and you complain of entrapment but it's not applicable and it's no good and you try to feint to the left and dart to the right but they are used to people trying to dodge past, they're not your average homeless joes, they're predacious street people, and one of them grabs you and so does his smell, the smell of a whole cattle-car of people in one man, and you can see the lice squirm in his beard an inch from your face as he bear-hugs you, and you can look into his eyes, one of them skyblue and the other the color of a spat phlegm; and the second guy who's lean and blue with tattoos from the waist up, he kicks you at the base of the spine again and again as you try to scream but the bear-hugger stuffs his beard in your mouth and with a strangely high-pitched giggle, says he always does that, as you struggle amazed not at his strength but at your own feebleness, and then the telling crack with another practiced workboot kick, the meaningful crack of your spine and the pain that in your mind is like a picture of jagged radiating three-dimensional arrows made of rusty iron, pain with weight, and the bearded one falls on you as you fall back and there's more cracking and crackling as you hit the hard ground of the ravine's lip and your head is hanging over the edge of the embankment, and the other guy grabs onto your neck and jumps off into the ravine, and that feeling is like a spin-painting with only the colors black and green, and the vertebrae come apart, and he swings from your head and neck as the other guy, drooling with laughter, holds on and the vertebrae pull farther apart and you remember when you were in kindergarten you drew a picture of a bear jumping over a fence only no one could make out what it was you'd drawn, and now other tramps come laughing, hooting, to swing on your head and neck and the vertebrae part completely and when they get bored they kick your body like a bean bag amazed that you're still alive, but you're not alive for long. That could happen to you. Be grateful that isn't happening to you. It could be. It's not. Be thankful.

2.

Be grateful that you're not a child in Thailand who's sold by his parents to a Bangkok child-brothel, and you're amazed that your mother kissed you goodbye as if you were going to visit a relative, as if you would see her again, and you thought that they would take the money from the man and then tell you to run away with them but they didn't even look back as you are led weeping, the weeping bone-dry, up the creaking wooden stairs in the narrow alley in back of the building, a squeezed building that would fall over but for the buildings on either side, and then they beat you the first time just to introduce you to beatings and to initiate you into the magnitude of your subservience but really it's a half-hearted beating compared to the second time when you refused to let the fat American fuck you in the ass while his friend, a tall skinny man who coos at you in an undertone as if convincing himself he's being tender, shoves a stubby thick member in your mouth and makes circular motions with his hips and, though you stomached that, when you felt the penetration from behind, you wrenched free and ran to hide under the bed and wouldn't come out till Kimaritchul, squat and strong, flipped the bed to one side and began—with a strangely anomalous look of patience in his eyes, like a horsetrainer, kicking you in the soft parts, very expertly, so as not to break anything but so as to introduce deep, deep bruises that hurt with your every movement all night long, each stab of pain speaking with Kimaritchul's unspoken voice, as you let the two men do what they wanted with you, after the skinny one made noises as if he disapproved of what the guard had done to you, and then goes on to fuck you till you choke and lose consciousness, but unfortunately you don't die, not till two years later when your kidney ruptures and they throw you in the canal. That's something to be grateful for: that's not happening to you.

3.

Be grateful that you're not recovering from your third diabetes amputation, leaving you one limb, your left arm, while the nurses, especially the one with the harelip and the dyed-blond with the long neck and slumped shoulders, give you filing looks, they're mentally filing you as human detritus that hasn't been picked up yet, filing you under hopeless and meaningless and simply a bothersome fulfillment of duty, that duty dwindling, on no one's instructions, day by day, the sponge-baths going from once a day to once every two days to once a week, the turning for bedsores following precisely the same declension, as if by clinical planning, the kindly remarks and encouragements and inquiries falling off to almost none, the eye contact vanishing entirely, the visits from the doctor also down to once a week, then once every ten days, the food which, after all, you can feed to yourself if they'd bring it, since you have one limb, even if you can't reach every part of yourself for a sponging without falling off the bed: the food coming only twice a day now and if you start whining about anything it comes only once; the television left on a channel that has gone off the air for good and then they say the TV is broken when it's not, and the talk about the lack of available beds, oh if only one would open up, within your hearing, their skill at indirectly conveying a sense of some imagined personal injury, their indifference to your tale of the night orderly who comes in and holds down your remaining arm and slaps you with a look of slack-mouthed concentration, four or five times before hearing footsteps and hurrying away, the nurse outraged when you try to tell the doctor she's forgot your insulin, the coma creeping up on you just as you smell the decay growing in your remaining limb . . . Something to be thankful for: that isn't happening to you.

4.

Thank your particular deities that you are not completely convinced, utterly convinced, granite-pillar and steel-brace convinced, that there is a large parasite growing in your intestines, a parasite that is a mutated variant on a tapeworm, but stubbier and thicker and intelligent, a wormish thing with jawparts like human fingers only translucent, rubbery, capable of grasping, and it's pushed its grip through the tissues of your intestines to grab some inner organ, sometimes your liver, sometimes your spleen, lately you suspect it's moved on to squeezing your bladder shut because you can't urinate, and your ankles are swelling and somehow this pleases it, and you can even hear it at times, as it can take words from your mind to give them back to you, to persuade you not to fight it, that's one of its survival adaptations, to whisper there are many parasites within all people, as everyone knows, flora the doctors call them, micro-organisms, and there are mites living in your eyebrows, and they eat dead skin and the fellows in your intestines help released trapped electrolytes from food and think of me as just another step, another kind of benign parasite, for if you relax and let me move freely I'll love you, I'll push in and out of you, and I'll reach out of your ass to caress your genitals, but only if you're quite still and trusting, you must surrender completely, and you must not scream when you see me. It whispers such things to you, but you're contemptuous of its sluggish efforts at persuasion, it is a thing of the lower orders and cannot persuade like a TV commercial can, or not as well as some commercials anyway, perhaps, and it cannot be trusted, and as the doctors are in denial, out of sheer ineffable horror, refusing to acknowledge the presence of the thing, you must, of course, cut yourself open with what over-the-counter topical anesthetic you can manage, and fight your own arm which tries not to cut any further as you penetrate to the layer of membrane over the intestines, but which you, in the unshakeable determination of your absolute will, overcome, triumphing as, lying in the bathtub naked and trying to staunch the blood with towels with your free hand, you cut with shaking fingers a long jagged rent in the large intestine, for a full fourteen inches, and lay the intestine open, and find the parasite within . . . is gone, is somehow gone, and as you bleed to death you think you hear it whispering from the drain. Be grateful that isn't you. Be thankful.

5.

Be thankful, too, that you're not trapped in the rubble after the terrorist bomb has reduced the building to a shuddering clinker of ragged stone, two days now, and the sounds of rescuers are very, very, very distant, eloquently distant, and you're in a chamber that was not made for habitation, under many tons of rock, with your arms and legs angled—unbroken!—in odd Jerry-Lewis postures, like a dancing Keith Haring drawing, only you're losing sensation in your legs because circulation is cut off by a stone that presses just hard enough, but your arms are aching with sensation, and, when you move, the rocks above nudge a little closer, a little lower, and small scavenging beetles begin to appear, you can hear their rattling legs on the stones, feel them brush past your mouth, your ears, and you can't feel them begin on your legs, there's no circulation there, but there's a sense of something flowing out of you down there, a coldness that seeps up from your calves to your knees, to your thighs, as you hear the child suddenly wake up and begin screaming for its mother, and you open your mouth to try to speak words of comfort but something chitinous climbs into your mouth and chokes you and . . . Be grateful, thankful, that isn't you.

6.

Be thankful for what you have; be grateful: You might be a child of ten and you might be that child in a leather bag, tied shut, hardly any room, a bag with holes punched in it, listening to the two men talk about police pursuit, feeling the van lurch left and right as they turn corners, hearing one of them say, with the joy of a lottery winner, ain't nobody coming after us, was nobody there to see the license number, no pursuit, Joe, we're home free . . . as you hear that the implications come alive in you and make you claw at the bag and try to scream through the tape over your mouth and one of them slams you through the leather with that two by four you saw just before they pushed you in and it knocks all the breath out of you and as you're getting breath back, each breath stabbing now, he says something about you better hold still in there, you better be glad you're in that bag there and not out here with me you little peter-pusher, and the other one says don't scare him no more'n you have to I don't want to have to gag him after we take him out, I want his mouth free after I take that tape off. But they're taking some kind of drug, you can't tell what, you hear them say crystal, and after they make those snorting sounds you can tell from their voices they're losing what control of themselves they have and you feel an icicle become part of your back and realize it's that sharpened screwdriver the red-headed man had, he's sticking it through the bag at random here and here and there, into you, just a half inch in here, and an inch there and it scrapes off your shoulderblade and he's laughing and his friend says wait, wait till we get to the woods, and when they do, when they take you out of the bag their faces hurt more than the tools and soon you beg them please, please kill me, but you don't quite die before they shovel the dirt over your eyes. But then you do. Be glad that's not you, be grateful, be thankful. We have much to be thankful for.

7.

Be thankful you're not running on legs that are losing their bones; that's how it feels, as you run, as if the bones in your legs are melting, you're sinking as you run into the street, because you've been running this way for two miles and you're fat and you're not a kid anymore as the truck chases you across the open desert, under a sun that never takes a breath, never relents, the pickup just ten feet behind, driving you ahead of it, with a man and a woman and three children in it, the children laughing loudest of all, as you fall in the cacti, naked in the cacti, and get up and run on, and on, stumbling and running, your feet ribbons of flesh, your heart almost louder than their voices and the gunning engine and they are calling you Mexi-nigger, Mexi-nigger you'd better get up but your bones have dissolved completely now and you can't get up and Dad lets the kids, even the girl, practice with the .22 on you, they shoot you in the hips and buttocks and you don't feel it much because of the exhaustion and the fear till one of the slugs hits your pelvis and splinters it and then there's nothing in all the universe but those splinters chewing out of your hip, nothing, anyway, till they lock the chains to your ankles and begin to drag you behind the truck, talking about how those ol' boys in Texas going to be startin' a fad, here, now son I want you to see what a fat Mexi-nigger's guts look like, whoa look at that and his shit too—
  Consider: that's not you. It could be you. It's not. Be thankful.

8.

Yes be thankful, you'd better be absolutely grateful that you're not in the bus when it goes off the bridge and fills with water and your little girl, eight years old, beside you, is looking at you with amazement because somehow you've made this happen and you'll never have time to explain that, despite pretending all her life that you could prevent things like this from happening, in fact, my little love, I was lying, all this time, something like this could happen anytime and only some perverse and unmappable grace prevents it from happening more, it's amazing when we're barreling along by the millions at sixty, seventy, eighty miles an hour on our steaming, tarry freeways that it doesn't happen more, it's amazing that cancer and plane-crashes and murder and war don't happen even more than they do, given that people are just mandrills with clothes on, my little sweet, so you should not be surprised, and I'm sorry I didn't prepare you for this; all this passing through your head in a split second as you see that look in her face right before the bus hits the estuary, slams the both of you off the ceiling of the bus with bone cracking force, and since your left shoulder shatters you have only your right arm to try to get her through the one open window within reach as water fills the bus, but there's a ferret-faced man, the one who said he was a lawyer, who's pushing your daughter out of the way so he can swim through, who's kicking you in the face to keep you from jerking him back from the window to let her through, and both of you are fighting underwater and beyond him you glimpse more than a dozen pallid faces with bubbles surging up from their mouths as they flap their arms and you claw at him to try to get him out of the way so you can get her through that window but she is clawing at you in desperation, clawing at your eyes, your own child without knowing gouges out one of your eyes in her terror, and then the darkness closes down on you both and it has nothing reassuring, nothing restful in it at all, but just a shattering emptiness and . . . Count your blessings, because that could be you: be grateful that isn't you . . .

9.

Be grateful, thank your ancestors, thank your stars, that you're not being strapped down in the metal chair, that you're not seeing those two distinct, sharp-edged expressions, either one or the other, on the faces of the people watching through the glass, either studied indifference or a fascination that's less than pornographic but not so very much less, and there are people murmuring to you just as if they care that you're about to be choked to death with chemicals, but they don't, not really, they don't actually care and they won't think about it after tomorrow or the next day, and the fact, the unblemished, untarnished certainty that you and only you have, that you're innocent, you really are innocent, not "they all say they're innocent," but authentically innocent, and that not only will it be believed that you raped and strangled two women whom you never saw or heard of till you were arrested for supposedly doing it, after someone stole your car and used it in the crime, someone who looks a little like you; not only will it be believed by the public, by history, that you are a murderer, but your wife, your children, your father and mother will believe that you are guilty, even though they made cardboard protestations to the contrary, ultimately they will believe it, and so the children will blame you for abandoning them, and no one will ever be truly sorry, except maybe the children, who will also hate you, no one will be sorry that you are now hearing the sound of the chamber door clicking shut, the last time you will hear a door shut, that you are hearing the sound of the cyanide capsules hitting the bucket to release the poison into the air; no one will really, not really care that you have only one last clean breath left and that the next one is like an animal clawing into your lungs as you shake and choke and shake and die knowing you are innocent and being killed for nothing. Be grateful, show some gratitude: that could have been you. And it's not.

10.
Be thankful, breathe a sigh of relief and nod your head in humble gratitude that you're not a neurotic fan of perverse dark literature, horror or crime or dark fantasy, a reader, at least today, of the obsessively-etched stimuli that is one of your few releases from the smothering sense of is-this-all-there-is in your life, that you're not that sort of person, reliant on occasional corrosive chemicals or puerile graphic images for relief from the inarticulate and undefined and never acknowledged knowledge that you are being hunted, something just out of the circle of your perceptions is hunting you: a fear; a fear of your own meaninglessness, your own irrelevance, your trappedness in a dead-end, soulless, monkey-masturbatory, mazelike civilization that you mock like a bad videogame even as you sock in another quarter, as your brain turns slowly, slowly inside your skull, scanning for an exit in an exitless world, as you lurch onto the next half-satisfying stimulus like the dying cocaine rat that pushes the lever; as you realize that your understanding of the unknown sculpture is really only of the chisel-scrapings at the foot of the sculpture, and you never have seen the sculpture, and that you're really truly trapped in a culture that, despite your arch commentary, your well-honed irony, your media-fed sardonicism, has conditioned and programmed you just as thoroughly as any shopping channel fixated Tennessee housewife; that despite your creative conceits you're probably going to degrade yourself for the opportunity to die in an upscale old-people's home instead of in an SRO hotel, probably of a painful and under-medicated cancer, after your youth is burned up in media dreams and gossip that has a life of its own and relationships that jar and sputter and circle blindly like bumper cars, and the loneliness of the long distance consumer, a hollow life in a hollow society of equally hollow people—Be glad and grateful that's not

. . . that it's not . . . not . . .

Oh. I see.

Oh, I . . .

I wasn't thinking. Ah. It is? Well . . . I . . .

Sorry.

Well anyway. There are, you know, other things . . . to be thankful for.

THE SEA WAS WET
AS WET COULD BE

Mary did not expect to survive so long after the airplane began to break up. But she did survive as she was pitched through the crack in the bulkhead, as the fuselage split in the screaming air and people clung to each other in despair. She survived to fall; first spinning, but then—by some serendipity of her flailing—to fall spread-eagled, like a skydiver with no parachute.

She was falling toward the sea. She could breathe. She was conscious. They hadn't been so very high, had been only a mile from the airport, reducing elevation in preparation for landing, but they were still over the sea. Then the bang, the crack, the screaming of air and children.

Somehow the bigness of what was happening overwhelmed fear. There was nothing left but to drink in these last few seconds alive—thinking: How alive I am, I've never been this alive, this awake! Was it always possible to be so awake? Now she saw the sea rushing up at her, waves taking on definition. And she thought she might survive if she went into a diving posture and aimed her fingers, with the hands together as if in prayer, down at the water. If she cleaved the water sharply enough, she thought, she might survive. She tried to angle herself that way. She put her hands together and aimed herself straight down and thought: I might—

That was her last thought before she struck, the word *might*.

Then she struck the water. There was a flash of sensation so powerful it could not be identified as pain. There was a white light. Then she was shooting down through the water, down and out, thinking without words that it had worked, that she had somehow cleaved it so fine that she had survived, even though she'd always heard that from that high up water would be as hard as concrete when you hit it.

It was true that her body was behind her, was spread out over the top of the waves, liquid to liquid, parts already nourishing ambitious seagulls, but she had kept going—like the time her brother had dived from a pretty high diving board and he'd been wearing Dad's swimming suit, a little too big for him, and the dive, the slap of the water, had pulled it right off him; and he was naked in the pool, and everyone laughed. It was like that, only it was her body that had been pulled off, wasn't it?

But no—she could feel her body now. She could feel it quite clearly. It was vast and shifting. It lapped on the shore nearby; it supported birds, on its surface, and a million million fish within it; she could feel each and every one as well as bigger things moving in her depths. She felt oil slicks on her body, and ships cleaving her back, and she knew that she had a new name, a name that was pronounced over and over again with waves and currents, a long name with an infinite number of syllables, and the speaking of it was never finished.

∞ ∞ ∞

REALLY, REALLY, REALLY, REALLY, WEIRD STORIES

About the Author
and the Stories

John Shirley has been weird for as long as he can remember and, for that matter, as long as anyone else can remember. There is some debate over whether this has been a boon or bane to his literary career. He's written fourteen novels–*Silicon Embrace* (Mark V. Ziesing) is the most recent; two will be reprinted this year, *Eclipse* (Alexander) and *Wetbones* (Leisure). There have been four previous collections as well, including last year's *Black Butterflies* (Mark V. Ziesing), which was selected as one of the "Best Books of 1998" by *Publishers Weekly* and included the International Horror Guild Award-winning short story, "Cram." Shirley now makes most of his living from writing not-always-weird screen- and teleplays.

As far as proving just how weird he is–the stories included in this collection alone are proof enough, of course. The earliest story collected here is early indeed–Shirley's first (or maybe second) published story ("The Word 'Random' Deliberately Repeated," 1973)–and the most recent is as recent as possible–a story written two days before I turned this in to the publisher ("Brittany? Oh: She's In Translucent Blue," October 28, 1998). With such a timespan (and wealth of never-before-published material) involved, it was thought information about when and where each story had first been published (or not) would be both interesting and informative. But, unlike other authors who have tidy files full of filed-by-date manuscripts and who carefully keep data concerning published work in triplicate along with duplicate copies of every magazine and book they've appeared in, John Shirley is, well, weird. He didn't always keep track–plus he's led this weird life, moved a lot, changed wives periodically (until he found the right one, Michelina, about eight years ago), etc. Just to find copies of some of the stories collected here, we had to turn to Shirley publisher/archivist/friend-for-years Steve Brown, who (we are thankful) had them in his files. One story came from a yellowing *F&SF* provided by devoted fan Shikhar Dixit. Many, of course, were in manuscript (or the digital equivalent) only, including one Shirley had told me on two different occasions to destroy. (Disobedience is often the highest form of loyalty.)

But, we did the best we could here in our own weird way.

—Paula Guran

REALLY WEIRD STORIES

"'I Want to Get Married,' Says the World's Smallest Man": *Midnight Graffiti*, ed. Jessica Horsting & James Van Hise, Warner, 1992

"Will The Chill": *Universe 9*, ed. T. Carr, Doubleday, 1979

"Tapes 12, 14, 15, 22 and 23": *Gothic.Net* (www.gothic.net), July, 1998; first time in print here

"Don't Be Afraid" is published here for the first time

"Lot Five, Building Seven, Door Twenty-three": *Dracula: Prince of Darkness*, ed. Martin H. Greenberg, DAW, 1992

"Kindred Spirits" is published here for the first time

"The Word 'Random' Deliberately Repeated": *Clarion III*, ed. Robin Scott Wilson, NAL, 1973

"Voices" is published here for the first time

"The Last Ride": revised from a story written in November 1989 that appeared in some *Penthouse* publication in 1990.

REALLY, REALLY, WEIRD STORIES

". . . And the Angel with Television Eyes": *Isaac Asimov's Science Fiction Magazine*, May 1983

"The Sweet Caress of Mother Nature" is published here for the first time

"In the Cornelius Arms": *Pawn Of Chaos: Tales of the Eternal Champion*, ed. Edward E. Kramer, White Wolf, 1996

"Quill Tripstickler Out the Window": *The Magazine of Fantasy & Science Fiction*, November 1981

"I Live In Elizabeth": *Heatseeker*, Scream Press, 1989

"Morons at the Speed of Light" is published here for the first time

"Silent Crickets": *Fantastic*, April 1975

"Screens": *The Magazine of Fantasy & Science Fiction*, April 1989

"Brittany? Oh: She's In Translucent Blue" is published here for the first time

"Ticket To Heaven": *The Magazine of Fantasy & Science Fiction*, December 1987

REALLY, REALLY, REALLY, WEIRD STORIES

"Ash": *Dead End: City Limits*, ed. Paul F. Olson & David B. Silva, St. Martin's, 1991

"Triggering": *OMNI*, January 1982

"Skeeter Junkie": *New Noir*, Black Ice Books, 1993

"When Enter Came": *Yellow Silk*, 1990

"What Joy! What Fulfillment!" is published here for the first time

"199619971998": *Three-Fisted Tales of "Bob"*, ed. Reverend Ivan Stang, Fireside, 1990

"Preach": *The Edge #4*, 1997

"Preach, Part Two: The Apocalypse of The Rev. John Shirley": is published here for the first time

"Modern Transmutations of the Alchemist" is published here for the first time

REALLY, REALLY, REALLY, REALLY, WEIRD STORIES

"Just Like Suzie": *Cemetery Dance*, Summer 1991

"Cold Feet": *One Dollar Magazine*, February 1974

"The Peculiar Happiness of Professor Cort": *New Pathways*, Fall 1988

"Tahiti in Terms of Squares": *Fantastic*, October 1978

"Equilibrium": *Heatseeker*, Scream Press, 1989

"What Cindy Saw": *Interzone #5*, 1983

"The Almost Empty Rooms": *New Dimensions 7*, ed., Robert Silverberg, Harper & Rowe, 1977

"Ten Things To Be Thankful For": *Gothic.Net* (www.gothic.net), November 1998; first time in print here

"The Sea Was Wet As Wet Could Be" is published here for the first time

∞ ∞ ∞

ABOUT THE TYPE

Really, Really, Really, Really Weird Stories is set in the typeface Savoy, a vaguely weird digital adaptation of Sabon. Sabon was designed by Jan Tschichold in 1964 and was, in turn, based on some of the sixteenth-century designs of Claude Garamond. The logotype used for the book title and chapter titles on interior pages is the somewhat-more-definitely weird Chapbook, a digital face designed in 1996 by Feòrag NìcBhrìde and based on the rough-hewn type of mid-seventeenth-century printed works. The logotype seen on the front cover was the work of the pegleg-sawingly weird Alan M. Clark, who incorporated it into his cover painting. Book design and typesetting is by the merely colorfully eccentric John Tynes, wot wot.